William C. Milne

Life in China

SALZWASSER
VERLAG

William C. Milne

Life in China

Reprint of the original, first published in 1859.

1st Edition 2022 | ISBN: 978-3-37512-709-1

Verlag (Publisher): Salzwasser Verlag GmbH, Zeilweg 44, 60439 Frankfurt, Deutschland
Vertretungsberechtigt (Authorized to represent): E. Roepke, Zeilweg 44, 60439 Frankfurt, Deutschland
Druck (Print): Books on Demand GmbH, In de Tarpen 42, 22848 Norderstedt, Deutschland

LIFE IN CHINA.

LIFE IN CHINA.

BY

REV. WILLIAM C. MILNE, M.A.

FOR MANY YEARS MISSIONARY AMONG THE CHINESE.

With Original Maps and Illustrations.

THE THIRD THOUSAND.

LONDON:
G. ROUTLEDGE & CO. FARRINGDON STREET;
NEW YORK: 18, BEEKMAN STREET.
1858.

PREFACE.

PLEDGED to the cause of Protestant missions in China by his earliest associations, the writer embarked for that country in the summer of 1839; and, with the exception of an absence of two years, continued to labour there till near the beginning of 1854, under the auspices of the London Missionary Society.

In prosecuting his mission, it was his lot to visit various places in China, *e. g.* Macao, Hong-Kong, Canton, Choosan, Ningpo, Shanghai; and to travel through the heart of three of her provinces, Chih-kiang, Kiangse, and Canton. A partial result of the observations, during this long period, made upon the Chinese as they are, is given in the following pages, arranged under five parts. The first part liscusses the common notions current in Europe and America about China and the Chinese, some of them eally untrue, and very unjust to the inhabitants of that empire; and in the other parts there is presented a ariety of positive information regarding Chinese life ind habits, which had been collected during a long esidence at Ningpo and Shanghai, as also in a journey f 1,300 miles across the interior. The sources of nformation were chiefly personal inquiry on the spot nd examination of native writers; and, except the short scraps acknowledged in the body of the work, and a few fragments in the second part now entirely re-written, but which originally were inserted by him many years ago in the pages of the "Chinese Repository," since defunct — nothing of what follows has appeared in print from the author.

The four maps which accompany the work are, on the whole, the most accurate hitherto published, being prepared by the writer himself after a very careful collation. That of the inland tour is the only one of the same route issued from the press so minute and correct; and as it is to be hoped that our relations with China, about to be materially improved, will likewise afford foreigners access into the interior of the empire, he trusts that this map, with his jottings *en route*, may form in future a valuable itinerary to Western travellers and adventurers. The names of places are given after Morrison's system of orthography—save such as have become part and parcel of the English gazetteer vocabulary, though mutilated imitations of Chinese sounds, *e. g.* Amoy, Chinchew, Canton, Macao, &c. In the map of China Proper, only the provincial capitals and departmental cities are inserted, also some important places known commonly to foreign readers; *e. g.* Shanghai, Swatow, &c.

The appearance of this little work has been delayed by circumstances over which the writer had no control; though perhaps fortunately, as it is issued at a time when public interest in matters bearing upon China is more eager than ever.

In concluding this prefatory note on the plan an

design of the book, the humble hope may be expressed: *first*, that it may do its part in diffusing in this country a more faithful and a juster knowledge of the Chinese people, and help to rid us of those false, as well as ridiculous, impressions so long encouraged regarding that nation and its social state, &c.; and, *secondly*, that this attempt may likewise aid a little in increasing or awakening the desire among the true philanthropists of the age to promote the cause of Christian civilization and pure Christianity in China. Should this manual in any manner forward these objects, the author will deem himself singularly happy.

WILLIAM C. MILNE.

SLOANE-STREET, CHELSEA,
February, 1858.

CONTENTS

PART FIRST.

WESTERN NOTIONS OF LIFE IN CHINA.

CHAPTER I.

CHAPTER II.

CHAPTER III.

PART SECOND.

REAL CHINESE LIFE AT NINGPO.

CHAPTER I.

CHAPTER II.

CHAPTER III.

CHAPTER IV.

CHAPTER V.

PART THIRD.

A GLANCE AT LIFE IN THE INTERIOR OF CHINA.

CHAPTER I.

CHAPTER II.

CHAPTER III.

PART FOURTH.

SHANGHAI.

CHAPTER I.

CHAPTER II.

CHAPTER III.

CHAPTER IV.

CHAPTER V.

PART FIFTH.

STATE AND PROSPECTS OF CHINA.

CHAPTER I.

CHAPTER II.

CHAPTER III.

LIFE IN CHINA.

PART FIRST.

WESTERN NOTIONS OF LIFE IN CHINA.

CHAPTER I.

ODD MANNERS—PIGTAILS—CRAMPED FEET.

Of ideas that most people in the West entertain about the Chinese, some of the elements may be said to be, odd manners, "pigtails," cramped feet, long nails, fans, paintings, rice-paper drawings, processions, concentric balls, lanterns, chopsticks, eating rats, mice, and bird's-nest soup, popular infanticide, and an utter want of benevolence.

In 1839, I carried with me to China notions such as these. From the first of my arrival I was curious to prove their truth; and now, following the order above given, I offer to the reader the result of observations continued during a residence of nearly fourteen years, hoping hereby to correct or confirm his preconceptions of the manners and customs of the Chinese.

Oddness of Chinese Manners.—In watching the "every-day life" of the Chinese, it is impossible not to detect analogies to habits everywhere else. Thus, other people dress, live in houses, eat, drink, marry, give in marriage, bury their dead, are courteous to strangers, are fond of fun, love their progeny, &c.;

and so do the Chinese. These are, as it were, instincts in the human race, which, like the instincts of the ant or the bee, have never changed since the creation of the world.

However, in habits general as these, there are incidental forms that may differ; and in China they *do* differ oftentimes so remarkably from the ordinary types amongst us, that, to one visiting that country, of all odd things there a Chinaman appears at first sight to be the oddest.

Not only in geographical position, but in notions and in practice, he seems to be at antipodes to "Western barbarians;" and what you have heard bruited abroad in your home circle of the strange contrariety in his habits to yours, you will, in time, find confirmed by his ways and manners.

To mention a few commonly noticed.—

In paying calls, *you* take your hat off, *he* keeps his cap on; *you* advance and offer a hearty shake of the hand to your friend; but *he*, as he advances towards the host, closes his two fists, and shakes his own hands.

At dinners (when you can afford it), *you* commence with fish and soup, &c., and end with a dessert of wines and fruits; but *he* just turns the tables, beginning with fruits, wines, and biscuits, and winding up with fish and soup.

At weddings, English ladies wear white; Chinese ladies cannot wear white, but other colours. Instead of young blooming bridesmaids trimmed in white, you may see old matrons rigged in black attendant on the anxious bride; and, for a honeymoon, the bride dispenses with a flight about the country to this and that spa, and satisfies herself with being caged up for the first month in her husband's house, and there is no need of any announcement when she may be "at home."

At funerals, black is not worn, but white; and the dead are shrouded not in white, but in the gayest dresses.

In amusements, it is not uncommon to see adults flying kites, and little urchins squatted on the ground looking on; and shuttlecocks are battledored generally not by the hand, but the heel.

In books, the name, when written outside, is inscribed on the bottom edge. The beginning of the book is what you would count the end. The running title is on the edge of each leaf. The paging is near the bottom, not at the top corner. Marginal notes are written at the top, not at the foot of the page; and in reading, you proceed from right to left, reading each column from top to bottom.

Miscellaneous.—The surname announced does not follow "the Christian name," but precedes it. In kissing, the fond mother holds up her lovely babe to her nose to smell it, as she would a rose. In moon-light, no matter how bright, you bear your lighted lantern about with you. The seaman, in naming the points of the compass, says, "East, west, south, north." In launching a vessel, she is sent into the water sideways. The horseman should mount his horse on its right side. The scholar, in reciting his lesson, does not face his master, but turns his back upon him. In parties, do not wear light pumps, but as thick-soled shoes as you can get; and, for blacking, they must be whitened with white-lead, and only the edges of the sole.

The Pigtail.—In the imagery of a Westerner, the badge by which the males in China are characterized is on his head. No sooner is the word *Chinaman* pronounced, than he stands before the mind's eye,—as delineated on the willow-pattern china vases, rice-paper pictures, &c.,—with a flow of hair depending from the back of the head. To produce such an appendage, the head is clean shaven in front and behind,—the crown alone being left untouched, from which the hair grows to its full length "unshaven, unshorn." This "pigtail" (as it is unceremoniously called by people from the West) on an average measures about a yard long; but it can be elongated by lengthening the braid of silk with which the hair is twisted, or by adding a tress to be purchased for a mite at any barber's shop.

Although in truth they belong to the exception, I have met with many natives who seemed really careful of the cleanliness and neatness of their coiffure,—early in the morning combing out the tufts, dressing them with an oleaginous stuff, and braiding the long black hair with their own fingers. In good society, the rule is to shave the head once in ten days. This is considered necessary both for comfort and respectability. To let the frontal hair grow long marks a man to be in mourning or in the depths of poverty.

On the pate of a newly-shaven youth, there is occasionally a peculiarity that may attract the notice of a keen-eyed visitor. When your table-boy comes from the barber's hands, with a well-glazed face and forehead, there is sticking round the border of his crown a circular ridge of bristles,—each hair short and stiff, and turned up like a fine-toothed comb. This that at first looks so odd, is explained on finding that the wearer is desirous to let the hairy border grow long enough to be braided with the main tress that flows gracefully behind. A very different solution this, certainly, from what I have seen in a book, published shortly before I reached China, entitled "Fanqui in China," in which the author remarks, "This I imagine to be the usual way of dressing the head by *single unengaged* youths, and of course must be very attractive," *i. e.* to the fair sex.

The common labourer often finds this ornamental plait inconvenient; yet, if at work, he can keep it out of the way by twisting it into a thick knot, or twining it about the head. Though at times an incumbrance, the poorest man is proud of this national badge, his queue. It is not unusual for a raw Briton on landing, to draw some sport from "John Chinaman's tail;" but very soon he is made to learn that he must not meddle too freely with a badge so sacred to his Chinese friend. "Noli me tangere," is the order of the tail as well as of the thistle. Yet vain as a native is of his appendage, he can turn it to purposes,—sometimes useful. A sailor at sea lashes his rough cap round his head with his tail. A crotchety pedagogue with no other rod of correction at hand, on the spur of the moment lays his tail over the head and shoulders of the stubborn scholar. And, for a bit of fun, a wag will play a trick on his companions by tying two or three tails together, and suddenly starting his comrades off in opposite directions.

The impression in Europe that the tail is universally worn by Chinese males, is on the whole correct,—being fashionable among native Chinese as well as Mantchoos. However, there are a few exceptions. The complete shaving of the head is distinctive of the priesthood in the Buddhist religion; while to let the hair grow long and bound up on the top of the head is the coiffure of the regular priests of the *Taou* sect. Very commonly you meet with wretched beggars who allow the hair to grow any length without cleaning or platting it; and the unsubdued mountaineers, called *Miaou tsze*, are said to be proud of what they consider a sign of independence, the unshaven head.

The long hair, worn perhaps in the manner of the Taouist priesthood, was from early times the habit of all China, until 200 years ago, when the new fashion was introduced by the Mantchoo dynasty on its taking possession of the throne. Two centuries have reconciled the natives of China to this badge of allegiance, and at the present time, more than ever, it has become the distinction between "royals" and "rebels." The insurrectionary movement—headed by the chieftain *Taiping*—goes by the name of "the rebellion of long-haired rascals," inasmuch as it insists on the re-adoption of the old style as the sign of admission within its ranks, namely, the natural growth of the hair upon the entire head, without being shaven, or cut, or platted, but bound in a top-knot. In one of the earliest protests issued by that brigand chief, with a catalogue of ten or twelve serious complaints against the supreme government, the first is, "that the Chinese from the outset had their own style of wearing the hair; but these Mantchoos have compelled them to shave their heads and wear a long tail, so as greatly to resemble the commonest beast." Upon this the following observations deserve to be quoted from the *Edinburgh Review*:*—

"As to this charge against the Tartar government, it must be observed that at its commencement, it only adopted the rule of almost all other dynasties in China at their foundation—the introduction of a slight alteration in the attire of the male population. The grievances here alleged might have been felt with some show of reason, and, indeed, in some places were avenged with great fury, by that generation of Chinese which had first to submit to wearing the tail, a badge of subjection under the sceptre of the Tartar conquerors, now adopted both by Chinese and Mantchoos. But, after a term of 200 years, to bring up this as *the first* in their list of grievances, sounds much like an effort to inflame the pride and animosity of the populace. This, indeed, cannot be denied, when we read their appeal in another part of their proclamations:—'Ye Chinese, *we* do most earnestly wish to save you. The majority of you are Chinese: yet how can you be so silly and stupid as to

* Art. "Political Disturbances in China," Oct. 1855.

BARBER'S SH

shave off the hair of your heads in submission to these Tartars, and adopt their style of dress? How can you be content to remain the slaves and dogs of the Mantchoos?' " &c.

The Cramped Foot.—While the badge of the man is in the head, that of gentility in the woman is in the foot. One of the earliest inquiries of a foreigner, when he visits that monster curiosity-shop—"the flowery land,"—is anent this point; and any new-comer from the West, be he never so modest, is sure to watch the pedicles of the first Chinese beauty or ugly he meets. But, should he bring up in the southern waters of China, the impression (common throughout Christendom) that the stinted foot is *universal* among Chinese women, is at once broken. The Canton boat-women (who are most expert at the oar) are the earliest to hail your approach to their shores, and they show by their naked foot that they find it more convenient to suffer this member to grow to its natural size. And, generally speaking, the female domestics of the Canton province prefer this freedom of nature. With truth, too, it may be averred, that among the lower classes, the popularity of this objectionable fashion is often but local. Thus, in Chusan and Ningpo, where I resided for eighteen months in 1842 and 1843, I can scarcely recall a single instance of a natural-sized foot among the women, even the maid-servants. But a subsequent residence in the north, particularly my travel through the interior of the Canton, Kiangse, and Chihkiang provinces, daily brought under notice females to whom the undistorted foot seemed indispensable for the sake of livelihood.

Among the camp-followers of the insurgent chief, who has been disturbing the heart of the empire, it was computed, in 1853, that there were, in the city of Nanking only, about half a million women, collected from various parts of the country. These females were formed into brigades of 13,000, under female officers.

Of these, 10,000 were picked women, drilled and garrisoned in the citadel. The rest had the hard drudgery assigned them of digging moats, making earthworks, erecting batteries, &c. Presuming that a good-sized foot would be a necessary qualification for a soldier's life in the Nanking garrison, or for engineering exploits in that singular campaign, we must give these Chinese Amazons credit for having the foot undeformed.

It appears that the Tartar families discountenance such a malformation among their daughters. Although Dame Fashion has occasionally tempted some of them to follow the manners and customs of the conquered race in compressing the feet, these misdemeanours (it is said) have been checked by the vermilion pencil of the emperor. Both in 1838 and 1840, his majesty had to sigh out, "*O tempora! O mores!*" and, issuing his orders for reform, he threatened the heads of families with degradation, if they persisted in irregularities of this stamp, and likewise warned the fair ladies, that, by falling into such low and vulgar habits, they would unfit themselves for selection as ladies of honour for the inner palace.

These remarks and instances go to show that there is a large and respectable minority of females in China with undistorted feet.

But as it is an error to say that the cramped foot is universal in China, it is no less a mistake to state, what I have seen in print, "that only parents of the wealthier sort can afford to their daughters the luxury of small feet." The streets and houses, in every town accessible to foreigners, abundantly testify how this fashion is mimicked by all classes. Even among the poor, who are likely to appreciate the value of preserving it in its natural size, there is another mode of calculating the profit and loss of the bandaged foot. When their daughters are given in marriage, "the golden lilies" (as their delicate feet are politely called) come in as a matter of no trifling pecuniary consideration. It is not at all improbable that many who have submitted to the torture till marriage, have felt it absolutely necessary to unloose the bandages and set themselves free, to assist their husbands in the garden or in the fields, &c. Yet it is unquestionable that among the lowest orders too, as well as the richer, the custom is popular and fashionable. In gangs of female beggars which have passed me in the streets of some of their cities, I have seen those whose bodies were covered with rags and vermin, but whose feet were bound as tightly and squeezed to as minute dimensions as you might witness in any wealthy family. Not unusually what to your eye seems a foot duly bound and bandaged, is all sham, and got up for the sake of aping respectability. A nurse in the family, in her evolutions by day, will sport quasi-cramped feet; but, when suddenly called up at midnight, will expose feet of ordinary and unmutilated dimensions. The pretence is admirably kept up, in some instances, by wearing short stilts, with small wooden feet in elegantly embroidered shoes. The writer has seen the part of a Chinese actress played, one of whose chief attractions was a remarkably small and elegant foot. The gait, the manner, were entirely feminine. However, it turned out to be nothing but imitation to the very feet,—all performed by a youth!

No one has ever been able to explain satisfactorily the reason for introducing this singular custom among the Chinese,—whether to imitate small delicate feet, or to keep women from gadding about, or to denote gentility and freedom from toil and hard work. Nor are the Chinese themselves agreed as to the precise date of its introduction, or the real originator of the hideous deformity.

Certain it is that the fashion is not derived by tradition from the first descendants of Noah's family. Some Europeans, I see, who conceive that there is no species of monstrosity but what must be laid at the door of the Tartar conquerors, boldly assert that the cramped foot was introduced by them 200 years since, when they mounted the throne of China. There is not the slightest foundation, however, for such an assertion. The written accounts of the natives, in tracing this custom, go much further back than 200 years. One author ascribes its origin to an infamous woman, Tankey, who lived B.C. 1100. She was empress at the time. Having been born with club-feet, she, by her marvellous influence over her husband, induced him to adopt her form of foot as the model of beauty, and to enforce by imperial edict the compression of the feet of female infants down to this imperial standard.

Others are of opinion that the detestable custom arose 1700 years after her, or A.D. 600. According to them, the then reigning monarch, *Yangte*, ordered a pet concubine to bandage her feet. On the sole of her shoe he had stamped the lotus flower; and each step this royal mistress took, she left on the ground a print of the lotus, or water-lily. On this account, to the present day, the bandaged feet of Chinese ladies are complimented as "golden lilies."

But another account maintains that the fashion owes its existence to a whim of *Le-yuh*, a licentious and tyrannical prince of the *Tang* dynasty, who held his court at Nanking about A.D. 916. It seems that one day, as he was amusing himself, the thought struck him he might improve the appearance of the feet of a choice favourite in his harem, by bending the instep, and raising it into an arch, in his imagery something resembling the new moon. How a resemblance was effected it is difficult to imagine. Nevertheless, the courtiers were so taken with admiration of this contortion, that the novel form was immediately introduced into their families.

There can be no doubt, I think, but in the estimate of the Chinese nation this artificial deformity is an essential among the elements of feminine beauty,—or, as a native writer says, "not to bind the foot is a disgrace." Mr. Lay has justly observed, "A foot two inches in length is the idol of a Chinaman, on which he lavishes the most precious epithets which nature and language can supply." In reciting the ravishing charms of their ladies, they seldom, if ever, forget to mention the extreme smallness of the foot. Indeed, the more reduced it is, the more graceful and becoming it is thought to be. But for us to trace out any physical beauty in this odious cramping of the female foot, would be an impossibility equal to that which a Chinese would feel in trying to detect any beauty in the shocking squeezing of the waists of English women into taper forms.

There have been amongst the Chinese themselves those who have been humane enough to deplore the unnatural mutilation, and have possessed the courage to condemn it. A talented writer, in the end of last century, in expressing his abhorrence of a custom so vicious, represents the Prince *Le-yuh* as the introducer of it, and on that account condemned him to endure a term of 700 years' punishment in one of the Buddhistic hells, which, he says, is but the first of a series of penalties awaiting the culprit through an interminable cycle of years to come. During the anarchy that prevailed at the opening of the present dynasty, a notorious robber-chief, who had a particular detestation of the club-feet of Chinese women, chopped off the feet of a very large number of females, and raised a vast pile of them. But the manes of those injured women are described not as crying for vengeance upon the bandit chief, but upon the head of that unpopular and unlucky Prince *Le-yuh*, whom they regard as the real occasion of their sufferings. Heaven is represented as responding to the appeal of these unfortunates by sentencing the tyrant to make 1,000,000 pairs of shoes for the women of China with his own fingers!

As to the age at which the foot of the poor girl is subjected to this cruel operation,—ordinarily it is about the sixth or seventh year; although, among the wealthier classes, shortly after the child has begun to walk. The notion of "iron shoes" and "wooden shoes" being used is, I apprehend, sheer figment in the brain of an over-imaginative foreigner. Only bandages are used. The object is not so much to make the foot smaller, as to cramp its growth into a certain shape. To force a contracted form, and to keep it in that shape, plain tight bandages are found quite sufficient; and these are not permanently to be removed until the desired figure be brought out. In notices of China, given a few years since, in "Annales de la Propagation de la Foi," the Journalist observes: "As they wear two pairs of shoes, one upon the other, and always keep one on, night and day, their feet are in the shackles." This does not agree with the custom of the people among whom I resided; and it is probable that the Romish missionary mistook the bandage on the foot for a pair of shoes.

Generally, the result of such binding is, that four of the toes are bent under the sole, the big toe only being left free, and the instep is forced up into a bulge. Accordingly, the walk of "the little-footed celestials" is a short and quick step, with a swinging of the arms, —precisely as in walking on one's heels. The Chinese compare this to the waving of a willow before a gentle breeze! Frequently, to support themselves in walking, these "waving willows" use an umbrella, make a walking-stick of an attendant, or lean upon the shoulder of a respectful grandson.

It cannot be doubted that cases of gangrene have occurred from such severe compression of the foot; and loss of both feet, or of life, and other evils, might be detailed as arising out of this pernicious rule of fashion. But, from all I have seen, I incline to the opinion that the injurious effects to life and health from this tortuous position, are not so certain as has been imagined. Mr. Lockhart, in his "Medical Missionary Report of his Hospital at Chusan, in the year 1840-41," observes: "Though several females came to the hospital affected with various diseases and with ulcers of the leg, only in one or two instances was there seen any ulcer or other disease apparently caused by the compression of the foot and the forced distortion of its bones. It cannot be said with any degree of certainty how far this practice is injurious to health; but it would appear, from the observation of numerous instances among different classes of society, both in children and adults, that it does not cause so much misery as might be expected from the severe treatment to which the feet are subjected in infancy. And torturing as this treatment of the feet would appear to be, and unsightly as are its consequences, it is, perhaps, on the whole, not more injurious to health and comfort than are the practices inflicted by fashion on the female sex in Western nations."

If there really be pain or distress in feet so tightly bandaged, it is marvellous to watch the evident freedom from both, shown by women who can walk several miles a day,—or by nurses, that seem to bear about their infant charges without discomfort,—or by maid-servants, who with apparent ease perform more than the ordinary amount of duties undertaken by English servants. There is nothing like the distress we should expect shown by the young women, who, with feet like hoofs, go through strange posture-making dances, or by the little girls that play about the streets and lanes.

Women are fond of playing at shuttlecock, and, for the battledore, use the cramped foot, but apparently without annoyance. I have seen, in a company of travelling jugglers, a woman raise a four-legged table upon her two club feet, balance it in the air, and turn it round and round upon her two extremities, but without manifesting pain.

To conclude this long paragraph on the foot fashionable among the fair sex in China, I must declare that any one acquainted with Chinese society should hesitate in saying, as has been said in the "Annales de la Propagation de la Foi," that "it is a great act of indecorum to look at a woman's foot;" and to such a one the fable will sound equally ludicrous (given in Murray's "China," vol. ii. p. 266), "that a lady presents her feet as the surest darts with which a lover's heart can be assailed."

CHAPTER II.

LONG NAILS—THE FAN—PICTURES AND RICE PAPER DRAWINGS—PROCESSIONS—IVORY BALLS—LANTERNS—CHOPSTICKS—RAT-EATING AND BIRD'S-NEST SOUP.

Long Nails.—In a European picture of a fashionable Chinaman, his fingers are tipped with lengthy nails. Certain specimens have come under my eye of nails cultivated to extraordinary dimensions, both among men and women in China,—to be interpreted as significant of an easy life, or of devotion to literature. Not unfrequent samples of affectation of gentility like this occur, especially amongst custom-house officers, copyists, writers, or pedants, that haunt the houses of wealthy foreigners.

I have met with one fellow who went by the name

"silver-nailed;" for, from their liability to be broken, he had to shield his talons in silver cases; and in one place I used to stumble on another, whose claws were so long that, when he walked abroad, he had to "sleeve them," or tuck them under his wide sleeves. Chinese do not clip, pare, or bite their nails, as foreigners do. But to wear inordinately long nails can, by no means, be said to be a very common practice in China. It is the exception to the general rule.

The Fan.—In the use of this there is no exception. It is a universal appendage with both sexes and all ranks,—in the southern parts, almost all the year round; in other parts, only in summer.

To a European, on his arrival, few articles will be more novel than the *fan* seen in the hand or the belt of male and female, rich or poor, soldiers, scholars, and priests.

The workman who can spare a hand, is industrious in flapping his fan with the one and labouring with the other. I have seen an officer going to battle waving his fan; and, on the authority of eye-witnesses of the attack on the Bogue forts in 1841, the native military were observed on those battlements coolly fanning themselves "amidst showers of shot and shell." Instead of a switch or cane, the fop in China flourishes his fan; and the schoolmaster turns it upon the cranium or knuckles of the offending pupil. It appears that the Japanese employ the article for a purpose never witnessed in the Celestial country, as Dr. Siebold says, "In Japan, a fan presented upon a kind of salver to the highborn criminal, is said to be the form of announcing his death-doom, and his head is struck off at the same moment he stretches it towards the fan."

The labourer, when he cannot use it, sticks it into the back of his collar or girdle, or "sleeves it;" but the man who can afford the luxury, slings upon his belt a worked silk case for his fan.

The innocent article now spoken of, has less variety in shape than in *the material of which it is made. Generally it is round, or leaf-like, or in the form of a* sector. The pattern is either stiff and open, or pliable and folding; the former made of silk, palm-leaf, or feathers,—the latter usually of paper, sometimes of fine goose-feathers, or of beautifully carved ivory. Besides being fashionable, one of the principal uses to which the fan is appropriated, is that of *a screen*. Everywhere, where people cannot afford something better, they may be seen treading the streets under a broiling sun, at 98° in the shade, with naught between their bare heads and the scorching sun but a plain fan. Natives fan themselves and their children to sleep. Quite as commonly it answers the purpose of a refrigerator to cool the person. But so employed, it is not flapped in the quick, hurried fashion of Europeans, which must occasion much exertion, and actually raise the temperature of the body. It is worked quietly, gently, regularly, without exhausting one's strength. If I mistake not, in the season of heat and musquitoes, no punishment could be severer to a Chinaman than to deprive him of this valuable implement. The bulk of the people, living as they do in narrow lanes, low houses, and unventilated rooms, during the extreme summer months find this article indispensable to their comfort.

The native passion for pictures, drawings, and autographs, has large scope in the various fans abroad. Made of silk and satin, they admit of a great deal of embroidery-work. Paper fans have fancy sketches on them, chiefly flowers. An infinite lot is constantly on sale with maps and outlines engraven of one or other principal city in the empire,—Nanking, Peking, or Canton; and, having every street and lane named, it forms a useful "guide" to a traveller visiting those cities. Others have the "lions" and scenes of particular localities sketched out. There are few that are without choice and classic sentences written on them. The English taste for preserving in albums the *souvenirs* of select friends, has its counterpart in the passion of gentlemen in China, who, to obtain the autograph of a friend, have only to purchase a plain fan, in which the "elder brother" is requested to pen a sentence or two, sign and stamp it with his seal. This done, it is kept or carried about by the owner as a valuable treasure,—a rare curiosity.

Pictures and Rice-paper Drawings.—The first few days of my sojourn at Macao convinced me of, what must be evident to a visitor at any Chinese port, the native taste for *pictures*, and the desire of shopkeepers to gratify what they well know to be a passion too among all strangers, for drawings, paintings, &c. But the best specimens to be obtained at Macao are not to be taken as fair samples of the native *unassisted* art. At Canton, Macao, and Hong-Kong, there has been for years so much imitation of foreign productions, and not a little improvement has gradually crept over the designs of the native artists, from the influence of Chinnery, an Englishman now deceased. That gentleman was for many years resident in Macao, and, much to his credit, lent his aid in suitable suggestions and instructions to some of the Canton draughtsmen; Lamqua, for instance, known to foreigners for his portrait-painting, and his younger brother, Tingqua, for his sketches and miniatures. The effect of this upon the native artists of Canton may easily be guessed.

Nevertheless, genuine specimens of uneducated artists are to be found in the south, but especially at the ports farther north.

The rude designs of their pencillings are such as may be seen on the commonest ware, the finest porcelain, wood-engravings, or wall-scrolls. Although the want of perspective is a glaring blunder in all their delineations, yet, from the wood-engravings in their topographics, or landscape sketches in their works on husbandry, which every foreigner meets with now-a-days, it is clear that experience has taught some of them, that, in describing the more distant objects, these should lessen in dimensions as they recede from the point of view. But they have not detected, that the more remote the objects become, to give effect to them, the more should their outlines diminish in distinctness. Well does Dr. Williams of Canton remark,* "Objects are as much exhibited as possible on a flat surface, as if the painter drew his picture from a balloon, and looked at the country with a vertical sun shining above him." Accordingly, in the grouping of different figures together, they fail ridiculously. Only in single parts and objects do they hit any likeness. In the ideography of their written language, the pictorial representations of some of their characters, though in short-hand, show a singular similitude to the objects intended; as 馬 for "horse," where the mane, tail, and legs, are marked, and 門 for "door," where the two posts of a gateway are outlined.

For fidelity in sketching *single* objects, and setting them off in colours, perhaps they are most happy in the painting of dresses, birds, insects, and flowers. Here they appear to copy nature with tolerable exactness, and are greatly assisted by their various bright and gay colours. Everywhere you find, from the pencil of Chinamen never instructed by a European master, pictorial representations of the attitude of birds and the position of shrubs, that will surprise and please you, as unexpectedly natural and drawn to life.

In their unassisted essays at portrait-painting they are certainly unsuccessful; their delineations of the "human face divine" are so expressionless, and of the

* "The Middle Kingdom," vol. ii. p. 173.

human figure so out of all proportion and unnatural. A piece with a group of human beings in it presents to your eye a caricature ludicrous in the extreme. Still, the Chinese are fond of pictures of men and things. Many a family, bereaved of its *paterfamilias*, is particular to have a portrait of the deceased hung up in the centre hall of his residence.

These may be had at any hour and any place for a mere trifle. Pictures for such an occasion are always on sale, though the only similitude they bear to the encoffined is a distressing opacity and lifelessness. Of course their great men come under the pencil of the artist; the fabulous heroes particularly. Recently, foreigners of all grades—sailors and soldiers especially—have not been less honoured, although presented in the most comic shapes and costumes; and British men-of-war, and "smoke-ships" or steamboats, are painted on paper fans and on cloth in shapeless forms and outrageous daubs. The fantastic forms and colours in which British subjects figure on their picture-books might suggest that the pencil had purposely drawn pasquinades and caricatures of Englishmen, if we were not convinced that the native artists are so far in the rear.

The local government of Peking has an "Imperial Hall," in which there hang "portraits of emperors, empresses, sages, worthies, and celebrated ministers."

Sir John Davis, in his "Sketches," observes: "It would be the highest and most criminal act of disrespect in the greatest of his subjects to possess a portrait or a visible representation of the 'Son of Heaven,' the Emperor." I apprehend this is not quite correct; for I am personally acquainted with native gentlemen, official and private, who have had possession of portraits of the Emperor, and have not concealed the matter. But, although they possessed these pictures of imperial majesty, there was no pretence that they resembled the person on the throne. Since my return to England, I find that, on the breaking out of the *Taiping* insurrection, the European world (certainly *not* the Chinese) has been entertained with portraits of the present reigning emperor and of his insurgent antagonist.* It is not at all improbable that the Chinese themselves have never seen those portraits: and, from the general style of portraits taken by the Chinese, it may be confidently asserted that these pictorial illustrations offered to the English public have nothing of similitude to the grand personages intended. Yet the writer of "Christianity in China," with the two pictures before him, separately engraven on his title-page, quietly sits down to elicit out of them the individual characters of the Emperor *Hienfung* and his rival *Taipingwang*, and draws a contrast in the following quotation: "Two portraits, one of the emperor in China, and the other of the insurgent chief, the crowned and the uncrowned; and, if we may judge from the physiognomical representations, we had almost said the woman and the man, the poltroon and the hero. Supposing the accuracy of the representations, we should deem the boy-emperor a weakling, and the insurgent chief a man fit to lead the armies of an empire against a Cæsar or a Napoleon. Commanding intellect, deep penetration, reflection, comprehension, intellectual resources, directness, determination, dignity, daring, —these are some of the attributes which the portrait of the insurgent betokens. It is the finest Chinese head we have seen; in fact, it can hardly be said to be Chinese."

Picture-painting in China is done on almost every kind of surface. On ivory, glass, and paper they are very successful. Paintings on leaves are remarkably curious, but rare, and high in price. The tissue on

* *Vide* Callery's "History of the Insurrection," &c., and "Christianity in China," published by Orr & Co., Edinburgh.

which this latter style is wrought is obtained from various kinds of trees,—leaves of very close network being preferred. After the soft part has been removed from the leaf by maceration, the reticulated skeleton is thoroughly dried and covered with isinglass, and then the colours are laid on with pretty effect.

But of their drawings those on *"rice-paper"* are most admired in Europe. By the name "rice-paper" the idea is conveyed that the soft, brittle ground of velvety surface on which the brilliant colours are laid, is made from rice-pulp. This, however, is incorrect. It is a pith of a plant of the bread-fruit genus, brought from the western parts of China, chiefly to Canton, where the manufacture of this paper and painting gives employment to several thousand hands. The outline is first laid on in Indian ink, by pressure. Then the rough delineation is filled up with the varieties of exquisite colouring matter.

Processions.—Without question the Chinese are fond of *processions*. But, from what I saw, they appear to me to be more *au fait* at them in the south than the north. Both at Macao and Canton, there are corporations that go to enormous expense in the outfit of these parades. Chiefly they are got up in honour of the *genii loci*, which for the occasion are ornamented and promenaded. The members of the clubs are dressed out very gaily, and march forth as attendants on their *penates*, with all the pomp and tinsel they can muster; silk and satin flags, most elegantly embroidered; bands of music; tables laden with sacrificial offerings, decked with flowers, images, and curiosities of every variety. To add to the diversions, groups of pedestrians are equipped in various military uniforms,—boys mounted on ponies or hobby-horses not larger than mastiffs, and aping the air, dress, and authority of mandarins, and young girls, like fairies, perched on twigs and branches of trees resting on men's shoulders.

Ivory Balls.—Next, what shall we say of the *carved concentric ivory balls*,—ten, twelve, or more, cut out, one within the other? It has long puzzled people how so intricate a piece of workmanship is fabricated. It has been conjectured, that originally they are balls cut into halves, so strongly and nicely gummed or cemented together, that it is impossible to detect the junction. And I have seen it deliberately stated, that attempts have been made by some to dissolve the union by soaking and boiling a concentric ball in oil,—of course, to no purpose.

The plain solution, obtained by myself from more than one native artist, is the following:—A piece of ivory, made perfectly round, has several conical holes worked into it, so that their several apices meet at the centre of the globular mass. The workman then commences to detach the innermost sphere of all. This is done by inserting a tool into each hole, with a point bent and very sharp. That instrument is so arranged as to cut away or scrape the ivory through each hole, at equi-distances from the surface. The implement works away at the bottom of each conical hole successively, until the incisions meet. In this way the innermost ball is separated; and to smooth, carve, and ornament it, its various faces are, one after the other, brought opposite one of the largest holes. The other balls, larger as they near the outer surface, are each cut, wrought, and polished precisely in the same manner. The outermost ball of course is done last of all. As for the utensils in this operation, the size of the shaft of the tool, as well as of the bend at its point, depends on the depth of each successive ball from the surface. Such is their mode of carving one of the most delicate and labyrinthic specimens of workmanship to be found in China or elsewhere. These "wheels within wheels" are intended chiefly for sale to foreigners: and numerous specimens annually are sent to England and America.

The Lantern.—There is another article on which there is no little ingenuity shown by the Chinese, namely, that which figures with some prominence in European notions of China,—*the lantern.* Probably no article of furniture in "the Celestial Empire" is more in use. Upon it, as upon other things, the native workman illustrates the skill and industry with which he can elaborate, and at the same time display a degree of taste in the variety of forms and the fanciful colourings in which the lantern appears. I am not now speaking of what is everywhere to be found—the plain candle or the simple lamp,—but what they call "*tung loong,*" "lamp-basket," "candle-cage," the cage or basket in which the light is lodged. It is of all sizes and shapes, and constructed of every sort of material. In dimensions, it ranges from the half-farthing toy for a child, or the penny hand-lantern for a poor man, up to the gorgeous specimen as large as a moderate-sized sitting-room, and measuring twelve or sixteen feet in diameter, or valuing about £100 sterling! As for *shape,* this article may be had in every imaginable form, round, square, irregular, and like to birds, beasts, and fishes. So, likewise the variety of material: the frame is generally of wood, or bamboo, or wire, or basket-work,—overlaid with silk, or paper, or glass, or horn, or cloth, or gauze, or glue; upon which we have decoration, or carving, or embroidery, or gilding, or painting.

In these "cages" oil or candle is used; but of *gas-light* they are totally ignorant. Their surprise and ecstasy in witnessing a good specimen of it is unbounded. A native of China, himself a great traveller in his own country, on visiting England in 1844, in company with me, was remarkably taken with this mysterious light. And in a few fugitive notes on England

and the English, published among his countrymen, he makes the following remarks on this great curiosity:* —"On the roadside there stand lamp-posts, with beautiful lanterns, that, when lit at night, illumine the whole expanse of the heavens. The gas which burns in these lamps is produced from coal, and, without question, is a most wonderful discovery; it jets forth a flame of light brighter than either the wax candle or the oil lamp can give. By it whole families enjoy light, and thousands of houses are simultaneously illuminated. In all the market-places and public thoroughfares, it is as clear and bright at midnight as at noontide, and, if I mistake not, as gay as our Feast of Lanterns. In fact, a city that is so illuminated might well be called 'a nightless city;' for you may wander about it till break of day without carrying a lantern, and, go where you please, you meet with no interruption."

Some lanterns are peculiar in construction. There is a handy one, the frame of which is upon hinges, or clasps. When not used, it can fold up, to be put into a corner or a travelling-chest. The one in general use is the transparent lantern. This is constructed of long, thin splinters, slit from bamboos, and woven into a network upon a plain frame. Such work gives employment to innumerable hands. Care is taken to have the open meshes of the lattice-work nearly of the same size. The whole frame is glued over, to keep the splints together; and when dry, a sheet of fine thin paper is gummed over the frame. A coat or two of glue and varnish is then brushed over the whole. This, on drying, gives a transparency to the lantern. To finish the article, a piece of wire is tied over the top, by which it is slung on a stick, long enough for the purchaser to hold it by as he walks about. Both the top and the bottom of the lantern are open. The

* See Chambers's Journal, No. 62, 1855, where almost the whole paper is translated.

socket for the candle is fitted in at the bottom, to be taken out and in at pleasure. To fix it in its place, this socket has a light frame of wire stuck in it, which rises up through the larger opening at the top, where it is hooked on to the lantern-stick.

There is what is called "the dragon lantern." This is brought out only in spring and autumn, at a festival observed throughout the empire, for propitiating some fabulous monsters of the deep and the valley. This huge "dragon" representative is composed of sixty or eighty painted lanterns, jointed together, each of the size and shape of a beer-barrel, with large tapers stuck in the middle. The length of the symbolical figure often exceeds 100 feet. At the one end there is an enormous head with gaping jaws; at the other a tremendous sweeping tail. To each joint there is fixed a pole for supporting the lengthy train. In that manner it is carried at night through the streets, or from village to village, the bearers as they walk in procession conveying to the corpus of the "dragon" a remarkably undulating movement, sometimes wriggling, sometimes writhing. As I have watched the "dragon procession" at night crossing a flat country and through dark lanes, it has had a most singular appearance, accompanied as it always is in Chinese waits, by men and boys shouting and screaming, with drums, gongs, and crackers, all out of tune.

Among lantern-curiosities in China, I must mention the *tsow-na-tung*, "the stalking-horse lantern," occasionally used on festive occasions. It is large, and sometimes made of glass, with sockets for lighted tapers interspersed within the massive form. The interior has three or four light circular frames of wire, the one above the other, according to the size of the whole figure, each balanced upon small pivots. In these wiry globes there are small wind-flaps, so arranged that the draught of air rushing up from beneath sets them in revolution; and upon these light cylinders there are perched figures of gaily-dressed women or warriors, horses, and other animals. It is a fanciful automaton, in certain localities very popular.

The common uses to which the lantern in China is put are numerous,—some quite unknown in the European world. At night, it is unusual for the humblest individual to go the length of a street without this article. Even when the moon is at its full, the lantern is considered indispensable. After a purchaser has selected his lantern, he has a painter to adorn it with flowers or figures, or some wise maxim, or he writes his own name upon it. Sedan-bearers and night watchmen always carry their lanterns; and officers travelling at night do not fail to display their titles upon huge "cages" borne before them. The lantern is made into toys for children, in the form of fishes, birds, and horses; and not unfrequently an urchin, yet scarcely able to walk, has his lantern-horse or phœnix.

But, will you believe it? I have been told by English officers, who themselves took part in repelling a midnight attack on the British troops in possession of the city of Ningpo in 1842, that, as the Chinese enemy, to the number of 3,000 or 4,000, attacked the city gates, they carried lighted lanterns overhead, so that they became marks for the British muskets!

Chopsticks and Food.—An essential utensil with a Chinaman is a pair of "chopsticks," as foreigners call them, from the nimbleness with which the instruments are used.* For the same reason, they go among the natives by the name *kw'ai tsze*, "quick lads." Originally they were designated *choo*, the character for which is compounded of the two signs for "bamboo" and "to help," meaning "bamboo aids;" called so,

* "Chop-chop" being used in the Canton-English brogue for "quick, quick."

probably,. because at first they were made of bamboo. In these days they are made of common wood, or the best ivory or silver. Chopsticks consist of two smooth sticks of the size of a long lead-pencil, the upper half square, the lower rounded. The two are taken up by the middle, and in the right hand. They are adjusted thus: the one "nimble lad," at its upper end, lies in the hollow of the thumb and forefinger, and at its lower is fixed in between the tops of the middle and third fingers. This one is stationary. The other "lad" is movable; it is held only by the tips of the thumb and forefinger. The couple act the part of pincers, and serve for picking up meat, fish, or vegetables already minced. In eating cooked rice, or any other grain, the bowl is brought to the mouth, and "the sticks" are used in a particularly dexterous fashion to shovel in mouthfuls of the grain.

In the higher ranks, Chinese tables are sometimes supplied with a kind of spoon, generally porcelain, rarely silver,—in shape resembling a child's "pap-spoon." It is fashionable, too, with the Chinese dandy to sport his "quick-lads' sheath" dangling from his girdle. Often this is a case ornamented with tortoise-shell, and not unusually it carries a long knife.

The question is oft repeated: "Don't the Chinese eat rats? Do they devour mice?" &c. On this, I observe, that in their cooking, and their articles of diet too, they can impart to us some suitable lessons, and instruct even a *Soyer*,—especially in places and times of scarcity. At the same time, I might give facts which would compel all to exclaim,—doubtless as a Chinese would exclaim of the English, if he were positively assured that we eat ox-flesh, or if the contents of our huckster sausages were exposed to his view,—"Non est disputandum de gustibus!" But of roasted rats and stewed mice, or of animals of this order cooked or eaten in any shape, I have never seen the semblance, never heard a hint among the Chinese themselves.

A man may be cast down to the lowest depths of poverty, when he is glad enough to scrape and swallow the dregs and offscourings about him; and, in a season of sore famine, hundreds in a town may be driven to devour what reptiles they may be able to catch. This may happen in any country;—but, for that reason, to rank such abhorrent articles among the daily provisions at a Chinese mess, is not only heedless, it is unfair.*

I find from the *Alta California* of June, 1853, that a crusade was commenced against the Chinese in California, and one ground of assault was the reported addiction of the Chinese folk to rats, lizards, &c. The editor of that paper wrote a leader on the 15th of June, of which the following is an extract:—

"If there is one class of 'nasty furriners'—as Paddy pronounced all the Mexicans during the late war—more ill-favoured, unfortunate, and forlorn among us than another, it certainly must be the Chinese. The length and breadth of popular sentiment against them in California is as a wide gulf, separating them more and

* In the Quarterly Review, January, 1857, there is a long and curious article on "Rats," in which the following instructive passage occurs:—"The *chiffonniers* of Paris feed on them without reluctance. Nor is rat-pie altogether obsolete in our own country. The gipsies continue to eat such as are caught in stacks and barns, and a distinguished surgeon of our time frequently had them served up at his table. They feed chiefly on grain; and it is merely the repulsive idea which attaches to this animal under every form, that causes it to be rejected by the same man who esteems the lobster, the crab, and the shrimp a delicacy, although he knows that they are scavengers of the sea. In the navy, they are not always so nice. An old captain in her Majesty's service informs us that on one occasion, when returning from India, the vessel was infested with rats, which made great ravages among the biscuit. Jack, to compensate for his lost provisions, had all the spoilers he could kill put into pies, and considered them an extraordinary delicacy. At the siege of Malta, when the French were hard pressed, rats fetched a dollar apiece; but the famished garrison marked their sense of the excellence of those which were delicately fed, by offering a double price for every one caught in a granary."

more every day from the hope of obtaining established rights and privileges as citizens in the state. The depth of degradation to which they are fallen in public opinion is as the bottom of a deep pit, considerably beyond the reach of means of extrication. They are sunk immeasurably lower than the native Indians, in the estimation of the miners,—lower than the beasts that prey upon the flesh of inferior animals; for the bear, it is said, will turn from tainted meat, whereas 'John' despises nothing of the creeping or crawling kind. Rats, lizards, mud-terrapins, rank and indigestible shell-fish, 'and such small deer,' have been, and continue to be, the food of the 'no ways particklar Celestial,' where flour, beef, and bacon, and other fare suitable to the stomachs of 'white folk' abound. It is not to be wondered at, therefore, that the habits of the Chinese in California should excite ineffable disgust, and turn the stomach of the stoutest Anglo-Saxon."

A week after, a reply from a Chinese appeared,—written, I believe, by a former pupil of the Morrison school at Macao. I make the following selection from it:—

"MR. EDITOR,—I am a Chinaman, and thank Shangti [God] that I am. I was taught to read and write after the English custom by a missionary at Macao, whom I also thank, as I can understand and appreciate the *numerous* acts of kindness shown to my countrymen by the great Fa Kee [American] people, especially the newspapers, whose delight it is to stigmatize my poor countrymen as a set of 'nasty furriners (*Alta*, 15th June), who are sunk so low in the depth of degradation that extrication is impossible—lower than the digger Indian, or the beasts of the field that prey upon the flesh of inferior animals;' 'despising nothing of the creeping or crawling kind;' 'rats, lizards, rank and indigestible shell-fish, have been and still continue to be the food of the no ways particklar Celestial;' 'utter inapplicability and aversion to follow those pursuits which our people insist they can only be useful in filling.' Now, what I want is your proofs to make good your unkind statements. When or where did you ever see any of my countrymen eat rat, lizard, or earth-worm? Have you ever visited any of our provision stores? Did you ever see anything of the kind? Did you ever take the trouble of investigating, as you ought to have done before condemning in such unfeeling language our manners and customs? Or why do you wish to create a feeling of prejudice against my country-men through the columns of your paper? Are we not already sufficiently ill-treated by those that profess to know better—so much so that we cannot pass along the streets without being subject to insult many times of the vilest kind? Now, that you may know the truth concerning some of our customs, know then (which likely you do know), that our empire numbers nearly, if not quite, one-half of the inhabitants of the earth; in many places it is so densely populated that it should not be considered a thing of such monstrosity that some would be compelled to eat *rats* to prolong their lives. But I have never seen it done, and I ought to know and understand as well as any one the manners and customs that have been handed down to us since the days of Hu-Lou Tue. Then, why should our whole race be reproached for doing what but a few ever did? and what you think are worms, &c., are nothing more than a species of crab or lobster, and other kind of meat cut fine and dried, which you are pleased to term rank and indigestible, fit only for the ostrich stomachs of 'John.'

"Now, is it not an admitted fact, that good health depends upon the kind of food used? Compare then the sickness and deaths of our countrymen to that of the would-be Christianized and civilized nations in California—their number is as eight to one. Now, who eats the indigestible food?"

It is not my object to lengthen this paragraph by

additional remarks on the diet of the people. I have only to add a word or two on "*bird's-nest soup.*" The natives are doubtless fond of gelatinous stews and broths. On this account, *fish-maws* and *sharks' fins* stand high in the estimate of gourmands; but neither so high as the edible "bird's-nest." When stewed, made into a soup, or mixed with other meats, this is by no means unpalatable, if my own taste can be trusted. "Much misconception formerly existed in regard to the substance of which these nests are composed; but recent scientific experiments have established the fact, that they consist of a species of seaweed [or rather of the mucilage of a seaweed], only found on the coast of Java and other islands of the Indian Archipelago. The quality of the nest varies considerably, according to the situation in which it is found. Those who are connoisseurs in the trade will select those nests which are found in the deepest recesses of the rocks. These are remarkable for their great transparency, and, from being continually exposed to an atmosphere that is impregnated with nitre, they necessarily imbibe a nitrous taste." *

The bird that supplies this whimsical luxury for the Chinese table is a small swallow, the *Hirundo esculenta*, which builds its nest on steep precipices and rocks that overhang the sea. It is found almost only in the islands of Malaysia. But the price paid to gratify this curious Chinese taste is very high. To procure the delicacy, the risk to life alone is tremendous,—from the lofty, deep, and dangerous caverns frequented by the swallows;—and, when brought to the Chinese market, the value is enormous,—the finest kind often being sold at £800 for only a hundredweight, or about twice the weight in silver! For this reason it can appear only on the tables of the wealthy, and is not a common dish with other classes.

* "Rambles in Java and the Straits," 1852.

CHAPTER III.

WHAT OF INFANTICIDE, AND THE WANT OF BENEVOLENT FEELINGS AMONG THE CHINESE?

Infanticide in China.—The crime of *infanticide* is a grave charge, which, for many many years, has been brought against the Chinese nation with some array of authority and solemnity.

It is thrown out from all quarters at random, and without the slightest reserve or hesitation. It has been the custom to expose it as the most horrible feature of Chinese life,—indubitable and not to be questioned, — that infanticide, especially of female children, is a universal crime among all classes, the poorer in particular. As a specimen of the accusation, take the following from a pamphlet published three years ago, entitled "The Chinese, a Book for the Day:"—

"There is, however, *one crime* which deserves more than a passing notice, because it shows that 'the dark places of the earth are full of the habitations of cruelty.' Female infanticide is perpetrated among the Chinese to a degree almost beyond belief. The practice is carried to such an extent, that it may almost be said to be patronized by the government, which does not interfere to prevent it. According to Barrow, it is tacitly considered a part of the duty of the police at Pekin to employ certain persons to go their rounds at an early hour in the morning with carts, in order to pick up the bodies of such infants as may have been thrown out into the street during the night. No inquiries are made, but the bodies are carried to a common pit outside the city walls, into which *all those that are living,* as well as those that are dead, are said to be thrown promiscuously! The same author states that the Roman Catholic missionaries attended daily at the pit for the purpose of rescuing some of the victims, and bringing them up in the Romish faith. Mr. Barrow further observes, that those of the missionaries with whom he had daily conversation, during a residence of five weeks in the emperor's palace, assured him that the scenes sometimes exhibited are such as to make the feeling mind shudder with horror. Dogs and swine are let loose into the streets at an early hour, before the police-carts go their rounds. He calculates the number of infants thus destroyed, in Pekin alone, to be not less than 9,000 every year.

The testimony of Barrow is of the last century. His visit to China was before 1800; and it is rather singular that not one, among the writers on China who have travelled in the interior since his day, has supported his statements by real facts. Not one has spoken of seeing carts running through the streets in the morning to clear away the dead bodies of these outcast innocents, &c.—not one. Besides, if the evidence of Barrow, like that of other writers, be examined, it is not of what he had seen, but only what he *heard*. Although he says he was resident in the imperial palace for some weeks, he never took the trouble to verify this rumour. He used to take walks and rides about the capital, but he does not mention ever having seen a single corpse of babe or adult.

Barrow asserts that police "carts go round the streets," &c.; but the streets in Chinese cities are generally so narrow that no cart can pass along the thoroughfare. As Tradescant Lay observes of Canton,* "The streets are so narrow, that no cart could pass through the principal thoroughfares; and, in the absence of sewers, all the excrement of the city is

* "The Chinese as they are," p. 47.

carried in large baskets, suspended from a pole, borne upon the shoulders of men who get their living by this kind of labour. I have met them more frequently than I wished at this necessary yet filthy task, but never saw the dead infants in their vessels, nor heard any of my friends say that such sights had fallen in their way."

Again, observes Barrow: "Swine are let loose into the streets," &c.—for what purpose, but to mutilate the helpless little ones by satisfying their ravenous cravings with their flesh and marrow?

But (to quote my lamented friend Mr. Lay once more) "in dealing with such a statement, one has only to remark that pigs have always the honour of being carried by two men when they happen to form a part of the passengers in the streets. It was never my good fortune to see any of these animals afoot, for reasons which will be obvious to any one who has visited a large town."

I would not knowingly conceal aught of the cruelties and sufferings of the Chinese; but, until I have better evidence than Barrow's, and as his bold assertions are entirely opposed to my personal investigations on the point, I have no hesitation in giving a flat denial to any assertion like his, intended to impress the European public with the notion that infanticide is practised among the Chinese with a shocking kind of system. Indeed, it is a question that gives room for inquiry whether this crime is proportionably greater in China than in some countries nearer home.

From what I have seen, in their families, of their parental affection, love of their offspring, and care of their female children, I assert it to be a foul slander on the Chinese people, to perpetuate in our publications stories which impress the youthful mind especially with the idea that they are so unnatural, wanting in feeling, and given to the slaughter of infants, that hungry hogs and dogs are trained to watch the dawn of morn as the hour for being let loose into the streets to cram their stomachs with shreds of outcast babes, and that dead-carts follow in their wake to scrape together the mangled remains of the poor unfortunates.

But "is there no infanticide in China?" Although I cannot recall a single instance of child-murder to which I can bear witness, from personal observation during my long residence in that country, and while I cannot relate one specimen of "the indifference with which the crime is regarded," I dare not say that this unnatural crime has not stained the hands of the Chinese. But that is not the question. It is averred that this is "a common practice" in China, and treated with levity by the people.

Are there no babe-murderers in England, or Scotland, or France, or Austria? Yet, who will presume to ground a general accusation against the daughters of Great Britain or France, upon the bloody crimes of a few who deserve only to have their names blotted out of the book of remembrance?

Suppose a native of China, a reader of English (of whom there are several now in China), were to peruse our daily journals for a month, and to note down the various cases that come up at the London police-courts of infant-exposure or infanticide—what should we think of his fairness and honesty, if he were to announce to his countrymen that the women of England and the fathers were a set of the most heartless wretches under the sun, for they were murdering their infants, male and female, right and left? Not less unjust is the fallacy to which many have come about the prevalence of infanticide in the Chinese empire, on grounds even more slender and shallow.

It is matter of regret to find that some who had learned this popular notion at home, although they have visited China, have not unlearned it there; which they might have done by impartial inquiry on the spot, and by the use of their eyes as well as their ears. That they adhere to it, can proceed from no other source than from either ignorance, or prejudice, or the tendency to retail fables,—not from personal observation. With all candour and frankness does Dr. Williams, of Canton (a gentleman longer resident in China than myself), observe of the Cantonese:*—" Investigations have been made about Canton, and evidence obtained to show that this crime is comparatively rare, and not at all countenanced by public opinion. The bodies of children are not as often seen in the lanes and creeks of Canton as those of adults; and the former are as likely to have died natural deaths as the latter."

There are well-meaning, but not judicious, philanthropists that have visited China, who may have ascertained from the lips of some natives that they have murdered one or two of their infants; but they have jumped to the conclusion, "*Ergo, all* the Chinese are babe-murderers!" They may have gone to other districts, the natives of which have scouted the idea of perpetrating this horrible crime; but why have the people in the former instance been believed, while the denials of the natives in the latter have been regarded as evasions of the truth, from fear of disgusting a foreigner or from shame of detection, and the entire population of 400,000,000 has been set down as giving countenance to infanticide?

Admit only that some parts of China, which are regarded by the nation itself as the poorest and most degraded of the eighteen provinces, have been fouled by this diabolical sin; then, it is published to the world (as Sir John Bowring has done recently), "it is *a common practice* in many provinces!"

Let it be granted, that, in certain places, at one time

* "Middle Kingdom," vol. ii. p. 260.

or other (say 150 years ago, when Kanghi sat upon the throne of China), what from sheer want or destitution, the lowest classes of those districts have been found guilty of this horrible enormity; but then (as Dr. Williams also justly remarks), from the conduct of these wretches of that date, "*the whole* nation (up to the present day) is branded as systematic murderers of their children!"

Let the real fact be announced that, in some parts of China there are conical mounds, or low buildings of brick (which I myself have seen), used as depositories of dead children; but the inference at once is made, that these must be the slaughter-houses of the little innocents of China: whereas the object of such erections is to provide poor parents with convenient places in which to bury out of sight infants that have died at birth or from disease. A statement to this effect was made two years ago by Sir John Bowring: "In many parts of China there are towers of brick or stone, where toothless—principally female—children are thrown by their parents into a hole made in the side of the wall."*

That sentence was penned evidently to confirm his notion that this inhuman practice is fearfully common in China; although, with the same pen, he writes that Chinese "parents are generally fond and proud of their children." But his Excellency does not appear to have inquired, and gives no room to the reader for a moment to suspect, if the "toothless children" died a natural death or not;† but writer and reader summarily decide

* Journal of the Statistical Society.

† In English law infanticide is a grave offence, but it treats the accusation with equal gravity (Taylor's "Medical Jurisprudence," p. 378); and "to provide against the danger of erroneous accusations, the law humanely presumes that every new-born child has been born dead until the contrary appear from medical or other evidence. The *onus* of proof is thereby thrown on the prosecution; and no evidence imputing murder can be received, unless it be made certain by medical and other facts that the child survived its birth, and was actually

that they all *did* die by violence at the hands of parents; or, as the *Times*,* on quoting the above passage, infers, "by a horrible inversion of custom, the Chinese seem to make arrangements for the death of children as other nations do for their lives. We have all heard of Foundling Hospitals, and of those apertures in the doors where an infant may be deposited when its parents discharge themselves of its care; but from the receptacles provided for discarded infants in China there is no return."

Further, it has been often said, and is extensively believed in Europe, that infanticide is treated with indifference both by the government and the people in cases of detection.

There is no doubt that, in some places, where terrible scarcity and famine have visited the people, many parents have, in a fit of desperation, exposed and even slaughtered their children; but at that the public mind has revolted, as will be shown in the next section. Foundling hospitals have long existed in China, and, on an emergency, temporary asylums have been set on foot.

Native tracts and official edicts (some of them of rather antique date) are met with against "the drowning of female infants." These may naturally excite suspicion that the crime has, at certain seasons and places, existed to an alarming extent; but their very publication, and those very institutions above-named, forbid the hypothesis that a practice so shocking to humanity "is regarded with indifference by the public generally, and is patronized by the government."

Sir George Staunton gives the following translation of a part of the 319th section of the Penal Code of China, and annexes a very appropriate note on the

living when the violence was offered it." Be the accusation against a nation as well as a person, "the *onus* of proof is thrown on the prosecution."

* March 12, 1857.

charge of infanticide against the Chinese :—"If a father, mother, paternal grandfather or grandmother chastises a disobedient child or grandchild in a severe and unaccustomary manner so that he or she dies, the party so offending shall be punished with 100 blows. When any of the aforesaid relations are guilty of killing such disobedient child or grandchild designedly, the punishment shall be extended to 60 blows and one year's banishment."

"It is manifest from this article," says Sir George, "that parents are not in any case absolutely intrusted with a power over the lives of their children, and that, accordingly, the crime of infanticide, *however prevalent it may* BE SUPPOSED *to be in China, is not, in fact, either directly sanctioned by the government, or agreeable to the general spirit of the laws and institutions of the empire.*"

The Want of Benevolent Feelings and Institutions in China.—But, besides the vague charge of infanticide, there is a general impression abroad, that a Chinaman is utterly destitute of the softer and generous feelings implanted in the human race. Cases are cited, the truth of which may not be questioned, of instances of inhumanity perpetrated by Chinamen. But acts of certain villains (be they ruffians in high life or among the humbler classes) are not to be charged on the entire people. Unfortunately, however, there has been too long encouraged, even among religious communities in our country, a taste for illustrations of "horrid cruelty" among the heathen, which tend much to breed disgust and dread, rather than awaken godly compassion or a fraternal concern to meet them as men and brethren on the same platform of probation. Indeed, is it not revolting, that, in our school-books, juvenile magazines, and addresses to children, there is too much done to pamper to this greed for stories of the cruel and heartless features in heathen nations?

Can this have a beneficial effect on the youthful mind? Tales of horror are not likely to move the fine and tender feelings of a juvenile heart. Besides, it is anything but fair to the rising race to choke their minds chiefly with monstrous and hideous notions of their fellow-men; as it is alike unjust to the pagan to prejudice the benevolent public by selections only from the dark side of his nature.

During my residence in different parts of China, one special topic of inquiry with me related to the existence and conduct of benevolent institutions among the Chinese; and, in giving in full the results of my observations on this point, I have no scruple whatever.

Having just dealt with the question of popular infanticide, I will now refer particularly to the existence of institutions for the protection of foundlings of both sexes, that exist in almost every chief city in the "Flowery Land."

The first of this class that I inspected in 1842, was in the city of Ningpo.

As I reached the building, I observed on the left of the outer porch there was a crib, large enough to deposit an infant. Over the chief gate there were emblazoned the characters for "nurture and protect infants," a sufficient index to the precise object of the institution.

On crossing the threshold, there opened a finely paved square. To the right and left, there were side doors with a tablet on each, denoting "milk-room," or nursery.

A number of coarse-looking women were peeping through the lattice, with babes at their breasts, and boys and girls at their heels. These poor foundlings formed a collection of the most dirty, ragged, little objects I have ever beheld. The nurses each had charge of two or three. At that time there were about seventy male and female children on the foundation. I gained admittance into the girls' nursery, where there were thirty domiciles, in two or three rows, running the one behind the other. The apartments occupied by the housekeeper formed a great contrast in order, &c., to the other parts of the establishment.

The object of the institution is to afford to outcast babes, or the children of destitute parents, the protection and nurture of a home. Boys remain under its roof until the age of ten or twelve, when they are hired out to service, or adopted by some childless parents; girls, until the age of fourteen or fifteen, when they are engaged as domestic servants, perhaps taken into concubinage, or oftener betrothed by a parent in behalf of a son or grandson. The institution is above 100 years old. It was erected in the first year of Kienlung's reign, when it numbered twenty-four small cabins. Since then it has been much enlarged, and now consists of 100 rooms, with public halls and superintendent's quarters.

The support it derives is from various quarters. Its annual income is from money laid out at interest, private donations, rent of houses, lands let out for return in kind or money, and yearly contributions made by each of the six districts in the department of Ningpo.

From "The Annals of Ningpo," published nearly ten years ago, it appears that the institution at that time owned more than 200 acres of land granted by the generosity of its supporters; and, in the fortieth year of Kienlung's reign, his majesty ordered the city and district of Ningpo to contribute annually forty stone of paddy, and the other six district towns of the same department respectively thirty-six stone of paddy, "so that the nurses and foundlings might be supplied with monthly rations, and whatever medicine they may require." Besides the resident manager, there is appointed a government inspector, who takes general cognizance of the affairs of the institution, principally to check extravagance, or prevent embezzlement.

Foundling hospitals in China are by no means of recent origin. A native writer, in one of the reports of the Shanghai Foundling Institution, observes: "I regard the plan of this asylum as similar to the method adopted during the *Chow* dynasty (B.C. 1120—B.C. 250), of relieving orphans in the spring and summer seasons. So likewise, during the *Han* dynasty (B.C. 220—A.D. 250), the emperors used to supply, from the public granaries, both orphans and those who had children which they had no means of supporting. Again, in the *Sung* dynasty (A.D. 960—1270), in one place and at one time, 500 acres of land were appropriated by government to the erection of buildings for the reception of castaway children."

Nor is it *rare*, as already intimated, to meet with institutions of this nature in other parts of China.

In Shanghai, there is one founded in the year 1710. The following description of it, taken from notes made during my last visit to it, in 1852, is extracted from *Chambers's Journal*, No. 135, in which I was permitted to insert it:—

"It stands in the south-east part, and near the centre of the city, in a retired lane; where, over an unpretending gateway, there is the inscription on stone, *Yuhyingtang*—'The Hall for Nourishing Infants.' The first thing that attracts your attention is a drawer at the right side of the entrance. Curiosity led me to pull it out, and I found it nicely wadded with cotton. On shutting it, I heard a bell tinkle inside the building; and it was explained to me that this drawer was meant for the deposit of any babe brought there by day or night. That due notice may be given to the inmates, the drawer, as soon as it slides back, touches a spring that pulls a bell; and then the porter hastens to open it, and introduce the live contents to the resident director.

"Upon entering the building, I counted twenty-four

indoor foundlings, chiefly infant girls, and among them maimed, blind, and idiots. To one child in particular my attention was called—a deaf mute eleven years of age. Of outdoor patients they had at that time 100 on their books. The nursery apartments were small, with cots humble, but sufficiently comfortable for the nurses. Some low empty barrels were pointed out, which, I was told, were used for lodging the little creatures, to relieve the nurses' arms when their charges became too heavy, or began to creep about. These child-barrels are about the ordinary height of a crawling infant, and full of straw, into which the piccaninny is put, and kept erect and out of harm's way. Of hired wet-nurses, I saw several, some of them in charge of two or three babes; and all were young, and appeared more healthy, clean, and good-looking than women generally of the lower orders. I was introduced to two resident officers, one a medico in his surgery, rather respectable in appearance and bearing. They informed me that, as the children grow up, they are adopted into families, or betrothed, or sent out to service. But no more accurate description can be given of the establishment, its objects and working, than in its annual reports, of which I have two specimens, one (for the year 1849) presented me on my last visit.

"Perhaps the most curious and instructive part of that report is the rules of the institution. A list of fourteen of these is given, which are too long and minute for more than a brief summary of the more important. These provide that the friends of the society shall meet every fortnight in the building, when, after paying their respects to the patron idol, they shall inspect the children, inquire into the conduct of the nurses, and give them their allowances in money and food. Under another head, the examination to be given to each foundling on entering is detailed in the following terms:—'The officers of the establishment must try to find out the year, month, and day of the child's birth; the lines and form of the fingers must be inspected;* likewise whether all the senses and members be perfect, and if there be on the body any scars or sores: all these particulars must be registered, and the child may then be given to one of the nurses to suckle.'

"Special attention is called to the hiring of wet-nurses, on which subject a whole paragraph is bestowed. 'Nothing can be so important in the rearing of infants as to select suitable wet-nurses. This ought always to be attended to with caution. Should any woman wish to obtain such a situation in our establishment, her own husband may come and give in her name, or a relative may do so, or a neighbour: but they must likewise stand security for her. The resident officers must then see that she is really able to suckle. If she be approved of, let her full name be entered on the lists; and when the foundlings are brought in, let them be distributed among these wet-nurses, as need be. Let there be constant vigilance to ascertain whether these women prove neglectful of their charge, or pass the children over to other hands, or exchange the children amongst themselves, so as to avoid trouble, or, what is worse than all, whether they have sent their own children into the building, and then offered themselves as nurses, for the sake of gain. . . . . It is the duty of the officers of the establishment to make all these inquiries. Should any of the nurses be charged with light offences, dismiss them at once, and appoint others in their stead; but for more serious offences, let them be handed over to the justice of the law.'

"The eleventh rule requires due clothing to be pro-

* The object of this is to prevent or detect any kind of smuggling or exchanging children belonging to the institution. Thus, prisoners and exiles have generally the wrinkles and lines upon their hands carefully examined and registered, to prevent evasion, &c.

vided for the children, and prescribes that 'in the third month there shall be given each foundling a calico shirt and a pair of trousers; in the fourth, a breast-bib and mosquito curtains; and in the eighth, a cotton jacket and petticoat, a cap, stockings, and a wadded coverlet. All these articles must have the mark of the establishment stamped on them, and whenever they are given out, must be registered in the books. The nurses are forbidden to pawn them. Each year, exactly as each season expires, the clothes must be duly changed, and should any child die or be adopted, they must be restored to the establishment.' Again:— 'An infant that has been deserted, has been deprived of the regard of both father and mother; but our institution engages to receive and train it up. Now, after that child has by adoption been transferred by us into other hands, if any one should falsely assume to be its father or mother, and by force carry it off, the only appeal against such savage villany is just to lay the written engagements between the board and the adopting family before the magistrate, and hand the offenders over to justice. Moreover, 'our asylum provides only for taking charge of deserted infants; so, should any persons recommend their own child to be suckled by the nurses of this house, on the plea that the mother is sick or dead, or bring any child of three years old and upwards that can feed itself and walk— no such case can for a moment be entertained, and we shall appeal to the magistrate for support.'

"Finally, 'as to the adoption by families of foundlings from our establishment—the male children must be adopted according to all the rules and rites of legitimacy, as if the adopting parents were childless; then there need be no more trouble about them. But about the girls, to prevent their being taken away merely to be reared for concubinage, or made objects of purchase, or reserved for other vile purposes, the superintendent of the institution, unless he be already thoroughly acquainted with the contracting parties, must first of all inquire about the occupations of the said persons, so that he may be quite certain that the child is not to be doomed to debasement of any kind. But even then, previous to any formal transfer of the girl, let due securities be taken from the relatives and neighbours of the parties. This being a point of first-rate importance, let the utmost caution be exercised in it.'

"One of the annual reports of this institution winds up with an appeal for increased support from the public in these words: 'Suppose that, for the sake of kindness to our fellow-men, especially those destitute creatures that are fatherless and motherless, every one among the benevolent in this neighbourhood were each day to contribute only one cash (or about one-seventh of a farthing), this would be sufficient to support all the foundlings in this house for one day. Now, it would be well if each person were not to set down a little good as *un*meritorious, or the most trifling donation as useless. Who knows but by this act you may lead others to follow your example? By the vernal breath from your own lips, either you may nourish a blade of benevolence in the field of happiness, or you may cherish the bud already sprouting. By promptly taking advantage of any opportunity when offered, for accomplishing your object, you may greatly promote the kind aims of this institution, at which we shall be mightily pleased.—Respectfully addressed to the public by the committee of the Shanghai Foundling Hospital.'"

Although infanticide and "the drowning of female infants," may have been, in certain places, or at particular times, the occasion of such solicitude and generosity on the part of the thinking public as to encourage the erection of Foundling Asylums,—it is scarcely to be doubted that the human heart in China, as in other parts of the earth, has had the spark of kindness lit up, if not fed, by the harrowing scenes that have often occurred, and unfortunately still happen in times of starvation and flood along the river banks. By these frightful visitations whole districts have been swept away, and hundreds of infants have been, not cast away, but left in the neighbourhood and grounds of "well-to-do people,"—in the last moment of desperation, by parents who could no longer endure the infant cries of hunger, and hoped that an unknown Samaritan might pass by to pick up the little charge and satisfy its cravings.

I remember well the spring of 1850, when, in consequence of severe famine in the interior, Shanghai and its environs were haunted by thousands of beggars. They were not people of the locality. They came from farther up the country,—many from the banks of the *Yangtze* and Yellow rivers. They covered the face of the country like locusts. And the wretched beggars, forming gangs and parties pressed with hunger, made their vociferous demands.

To relieve the distressed multitudes, *charities* were solicited by the provincial and local governments, and the smallest contributions were encouraged. The rich gentry and the middle classes all united in the good work,—opening subscription-lists and grain-stores. In some instances, contribution-lists were opened in shares not exceeding 100 copper cash, or about fourpence. The foreigners were glad to throw their mites into the benevolent scheme. But not the least important and effective was a temporary asylum got up by the native gentry of Shanghai, solely for the shelter and support of destitute *children*. It lay outside the south gate of the city, and was called the "Asylum for Outcast Children."

Having had a good opportunity, by personal inspection, of acquainting myself with its object and operations, I can readily speak of it. The asylum was but temporary,—only for a few months, to meet the peculiar exigencies of the juncture. The range of buildings was run up in a few days,—extending over four acres of land. It was divided into one hundred apartments, all on one floor,—some fifteen feet square, some thirty feet. They were flagged below, where the children ate and played; had lath partitions, and were fitted up with sleeping-compartments raised a few feet above the ground. The number of children, when I visited it, amounted to 2,000, one-third of them girls. Each child was well clad, and seemed well fed. A ticket was put on each, and a minute registry kept of the place from which the child was brought; so that, on the breaking up of the asylum, it might be restored to its proper guardians. They were portioned off in twenties for each compartment, and placed under an aged matron, who had the charge of their food, clothing, medicine, &c. The average ages were between three and ten. It was said, those found under three were sent to the Shanghai Foundling Hospital already spoken of, and any above ten years were declined. Wherever the innocent little sufferers were found, they were taken up and minutely questioned as to age, surname, and parents. I fully believe that of this family of children, numbers were not cast out by the parents to the intent that they might not live, but were sent out or left on the roadside in the expectation that their offspring might live on public bounty, fed and clothed, as was done in this institution. This act of benevolence on the part of the Shanghai natives was unsuggested by foreigners. It was set on foot by themselves, encouraged by the local magistracy, and carried out by the united effort of a kind-hearted public. And I must add that the entire order in the establishment was, as far as my inspection served, most surprising, and the arrangements admirable.

Of other philanthropic societies, I give the following, as found during my residence at Ningpo, with additional notes collected subsequently.

1st. The *Tsing Kiehtang*, or "Virtuous Hall," is a retreat for poor widows that have lost their earthly all. The building at Ningpo had been erected under the sanction of government, but chiefly by private contributions. Admission is also granted to maidens whose intended husbands have died prior to marriage, and who have, in consequence of their bereavement, taken upon them the vow of perpetual virginity.

In most of their principal cities, some provision is made for destitute *widows*. At Canton, for instance, there was a fund for the relief of this class, which was of comparatively recent origin, opened only in 1820. The government united with the gentry in supporting and managing the fund. The allowance to the widow was small, only £1. 13*s*. per annum, but enough to supply her with some food for a time. The number on the fund has amounted to 1,500 women. Not long ago, the public authorities made loud complaints that some of these widow ladies, on getting married again, sold their tickets instead of returning them, and that the relatives of others who had died had done the same. This formed a kind of parish relief in Canton; yet those who had kindred on the spot did not like the exposure of their names and circumstances—points elicited in getting these alms; so that the chief applicants were widows whose relations lived at a distance from the city.

2nd. The *Yangtse-yuen*, or the "Provident and Relief Asylum," at Ningpo, was a government building, designed to afford shelter to the infirm and disabled. Here the halt, the maimed, the lame, &c., met to sympathize with each other and receive a slight expression of paternal concern from the heads of government.

The larger cities throughout the empire—where both poverty and wealth are stalking through the streets—offer some such refuge to the numberless objects of pity that float about the lanes and alleys. However, as in every other land under the sun, the arrangements are by no means adequate to meet the necessities of indigent refugees, or to suppress beggary. According to some intimations, it appears that only "a limited number" is statedly favoured with provisions from the Imperial treasury, while "the excess" only just tastes of the good things the Imperial heart would confer if the coffers of the nation were fuller. As soon as those on the list die off or disappear, their places are readily filled up out of the mob of clamorous candidates. There seems to be one individual appointed by the local authorities to superintend and keep in order the inmates of this retreat. If these, his *protégés*, be found begging in the streets, or rather, if complaints be reported of their noisy alms-begging, he has authority to check their vagrant and violent dispositions.

Thrown as they all were into one building, itself comfortless, inconceivably so from the dirty and irregular habits of its occupants,—respectable natives of Ningpo, though themselves not of the "first water," spoke of it with significant shrugs and gestures, so that I cannot hold out the notion that, in neatness, order, and cleanliness, it can resemble the "poor-houses" of Great Britain. However well becoming a patriarchal government as that of China, various circumstances render this provision for the outcasts of society almost useless and inefficient. Not the least drawback is the notorious and devilish cupidity of the managers, who do not hesitate to enrich themselves by drawing largely upon the public allowances for the famished and helpless. Doubtless, too, this passing remark may fall on most of the philanthropic institutes in the empire of China.

As a natural consequence, observe the crowds of pitiful objects in human form that haunt the streets and parade from shop to shop, house to house, raising their importunate and ceaseless din for "cold greens," "cold rice," "cold tea."

STREET BALLAD SINGERS. CHINESE AIR.

Early in the morning, no sooner has the bustle of business begun to wake up within the city walls, than (as I have repeatedly witnessed, at Ningpo for example) bands of blind, lame, and scurvy beggars enter in Indian file, and divide off at certain points in gangs, to press their claims on the pity and the purses of shopkeepers and householders.

The utility of music is fully appreciated by these beggars, as valuable in expressing their wants and in exciting the pity of passengers; but to European notions of harmony, it does not deserve the name of music. Nevertheless, however unscientific Chinese music may be, its power of association over the people is marvellous; for a native of the "middle kingdom" would far rather hear a band of their ballad-singers whining their unearthly twangs, than listen to the heavenly warblings of the nightingale of the West, the far-famed Jenny Lind.

If you can master it, as a specimen of their vocal music, take the Chinese air in the opposite page set to English notes. The Chinese words are placed underneath, and the following may be given as a general translation.

THE SONG OF THE FUNG-YANG BEGGAR.

*Fung-yang** bright,—fair to view,
During ten years' reign of the Emperor Choo:
Then came deluge, three years' drought too—
Three years' locusts,—woe after woe.
Rich man field sold, poor man child sold;
Childless and landless, too, wretched I,
A houseless wanderer, must beg or die.

Besides vocal music, playing on instruments is also called into use by these pilgrim-beggars, in order to call the attention of passers-by, and dispose them to the exercise of charity. On approaching, you are flattered

* A district in Nganhwuy province.

and entreated. Should your hand move quickly and be liberal, ten thousand blessings are lavishly poured on your happy head; but ill-luck to the hard heart and hand that withhold a cash.

Liberal almsgiving is not unusual in China. At Canton, a rich lady, during the cold weather of 1832, distributed 500 warm jackets among the aged and infirm poor of that capital; and at Shanghai, in the far north, it was no uncommon thing, in the depth of winter, to find a merchant, or some benevolent family, or a committee of natives, subscribing to supply the destitute with clothing, and get up "kitchens" for boiling rice and tea, to be distributed by tickets among the poor multitudes.

In this manner, the wealthy occasionally devise liberal things for their fellow-creatures, and gain for themselves the smiles of the emperor, as well as the benedictions of the poor.

Drought, inundation, hailstorms, pestilence, and war call forth from time to time the special benevolence of the imperial government, as noticed in the Peking Gazettes, along with the sums of money or supplies of grain granted.

Thus, in 1842 and 1843, owing to the distresses in which especially Ningpo and its neighbourhood had been involved in the broils with England, the emperor resolved on soothing the people there with tokens of royal bounty, and distributed a sum of money among the unfortunate classes in the several cities of *Ningpo*, *Chinhai*, and *Tinghai*, where they had been haunted by the horrors of war. Those whose claims were acknowledged by duly appointed commissioners, had the character 查 marked over their doors, denoting "examined and approved of." And in my daily walks in Ningpo and its suburbs, my eye used to fall on hundreds of these official marks. The distribution was to continue for three months in succession. In the department of Ningpo, it was calculated, by one in authority, that, in 1843, there were 200,000 of these beneficiaries. Farther north, in the province of *Kiangsoo*, that same year, and in consequence of similar disasters, notwithstanding the enormous draught made on the imperial treasury by the demands of the British government, in consideration of the distresses of the people the government sold rice out of the public granaries at half-price for four months, which tended much to the relief of the lower classes.

With the Kwangse insurgents, it has been a favourite accusation against the reigning dynasty, published in their national protest, that, "Whenever there is famine from drought, the emperor does not show a particle of commiseration for the people; but, while multitudes are starving to death or wandering about in search of food, and the bones of those that have perished lie about exposed like grass on the earth, these Mantchoos just sit and look on, only too glad to see the Chinese population gradually diminishing." The facts I have already mentioned give the lie to this. It is known, also, among the people, that the policy of the imperial government is to exhaust all means to soothe and supply the people in distress. Doubtless, in many cases, through the knavery of the intermediate agents, embezzlement and oppression exist, so as completely to thwart the intentions of the imperial heart. But more facts on the other side could be given indicative of the paternal regard of the throne for the people. It is only in 1849, that, on account of a violent inundation near *Soochow*, the Paris of China, the poor outcast peasants there, and others, had, for four months successively, a monthly allowance from the imperial treasury of 900 cash, or 2*s.* 6*d.*, to each adult in distress; and 600 cash, or 1*s.* 8*d.*, to every young person.

One line of conduct pursued by the military leaders of the English forces in 1842, at such places as were visited by them,—that proved successful in reconciling myriads of the poor to their misfortunes, and in gaining a good name for the conquering heroes,—was the liberal and cheap distribution among them of rice found in the government granaries which fell into British hands. On more than one occasion, I have been present at a "rice-dispensary," opened at *Chinhai,* during our occupation of that citadel. The claims of hunger, as well as the low price of the rice, urged the starving population of every age and sex to hasten to their "barbarian" friends, from whom they received this timely token of concern for their terrible wants; and the name of *Lopat-tan* (Robert Thom), then acting Chinese interpreter and magistrate at *Chinhai,* who headed this charitable movement, is deeply engraven on the memory of hundreds and thousands in that vicinity.

3rd. *Medical Dispensaries* exist in this country for the purpose of examining the sick and diseased, and administering medicine free of charge. I was not able to find any special institution of this character at Ningpo, except a branch department connected with a general benevolent society mentioned below; yet I have good native authority for saying that they exist in cities of the first magnitude. But, from all accounts, it is to be apprehended they are inoperative, on account of the narrow and illiberal principles on which they are worked.

In a native description of the city of Canton, I find that, "some centuries ago, a public medical dispensary was got up, with a view to furnish the poor sick with medicines;" but, adds the author, "for a long time the establishment has been closed." Up to 1853, there was a public dispensary at Shanghai, raised, supported, and managed only by the native residents. It was set on foot in 1845. The report for that year observes: "In the rivers about Shanghai, we have the day and night tides; but in the branch streams and canals, where there is no tide, the water becomes stagnant. The water of the wells is affected in the same way; and, accordingly, the people who live in those vicinities suffer from the damp and malaria, and are cut down by disease. . . . . . Hence, during the summer and autumn, much sickness prevails among them. Those who have the means perhaps call in a physician. This is all very well. But, when the poor are victims to these malignant influences, and are unable to procure medical aid, how terrible are the consequences! Now, is it not far more praiseworthy to provide for people when they are alive, than to do so by procuring coffins for them when they are dead?"

These imperative reasons, it is stated, induced many benevolent individuals to open the dispensary. By the printed report of 1845, above 13,000 patients attended during the first three months. The regulations of the establishment are most punctiliously laid down on black and white, of which I can only offer the reader the essential points; namely, that "as it is a benevolent society, in the expenditure there must be marked prudence and rigid economy:" that "the physicians, on giving advice, are not to take fees:" that "each patient must be attended to in turn, and not strive to be seen before his turn:" "the physicians must not either, on account of wind or rain, absent themselves from their posts." Twenty-nine practitioners are named as having severally given their aid for the year. The subscriptions for the year exceeded £150; still a small balance remained after deducting the expenditure. Two-thirds of the expenditure went to defray medicines; the remaining third was spent on "miscellaneous expenses," or expenses on account of the officials about the establishment—the list of which may amuse the reader:—

"Dinners for physicians and attendants; flour cakes for dinners and luncheons; dinners to the apothecaries; physicians' boat-hire and postages; altar candles; tea; tobacco; 200 writing-pencils, and 400 ink-sticks; five subscription-books; paper for writing prescriptions on; folding paper for making up medicines; red placards; seventy prescription-books; registry-books; powder-envelopes; tickets for patients; cooks' wages; paper on which to put plasters; seven teapots; twenty towels; subscription-papers; engraving physicians' stamps; rice-baskets; and twenty-two tobacco-pipes," &c.

4th. *An Asylum for the Blind* existed in Canton in 1832, a notice of which I extract from the first volume of the Chinese Repository:—"The magistrates have issued a proclamation concerning this governmental institution, requiring all the blind to appear in person and show their tickets for examination. There appear to be 2,394 blind people, both men and women, that receive an allowance of something under one shilling a week. This is insufficient for food, and they are allowed to beg, sing, &c., for the sake of additional subsistence."

5th. There has been also a *Leper Hospital*, or *Ma fung yuen*, at Canton, where leprosy of the most hideous and incurable form has numerous victims. In 1832, the patients here numbered 341; supported at an expense of only £100 per annum!

6th. *A Vaccine Establishment* has been maintained at Canton by the natives since 1805. Vaccination was first introduced among the Chinese by Alexander Pearson, surgeon of the East-India Company's factory at Canton. Dr. Pearson also opened this "Vaccine Institution," and wrote a short treatise on the theory and art, which was translated into Chinese by Sir George Staunton. Since then, however, it has been entirely maintained by the natives themselves, who learnt the art from Dr. Pearson of checking small-pox by vaccination. Native practitioners attend regularly. The merits of this novel introduction are wide-spread through the most important districts. In other parts of China, inoculation is said to be practised among the Chinese, occasionally on the tender lining membrane of the nostrils.

7th. There used to be at Shanghai a *Humane Society*, or *Kew-sang-chuh*, a society to rescue drowning people. I know not whether it exists now; but, previous to the occupation of the city by the piratical brigands of 1853, the institution stood on the bank of the river outside the great east gate.

It provided that, in case any person fell into the river, boats should be at hand to pick him up. If picked up, means for restoring life were adopted,—such as placing the unfortunate man on his back, and inverting a large boiler over his abdomen! The result expected from this operation is, that the water by which the patient has been choked will ooze out at the nose, "on account of the connection between his distended abdomen and the empty space of the boiler!" Another mode, recommended in the prospectus, for restoring animation, is to "hang up the patient by his feet on the shoulders of another man, and then stop up the anus with a lump of cotton, as a motion might prove fatal. The consequence will be, that water will flow out of the mouth, and thus life will be saved!"

8th. *Almshouses for old men*, erected and supported by public contributions, exist in most of the principal towns. At Hangchow, in 1843, they boasted of 500 "destitute aged men" belonging to such an institute, enjoying the shelter and protection necessary and suitable at their time of life.

9th. At Shanghai, the writer found two benevolent institutions of a general character,—the one in the south part of the city, called *Tung-shen*, or "United Goodness Hall;" the other outside the north gate, the *Tung-jin*, or "United Benevolence Institution."

The latter seemed to be the more prosperous, yet their objects were one and the same; the following for instance:—To show pity to the widow; to provide for aged men; to distribute coffins among the poor; to look after the cemetery for the poor; to supply water in case of a conflagration; to support the free schools; to supply the poor with warm clothing and food in winter.

10th. But at Ningpo there was the *Te-jin-chuh*, or "Practical Benevolent Society," which particularly attracted my attention.

It was set on foot in 1834, chiefly at the instigation of two native gentlemen, who contributed largely of their own property, and induced many wealthy citizens to join them in some effective measures for the relief of the popular misery, then aggravated by the hard times of that year. Its precise views may be understood from this digest, drawn out of its report of 1836, which I have lying before me. Its *objects* are:—

"*To take care of outcast infants.*"—The report states that the founders had their pity moved by the harrowing scenes of famished, screaming, and pining babes which, having been deserted by parents in consequence of the severe famine of the season, they saw lying along the roads and highways.

"*To provide raiment for the poor during the cold winter.*"—The report intimates that, in 1835, grants of clothes were made to the Foundling Hospital and to numerous beggars in town and country,—to the latter especially, a coarse paddy-sack covering the whole person.

"*To supply the poor with coffins.*"—By printed statements in my hands, it appears that, in that same year, 151 coffins were provided for destitute families, at an average expense of five shillings.

"*To bury those found dead, at least those unrecognized.*"—Under this head the society had, in 1835, to provide for 279 adults and children.

"*To gather the scattered bones of the dead,*" lying about the burial-grounds. This is a mark of respect periodically paid to the relics of those who already have been committed to the dust, but whose coffins, from age, have broken up. When the bones are collected, they are transported to the cemetery belonging to the society. The coffins in which the scattered bones are placed are not large, and one year they numbered 647.

Perhaps the most forbidding spectacle witnessed in the neighbourhood of a Chinese city (*e. g.* Ningpo) is the exposure of coffins, many of them old, dirty, and dilapidated. Those I encountered in 1842 and 1843 lay chiefly along the foot of the ramparts. Some had gone to pieces from sheer rottenness, and others (especially the more recent) had been rummaged by thieves and hungry dogs. But these coffins, which form so unpleasant a part of a traveller's prospect in China, generally contain the remains of the poor. The respectable portion of the community, so religiously careful of the relics of departed friends, erect "family tombs," which, both within and without Ningpo, are denoted by small conical mounds, in the shape of a sugar-loaf, covered with green sod, and encircled with junipers or the common pine.

Charity Hills, under the supervision of the above society, are appropriated for the burial of the friendless and moneyless.

In Ningpo, there are two lots of ground—one to the east, the other to the west—both the property of this society, and set apart for the purpose specified. While walking on the walls of Ningpo, it was no unusual thing for me, at different parts within and without the ramparts, to stumble on heaps of coffins that seemed recently collected. This was soon explained by meeting with the report of this society, which at certain times sent its agents out to pile together the coffins of the poor, for the purpose of transporting them by boat to the "Charity Hills," where they were buried at the expense of the society.

"*To dispense medicine to the sick poor.*"

"*To distribute tea in the summer, and provide firewood for preparing it.*"

One more object of the institution is, "*To gather, for burning, paper with written characters.*"

Accordingly, the society sends forth its bearers, to go from house to house, lane to lane, street to street, and pick up all the scraps and fragments of written or printed paper that are lying about. In this way, one year it collected fifty hundredweight of such paper rubbish. Nor is this "good deed" (for so the Chinese believe and designate it) confined to any particular society. There are many private individuals who, supposing it to be in the eye of their gods a meritorious act, of their own accord distribute collectors of paper scraps round the city, pay their wages out of their own pockets, and, on getting the gleanings, have a regular bonfire. The bearers employed carry large hampers, with the announcement written on them, *King-sih ts~e-che,* "Be respectfully careful of paper with written characters." This explains a sight occasionally noticed in the city streets,—a man carrying huge baskets of loose paper. The respect of the Chinese, the well-bred especially, for written or printed paper exceeds all bounds: it is sacred to an extreme. Hence the complaints often made at the outrageous treatment of written and printed paper at the hands of foreigners.

But, in winding up a list of benevolent movements among the Chinese themselves, I must not omit an important item—

11th. *Educational Charities.*—At Ningpo there was a two-hundred-year-old building, originally named "The Charity-field College," whose prime object was to assist the poor and illiterate in their education.

During my residence I saw little but its ruins; for, having in the war with Britain been temporarily occupied by a Chinese officer, it shared the fate of all other official residences when it fell into the hands of the victors. Throughout the country, as in places like Canton, Hangchow, &c., charity schools are entirely supported by private subscriptions. The native description of Shanghai mentions several free schools there, although little trace of them at present remains.

From the preceding notices, it will be seen that the sweeping charge against the Chinese, as having no notion of, and never providing means for, relieving the poor and destitute, is unjust—it is unfounded. Here we have various schemes for the protection of infants, widows, and the aged, to provide for beggars, to shelter the houseless, to rescue life from fire and water, to meet the wants of the blind and the leper, to check smallpox, to supply medicine, food, and clothing, to aid the indigent scholar, and to afford to the destitute the rites of sepulture. Although it must be allowed that the demand for relief is not adequately met, and that the good intentions of the institutions named have been, in many cases, wofully thwarted through the venality of the managers or the indolence of the supporters; yet, it must be obvious, that the dictates of human instinct have been whispering in the hearts of the Chinese, long before China was opened to foreigners, and have suggested schemes of philanthropy really judicious and appropriate. Let Gospel Christianity enter with its generous influences into the empire of China,—let but Christianized civilization insinuate itself into that "hive of nations,"—then, instead of streamlets, the flood-gates of genuine benevolence shall be opened among the people; and through them shall issue the pure rivers of charity, humanity, and "brotherly love."

PART SECOND.

REAL CHINESE LIFE AT NINGPO.

CHAPTER I.

MY FIRST APPEARANCE IN THE CITY—CALLS ON THE NATIVE OFFICIALS—FLOWER-GARDENS—TEA-HOUSES—MILITARY GROUNDS—CITY WALLS—MOSQUE—TAOUIST, BUDDHIST, AND CONFUCIAN TEMPLES—ICE-HOUSES.

Having canvassed and discussed the general views entertained by "outer barbarians" about "the Celestials," may I invite the reader now to accompany me to some parts of China, hitherto rarely visited by foreigners, where he may have an insight into the real condition of "the Chinese as they are."

The years 1840 and 1841 had been spent at Macao; the greater part of 1842 at Tinghai, during the occupation of Chusan by the British troops; and, on the termination of the rupture between Great Britain and China, I embraced the earliest opportunity of seeking a residence at Ningpo, one of the chief cities of Chih-kiang province. Any good map of China presents a coast-line approaching a semicircular curve, near the centre of which, in lat. 29° 58′ N. and long. 121° 22′ E., lies the said city. During my stay at Tinghai, I had made friends with a few of the leading men at Ningpo, and felt encouraged to take the step. In forming my plan, I was fortunate to have the aid of Woo,* a native tutor

* This is the Chinese native whose paper on "England and the English" appears in Chambers's Journal, March 10, 1855.

of the language, in whose judgment I had good reason to confide, and of whose uniform kindness and fidelity during a term of eleven years, I am happy to bear a grateful testimony.

In taking this course, the objects were to increase my knowledge of the colloquial dialect, and—intercourse with the people being less fettered—to carry out the purpose of my mission.

Accordingly, I embarked at the Tinghai wharf, in a common passage-boat, on the morning of the 7th of December, 1842. The boat having taken in its complement of passengers (all natives but myself), passed under "Joss-house-hill" at eleven o'clock, and, with fair wind and tide, entered the mouth of the Ningpo river at four that afternoon.* By six, we landed at "the Chusan wharf," just by the fork of the river, called *Sankiang-kow*, or "the mouth of three rivers." †

As soon after landing as possible, I made my way for the west gate of the city, within which there is a lagoon called *Hoo-se*, on the eastern bank of which stood the family residence of Dr. Chang. This was a native practitioner I had met some months previously

* The distance between Tinghai and Ningpo is reckoned by the natives at 180 lee, or, giving 3⅓ lee to a mile, 54 miles.

† Called so from there being at this point a junction of three streams. To the north west there is a large stream running down through the districts of *Yuyaou* and *Tszeke*, variously called the *Yaou* river, the *Shun* river, or the river of *Tszeke*. To the east there is another stream, known as the *Yung* river, which name it retains only the distance of ten miles above Ningpo, when it branches off in two lines, one to the south-west under the name of *Yung* river, another to the south-east towards Funghwa, borrowing its name from that district. Where the *Yung* river unites with the *Funghwa* stream, it occasionally is spoken of as the *Pihtoo* or "North-ford river." At the eastern angle of Ningpo, this twin tributary joins the river of *Tszeke*, and these joint waters flow north-east and north in a deep channel, until they enter the open sea at Chinhai, at a distance of eleven and a half miles from the point of confluence. From Ningpo to Chinhai, the river has various names: the *Yung* river, the *Tatsieh*, and some parts the *Siautsieh*. In English charts I find it called *Takiah* and *Tehiah*; correctly given, it is *Tatsieh*.

at Tinghai, between whom and myself there had grown a warm friendship. The sight of a solitary Englishman in the streets, a good while after sundown, created some stir. Curiosity was awakened; and police-runners hastened with most pressing inquiries, who I was, and what my object in visiting Ningpo?

I jostled through the crowds, and at length, after a weary trudge through innumerable streets and lanes, reached my friend's house safe and sound, heartily welcomed by himself and family. However, I had scarcely been seated, when messenger after messenger from the principal offices arrived, repeating the inquiries about my name, objects, and attendants. Perceiving the anxiety that was abroad in consequence of my sudden appearance, I thought it advisable officially to apprise the chief officer, the prefect of the department, of my arrival, and intrusted my host's eldest son with my card and compliments for his worship. The youth returned in an hour with the prefect's card and congratulations; and, in the course of the same evening, one of his confidentials came with kind messages, and an invitation to wait upon him the following day.

On awaking next morning, I was rather taken with the pleasant site of my host's cottage, built on the side of a busy road and the brink of a city lake, at times the scene of much life and gaiety, and its open front set with a row of overhanging willows that threw an agreeable shade over the humble dwelling.

While we were at breakfast, the few, who from an early hour had been loitering about the house to catch the first glimpse of the foreigner, became a multitude. The door-screen was of no avail; and the paper windows were all pierced. Each hole and corner showed an eye of curiosity.

The venerable doctor entreated his fellow-citizens to be a little more polite to an English visitor, and tried to remonstrate with some for their want of good breeding. But it was all unavailing. The people would gratify their curiosity if they could; and the crowd still increased. However, there was no noise, no rushing, no crushing. They looked on in silence, wondering, as they made observations, how unlike the foreigner was to the representations they had seen in paint or read in proclamations;—his face a little different from theirs; his hair and his dress very different. But he was not "red-haired." He was not "without joints." He was not "black-faced." He was not "a bear" nor "a monkey." He was not "fierce," nor was he "a devil." He could sit and talk Chinese. He was there eating Chinese food with Chinese friends, and could use the "quick lads" as well as any of them. "Well! is this really an Englishman?"

After breakfast I started on foot to the office of the prefect, Shoo-Kungshow, whom I had yesternight promised to visit. My aged friend Woo-siensang and Dr. Chang accompanied me. As all the official residences in the city and neighbourhood had been destroyed during the war with England, his worship was occupying a temple not far from the west gate, "the *Wanchang Koh*." The outer court of the building was very noisy with the hum of attendants, eagerly rushing forward to get a glance at the new arrival. In due form I was ushered into the audience-room, by having cards sent in, &c. The room was quite cheerless and cold, destitute of ornament, and possessing only a row or two of cumbersome chairs. On his worship entering, he seemed greatly pleased to see me, and, what satisfied me more, he treated my teacher with marked respect; for before the treaty at Nanking, a native teacher would probably have been seized and imprisoned for being seen in company with a foreigner. The *ta-laouyay* (the style of addressing him, equivalent to "your worship") was a short thick-set man,—head large,—face round and honest-looking,—features deep,—countenance intelligent and agreeable,—eyes large, black, quick, and expressive,—beard jet, long, and pointed, and his upper lip overhung with tremendous moustaches. He wore an official cap, which had a fine plume of peacock-feathers behind, and was topped with a transparent crystal ball denoting the fifth rank of nobility. His dress was not gaudy, though of rich dark-coloured satin; around the neck there was slung a string of large elegant beads, that fell over a square breastpiece of beautiful embroidery,—a duplicate of which was sewed upon his tunic, the one in front, and the other behind. On this breastpiece he had the badge of his order embroidered, the *pihhien*, "silver pheasant." His voice was musical; and, when he spoke, it was with an air of authority. At first his utterance was to me indistinct,—partly from not being accustomed to the accent of Kiangse, his native province. He was only fifty-three years of age, — an inquiry on which point (according to Chinese etiquette) was almost the first question that passed between us.

In his deportment, he was dignified but not supercilious; bland and affable, but by no means familiar; and even now the favourable impression on my mind is as fresh as on the day it was made. Shoo-Kungshow was an officer often spoken of among the English during the war, and doubtless is still remembered by some as "the fine old fellow."

Two topics in particular engrossed our conversation at this interview. One was *geography*. He showed me a Chinese manual of geography in his library, which was exceedingly imperfect and erroneous. Accommodated entirely to the narrow and exclusive views of the Chinese, it contained a most defective outline of the divisions of the world. The other subject was suggested by his being informed that I was neither a merchant, nor a soldier, nor a civilian. "What then?" "A minister of Jesus Christ's religion." On finding that I was not a Romanist, he expressed surprise that, in Western lands, we should have two different religions professing the name of Jesus. He asked what was the real point of difference,—at the same time conjecturing it might consist in the one system inculcating the worship of the cross as he had witnessed among the Papists in China, and the other declining to pay such homage. I endeavoured to explain a few of the prominent features of disparity, and entreated him to discard the notion that Popery was one with the genuine religion founded by Jesus himself.

On leaving the prefect, his worship expressed gratification in at last meeting with one who was not a soldier; for he had seen too many of that rank during the last two or three years.

Koo, an officer inferior to the prefect, though one of his official confidants, then led me into his worship's summer-house, where I was entertained with great urbanity, as well as with a profusion of tea, wine, cakes, fruits, &c. While sitting there, a man rushed in and dropped on his knees before Koo-laouyay. He was a *Han-Kan* or "Chinese traitor," that had been proscribed during the late war, for aiding and abetting the British. By the treaty of Nanking, the imperial reprieve had been obtained for all this class, and passes had been sent to each. Mr. Koo immediately requested him to rise from his kneeling posture, and handed him to a seat, when he joined us in tea and talk. This officer, Koo, called on me next day; and, in his manner and inquiry, evinced no little candour and curiosity. He was particularly searching in his questions about England and other Western countries.

Having gone the round of etiquettish visits, the rest of the day was spent in looking round the city, my friend the doctor volunteering to act as guide. This was somewhat to my advantage, for the aged man did what he could, by suasion, to keep at a distance the crowds that collected round to see a single stranger from a far country treading through the heart of their city.

In the course of my wanderings I called at the residence of Mr. Lin, a gentleman of extensive reputation and large property. He chanced not to be at home, yet I was invited to look through his flower-garden, so highly spoken of by the citizens. The taste displayed in laying out these narrow grounds was certainly wonderful, as well as the skill in grouping together in becoming proportions a complete epitome of rural scenery. Here there was a lake with its islets, there mountains, hills, and dales, orchards and jungles, barren rocks and green swards, pebbly paths and chunam walks, all compressed within less than half an acre of land. Everywhere the eye fell on elegant slate slabs, squares of marble, needles of petrified wood, stunted firs, forced peach-trees, Japanese dwarf cedars, and bamboos, green, black, speckled, square-stalked and round-stalked, &c. &c.

The rich, when they can afford it (and if they have a t-ste for it), have their grounds laid out much in the style I have described, not improbably for the sake of affording the females and children in their establishments means for recreation. Such attempts to bring within a narrow space an epitome of rural nature have been highly successful, and present an agreeable miniature of the picturesque scenery in country life to those that are confined within closed doors. In the midst of these tasteful arrangements, it is not unusual to erect a summer-house for study or amusement. A small lagoon will invariably be found in such charming resorts, where goldfish and other varieties are reared, and the water-lily in particular, a favourite with the Chinese for its wide open leaf and its fragrant flower.

Leaving the elegant mansion of Mr. Lin, I called

on another gentleman of property, Mr. Tang, famous among his townsmen for his pencillings of the chrysanthemum. His manner was dignified and kind. The ladies of his family seemed curious to have a look at the stranger. It would of course have been out of place to introduce me to their gaze; yet, ever ingenious in devices to gratify inquisitiveness, they contrived to prick the paper windows and peep through. Mr. Tang observed this, but made no objection to it.

Wearied with my walks, I hastened back to my lodgings; but at even I wandered abroad to have a look at the "tea-houses" of Ningpo, generally frequented after sunset. Being at a distance from the heart of the city, where "tea-houses" and "eating-houses" abound, some of them very respectable, I found myself in one of a low order, with furniture wretched, tea poor, and company low. This is not to be taken as descriptive of the general character of these convenient establishments;—by no means. And although those of the lowest rank may bear an affinity to the grog-shop in England, there is the marked difference in *the beverage*. I have without doubt seen strong drinks too freely used in some of these nominal "tea-houses;" yet the common draught is that which "cheers but does not inebriate." Very large shops appropriated to tea-drinking are to be met with everywhere in Chinese towns, occupying extensive flights. On the floors of these rooms there stand square wooden tables, with benches and chairs sufficient to accommodate four or six people; and at the further end, there is the kitchen with ovens and stoves duly arranged, and bearing huge kettles, massive teapots, monster caldrons as large as yourself, all filled with hot water. Usually there is a goodly staff of waiters moving about, vigilant in their attentions, carrying small trays, with teacups of the warm decoction and plates of cakes and dried fruits, &c. Less than a farthing will obtain a refreshing cup of comfort. At every hour, morn and evening especially, the rooms are crowded. There is no prohibition of tobacco-smoking or gambling, but the reverse. Nor is there any restraint on loud and noisy conversation. Labourers and passengers are constantly dropping in for such appropriate conveniences, as are offered in the shape of basins of warm water and rough (rather coarse) towels, for washing hands and face. Often music is conducted within, and, much like resorts of the same class in Europe, the tea-drinking houses in China form the evening refuges of the working classes for news and gossip, amusement or recreation. Accordingly, at that hour, you may see whole tables occupied by dice-playing and other games. Frequently, on winter nights, they are converted into rooms, where a man, popular for his powers of mimic and comic, is invited for a few pence to hold forth, and will rivet an audience for an hour or two by his recitals of strange legends and tales from ancient history. Besides, it is not uncommon for disputants to refer their quarrels to a "tea-shop assembly;" and I have known cases of libellous slander taken by the plaintiffs to a gathering in a tea-drinking establishment for adjudication.

"Eating-houses" sometimes are connected with tea-houses. In these a substantial meal can be had at a moment's notice. Some of them occupy large and commodious buildings. I have been in several that were two stories high, with the *restaurants* above and kitchens underneath. The bill of fare offered everything in season, at moderate charges. Those of the better class that I visited were well fitted up, and in most points corresponded to establishments of the same name amongst ourselves.

One word or two about *tea* and the *mode of making it.* They have varieties of tea; but an officer I once visited produced a valuable packet of "*strengthening* tea," prepared in Yunnan province, and of great repute as a medical preparation. It looked much like common black tea, made up into round balls with paste or gum. But the taste of the infusion was exceedingly bitter. After descanting at some length in a rhapsodical strain, on the virtue of the beverage, he abruptly proceeded to assure me that there was another species superior still, indeed unequalled by any other tea for flavour, fineness, and scarcity; namely, "the *monkey tea*." This, he added, could be obtained only in small quantities, and in select spots. Growing on heights inaccessible to the foot of man, and approachable only by the sagacious brute whose name it bears, he said it was collected by certain of the monkey species trained first to climb up the most lofty precipices, and, after filling their pouches with the delicious herb, to descend again to empty their contents into their master's baskets! The delicacy of the tea he pronounced to be beyond exception, and its value very high. Having himself tasted its sweets, he deplored that he had it not in his power to treat me with a cup of the prime draught. On referring to Le Breton's "La Chine en Miniature," I find the following notice of the same article: "Dry and elevated situations are much more suitable for the cultivation of tea than low and damp ones; the consequence is, that the in-gathering is often very difficult, especially that of the best kind of tea. Men could not, without the greatest difficulty, hold on at the sides of the peaks; one false step might be the cause of severe wounds, or at least injure or tear up the young trees. Sometimes the sides are so sharp and pointed that it would not be possible for men to climb up.* To overcome this difficulty, a singular expedient has been resorted to. Monkeys are dressed so as to be

* I have been told by some natives, who believed it, that there are tea-shrubs whose situation is so much elevated beyond the reach of man, that their leaves can be found only by the wind driving them from the top to the base of the mountains, where they are picked up by the proprietors of tea-plantations.

able to climb, and to gather the leaves off the tea-branches. One can easily conceive how difficult it is to have to make use of such helps, for the monkeys can only be guided on such occasions by an instinct purely mechanical. When they have descended the mountain that they have climbed with the help of cords, they receive for a reward some dainty for their taste."

The common mode of "making tea," among the "tea-drinkingest people on the face of the earth," is simply to put into a cup as much tea as you can pinch up with your fingers, pour upon it water at the boiling point, and cover the cup. The beverage is then sipped at pleasure, and a second edition obtained by repeating the application of boiling water.

In families and shops, where visitors are constantly pouring in, a commodious teapot full of the decoction stands on a counter or a convenient side-table, surrounded by a bevy of teacups, to oblige the thirsty customer. *Rain-water* is the universal favourite for preparing the draught; hence, in economical families, huge monster jars are constantly standing under the eaves of the houses, to catch every drop of the "heavenly rain." Strong tea is not preferred by the Chinese, black tea being the rule, green the exception. When decocted, it is drunk without any admixture of *milk* and *sugar*. These are used only by foreigners, and probably to mollify the *désagrémens* of the "black draughts" they are so fond of "masking." As to sugar and milk, the former is superabundant in China, and used for every imaginable purpose except tea-drinking; but you will live long enough in the "flowery land" before your ears are startled by the milk-whoop, which in England is the morning salute to wake up the kitchen and nursery-maids. I am now speaking of the Chinese, not of the habits of foreign visitors, who in this respect show that they will not always do in Rome as Rome does; for they will have milk even in milkless China, and at length those tremendous water-buffaloes (which one at first sight scarcely knows what to call, — hippopotamuses or rhinoceroses) have been trained and are drained to supply foreign tables at the several settlements, with thick milk for tea and coffee.

The first time I caught sight of milk in a Chinese street, it was in the hands of a female carrying a cup of what I thought to be the genuine unchalked article. "Excuse me, but what is that?" said I. "It is milk," she replied. "What milk? cow's or goat's?" "Woman's milk, sir." "Woman's milk! for what use?" "It has been bought for an aged neighbour." "And what's the price of that cupful?" "About eighty cash." Subsequently I discovered that it is not unusual for nursing women to sell their own milk, for motherless babes or octogenarians in second babyhood, the nurses drawing their own milk to vend it at 2*d*. or 3*d*. a cup.

After my first day at Ningpo had passed off in rambles among official residences, flower-gardens, and tea-houses, the second was occupied with another series of excursions, all diverse and instructive. Only two minutes' walk from my habitat, there was a parade-ground for military exercises. Ascertaining that the horse-archers were out, I hastened to the spot immediately after breakfast. The ground occupied was perhaps 200 yards long by 50 broad. The officers present were of an inferior grade, ensigns and serjeants, except the military judge that was seated under a canvas canopy. The archers were drawn up two deep, and called out in companies of eight men, to receive orders on their knees. They then went onward to the spot marked off, one after the other mounting his steed, setting it at full gallop, and firing his arrows. As each man shot off his handful, he returned, and kneeling before the superior, received his reprimand, or instructions, or approval. The bull's-eye, about sixty yards off from the canopy, was represented by three red balls, painted one above the other upon a square sedge-mat nailed to a bamboo frame. The aim was to hit any of the balls, especially the centre one, while the horse was racing along the course. Some proved bad shots, others good, and every successful hit was announced by drum-beating.

The freedom I had in watching this review, formed a marked contrast to the restraints that not long before were laid on foreigners at Canton, who had expressed a wish to be present at one of their grand military exhibitions. As that proclamation reads,—"The local authorities think, very properly, that it is their duty to keep a strict guard against their foreign visitors: accordingly, the Cheheen of Nanhae a few days ago issued a proclamation forbidding them to repair to the parade-grounds to witness the military reviews which were there soon to take place. Two reasons were offered for this prohibition: first, lest having swords with them they should suddenly get into a rage and injure the by-standers; and in the second place, lest they themselves should amidst the crowds be trodden under foot: for these considerations, the Cheheen orders the hong merchants and linguists to do their duty, and prevent the foreigners from transgressing their proper limits."

Ten years after, I had an opportunity at Shanghai of attending a military parade of infantry and artillery, got up in preparation of the descent of the Kwangse rebels; but the continued want of discipline was astonishing. There were five companies of the *red, blue, white, yellow,* and *black* flags respectively; with fifty privates, also one piece of artillery and gunners, in each. The evolutions and revolutions were destitute of rule and order. Besides artillery, there were ginjall and musket bearers. The muskets were of horrid material. The guns (130 lbs. in weight) were dragged by six men.

The cleaning-rods were bamboos pointed with stiff hair; the ramrods nothing but bare poles; and the cannon-matches cords of tow. The ginjalls were heavy, like field-pieces, and had to be borne on two men's shoulders. The soldiers had no regimentals to distinguish them, except perhaps that they had no rags. They wore red tasselled caps, each with a bit of cloth hanging on to his tassel, and coloured according to the *red*, *blue*, &c. company to which he belonged. The officers literally were of the "Society of Odd Fellows," all tucking up their petticoats and robes, flaunting about, cutting military capers, shouting out the word of command in a most discordant fashion, and breaking up to refresh themselves with tea and tobacco.

To return to Ningpo: 'When the "archer-parade" was over, accompanied by Woo-siensang, I sallied forth to the great city walls, intending to make their circuit. The entire circumference approached five miles; the average height twenty-five feet, exclusive of a parapet five feet high; the width of the wall on the top fifteen, at its base twenty-two feet, the *matériel* solid,—the lower part of stone and granite, the upper brick. Some parts were greatly dilapidated; and occasionally the ramparts so overrun with grass and weeds that I could with difficulty thread my way. In the wall there are six gates, each of them double, the inner supported by an outer one at a distance of at least twenty yards. The line of wall that runs off from the one side of the inner gate towards the outer, is the leading wall. This, describing a section of a parallelogram, meets the inner gate round at the other side. At the point of the inner gate where the two parts of the leading wall approach each other, an arch is thrown across to join them, called the "moon-wall." Over each gateway—inner or outer—a guard-house stood, that on the former being the larger, and two stories high. During my residence of seven months in Ningpo, these stations were unoccupied by guards, even at night. The city gates were generally closed a little after sunset,—though opened to any one who would pass a bribe of a few cash into the porter's fist. I did not find here, as I subsequently found in other Chinese towns, that many dwelling-houses were built on the walls, or even contiguous to them. On this account there was a clear walk along the base of the wall within the city, eight and ten feet in width.

Casting my eye over the interior of the several guard-houses as I passed along the walls, it was impossible not to scan the traces of Englishmen that had been there. Our British soldiery, many months stationed there during the war with China, had beguiled their tedious moments by scribbling lines with lumps of charcoal, or scratching ungainly figures with their bayonets. Nor is this a trick confined to Europeans. Side by side with their delineations, I deciphered the figurings of Chinese too, who seemed equally off-hand in writing names on walls, or cutting them out upon wood.

Nor was I less surprised here, as in other cities in China, to witness on the gateways numerous placards of different sizes and attractive shapes,—pasted up to apprize the "gentry and citizens," or "ladies and gentlemen," of "religious services," "theatrical shows," "magisterial orders," "medical feats," &c. The rage for advertisement in China is quite as prolific as elsewhere; and among other curiosities in this class of production, I have seen fiery squibs on public characters, sober admonitions on sundry subjects, and quack puffs in every line of business. As in Europe, so in China, objection is taken to the placarding of bills upon private premises; and you meet with notices to the effect, that "Bills pasted up will be daubed over," —"Placards will be torn down,"—"You are not allowed to placard," and sometimes the polite request "Pray do not paste your bills here."

STREET DRUGGIST

During these perambulations, on spying a large lofty building in the heart of the city, I made for it. It was "the Drum-loft," an arch of wide span, surmounted by a guard-house. Standing as it does in the centre of the city, where the principal streets meet, the scene around was bustling and lively. According to the local records, this loft existed prior to the fifteenth century, and has undergone a variety of changes. The object of the monument is denoted by its singular appellations, "the observatory," "the sea-sun radiance loft," and "the clear distance;" showing that the building was originally built for a guard-house, or a prominent part from which the surrounding country could be watched, in protecting the interests of the city and inhabitants. The popular name "Drum-loft" is given to it from a huge drum kept there, to be used by the city watchmen in their ordinary night beats, especially in cases of emergency from foe or fire.

From the "Drum-loft" I hastened back to the walls, where, as before, I met with few people,—these only such as had run up from the streets below, with a vacant curiosity gazing at a plain Englishman. More frequently I came upon lean horses, here and there grazing in solitude on the ramparts. Outside the walls, there is a moat of some extent that well nigh encircles the city. The northern and eastern faces of the city, supposed to be well enough guarded by the river, have no moat. But commencing at the north gate, it runs along the foot of the wall, west, south, and south and south-east, until it stops at what is called "the Bridge-gate." This gives it a length of about three miles. It is deep, in some places perhaps forty yards wide, well supplied with water from the neighbouring fields and river, and daily navigated by small boats.

"The Bridge-gate," one of the two eastern gates in Ningpo, is called so from a floating bridge thrown across the river right opposite. The bridge measures

200 yards in length and nearly six broad. It consists of planks firmly lashed and laid upon lighters, of which I counted sixteen closely linked by iron chains. Occasionally it was opened at a certain part for the passage of boats plying up and down. There was a busy market upon it, and the passengers were so thickly jostled, that no man had time to gaze about him. It led into a bustling and populous suburb on the other side of the river.

On this first visit to the walls of Ningpo, the scenery around was, I must say, agreeable; nor was it less so in my subsequent strolls here. The vast plain around the city was a magnificent amphitheatre, stretching away twelve, fifteen, and eighteen miles on the one side, to the foot of the distant hills, and on the other to the verge of the ocean. Many a pleasing and curious object arrested the eye. Turn it from the north-west, round by the south and south-east, there lay before me canals and water-courses, cultivated fields, snug farm-houses, smiling cottages, family residences, hamlets and villages, family tombs, monasteries, and temples. Towards the east, the vision was bounded by rising mountains; but between them and me the land scenery was much the same as already described, only that I could see more distinctly the river swarming with boats, and its banks studded with ice-houses. Nor was my curiosity less amused or gratified as I turned the eye from without to look within the city. There, there were single and double-storied houses, low and irregular; heavy prison-like mansions, family vaults, temples with their glittering roofs, official residences, examination-halls, and the sombre pagoda of Ningpo, to all which I must defer my visits to another day; for, worn out with this weary tramp on the city walls, I had to return to my host's dwelling for refreshment.

I have been particular in giving my jottings on the

walls of this city, that I might acquaint the reader with what may be regarded a good sample of a walled town in China; for almost every town, even of "the third," or lowest class, is, or has been at one time, walled. Yet it is not pretended that my rough description of Ningpo, though it be a city of considerable importance, can approach the reality in such large capitals as Nanking, Nanchang, or Peking.

On reaching my lodgings, I found awaiting me a mark of respect unexpected though agreeable. Shoo *ta laouyay*, the prefect, had called to see me. It is a rule among officials to return calls, in person or by proxy, the second day after the visit. I looked for nothing beyond the proxy. But while I felt honoured by his worship's personal attentions, I was specially pleased at it as an additional sign of the breaking up of official exclusiveness and vanity. The prefect came with his usual retinue of criers, lictors, chain-bearers, and other attendants.

Chinese magistrates rarely, if ever, go out, on duty at least, without a crowd of *attachés* of various orders. First, you have "ragged rascals," with ornamental flags and poles, large lanterns, and red boards having the rank of the officer painted on them, running and shouting to the street passengers—"Retire, retire! keep silence, and clear the way!" Gong-strikers follow, denoting at certain intervals by so many strokes, their master's grade and office. Next come chain-bearers, rattan-bearers, whip-bearers,—significant of his judicial power. Alongside of the magisterial chair there are servants trotting on foot, with umbrellas, pipes, and card-cases. The rear is brought up by one, two, or three seedy bamboo chairs, occupied by secretaries, scribes, and hangers-on. The number of chair-bearers depends on the rank of the officer. Most of the attendants wear red-tasselled caps. During the war with China, the English entertained the notion that every Chinaman that flourished a red tuft on his bonnet must be a soldier, or one connected with native officials. So firmly did this idea seat itself in the minds of some of the British leaders of that expedition, that not a single individual on the island of Chusan was permitted to wear a tasselled cap; and whoever might be seen with it in his hand, or in his house, was at once suspected and seized. If the hovel of a native happened to be searched, and a red-tasselled cap—never so torn, dirty, or musty—was found in a closet or a corner, it was concluded indisputable that the poor inmate was a soldier, a kidnapper, or a disturber of the public peace. Indeed, for some time after the close of the war, while Chusan continued in the hands of the British, not a man of peace was allowed to sport such caps, not even the messengers from Ningpo sent by native officers with messages to the foreign authorities at Tinghai. Such a course was followed in consequence of an erroneous impression. This kind of cap is worn not by the soldiery only, but by gentlemen's servants, the messengers of officers,—even the lowest menial when he pays a visit of ceremony or celebrates a festive season. The cap is of cloth in winter,—of straw in summer,—with a tuft of red silk on the crown. As festivities are by no means unfrequent during the year, a cap of this sort is an appendage necessary to the wardrobe of every police-runner, or chair-bearer, who ranks in the lowest of the plebeian classes.

On the first Sunday after reaching Ningpo, I had an interesting visit early in the morning from one of the two Mohammedan priests connected with the mosque in the city. It was quite a treat to hear a Chinaman converse about the One living and true God, the commandments of Jehovah, and some of the patriarchs of the Old Testament. He spoke decidedly on the irrationality and wickedness of worshipping a plurality of gods, adducing the express command of Jehovah that he himself alone should be the object of adoration. Of Jesus Christ this individual appeared to know little beyond the name.

My interview with this junior priest encouraged me much on a subsequent occasion to visit the mosque itself. Over its entrance were engraven the characters "*Hwuy Hwuy Tang*," "The Mohammedan Temple." In the first visit, I was fortunate to meet the senior priest, a native of Shantung, though of Arab descent, his ancestors having come from *Medina*. He himself was able to read the Koran, and talk Arabic with a degree of fluency; but of Chinese reading and writing he was as ignorant as an Englishman in England, although he had been born in China, could talk Chinese, and was a minister of religion among the Chinese. He lamented much that there were so few adherents to his creed at Ningpo, where they did not number more than twenty or thirty families, one or two of them of official rank. From this interesting man I learned that the stronghold of Mohammedanism lies in Hangchow, the capital of Chihkiang province, in which there are several mosques. His reigning desire was to make a pilgrimage to Mecca; and with this view he put the minutest inquiries as to the distance of that city, and the length of voyage, &c.

He took me into the place of worship, adjoining his private residence. On ascending a flight of steps, I was brought under a plain roof. Beneath this I observed scattered up and down, a quantity of old furniture and agricultural implements covered with dust. To support the roof there were pillars, ornamented with sentences from the Koran. As soon as I entered, my attention was attracted by a pair of small doors in the wall, within which I was told was the sacred seat, and on one side of it a little book-case, with the Mohammedan Scriptures in twenty-four parts. He showed me his canonicals,—simply a white robe and a pointed turban,—

never worn but at religious services. He told me they professed to hold one day sacred in seven; but if the followers of the Prophet had any urgent secular business on that day, they did not trouble themselves to attend service. Happening to see on the threshold a tablet, called *Lungpai*, the "Dragon Tablet," similar to that found in any Chinese temple, with the inscription upon it—*Hwangti, wansui wansui, wanwansui*, equivalent to "The Emperor, the Everliving," &c.,—I pointed it out and asked him how, if he regarded the spot as consecrated to the worship of *Aloho,*—the name he gave to the One living and true God,—he could permit such a tablet to stand there. He protested that he did not, and never would, pay religious homage to such a tablet or to any human sovereign. In evidence of the truth of his asseverations, he pointed to the low place given it on the ground floor, so far removed from the sacred seat. Further, he explained, that it was placed within the precincts of the mosque only for expediency's sake; for, if he and his disciples were charged by the enemies of Mohammedanism with disloyalty, they had only to appeal to the presence of the tablet.

On the fifth day of my residence at Ningpo, I had a message from the commander-in-chief of the Chihkiang province—his head-quarters being then at Ningpo,—inquiring if I could supply him with a glass for a damaged telescope. It was entirely out of my power to meet this request. I could only offer to send it to Hong-Kong to be repaired. But this did not suit his excellency. When, subsequently, I called upon the commander-in-chief, I found him an aged man, of a tall figure, and affected with paralysis of the right eye. His speech was slovenly, his manner indolent, though his notions sounded high and aristocratic. He wore a handsome red dress, and his official cap had a red coral button, with a slender plume of peacock-feathers. The attendants immediately about his chair were ensigns, sergeants, and corporals, with brass and opaque buttons.

About the same time I took the opportunity of waiting on several other mandarin authorities in Ningpo,—of which visits I offer the following summary. There was one of the name of Luh, who, during the peace negotiations with Great Britain, had fallen under the Imperial ban and lost his honours and office. Although the flush of health was diffused over a fine oval countenance, it was evident he was much depressed in consequence of his recent degradation. The reputation in which he stood among his countrymen as a scholar was high. He was spoken of by the Ningpo citizens as one who had been very efficient in his department, and his removal from office was much regretted by the people. Ever since his return from Nanking, whither he had been summoned in the summer of 1842 by the Imperial commissioners to assist in forming the treaty, he had conducted himself towards the English with uniform courtesy, as I can testify from personal knowledge; and in losing him they also were deprived of the services of an enlightened Chinese friend.

While I was seated in Mr. Luh's audience-room, Le-joolin, the successor of my friend Shoo-kungshow, entered. Being not above thirty-three years of age, he was considered one of the fortunate men of his day, to enter at so early an age upon an office of such high importance. I was informed it was his literary attainments that had obtained for him favour at court. At nineteen he took the second degree of literary honours, and was at once appointed to the mayoralty in a neighbouring city. In his remarkable intelligence and unassuming kindness, there was reason to hope that he would aid in promoting a liberal policy towards foreigners.

But my visit to a neighbour of Messrs. Luh and Le

was attended by impressions the reverse of all made in my interview with those gentlemen. His name was Lung, then acting the part of mayor in Ningpo. His long, lank figure,—supercilious look, and affected condescension to speak with a foreigner,—chilled me, and awakened a suspicion that he was a man capable of doing dark deeds. Of this I had a melancholy proof that very day on leaving his office. In front of Lung's visitors' room, my eye caught a group of people collected in the middle of an area. As I approached the spot, I saw an unfortunate culprit, with his knees bared, kneeling on a coil of iron chains. He was fixed in that horrid posture by having his hands tied behind his back to a stake that was held firmly in the ground by two men. If he swerved to the right or the left, a man on either side, armed with a whip, forced the tortured culprit back to his perpendicular position, by a lash or two on his bare head. The agonies of the poor fellow were evident, from his quivering lips, pallid countenance, and tremulous voice imploring relief, which was refused with the cold mocking command, "Confess or suffer." I left the spot speechless.

To leave this "chamber of horrors:"—Situate within the north gate of Ningpo, there were under one roof two temples of the Taou sect, called the Yushing Kwan, which I repeatedly visited. Though the flight of buildings was extensive, and there were not many priests about, everything seemed in good order, probably owing to its having been recently tenanted by some officers of state; for when official residences are scarce or in ruin, temples, monasteries, and even nunneries, are converted into officers' apartments. The authorities of Ningpo, having by the ravages of 1841 and 1842 been thrown out of house and home (for our British troops, although they spared private, did not spare official residences), were for a year or two obliged to bury themselves in the halls and cloisters of the priesthood.

On my first visit, I found the Yushing temple lay close under the walls, and sheltered at the back by a thick grove of trees. The avenue from the outer lodge to the *sanctum sanctorum* was clean and cool,—overhung by the branches of lofty trees that rose up on each side of the walk, and threw a sombre quiet over the whole place. The chief priest, a man of short stature and slender make, but venerable in appearance and genteel in manners, politely volunteered to show me round the building. I passed from one corridor to another, but, throughout the immense building, met with only half a dozen inmates of the sacerdotal order. The spacious chambers and halls were occupied by sculptured, carved, or merely painted images, of all sizes, shapes, and ranks, young and aged, animal, human, devilish, and imagino-divine. A few of the inscriptions were awfully misapplied. At the entrance-gate, for instance, this line ran below an ugly three-eyed monster, "The three eyes that neither good nor evil can evade."

A little way on from this I observed another large gateway, belonging to the temple of Lew-tsoo. Within that entrance, and under cover, there were seated four huge figures, "the four great Kin-kang,"—probably standing there to the present day. One carries a lyre, "at the notes of which," they say, "the ears of the whole world are awakened." Another, with a black and ferocious face, flourished a drawn sword. A third sported a big umbrella, and is said by the simple elevation of this instrument, to have power to draw down to earth storms of thunder and rain. The fourth twists a long snake round his arm, to denote skill to tame wildness into submission. They were arranged two on each side of the passage. In the centre gateway, an image faced you exactly as you entered, very stout and with the breast and upper abdomen exposed, seated on a large cloth bag, laughing and looking right jolly, with the two words inscribed overhead, *Chih siaou*, "the ever-laughing one." This is a representation of "the Buddha that is to come." Behind him there was an erect idol, called "the Wei-to image," or "the Hoofah wei-to," as he is said to be "the protector of the Buddhist faith." He was clad in armour, and seemed ready for the offensive or the defensive. Within there was a crowd of other images, chiefly canonized heroes and disciples of this popular superstition.

Passing from that point, I made for a Buddhist monastery close by,—the Yenchingsze. There I found fifty priests. Adjoining it there was another, called Kwantang, still larger than any I had seen, and more ornamented. The images of Buddh here were the most gigantic I have ever set eyes on in China—the three principal representations of Buddh—the *Shihkia*, the *Wanshoo*, and the *Poohien*. Just behind that triad, there stood the "Thousand-handed Kwanyin," the Shiva of the Hindoos. On each side of these *dii majores*, there was a row of nine figures to represent some celebrated hermits and deified genii, called "the Lohan," all in various postures and with different features. The priests spoke with regret at having lost an enormous metal bell that belonged to their temple, and which was carried off by the British when Ningpo fell into their hands. "That bell of Ningpo" now figures in the British Museum.

When I visited this temple, there were only fifty or sixty priests, who had come from different parts of the empire. Occasionally there are above 1,000 within these walls, whose sleeping-berths seemed destitute of every vestige of comfort, while the mess-room and kitchens looked the very reverse. In one of the kitchens a huge boiler was pointed out, in which, they said, as much rice could be boiled at one time as to feed about 2,000 persons. The head priest invited me into his sitting-room, where we conversed on a variety of subjects. He and his attendants listened to my remarks on the existence of the only true God and his claims to our homage; and, touching the Saviour Jesus Christ, it appeared they had obtained, at different times, some portions of our Sacred Scriptures and of Christian tracts in Chinese.

Without speaking of the difference in their doctrines, ceremonies, and canonicals, the marked distinction between the Taouist and Buddhist priests that I encountered on this occasion was this:—The priests of Buddha had their heads clean shaven, without a relic of hair left. Those of the Taouist religion, however, shaved as their countrymen generally did,—nourishing the hair upon the crown of the head, until it became long enough to make a *kondeh,* which they fixed with a hair-pin; so that the only difference from the commonalty was in the Taouist priests tying up the hair in a tuft on the crown, while the people generally let it dangle in the form of a queue.

To pass on to other buildings in this city worth a visit: There was "the palace of the God of the Eastern Range."—In China there are "Five *yoh,*" or ranges of lofty mountains, that have given rise to a good deal of fabulous matter; the Eastern chain, the *Taishan* mountains, in Shantung; the Western chain, the *Hwashan,* in Shense; the Southern chain, the *Hungshan,* in Hoopih; the Northern chain, the *Hanshan,* in Shanse; and the Central chain, the *Sungshan,* in Honan. Each is supposed to be the residence of a presiding deity.—To the resident genius of the Eastern range this building is consecrated. It lay to the south of the "Bridge-gate," from which I discovered a path close under the city walls leading direct to it. The range of the edifice was long. It bore an elegant front, decorated with a group of handsome reliefs, among which was embossed in gilt its name. On entering, I found it almost deserted. None of the regular priesthood made their appearance, nor were votaries to be seen. The only persons to be descried (except the door-keeper) were mat-makers. It appeared to be more a mat-mart than a sacred building. The images were dusty and filthy, besides showing other signs of disuse and neglect. On pushing my way to the extreme end, I espied a gallery of idols, and attempted to ascend the staircase. As the doors were barred, admission could not be gained, and my attention was called to two notices, the one placed at the bottom of the right-hand flight of steps, warning "(those that eat) strong meats (and drink) wine not to enter:" the other upon the opposite side, advising "the unclean" person hastily to retire. Passing out to the street, I perceived a wicket on the right hand of the principal gateway. It was opened to me, and I was invited to look on illustrations intended to depict the terrors of hell. The apartment, a dark, dreary cell, is called *teyoh*, "the earthly dungeon." In the centre of the ground-floor there were images of hideous aspect in threatening attitudes, and behind them groups of small figures in stucco relief plastered upon the wall, to exhibit the pains and penalties of hell. These were arranged in three or four rows, rising one above the other until they reached the ceiling. Each group had its judge, criminal, executioners, and peculiar form of punishment. The judges were attired as officers generally are, and the executioners as police-runners. The grade of penalties was varied according to the heinousness of the culprit's crime, and the horrors of future punishment were depicted before the spectator in every possible form. To be whipped, to be bastinadoed, to be seared with red-hot irons, to be strangled, to be speared, to be beheaded, to be sawn asunder, to be flayed alive, to be squeezed, flattened, and crushed between two thick planks, to be slit up, to be bored through and through, to have the eyes dug or chiselled out, to have the limbs torn off one by one, to be plunged from a cliff or a bridge into a dungeon below, or into a rapid torrent, to be pounded in a heavy mortar, to be boiled in a hot-water caldron, to be burnt up in a furnace, to be baked at the stake, to have hot liquids poured down the throat, &c. &c., constitute the ideas of future punishments indulged in the books of this school, a counterpart of the torments inflicted by the Inquisition in Europe upon the magnanimous adherents to the Protestant faith.

En route I visited the T'ienyih-koh, a valuable repository of Chinese works, chiefly those published anterior to the opening of the present dynasty,—a collection said to belong to the Fan family, a member of which was keeping it. The works were arranged in 300 classes, and the cases in which they were deposited were closely shut, to be opened only on special occasions.

Turning from this spot, I bent my steps to the T'ien-fung t'ah, named by foreigners the "Tower of Ningpo," the "Pagoda of Ningpo," or the "Ningpo Obelisk." As you ascend the river from Chinhai and come within five miles of Ningpo, this is the most prominent object that arrests the eye; and, to foreigners who visit the city, it is a point of no little attraction. As soon as they enter the east gate of the city, they make for it, and wend their way in a south-west direction. After shaping their course through numberless streets, it abruptly bursts upon their view, rising 160 feet over their heads, and towering high above the surrounding houses. This pyramid is hexagonal, and counts seven stories and above twenty-eight windows. At every window there is a lantern hung up; and when the obelisk is illuminated, which I have seen only once during my stay, the scene is very gay. On my visit, the building was in much need of repair, as it was daily becoming more dilapidated, and had already deviated considerably from the perpendicular, so that it might not inappropriately be called "the Leaning Tower of Ningpo." As it was in the keeping of a Buddhistic priest who lived in a monastery behind, I was under the necessity of awaiting his arrival. He, poor man, found it advantageous to keep the keys. It was in that way alone he could secure the largesses of his foreign visitors. By ascending a flight of narrow wooden steps that ran up in a spiral course through the interior of the column, I reached the uppermost story, from which one of the finest views one could desire opened :—the entire city and suburbs beneath; the valley of Ningpo, with its hamlets, villages, hills, mountain rivulets, and rivers all around; and, away in the distance, bounding the horizon, chains of mountains on the one hand, the sea with its islands on the other. Within the tower itself there was nothing to interest a visitor except the scribbling of Englishmen, some of whom seem to have been very solicitous to register their names on its dome for the benefit of posterity. The following was one of the many scratches :—

"P. Anstruther, prisoner, { September 16th, 1839. / February 23rd, 1840.
"P. Anstruther, free and master, October 13th, 1841."

in which a *lapsus manus* had entered an ante-date of 1839 and 1840, for 1840 and 1841. On descending from the lively spectacle I had been witnessing above, I found myself among "heaps of the slain;" the poorer classes having selected the outer base of the edifice, as a suitable spot on which to deposit the coffins of their dead.

The date at which this tower was founded is exceedingly antique, indeed more ancient than the city itself. The district of Ningpo, in the time of the original Han dynasty, or at the opening of the Christian era, was very small. During the seventh, eighth, and ninth centuries, it rose in importance. At the commencement of the tenth century, and in the reign of Taitsoo—

the first monarch in the line of "the Five Dynasties" which successively contended for the mastery—it was organized a larger district. During that emperor's short sway, the foundation of the city walls was laid by Hwangshing, a native of the place. But the "Tower of Ningpo," had been reared one hundred or one hundred and fifty years previous to that event. In raising this superstructure at that anterior date, the object sought for accorded precisely with the belief, which at the present day obtains through the whole empire, that the presence of such an edifice not only secures to the site the protection and favour of heaven, if it already bears evidence of enjoying it, but represses any evil influences that may be native to the spot, and imparts to it the most salutary and felicitous omens. The tower has stood for the last 1,100 years. But its history during that period, as given in "the Annals" already referred to, has been much chequered. It has fallen to ruins and been rebuilt. It has been burnt almost to the ground and been reconstructed. It has been struck by lightning and been repaired. Its pinnacle has been blown down in a hurricane and has been restored. Some portions of it are now undergoing amendment. But its days appear to be numbered, and ere long its downfall may be announced.

Still pursuing my walk, I came to Hien-Hiohkung, "the District Literary Hall." Each department in the empire owns a literary hall; so also does each district. Accordingly this city, being both a district and a department city, has two such halls. The district college was laid in ruins amid the disasters of 1841, and, when I visited it, was rising out of a mass of wrecked materials into a neat, orderly, attractive range of buildings. In these days, there is more name and show than reality or utility in such an institute. It was originally designed to be the residence of the literary officer, or government superintendent appointed to preside over the interests of learning in the district, but especially to patronize and promote the studies and views of those candidates who should be so successful as to take the first degree. Here they were to pursue their daily studies, and to undergo their monthly examinations, under his immediate inspection. But, from the degeneracy of the age, it has almost become the seat of a sinecure.

The *Department Hall,* dedicated to Confucius, is a magnificent flight of very roomy buildings in the northern quarter of the city. It was occupied by the British officers in 1841. Its first foundations were laid in another part of the city, in the eighth century of the Christian era. It was removed to its present site three hundred years afterwards. There was little to interest the eye here beyond the extensive grounds, the capacious and vaulted halls, the gilded, carved, and decorated roofs, the pillars, walls, and tablets, commemorative of the virtues and honours of Confucius and his earliest and most renowned followers. The central tablet of all, raised upon an elevated stone pedestal, bore the following inscription:—"*The Spiritual Seat of the Most Holy Teacher,* CONFUCIUS." There was no image; but before this tens of thousands have paid divine adoration and worship, and a native of Ningpo informed me that "annually, at the opening of the spring and the autumn seasons respectively, before this shrine they offer up to the most holy sage one cow, one sheep, one pig, with a certain number of pieces of silk and a variety of sacrificial vessels filled with grain, dried fruits, and vegetables."

Rambling out of the city, I got into lumber-yards, dockyards, &c. and, among other curiosities, found *ice-houses,* on the banks of the river. Most of these ice-depositories were not built under but *above* ground, generally on a platform of earth, so elevated as to be out of the reach of the freshes of the river and neighbouring swamps. Upon this mound a bamboo frame was thrown and closely thatched over with paddy-straw. The ice had been taken from the surrounding fields, tanks, and ponds, which the proprietors of the ice-stores filled with water during the frost. When of a sufficient thickness, it was collected; and as it was brought in each layer was covered with dry straw, to preserve it during the summer. Every ice-house had its drain to carry off the meltings. The article was not used by the natives at Ningpo, except as an antiseptic for flesh and fish during the heats of summer. The people knew nothing of cooling liquids, except as they had observed foreigners use ice for that purpose; and they were quite content to sell me a basket of it for 3*d*. or 4*d*., a charge by no means extravagant during the dog-days. The population of Ningpo was supplied with fish caught several leagues from the coast; and as without ice it would have been altogether impracticable to bring it to town in an eatable state, the fishermen were regularly supplied with it from these houses. To keep the article from dissolving, the hatchways of the ice-junks were covered with straw and mats, constantly kept moist with sea-water. In a journal kept during one of the Burmese embassies from Ava to Peking,—translated by Lieut.-Colonel Burney,—the following odd paragraph is to be found:—"For the use of the Chinese emperor in the hot season, the ice in the lake to the north-west of his palace-inclosure is broken open, as we saw, with hatchets, and axes, &c.; and pieces about three or four cubits thick and two or three long, have holes made at one end, as is done by us to logs of timber, and are conveyed by ropes and put into the moat surrounding the palace-inclosure. This ice melts and becomes water, in consequence of the increasing heat in the month of March." In this manner his Imperial majesty is *iced* during the summer!—at least so imagination would have it.

CHAPTER II.

PUBLIC FEELING TOWARDS FOREIGNERS AFTER THE LAST WAR—RESIDENCE IN A CHINESE FAMILY—LODGINGS IN A BUDDHIST MONASTERY—IN A BUDDHIST NUNNERY—AT A CHINESE MERCHANT'S.

PICTURE to yourself an Englishman 17,000 miles away from home, residing in a large Chinese city that was surrounded by a ponderous wall of five miles' length and occupied by a population which till recently had been driven out by British fire and sword,—an Englishman living among a people, not only unable to sympathize with him, but totally different in language, habits, dress, religion, and notions, many of them too (in consequence of the late disasters of war) overwhelmed with sorrow, or overawed with fright, or burning with hatred, or gnawed with envy, or reeking with vengeance,—a single solitary Englishman living there alone and companionless; and by sympathy you may be able to realize something of the position in which I found myself at the close of 1842.

When I had been some time there, it was of no little interest to watch their various expressions of feeling about foreigners.

Once, as I tramped down a long lane between two rows of heavy-built mansions, I met a party of rough stalwart Chinamen, and passing them, saluted them with a friendly word. They did not return it, but looking back at me, said to each other, "Oh, but for the Nanking treaty, what a chance to catch that fellow!" I replied with a smile and a bow.

At other times, a term of reproach like *fan-kwei*, "foreign devil," fell on the ear. I could forgive this.

It was only a traditional vocable, which most of them had got from their fathers, but was not intended by themselves as an insult: so that generally I took no notice of it, except with a significant look or by asking the offender if he knew the meaning of his language.

More frequently I was struck with symptoms of excessive terror shown by the commonalty, particularly during the first part of my stay. Indeed it was painful to observe the undue timidity that men, women, and children of all classes evinced at the sight of the foreigner. Everywhere I was at once recognized by the tight trowsers, long black coat, and English hat. At fifty yards off, my appearance was the signal for women to bolt into their houses with their screaming children and bar the doors. When I trudged along the paved street, every passenger seemed as if he wished he could shrink into a nut-shell. One dared not look me straight in the face. Another stole a side glance at my hand or umbrella, imagining that my stick concealed a spring gun, or my very fingers could be turned into pocket-pistols. A third, as he shuffled past, would put his coat-sleeve (or, if he had such a thing, his handkerchief) up to his nose, and when he had got clear of me, he would spit; for he had heard, and suspected it was too true, that about "these outside barbarians" there was a dangerous and infectious malaria. A crowd of gaping mouths and staring eyes would follow at a distance; but the least halt I made scattered the multitude, and sometimes I found myself standing alone wondering and amused at the strange effect.

No doubt, much of this probably was to be traced to the prowess and triumph of the foreign sword. But certainly the marvellous tales, circulating among them about their formidable foes, must have added no little to their consternation when they saw them face to face. Thus when Chusan was first taken by the English, in 1840, of the stories their appearance occasioned some were supremely ridiculous;—such as, that they had legs without joints,—their limbs were so stiff that if they fell, they could not rise,—they were stone blind,—their faces were perfectly red, and the hair of the head fiery,—in their native country they had no moon, no sun, no stars, no sky,—being destitute of the medicinal rhubarb, they were affected with eternal costiveness,—the troops of India (which accompanied the expedition) were amphibious animals, living seven days in the sea and seven on shore,—and the British troops were so easily affected by cold, that the winter frosts of Ningpo and Shanghai would assuredly destroy them. Other more extraordinary descriptions of the English were given out by the government officers, purposely to fire the soldiers with courage and fill the people with contempt of foreigners, though really more calculated to frighten them. The consequence was, that, when the Chinese "braves" went out to meet those English monsters, they were taken with more than sudden amazement at finding them so sleek, nimble, hardy, dexterous, dauntless, and victorious,—the very reverse of what they had heard or expected,—and the nervous system of people and soldiery sustained a shock from which they could not soon recover.

The cowardice which the Chinese military in general showed during the struggle with England, certainly lowered them much in public estimation; and ever since that trial of strength and courage, the native soldiery, always dreaded for its oppression, has been despised for its want of manliness. The citizens of Ningpo themselves related some amusing stories of their military leaders disguising themselves in sackcloth, or coarse hempen garments, and straw sandals, to elude the pursuit of the British. A Chinese eye-witness of the scene used with great humour to recite the following story:—While H.M.S. *Cornwallis* and other vessels of war lay abreast of Nanking during the truce, when the negotiations for peace were in course of deliberation, the garrison of that capital was, on one occasion, thrown into tremendous confusion from the roar of British cannon suddenly bursting upon their ears. It was a salute. But imagining that, in defiance of truce engagements, the English broadsides were opening on the citadel, the brave-hearted sons of *Han* threw off their heavy boots in the open streets, rushed through narrow lanes and dirty canals, and ran for their lives as they best could.

On a certain evening I went to a temple, as spectator of some religious ceremonies, accompanied by the native who was fond of telling the above anecdote. There happened to be two petty officers there who were anxious to get on the same gallery with me; but, as there was no room, claim for admission was refused by my friend, who well knew who the applicants were. Upon this, however, their quiet request rose to a stormy demand that the gallery-doors should immediately be opened, as the gentlemen outside were of such and such a family and rank, &c. There was no denying this. But my guide, who was sitting by, whispered to me, loud enough for them to hear as they walked in, "Yes, you press these claims now; but 'tis no sooner *p'ung* than you *p'ang!*" This was to them very cutting, but occasioned much merriment to the crowd around, as it was accompanied by gestures remarkably expressive; *p'ung* in the patois denoting the firing of a gun, *p'ang* the flight of defeat. Next day, a town policeman appeared at my lodgings to inquire who that Englishman might be, whose friends refused admittance to the officers that visited the temple on the previous night. Dr. Chang replied (without my sanction), "That Englishman's name is *Mei* [which was my surname], and he is the friend of the great civil officer *Ma* [Morrison], the Secretary to his Excellency *Puh* [Pottinger], who is the Plenipotentiary of the British sovereign and the intimate friend of *Eleepoo, Keying,* and *Niukien,* the commissioners that assisted at the formation of the treaty of Nanking." The messenger went away thoroughly cowed, and nothing was heard from his masters after that.

The breaking of national conceit and pride was one decidedly beneficial effect of the terrible chastisement which Great Britain inflicted on China in the last war; and, if I might here sum up the notes subsequently made on the same score, especially at the northern ports of China, I could not do better than quote the closing paragraph of Mr. Macaulay's speech in the Parliament of 1840, when the question of that war with China was brought before the House, every word of which is a prophecy already fulfilled :—" I have done; and have only to express my fervent hope that this most righteous quarrel may be prosecuted to a speedy and triumphant close, that the brave men to whom is intrusted the task of exacting reparation, may perform their duty in such a manner as to spread throughout regions in which the English name is hardly known, the fame, not only of *English skill and valour,* but of *English mercy and moderation;* and that the overruling care of that Providence which has so often brought good out of evil, may make the war to which we have been forced, the means of establishing a durable peace, beneficial alike to the victors and the vanquished."

Naturally enough, under the circumstances in which I was placed at Ningpo, the appellations and epithets by which the Chinese specified foreigners came up as a point of interesting inquiry, especially as illustrative of their views and feelings towards strangers from distant lands.

There are expressions used in official writings, such as *e-jin* or *wai-e.* These at one time awakened suspicion in our government, and recently led to a smart discussion among foreign sinologues; but the upshot of the inquiry has been to ascertain that the term meant no more than βαρβαρος, as used originally of those who were not "Greeks," or unable to speak the Greek language,—"Gentiles" as opposed to "Jews," and "foreign" in contrast to "home." So with other phrases in Chinese books. In easy writing and talking, they also designate them "outside people," "people from afar," "travelling strangers," "people of the western ocean," "outside foreigners."

In naming the nations to which foreigners separately belong, sometimes there is an attempt to transfer the proper name, e. g., *Yingkihlih* for England, *Amiliko* for America, *Holan* for Hollanders; at other times, the nations are described by their flags, e. g., *Danes* by *Hwangke*, or "yellow flag,"—America, by *Hwake*, or "flowery flag,"—Prussia, by *Tanyingke*, "the flag of only one eagle." In official documents that pass between the Chinese and English governments, England is designated the *ta ying kwah*, "the great Eng(lish) nation." With polite Chinese who converse about England, the same style of address is not unusual. There is the phrase *Hungmaou*, "red-haired," applied to foreigners of all classes. This probably arose from the Dutch being among the first to open trade with China. It appears that, when they visited the empire three hundred years ago, they excited the wonder of the Chinese by their reddish hair; hence, the name given to them and other subsequent visitors indiscriminately. A Chinese work, alluding to their arrival, says, "Their raiment was red, and their hair too. They had bluish eyes deeply sunken in the head, and our people were quite frightened by their strange aspect."

In the south of China, at Canton especially, foreigners are assailed by the opprobrious epithet of "foreign devil," &c. This, during the war with England, crept into the vocabulary of the people in the north, and has not yet been erased. There they sometimes are designated "black devils," &c. But I am happy to say, that in the north less than in the south is the ear of the foreigner offended by nicknames for which there can be only the apology offered above.

I have heard myself called a Weitsze or a Wotsze. On inquiry, I ascertained that this is a name applied by them to nations lying on the east of the empire,—to the Japanese, for instance, who amongst the Ningpo people have long been known by that term. The Portuguese, who of foreigners were the first to trade three centuries since at this port, were likewise designated "Wotsze." It was to be expected that, ignorant at that time as the Chinese were of geography and of the geographical position of Portugal, they would give the same name to all foreigners who then made their appearance on the eastern coasts. From further inquiry, I learnt that many of the people in the Chihkiang province have not yet been so enlightened as to relinquish that appellation in speaking of foreigners; and when at Ningpo, I found that at Hangchow foreigners generally, the English in particular, still were designated Weitsze.

Perhaps the most singular name by which to denote a foreigner, especially an Englishman, is "I say." This was quite common at Chusan and Ningpo during the occupation of those cities by our troops; and in some localities it has got into the local brogue as a foreign name for a foreigner. The derivation of the name is as odd as the word itself. During the war, wherever our troops settled down in quarters for any time, boys and other parasites crept into their cantonments, ready at any notice to help our troops as servants, &c. They could not fail to catch the very common ejaculation, "I say," "I say," with which the sailor or soldier saluted his comrade, and the natives concluding it to be a friendly name, it came to be a usual designation for a foreigner, introduced into Chinese sentences. For example (giving a translation of some sentences), "There was a red-coated *I say* sent me to buy a fowl;" "Did you see a tall *I say* go along here a while ago?" I was passing the police-office at Tinghai one morning, while military law reigned in that district; a thief had been caught and was tied up to be publicly whipped; as the lash was applied to the fellow's naked back, he roared and shouted frightfully. He appealed to his gods first, but finding this appeal of no service, he thought he would try the "I says," who were thrashing him. During the punishment, he continued calling out "Poosah, poosah! Omi-to-fuh, omi-to-fuh! I say, I say! O I say, I say!"

Being still a guest under the roof of Dr. Chang, I took care every day to return at sunset from my usual perambulations. On one of these evenings I observed that, after being himself absent all day, the aged doctor returned late, sighing often and groaning deeply. I perceived there was some fresh burden on his mind. This was confirmed by his calling my teacher aside. To him he explained his troubles, the particulars of which he requested might be communicated to me. Being an intimate friend and confidant of the prefect Shoo, Dr. Chang had been early that morning summoned by his worship to a private audience, during which he had to break the news that had just reached him, of his own degradation from office, the forfeiture of all his honours, and his committal to the Board of Punishment.

The alleged occasion of such summary punishment was, not his well-known disposition for a peaceful termination of the differences with Britain (his utmost efforts to promote which had been put forth during the friendly conferences at Nanking), but his having lost his ground at Tinghai, when that city was attacked and carried by the English in the autumn of 1841. He had superintended the erection of the defensive works on the island of Chusan, and was now made responsible for their loss. After that disaster, he had twice attempted self-destruction, but, through the prompt remedies of his close attendants, he had been restored. That he had survived the disgrace was no small item in the charge against him. Had he fallen in battle, it was said, his manes would have been raised to high honours and his heirs to official rank.

Before proceeding with the history of our fallen friend, one word about suicide in China. The popular modes of self-destruction are drowning, hanging, and swallowing opium or gold-leaf. With officials, the first and the last are the most respectable methods. During the war with England, when their reverses were frequent, the military officers in numerous instances effected self-destruction in one or other of these ways. Various accounts are given of the use and effect of gold-foil for the purpose. One has it, that a quantity of the flimsy leaf made up into a large bolus, is swallowed: when a cupful of water is drunk, it expands the gold-leaf in the stomach, which distends so as to occasion speedy death. Another account explains, that a bundle of the loose foil is thrust down the throat to produce suffocation.

One other mode of self-destruction is reported among the people as a fact, though it sounds fabulous to us. There is a bird called the *Sienhoh,** on the crown of

* I saw a pair of this ornithological curiosity at Ningpo. They were natives of Siam, and resembled the crowned crane, or *Grus carunculatus*. They were both young, male and female, nearly of a size, and had very long legs. The head was of a most handsome black, forking behind, having on the crest a scarlet skin. The rest of the body was white, except the secondaries of the wings which were not red, as represented in some Chinese drawings that I have seen, but black and overlapping the tail. Upon the embroidered breast-pieces of dresses, worn by the highest nobles of the state, there is a copy of this singular bird elegantly worked. A native work on the ornithology of China, which I have examined, gives some curious and prodigious stories about

whose head there is a beautiful scarlet tuft of down, or velvet skin, to which, the natives believe, the poison of the serpent it is fond of eating determines. This downy crest is often formed into a bead, and that bead is concealed in the ornamental necklaces of the high officers, for a suicidal purpose in case of imperial displeasure, which (as report goes) is easily effected by merely touching the venomous bead with the tip of the tongue, when death follows instantly.

From his rank being a lower one than that which could entitle him to wear that style of necklace, Shoo had not had the privilege of adopting this aristocratic mode of doing away with himself; although he ventured on the other expensive and hazardous form of suicide by gold-leaf, from the consequences of which he had been rescued by the timely aid of friends. At last he fell into a calamity considered worse than that.

Poor unfortunate man, he was stripped of his badges and plumes of honour. Already his fawning visitors began to shrink from him, and the heart that yesterday beat high with expectation, to-day sighed and sank in despair. In the course of the evening, while these explanations were given, I received from the degraded official a present of cakes, oranges, and hams, one of them the ham of a Shantung dog. A kind message accompanied the *donum* to say that, under his altered circumstances, he could not venture to invite me to dinner as he had wished.

A few days after, I embraced an opportunity to wait on the downcast Shoo. Shorn of all his official ornaments, buttons, feathers, &c., he looked a fallen chieftain. As soon as the usual civilities were over,

this fowl:—that it can live one thousand years; at sixty years of age it can sing regularly and beautifully every hour of the day; that on reaching its one thousandth year it can mount trees, but never before that, &c.

he significantly shook his head, exclaiming, "Ah, we officers of the middle empire are badly off! But thrice happy your people and princes, with just laws and equal privileges!" His worship then entered into a detail of his disasters.

By his learning, suavity, and justice, Shoo had secured for himself a good reputation in Ningpo, and made many personal friends. Of course, much anxiety was felt for him among the householders. More than once, the citizens forwarded petitions to the governor of the province, seeking his interference on behalf of Shoo-Kungshow. The views of the community thus intimated, were seconded by a deputation of wealthy inhabitants, who expressed their readiness to pay a heavy ransom for his life. It seemed the governor had gone as far as he could in interceding on his behalf, but failed. In proof of the sincerity and earnestness of his well-wishers, the Ningpo residents opened a subscription to redeem the life of their favourite officer. During those few days of intense anxiety, subscription-books were circulated through the city, with a page in each copy appropriated to the several trades and classes of merchants. In this way the lists began rapidly to swell; but, in consequence of information from head-quarters, founded on peremptory instructions from the Imperial cabinet, these benevolent proceedings were put a stop to; and every person looked on Shoo as a fated man.

Several of his personal friends called on me to see if I could advise a *dernier ressort.* I knew that Shoo was a universal favourite among the officers of the British expedition, and was well known to the heads of that expedition, especially Sir Henry Pottinger her Majesty's plenipotentiary. As Sir Henry was at the time in the south of China, holding frequent interviews with the Imperial commissioners appointed to complete the treaty with England, I recommended that the principal inhabitants of Ningpo should draw up a petition in favour of Shoo and forward it to the British plenipotentiary, requesting him to intercede with the Chinese commissioners on his behalf. They adopted the suggestion, and I had the happiness to transmit their petition to Hong-Kong, the seat of Sir Henry's government. Shortly after, I received a reply from Sir Henry's private secretary, to intimate that "Sir Henry needed no petition to make him speak expressly in Shoo's favour," so highly were his abilities and services valued.

That native officer's life was spared. He survived his disgrace and lived for some time after, conscious (I believe) that none were more anxious for his safety than Englishmen, and none more successful in interfering for his rescue.

From the day of my arrival, the worthy prefect (now degraded) had been kind in his attentions, and encouraged my residing at Dr. Chang's, till he himself should be able to select better quarters for me. He had not succeeded, however; and, from the circumstances that had befallen him, he saw it prudent to desist from further search. Apprehensive also that his friend Dr. C. might get involved in a similar dilemma, he advised me to remove from his residence and occupy quarters without the city.

It appeared but prudent to leave the doctor's homely cottage as early as possible; though I felt a strong repugnance at quitting the city altogether. Accompanied by my steady teacher and guide, I went to the *Kwantang* monastery, where the chief priest, a man advanced in years but of very lively temperament, conducted me round the building, and showed me the various chambers and attics. On naming the object of my visit, he candidly stated that the objection he had to my living under the same roof was that females of Ningpo, who formed the majority of the worshippers in these temple-premises, would desert the building on the first rumour of an Englishman tenanting any portion of it, and the earnings of the priestly office would be endangered. Of course I could not urge my proposal.

My anxiety to hold quarters within the city arose, not so much from a view of the advantages that a missionary enjoys in this situation, but from a conviction that, among a people like the Chinese, the sooner a precedent such as this is admitted, the better for all parties, native and foreign. At present it appeared that no alternative was left but to retire quietly to the suburbs, and subsequently to embrace the earliest opportunity of returning into the city.

Upon quitting my kind host's roof, I took possession of the back apartments in one of the temples in the southern suburbs of the city, temporarily appropriated by the Ningpo authorities for the use of foreign visitors from Tinghai. There were two buildings contiguous to each other. I selected the Laouhwuy-kwan, "the old Club House."

Among native residents and merchants, who come from one province to another, it is common for those of the same province or department to contribute towards the erection of a temple on the spot where they are engaged in business. The temple is dedicated to the god of their native place or province, for the sake of gaining whose graces service is conducted by duly-appointed priests. Theatrical plays are likewise acted within the building, both to amuse the public and to gratify the god-idol. The order of priests depends chiefly on the religious profession of the contributors. But not unfrequently the custody of the building and the performance of the ceremonies are left with a layman, denominated the *tsaikung*, "master of ceremonies," whose habiliments are not peculiarly distinctive. The erection in which my lot was cast, was one built and supported by voluntary contributions. The chief patrons were Fuhkien men, who had contributed 6,000 dollars towards the structure. "Assembly Halls" of this form differ little from a common temple, with a spacious open area in the centre, and built all round with upper galleries and commodious rooms. Certain compartments are generally appropriated to strangers who may be making a passing visit—strangers especially from those districts to which the patrons of the building belong. These halls are remarkably convenient for travellers speaking the same dialect, coming from the same localities, and probably engaged in the same commerce, but without any family connections in a place, and ignorant of the *locale* of lodging-houses. In some respects they answer to European club-houses, or resorts for people to hear news and obtain market intelligence from the interior.

Into the upper rooms of this building I moved my baggage, and contrived to make myself pretty comfortable;—one of the large rooms being divided into three compartments by suspending sedge mats from the rafters, so that, between my teacher's chamber and my own, there was a sitting-room. In edifices of this order, the members of the club usually set up for the principal object of homage the image of the presiding genius of their native place. Besides that *genius loci*, there were several others occupying various parts of the building. In the compartment partitioned off for myself, there sat the idol, *Wanwang*, the calm, quiet-faced "Prince of Literature."

Having enjoyed the company of that personage for some time, I must not pass him by without a remark. He flourished originally 3,000 years since, and continues to maintain an unsullied reputation in the literary world, as the author of the *Yih-King*, "the Book of Changes," the earliest and the most mystic of the Chinese classics. That work was composed by him during a three years' imprisonment, under the reign of the last emperor of the *Shang* dynasty, who earned an infamous celebrity by his follies and crimes. In it he developed the eight diagrams of *Fuhhi* into sixty-four combinations; by ringing the changes around which combinations there are no less than 16,777,216 variations formed. This curious relic of antiquity professes to treat of the first cause, as founded on the Chinese system of dual powers, the *yang* and *yin* principles, the grand male and female vivifying elements in the creation and subsistence of the material universe. All the phenomena of nature are traceable to this duality, or to the multiform changes of the cabalistic diagrams connected with it. The principles of human conduct, good or bad, are likewise deducible from the successive evolutions of that dual system. Into the hidden meaning of this celebrated classic, Confucius himself spent many years of inquiry, and with the author's own remarks there is now incorporated the addition of a commentary from the pen of Confucius. The students of said antique work depend on the annotations of that sage for clearing up the aphoristic expressions. But a native catalogue published in China (with all the books of the four department,—classical, historical, professional, and *belles lettres*), mentions no fewer than 1,450 distinct works on "the Book of Changes," in the form of treatises, memoirs, expositions, commentaries, &c. A writing like this, bearing the stamp of the remotest antiquity, and clothed in language of which their most sage philosophers could scarcely decipher the mystic lines, is the very book to please the Chinese mind and enlarge the native bump of veneration. Besides, it has given vast encouragement to the art of divination from shells, marks, letters, &c. Indeed, anything and everything of the most fanciful and superstitious form has found its original here; and the whole art of divining is ascribed to the god of literature as its inventor. The author of the strange and curious fragment I have been speaking of, has of course for ages been canonized, and is pointed out among the *élite* of the Chinese pantheon. It was the same god of learning that shared the apartment I had appropriated for myself in the "Old Assembly Hall."

But, besides the companionship of that eminent prince of literature, I found another set of messmates, far more vivacious and amusing as well as disturbing; for in my lodgment I had been anticipated by a populous colony of rats and mice. The size of these visitors was certainly monstrous, as their number was overwhelming; and there was no keeping them out during the night. The tricks they played, too, showed no little daring; and not inappropriately they have been designated "the cavalry of Ningpo." The dexterity with which they bounded from beam to rafter was surprising. They were equally expert in rattling over my furniture at pleasure, and they seemed to scour, in regimental squads, every nook and corner of the apartment. Their squeals of pleasure as they pitched into my provisions were truly amusing, and their screams of rage or pain as they pitched into each other were equally annoying. But it was not the least of nuisances, just when one was dropping off to sleep, to be aroused by having the face licked by their slimy tongues, or pawed by their cold extremities.

Rat-destruction would have been an endless job and of little service, as the places of the slain were instantly occupied by successors, determined to wreak vengeance for the blood of their comrades. If rats were a favourite dish at a Chinaman's table, assuredly the rats of Ningpo must have lost their popularity with the residents there; for in number they not only never decreased, they seemed daily to multiply. Rat-catching gives employ to certain hands here, for the purpose of supplying a limited market for ratskins, to be used in various forms.

Often as I have paced the streets in China, my attention has been arrested by the tinkling of little bells, giving notice of a rat-catcher approaching. Here he comes with a pole across his shoulder, on each end of which there hangs a frame with an exhibition of dead rats, poisoned rats, stuffed rats, dried rat-skins, and flaming labels to advertise his office as rat-catcher, There are passing travellers who have seen spectacles of this kind on arriving in China, and, having heard beforehand that the Chinese devour everything, rats and mice among the rest, have concluded that those rumours were confirmed by such a sight. On returning home, these gentlemen have published notices of their visit to Chinese towns; and, by inserting pictures of a man going to market with strings of rats and mice hanging by their tails to a stick across his shoulders, they perpetuate the idea, especially among young people, that these form common articles of food for the "celestials."

In a few days it came to be bruited abroad among the Buddhist priests, that Mei-siensang was tenanting one of their temples; and soon I felt apprehensive of being pestered as much by swarms of priests as of rats. On the second day of my residence at this monastery, five Buddhists of the sacerdotal order waited on me. They were inquisitive about my dress, boxes, books, &c. &c.; but began to feel some interest in trying to satisfy me, when they found I was, on the other hand, as curious to know particulars about them.

From inquiries then made and subsequently confirmed, it appears the larger majority of bonzes come from the lowest classes of society,—perhaps fatherless, and given up to the service of Buddha by a destitute mother for a few pieces of money, or, as often happens, sons sold to the shrine of their god by both parents, only because they are poor. These five individuals themselves assured me that they had each entered the priesthood at an early age and in orphanhood,—one at six, a second at eight, a third at ten, the fourth at twelve, and the fifth at fourteen. On another occasion I was informed of a mother having sold a child only five years of age, to be trained to the priesthood, for the trifle of ten dollars, or scarcely £2 sterling. There are priests I have met with who have taken the vow late in life: for instance, one at Tinghai, who had married and begotten two sons before he took the vows of priesthood. He told me his wife was dead, but he seemed utterly unconcerned about his sons.

After a week's residence in this suburban monastery, finding it anything but convenient, I resolved to seek other quarters, and succeeded in ferreting out apartments within the east gate. At this time I chose a wing adjoining a Buddhist *nunnery* dedicated to the goddess Kwanyin. The rooms had lately been occupied by an officer of the civil department. Being now vacated, I engaged, at ten dollars a month, a kitchen, sitting-room, and two bed-rooms. As soon as the terms of agreement were drawn up, I deserted the monastery, which I had been occupying for seven days.

However, the monks of Buddh were reluctant I should leave them without a parting feast. I was too glad to accept the offer. As we sat down to dinner, in appearance there was nothing to distinguish the viands from what one ordinarily meets with at the tables of those who have "not come out of the world." The Buddhists invariably prate of having separated themselves from the commonalty, and, in proof, talk of having given up for aye the unclean things of a grovelling world. They profess entire abstinence from blood and racy food, flesh, garlic, or animal oil. I have known them even refuse to drink plain tea out of a cup or teapot of mine, afraid lest there should be any contaminating stuff in it. Nevertheless, rigid though their principles be, and austere their professions, I am compelled to testify, from what I have seen of the practices of these priests, that they are rather loose and inconsistent in common life. The head priest in this very establishment gladly accepted from me a present of a ham; and a junior in the building informed me that, during their minority, priests are permitted to indulge in the rich treats of the table. It was with the assistance of this young priest that my daily meals were cooked as long as I lodged here. And if rumours are to be received, the high monasteries in the interior of China are notorious for the sumptuous living of the inmates. I was particularly amused, on this occasion of their giving me a dinner, to see how the fraternity sought, even with their simple materials of bean-powder, vegetables, &c., to conform as far as possible to what they of the world eat. At first sight the dishes seemed similar to what one finds at any other *table-d'hôte;* and, until I had examined and tasted them, I thought everything before me was very flesh—very fowl. The skin of the chicken appeared to perfection, and I had before me what seemed the pimply morsel; but it turned out to be a square of consolidated bean-pulse, the upper layer of which had been impressed with a rough towel! We had "mock fowl," "mock mutton," "mock bird's-nest," "mock etcetera." The wine, however, was neat and unadulterated, a strong spirit distilled from rice, the best of which goes by the name "Shauhing wine."

In the middle of dinner, about 7 P.M., my servant, who had gone on with my baggage, came to inform me that the lady-abbess, in charge of the rooms I had taken, sent a request that I would delay my coming for a day or two. She felt desirous to make further inquiry about her new lodger, and to satisfy some misgivings she had at having given up the apartments to a foreigner. But it was too late. All my luggage had been moved, and it only remained for me to move my person. The head priest from whom I was about to part, on being apprised of the dilemma, volunteered to accompany me and stand surety for my good character. Prudence dictated that I should occupy the new lodgings without delay, and within fifteen minutes I found myself at the principal gate of the nunnery.

When I entered I was introduced to the abbess. She doffed her skull-cap, and made a respectful bow with her bald pate and closed fist. On returning the courtesy, she began to make inquiries about my age, family, calling, and objects, to all which I answered apparently to her satisfaction and agreeable surprise too, on finding that I could converse with her in her own tongue. She was evidently relieved by this interview, as well as by the recommendations of the priest. When her mind seemed at rest, she brought in a tray of tea and sweetmeats. The nuns under her care, nine in number, were hanging about the door; and, at last, the *supérieure* gathered courage to introduce her pet disciple, a girl of twelve, who had been for six years under her instruction, but not yet fully initiated. In a short time the timidity of the abbess entirely wore off. However, the curiosity which she and her pupils, during the rest of the evening, evinced about everything the foreigner had brought, became so prying and disagreeable, that their adieu was hailed as a timely relief. My small stock of tracts was opened, and I was gratified to find that all the nuns were able to read. I gave each a copy, and we parted for the night good friends.

In a day or two the nuns also sent me a dinner, not merely to conciliate my good-will, but also to get a few dollars. Dependent people in China often provide dinners for their patrons or their superiors, solely with the view of drawing on their purses; a strange practice, acknowledged and supported by common consent. But the repast provided in this case was all vegetable —

vegetable — vegetable; precisely similar to what the priests had entertained me with a week before, but got up with more care and at greater expense. It was very, very tasteless, to be sure, and utterly devoid of relish. Such an attempt to imitate animal diet may please the fancy, but it will not gratify the palate. As the Chinese conclude by eating rice with a light soup, rice came on the table in the regular course, and some liquid in a centre bowl intended to represent a dish of soup; but, could anything be more emetical?—it was nothing save lukewarm water—genuine, limpid, unadulterated *warm water!*

After I had been three weeks in possession of my quarters at the nunnery, the lady-abbess broadly hinted her wish that I should look for other quarters, and, prostrating herself before me, knocked head and implored that I would forthwith quit. On perceiving the great anxiety that my presence on the premises occasioned, I assured the landlady that I would not trouble her with my presence longer. She had endangered her gains by admitting me under her roof. Besides, there were prudential reasons that induced me to hurry off. Circumstances came to light not much to the credit of these ascetic ladies, which forced me to suspect that their course of life was a burlesque on professed purity and continence. Yet, after all, it is a difficult thing in China to fix on a locality free from some *mala fama,* true or false.

Before taking leave of them for good, I must offer a digest of particulars that I collected about Buddhist nuns and nunneries in China, during so fit an opportunity of learning something about them.

That building was called the nunnery of *Kwanyin,* being dedicated to the idol, also titled in European writers the "goddess of mercy." The full designation of the idol is *Kwan she yin,* "observing the world's sounds." It is represented as a female with a child

in her arms, who is supposed to extend her patronage to all that in trouble or difficulty raise the cry for compassion,—being one of the numberless objects of idolatry introduced from the West by the Buddhists. It is one of the few female deities in China; and no other idol meets with more respect and honour throughout the land, nor is there any other so frequently invoked in favour of frail humanity, as women form the overwhelming majority of the devout, and *Kwanyin* is the special patroness of the weaker sex, especially in the hour of child-bearing.

The great allurement presented by the supporters of Buddhism to the mind of the aspirant who would consecrate herself to the altar of the goddess, is the absorption after death into the unknown Buddha;—a matter that, the more mysteriously it is represented, the more taking it is to the mind of the ingenuous but credulous candidate. That sort of personal advantage is held out by the institution to facilitate the succession of an order of priestesses who can gain access where the formalities of society cannot admit the stranger priest, and who are qualified to work with dexterity and impunity upon the feelings of a class the most susceptible of religious impressions.

To maintain a female order of priesthood, the rooms of "the annihilated" or "absorbed" (as they will have it) must be filled up either by purchase or by self-dedication. In the case of purchase, babes and girls of tender age and good promise are preferred, and bought up at a low rate. To my personal knowledge, a sweet child only four years of age has been offered by its own mother to an abbess for the paltry sum of eighteen shillings. There are some, however, who are dedicated by their parents from birth, irrespective of emolument; and others, on coming of age, voluntarily consecrate themselves to the service of this deity. When the case is optional, it arises often—if not always

—from being thwarted in some of their prospects or wishes. I have seen a blooming "religiosa" of nineteen, who had "left the world" to take upon herself the vows of perpetual virginity, in consequence of the untimely death of her intended husband. That nun had small feet, her pedicles having been bandaged prior to her misfortune. But of nuns that I have met at Ningpo or elsewhere, there are very few with the cramped foot; those marked with this deformity having probably taken the veil of their own accord and without compulsion, after having reached the years of discretion.

In general the candidate is not admitted into full orders until she attains the age of sixteen. Prior to this, and indeed from the very commencement of her ascetic life, she assumes the garb peculiar to the sisterhood. The chief apparent distinction between the novice and the sister in full orders, is that the head of the latter is wholly shaven, while the former has only the front part shaven. The younger nuns have platted queues flowing down behind. The habit which this devout class wears, on the whole so much resembles the dress of the Buddhist monks, that in many cases it is impossible at first sight to distinguish the two orders. The nuns have clumsy shoes, long stockings and garters, full trowsers, short jackets and wide sleeves, with bald heads, and tiny skull-caps,—precisely as the priests. Yet it must be owned the sisters have smoother faces, softer looks, sweeter voices, and perhaps are more tidy than the *fratres*. If report is to be trusted, the nuns of Soochow have reversed the rules of their order, and, throwing aside the rough hempen cloth or coarse material assigned to the self-denying sisterhood, prefer silks and satins for dresses.

When a young woman has bared or shaven her head, or, according to European phraseology, "taken the veil," she is required to live a life of devotion and self-mortification. She must eat and drink sparingly, and her diet must consist only of plain vegetable. Strong meats and drinks are to be avoided as deadly poison. The business and cares of this life are not to engross her attention. She has retired from it, and she must be fitting herself for eternal canonization. Nothing should occupy her thoughts or engage her affections but the service of the temple in the precincts of which she lives, and acts of benevolence and compassion. Religious exercises are daily to be conducted by her; the furniture of the small sanctuary connected with the convent has to be looked after and kept in order; and the men or the women who come to worship at the altars and to ask guidance or comfort are to be assisted. If there be leisure, the sick and the poor must be visited; and all who place themselves under her spiritual direction, it is presumed, are to have a vital claim on her regard. That she may live a life of seclusion and self-denial, she has to pledge herself to inviolable maidenhood. The thought of marriage must not enter her head, and the society of man (except worshippers) is to be shunned. Upon her death she is to be swallowed up in nihility.

While I resided at the Kwanyin convent, it had altogether ten nuns, whose ages ran between seven and twenty-five. Spite their spare diet, they all looked fat, plump, and hale, with the exception of the two youngest. The abbess was about forty years of age, and more masculine in temper than any Chinese woman I had yet met with. She was of a most passionate turn, and I have repeatedly watched her anger, when roused, rise to a fearful pitch. A thorough scold, she kept her pupils in perpetual awe. Her avarice was voracious, and her deceitfulness dark and deep; and, though she appeared most fastidious in avoiding animal food and everything of a strong flavour, she was in the habit of plying herself with ardent spirits, distilled from rice, and at times appeared to be rather under its influence.

The daily services in the place were conducted morning and evening; but at the usual exercises I rarely saw more than two officiate. On special occasions, occurring every month, there were services that occupied the whole day. At some of them they were aided by sisters from neighbouring nunneries, and not unfrequently priests were called to join in the sacred concerts; in which case the priests and priestesses occupied separate apartments, but proceeded with the chants in unison.

Their sacred books consisted of many volumes, printed in large text and on fine paper. For these they have the profoundest respect. I happened to purchase a copy from them, but they would not part with it until they had importuned me to give it an elevated place on my bookshelf, and, to make sure of it, had placed it there with their own hands. The rapidity with which the pages and sections of their liturgy were hurried off at their religious services was amazing. Both old and young appeared equally expert in the recitations; yet there was nought of a devotional spirit about them, and their demeanour was far from devout. Repeatedly I have watched a choir of juvenile nuns meet to pay religious homage to the stock on their shrine; but they were merry, tricky, flirting, and frolicsome as any party of girls keeping the birthday of a schoolfellow. In their liturgical forms, such as this was recited, to them as unintelligible as to us, though laudatory of their goddess Kwanyin—

> "Sew-le sew-le, mo-o, sew-le, sew-sew-le sah-po-o,
> Sew-to-le, sew-to-le, sew-mo-le, saou-po-o,
> Nan-woo-sau, mwan-to-muh, pwan-nan-yen, toh-loo, toh-loo, te-me-sah, po-o."

Much time being spent in reading and reciting prayers, canticles, &c., the candidate, before she can be admitted into full orders, must undergo an educational training;

and, with this view, many pursue the elementary course usually adopted through the empire, learning the Trimetrical Classic, Four Books, &c., and acquiring the ready use of the pencil. Some nuns are reputed as being well read in the lore of the country.

Those among the laity (females especially) who have placed themselves under the spiritual instruction of a nun, are expected to put implicit confidence in her as a teacher and priestess. Be the devotee a man or a woman, the chosen preceptress gives the individual *a new name.* Each nun is on the alert to cultivate the acquaintance of the disciples she makes, and to swell her list of friends, as her private support principally depends on them.

In this nunnery of Kwanyin I saw a slab behind the altar, with the names of subscribers all cut out on it. Visitors from town or country, by no means scarce, used to leave a little in money or kind; and, what with gifts and donations, the means of subsistence were not lacking in this establishment. It had besides some property invested in lands and houses. And the wing of the convent which I occupied was entirely appropriated to lodgings for country visitors, let out at a moderate charge, and capable of being made comfortable, if one were not constantly subject to annoyance from the boisterous money-seeking landlady.

I have above mentioned that *special* services occasionally devolved on the nuns. These were generally got up by the patrons of the order, under circumstances of calamity or prosperity, or when the abbess was successful enough to work up the superstitious feelings of a husband by means of a nun-ridden wife. Any person who engaged the religious performances of the nuns, was called upon to appoint the number of sacred books to be recited. For this he had to pay a certain remuneration, according to a scale of charges. At each service the nuns respectively received a small premium, for pocket-money, not exceeding three-pence.

In the district of Ningpo, I was told there were thirty nunneries and about 300 inmates. But the estimation in which this religious order is held is exceedingly low. They are described amongst their countrymen as a class of women almost on a footing with those who are lost to the most delicate and chaste feelings, that are the glory and protection of woman. Like the male priests of the Buddhist religion, they are not only not respected by the populace, but are detested for their profligacies, and dreaded for the influence which they are supposed to exert on one's destiny by familiar intercourse with the spirits of the invisible world. Hence the common saying, "To meet with a nun in the street will be unlucky to your errand." Such was the infamous profligacy, in 1840, of the dressy, *opium-smoking* nuns of Soochow, the capital of Kiangsoo province, that the notorious Yu Kien (who, in 1841, hastened down to Chinhai, as Imperial commissioner, invested with full powers to exterminate us English by fire and by sword), broke up their establishments and disbanded the sisterhood in that city.

To complete this notice of Chinese nuns and nunneries, I must say a word about the two junior inmates of the Kwanyin convent, already alluded to. The younger died while I was residing in the establishment. She died at the early age of seven, and had been an inmate scarcely one year. When I came first, she was suffering from ulceration of the bowels. On the abbess hearing that there was an English physician visiting Ningpo, she applied through me for his assistance. Dr. Johnson, of the Madras Rifles, was then on a visit of a few days, and cheerfully gave his advice, and prescribed from his own stock of medicines for the poor sufferer. But unfortunately the child was beyond remedy, and death had fastened on her vitals. One morning, while the elder nuns were saying that the child was sleeping soundly, they seemed unaware that the sleep of death had stolen upon her, until they found she was insensible to sound and touch. When they ascertained this, the *supérieure* had the body removed out of the house, and put behind, in a common wood-cellar, there to expire unnursed, unattended. *Aluh*, her senior in age, though still a girl in manners, was devotedly attached to her dying companion; yet she was not allowed by the lady-abbess to watch over the closing moments of her playmate. When the dead child was laid in her rude coffin, the housemaid was ordered to cast into it a doll with which she had daily played; and, after certain incantations to quiet the spirit of the departed and to bribe away any demons lurking about the spot, the coffin was carried out and laid under the city walls, to be removed by the officers of a charitable institution.

Aluh was twelve years old. Her father used to go about Ningpo, hawking turnips and greens; but on his death the mother sold the child to the nunnery at the tender age of four. In her countenance there was something peculiarly striking—there was so much intelligence and cheerfulness—to which her wearing sickness added a mournful interest. She was a good reader of Chinese, and able to write too. Often she stole into my sitting-room to look at my books, and would sit for half an hour at a time to inquire about England. She seemed glad to read a tract now and then with me, and to converse on the religion of the Saviour, — a topic that came up naturally enough, especially as her state of health could not but awaken apprehension that she would not long be a survivor in this world. Though she listened with some interest to my explanations of gospel truth, it was painful to detect the thick films of prejudice induced by the idolatrous system in which she had been trained. A few weeks after I quitted the nunnery, I was distressed to learn that *Aluh* had crossed "the bourn."

Through the mediation of several Chinese friends, suitable lodgings were found for me within the city, not far from my former apartments, and made as snug as Chinese can make such things. I moved into them in the middle of January, 1843.

The landlord was a merchant of property and respectability. During the occupation of the city by the British, he contributed a good deal of his estate to levy a militia,—one of many fruitless measures adopted in those days to repel their foreign foe. Under the suasion of my personal acquaintances, he consented to let me have the use of seven rooms, besides cookhouse, &c., at the monthly rent of ten dollars. This he afterwards lowered to four dollars. When the first monthly rate came due, he positively declined to accept any remuneration, and begged me to let him have the opportunity of showing me this mark of kindness. Up to the time of my occupying his rooms, he had been afraid of Englishmen; but, after having seen several gentlemen of the naval and military service who now and then visited Ningpo and passed an hour with me, their urbanity wore off his timidity, and he soon perceived that really the English were not so savage and barbarous as he had imagined.

My occupation of these apartments continued undisturbed until I quittted the city the following July.

CHAPTER III.

A MANDARIN DINNER—INTERVIEW WITH A FAMOUS KIDNAPPER—NEW YEAR FESTIVITIES—CHINESE ALMANAC—WHIPPING IN THE SPRING—FEAST OF LANTERNS—APPEARANCE OF A COMET.

NOT many days after installing myself in the new quarters, a party of English gentlemen visited Ningpo. In need of a guide and an interpreter, they requested me to accompany them to the residences of the Chinese officials. I was happy to render what aid I could; and subsequently was gratified to find that the courteous treatment which these gentlemen received at the hands of the native "big-wigs" produced a rather favourable impression on them. They expressed themselves not only pleased, but surprised, at the handsome manner in which they had been entertained.

There was one particular, among others, on which my friends got some new light. They were invited by the chief officer to take an ordinary tiffin, and were glad enough to have an opportunity personally to witness a real curiosity,—a genuine feast at a native table; although they had no intention of dipping into dishes which they supposed would consist only of puppy-flesh, earth-worms, rats and mice swimming in liquid hog's-lard. What was their agreeable surprise, then, to find the viands totally different to their preconceived notions, excellent as well as various! First came hot rolls and sweet cakes; next, sweetmeats, varicoloured eggs, and candied marrow-bones; then, duck, fowl, beef, kid, and pork; lastly, fish, soup, and rice. Besides, the table was loaded with fresh and dried fruits and abundance of the best wine the Chinese can boast of. The only "*amari aliquid* which disflavoured their fountain of contentment" was that, while each had a plate, a bowl, and chop-sticks, we all had to take in common out of one central dish. Having for some time got accustomed to the use of the "quick lads," I managed to supply myself readily. But my companions were not equally nimble in plying their "sticks." However, Chinese spoons and silver forks of native work were brought to their timely assistance; and at the end the English visitors, gratified with so ample and substantial a repast, parted with the officials of Ningpo on very good terms indeed.

Our host, Luh, the chief officer, was at the time unfortunately suffering from itch, and perceiving that there were two medical men in our party, he was by no means shy in revealing his complaint. They promptly prescribed the usual remedies. But, on receiving the medicine prescribed, the *Taoutai* (his title) felt much surprised at the beautiful lemon-tint of the sulphur, in this respect so vastly superior to the unclarified mineral found in the native drug-shops. Nor was he less amazed at learning that he was required to *swallow* sulphur, which he had heard of being applied only externally. After his foreign physicians had left the city, his excellency sent a special messenger to me three distinct times, to make sure that the article was really to be swallowed; for he insisted that, "as the sulphur is heating, it is inadmissible into the internal system."

About this time I formed acquaintance with Mr. Le, formerly in office in the province of Nganhwuy. What particularly took my fancy in this man was his frank and undisguised avowal of political opposition to, what he considered, English encroachment on the grand prerogatives of the Emperor of China. He protested he was still for war, and prophesied that, though peace between the two countries might last awhile, the tug of war would soon be renewed.

During the struggle with Great Britain, he had become conspicuous in the kidnapping department; and he now openly acknowledged that, in the spring of 1842, he had concerted plans for my abduction, in consequence of information obtained from a Chinese lad, who, while in my service at Tinghai, had been kidnapped and carried to Hangchow. This naturally brought to my mind a fact that occurred a few weeks after my servant had been waylaid. I related the same to Mr. Le, greatly to his amusement; and I mention it here at some length, both on account of my singular deliverance and the ludicrous *finale* to circumstances otherwise anxious and perilous.

In the early part of that same year, it was by no means uncommon to hear of British soldiers or seamen being kidnapped at Tinghai, and carried to the mainland for imprisonment,—perhaps something worse. If I mistake not, it was (and I may add *is* now) the only effective plan the Chinese adopted for annoying their foreign aggressors. Besides, it was then a rather lucrative employment to the successful kidnapper,—a good reward being offered for a live Englishman, or an equivalent for his bleeding head.

At that time, as I was residing alone, and, without a messmate, occupied a lonely cottage in a Chinaman's kitchen-garden in the heart of Tinghai, some friends in her Majesty's 55th regiment felt somewhat concerned about my solitariness, and proposed that I should share a berth in their rendezvous. Their great and uniform kindness to me, for which to the present hour I am deeply sensible, was politely declined, as I felt no cause of apprehension, and was desirous to pitch my tent as long as I could among Chinese. My *locale* was in the compound of a respectable citizen, whose confidence had already been tried, and whose honour was pledged to render me all the security in his power; and so I determined to continue the tenant of my humble lodgement. The gentlemen of the 55th insisted, however, that I should take with me some weapon for self-defence, and I was persuaded to accept a double-barrelled horse-pistol, loaded and primed.

The bed-room that I occupied had four doors in it, and as many windows; but was without a lock or iron bolt, and provided only with wooden snaps: so that, whenever I retired to rest for the night, in order to make myself secure, I piled up chairs, boxes, and sundry pieces of luggage against the doors and windows, that in case of an attempt at violent entrance, I might be aroused.

For several nights in succession I slept with the loaded pistol by my pillow. But on one Sabbath evening—dark, gloomy, stormy, and threatening—the impression came over me as I retired into the room, that, on a night so favourable for kidnapping as that was, some attempt might be made to carry me off, and that probably, on the fright of the moment, I might use my formidable weapon and bring a fellow-creature down to the ground, or hurry him into eternity. *Instanter* I resolved to risk my own safety rather than incur the horror of killing a man and a brother. So, throwing the pistol into the bottom of my box, I locked it up. After adopting the usual precautions with boxes and baggage, I laid myself down and slept comfortably for a few hours.

Somehow, about one o'clock in the morning, I awoke; why, I knew not. The wind was howling over the roof; the rain was pouring down in torrents; the thunder every now and then pealed forth; and sleep had fled from my eyelids. But my drowsiness was startled by low and suppressed murmurs. Raising myself on my pillow to listen, I discerned there were whispers outside—strange, unusual sounds—the voices of Chinese, consulting, aiding each other. They were already in the garden, and in a few seconds they might be within reach of me. The pistol was in the box,—but no time was to be lost in reopening the trunk. In a trice I leaped out of my hammock, seized a huge bar, rushed to the window, rammed it against the frame, and shouted out the English soldier's night salute—"Who comes there?" The effect was that of an electric shock. The rascals took to their heels, and made their flight complete; leaving behind what was too significant —a bag and a sword! I could not but thank God for my escape, and theirs too.

By this time the servants were all up, in greater alarm than myself,—the watchman especially, whom I caught in the arms of Morpheus. The morning not having yet dawned, and the night being still bleak and awful, I warned the servants in the cottage to keep a look-out; as, in all probability, the fellows might muster courage to renew the attempt. Upon this I threw myself back into the Chinese cot. However, by this time my warlike disposition had got roused; and the pistol, dragged out of the portmanteau, was placed by the bedside as usual. One hour passed away, still very sleepless. At last my teacher came creeping into the room, and fluttered out the whisper, "They are coming again, they are coming!" I allayed his terror with the assurance that I was quite ready for them now. Following him with the cocked pistol, I went to the back premises. There I saw in the twilight what my domestics saw,—two men on the wall, the one helping the other down. Crawling under a hedge between me and them until I got exactly abreast of them, I halted. I levelled the pistol at them, hoping only to graze them. As before, I bawled out, "Who comes there?" To my horror the pistol went off! It dropped out of my hand, and I thought to see one, perhaps two, human beings also drop. But, still there they are as before, aiding each other over the wall! Now imagine, good reader, my surprise and relief at the ridiculous close to the whole affray; for, as twilight advanced, I beheld, and lo! the men I had been shooting at were two branches of a tree, overhanging the wall, quietly and regularly moving with the morning breeze!

When I related this story to Mr. Le himself, it occasioned him no small merriment; and ever after, notwithstanding his patriotic antipathy to the English, he treated me with remarkable courtesy, as if to make the *amende honorable* for the annoyance he had perpetrated by his kidnapping tricks.

Like other Chinese, in mark of respect, he invited me to dine with him on an early day after our acquaintance was formed. On this occasion I met at his table with a peculiar dish, which I have never seen under the roof of any other host, though I was informed that it was not a monopoly of Mr. Le's taste. When our party of six had seated themselves at the centre table, my attention was attracted by a *covered* dish, something unusual at a Chinese meal. On a certain signal, the cover was removed; and presently the face of the table was covered with juvenile crabs, which made their exodus from the dish with all possible rapidity. The crablets had been thrown into a plate of vinegar just as the company sat down—such an immersion making them more brisk and lively than usual. But the sprightly sport of the infant crabs was soon checked, by each guest seizing which he could, dashing it into his mouth, crushing it between his teeth, and swallowing the whole morsel without ceremony. Determined to do as the Chinese did, I tried this novelty also with one—with two. I succeeded, finding the shell soft and gelatinous, for they were tiny creatures, not more than a day or two old. But I was compelled to give in to the third, which had resolved to take vengeance, and gave my lower lip a nip so sharp and severe as to make me relinquish my hold and likewise desist from any further experiment of this nature.

My engagements being numerous and my hands full, the days passed so rapidly and pleasantly away, that, almost before I was aware of it, I had nearly got to the close of January, 1843.

That month was the twelfth moon, during which every one was occupied with preparations for the approaching new year: in describing which, the expressions of the vocabulary are numerous as well as significant; *e.g.* "thanking the year," "attending the old year out," "making presents to it," "parting with the year," or "keeping it in," &c. From the nineteenth of this moon, the government offices were closed for thirty days, the adjournment being ushered in by the clumsy and cumbrous ceremony of "putting up the seals of office." During that crisis presents were most abundant amongst the wealthy,—passing from hand to hand with speed and in number beyond calculation. The city officials were remarkably attentive to me at this season, which ceremonial courtesies I was glad to interpret as tokens of friendship. Their gifts consisted chiefly of packets of tea, fruit, and sweetmeats; the lots being made up of *even* numbers, from the prevalent superstition among the Chinese, that in an odd number there is bad luck, in a complete number good. That rule is almost universal on festive occasions, especially at the opening of the new year. On the other hand, in making presents at a time of mourning for a deceased friend, or at the anniversary of his death, which it is not unusual for them to keep,—the odd number prevails.

As to the celebration of the new year, I now had ample opportunities of observing the family ceremonies and festivities, which in every case were as extensive as their means could afford. The domestic preparations continued through the whole of the last month of the old year. First, there was the working up of the *nien-kaou*, the *tsiehtsieh-kaou*, "the yearly or the season cakes." It was a composition of rice-flour and water, worked with the hand like dough; which, after the mass had gone through sufficient manipulation, was put on trays to be reduced into cakes of various shapes and sizes. Bakers and confectioners had their hands full. But in families particularly, at a time when there was a general gathering, the manufacturing of this favourite cake gave ample room for the services of women, children, boys, girls, and servants. Every household was busy at it, and no little fun and frolic enlivened their gay circles. Often the quantity stored up was immense, and the display of forms and devices of the rice-dough was to a Chinese eye attractive;—each piece impressed with a red stamp, or decorated with figures from a vermilion pencil. Previous to eating the cake, it had not to be baked, but to be sodden in hot water with sugar, and sometimes in hot wine.

On the 23rd of the last month, or a week before the old year died out, a kind of family service began, called *tse tsaou*, for "sacrificing to the kitchen god." This *lar* was represented by a small image, sometimes by a rough drawing, stuck up in a niche over the oven. It first underwent a thorough scouring, to clean off the soot which had been accumulating upon it during the previous 360 days. Some of the "too superstitious" had the idea that, after this purgation, it ascended up to the court of heaven, to join the annual divan of tutelar deities, and to render its yearly account of the acts of the family over which it presided. It was thought too that it had a furlough of seven days from its murky duties, which were to be resumed on the first of the coming year. I likewise found that it was not an unpopular notion that the *dii majores* visited the earth in a body at this period for an entire week; and many natives gave this as the reason for being so particular in setting their houses to rights, and keeping the premises clean and orderly at so memorable a time. During the hallowed interval, special pains were taken to keep the ground undefiled by any sort of nuisance. Scrupulous care was everywhere paid to *tanchin*, or "wipe down dust" and cobwebs, an operation very desirable and needful. There were likewise thank-offerings and oblations without end to the various *lares* and *penates*, accompanied as usual with firing of crackers and gong-striking, &c.

On New-year's Eve, the city was one scene of life and activity;—people running from shop to shop paying debts or collecting arrears: crowds hastening to the country to rejoin their families; multitudes hurrying back to their rural cots, with the purchases they had been making for the approaching festivities: and thousands returning to town to spend the holidays with relatives and friends. The retail houses were overflowing with customers; and it was an object with sellers to clear off their goods as speedily as possible, and with purchasers to supply their wants at an unusually low rate. The quantity of money that circulated during those twenty-four hours must have been enormous; and, in many cases, it was attempted to prolong the closing day to an unwonted hour, especially by those who were unable to gather in their dues.

In the family residences, the scene on this evening was no less animated. Dr. Chang had invited me to spend the early part of that night in his family, and I availed myself of his offer, as it gave an opportunity of observing the ceremonies in the domestic circle on New-year's Eve. When I reached his house, 7 P.M., I found the members of the family dressed out in their best attire. The principal room was tastefully lighted up, and the furniture looked unusually tidy. In the centre there stood the ordinary table, *pro tem.* converted into a ceremonial one. At the top of it there was set a high chair, over the back of which were thrown three distinct scrolls, with uncouth paintings, to represent "the most Celestial and Superb Shangti," an honourable designation adopted by the Taou sect in speaking of Yuhhwang, their chief deity. Before these daubs three teacups were arranged, and three cups of wine, offerings being usually arranged before their idols in triplets. Further on there were twelve wine-cups set, to denote, as they said, the several months of the year; and the table was amply supplied with fruits, unseasoned vegetables, incense, candles, wine, sugar, new-year cakes, ornamented candles, and last, but not least, the "fuhle" offerings.*

At the foot of the table and on the floor a red cushion lay, upon which the worshippers had to kneel. It was a moving spectacle to witness the aged patriarch repeatedly kneel at this ceremonial altar, bowing his venerable head to the earth, and for some minutes continuing in a kneeling posture, with his eyes cast to the ground and his lips moving as if in silent prayer. It was the most reverential act of worship I had yet seen any Chinese engaged in. I had been spectator of hundreds of worshipping natives; but there was with them a want of devotion, earnestness, and sincerity, the reverse of what now was presented to my view. After each of his sons had succeeded Dr. Chang in their acts of obeisance, the painted scrolls were taken outside and burnt, along with a heap of silver-paper, the combustion being announced by firing three heavy crackers. A cup of wine mixed with the "fuhle" offerings was emptied out upon the roof of the house, which trifling act was interpreted as denoting their gratitude to the demi-god Shinnung, for having taught

* The "fuhle," or "offerings denoting happiness," ordinarily are of three sorts, "fish, pork, or fowl," although Kanghe's Dictionary says, "beef, mutton, and pork." But the rule is not fixed.

mankind to cook food, instead of eating it raw and undressed as people once on a time used to do. In the cook-house, there was a sacrifice offered to the god of the kitchen, on his imagined return from heaven. At this time he looked clean, was illuminated by two or three burners, and had six plates of vegetable stuff lying before him. Then followed the devoirs to the ancestors of the male branch only, represented by eight portraits. The deceased respectively were served with a bowl of rice, a cup of wine, and a pair of chop-sticks. At this part of the ceremony, the arrangements of the table were not materially altered, and the devotional feelings of the worshippers did not seem to decline. The solemnities were then closed by the whole party sitting down to a hearty supper. Thus ended the old year.

With equal vigilance and punctuality the new year was watched as it opened upon the world. They "sat it in,"—men, women, and children. At its earliest dawn, there was presented to each one a warm dish of new-year's cake soaked in wine syrup; and as the sun rose, the several members of the household sallied out to pay their respects to the family and city gods, deceased ancestors, and surviving relatives. Sunrise was the general signal "for paying the compliments of the season;" and throughout the merry season, which was spun out to eight or ten days, there was nothing but a round of friendly calls and feastings,—all classes being most polite and complaisant to each other. On New-year's day itself, one was not much troubled with calls, except from intimates;—most men having enough to do in watching the entrance of the new year and paying their dutiful attentions to the members of their own families, while many, fatigued by the watchings of the night and surfeitings of the morning, were obliged to go to bed at noon. In lieu of personal visits, a convenient proxy was adopted by private individuals, and chiefly by merchant firms and public institutions, in sending merely complimentary cards by the hands of their servants, who slipped them under the doors; so that when I started on my morning cruise of friendly calls, I stumbled on heaps of cards lying in the passage-way. It was on the second day that the inhabitants themselves began to stir out, dressed up in the finest suits they could afford.

During the first two or three days there were no shops open, except the stalls of fruitsellers and fortune-tellers; in anticipation of which the people generally had laid in a good stock of fresh and salt provisions for at least one week. Otherwise, hapless the lot of the improvident at this period; and most unfortunate was the situation of an English party, which visited Ningpo at that time, and, ignorant of this custom, could with difficulty scrape enough for a few days' subsistence.

From the first to the close of the month, there was an incessant din of gongs, drums, violins, and crackers; with feasting, gambling, and play-acting. No business of importance was done for ten days, and, before any shop could resume its trade, the master had to consult the stars for a lucky day. The public offices were opened on the 20th; and this *Kai-yin*, "opening the seals," was a breaking up of the gala season with which the new year had been celebrated.

Throughout that interesting period, I had many "golden spots in time" for recommending the doctrines of Christianity. Frequent conversations with officers, merchants, and mechanics, directly led to the great subject of my sacred mission. There was no opposition to the broaching of the vital truths of the Gospel; but usually they were curious to know something more about them. Occasionally a defence of their idolatrous practices was attempted; yet never was a tract or Christian book declined or treated with slight. Still their pride grasped at the lame and sorry apology of "local custom," "common usage," popular habit," and "traditional practice," the rule of conduct to a Chinese in religion as in politics.

The most commonly-circulated work amongst the natives at this season of the year was the almanac; which for that same year divided it into twenty-four terms, their usual division of the year to express the several periods of the sun's passage through the twelve signs of the zodiac. The distinct names of these terms are applied to the day on which the sun is in the first and the fifteenth degree of a sign of the zodiac; consequently, in reckoning by the lunar year, their places in the calendar change every year, but in the solar year of Europeans they fall more uniformly upon the same day in successive years. When an intercalary month occurs, the terms continue to be reckoned as usual; by which arrangement the first term sometimes falls into the twelfth moon, making twenty-five terms in a year; but most usually it is on the first moon. Some of the terms are sixteen days in length and some fourteen, but the average is fifteen. They correspond to our months nearly as follows, and fall in the signs given below:—

SPRING SIGNS.

				The sun in Aquarius.*
1.	February	5th	Lih-ts'un	1st moon.
2.	,,	21st	Yu-shuy	The sun in Pisces.
3.	March	6th	King-chih	2nd moon.
4.	,,	22nd	Ts'un-fun	The sun in Aries.
5.	April	6th	Ts'ing-ming	3rd moon.
6.	,,	22nd	Kuh-yu	The sun in Taurus.

* The zodiacal marks adopted in Chinese almanacs, although representing objects selected from the zoological world, differ considerably from the signs used amongst us. They distinguish them as follows:—1st, the Tiger; 2nd, the Hare; 3rd, the Dragon; 4th, the Serpent; 5th, the Horse; 6th, the Sheep; 7th, the Monkey; 8th, the Cock; 9th, the Dog; 10th, the Boar; 11th, the Mouse; 12th, the Cow.

SUMMER SIGNS.

1. May	7th	Lih-hia		The sun in Taurus.
2. ,,	22nd	Siaou-mwan		4th moon.
3. June	7th	Mang-chung		The sun in Gemini.
4. ,,	22nd	Hia-che		5th moon.
5. July	8th	Siaou-shoo		The sun in Cancer.
6. ,,	21st	Ta-shoo		6th moon.
				The sun in Leo.

AUTUMNAL SIGNS.

1. August	9th	Lih-ts'ew		The sun in Leo.
2. ,,	24th	Chu-shoo		7th moon.
3. September	9th	Pih-loo		The sun in Virgo.
4. ,,	24th	Ts'ew-fun		8th moon.
5. October	9th	Han-loo		The sun in Libra.
6. ,,	24th	Shwang-kiang		9th moon.
				The sun in Scorpio.

WINTER SIGNS.

1. November	8th	Lih-tung		The sun in Scorpio.
2. ,,	23rd	Siaou-sieuh		10th moon.
3. December	8th	Ta-sieuh		The sun in Sagittarius.
4. ,,	22nd	Tung-che		11th moon.
5. January	6th	Siaou-han		The sun in Capricornus.
6. ,,	22nd	Ta-han		12th moon.
				The sun enters Aquarius.

In the nomenclature of the annual terms there is a reference to variations in the seasons of the year; and as it may be interesting to have the native interpretation of the particulars in the preceding tables, I append the following brief analysis, translated from a native work.

SPRING SIGNS.

1. *Lih-ts'un*, or "beginning spring," to celebrate which they have an annual festival, somewhat resembling the procession of the bull Apis among the Egyptians, connected with the opening of agricultural labour for the current year.

2. *Yu-shuy*, or "rain-water," *i. e.* the vernal showers that begin to develop and nourish universal nature.

3. *King-chih*, or "exciting insects;" for, according to the native entomology, this is celebrated as the time when reptiles and insects of all kinds are "aroused by the thunder-claps of spring out of the torpor of winter, during which they have been embedded in clay."

4. *Ts'un-fun*, or "vernal division," or "the vernal equinox when day and night are equally divided."

5. *Ts'ing-ming*, or "clear brightness," when "the wind and sun are pure and genial, and the spring light is clear and cheering. During this term the most religious attention is paid to the sepulchres and manes of departed friends."

6. *Kuh-yu*, or "grain rains," to be improved for scattering and sowing seed.

SUMMER SIGNS.

1. *Lih-hia*, or "opening summer."
2. *Siaou-mwan*, or "little filled;" the wheat by this time has gradually got ripe and full.
3. *Mang-chung*, or "busy in planting," when the husbandman is fully occupied in transplanting the paddy.
4. *Hia-che*, or "summer point," or æstival solstice, when the length of the summer day is greatest.
5. *Siaou-shoo*, or "little heat," *i. e.* the gradual rise of warm temperature.
6. *Ta-shoo*, or "great heat," during which the temperature waxes exceedingly hot.

AUTUMNAL SIGNS.

1. *Lih-ts'ew*, or "the beginning of autumn."
2. *Chu-shoo*, or "the extreme height of the hot temperature."
3. *Pih-loo*, or "white dew begins to fall."
4. *Ts'ew-fun*, or "autumnal equinox."
5. *Han-loo*, or "cold dew:" the falling dew gets gradually colder.
6. *Shwang-kiang*, or "the descent of hoar-frost."

WINTER SIGNS.

1. *Lih-tung*, or "the opening of winter."
2. *Siaou-sieuh*, or "little snow occasionally."
3. *Ta-sieuh*, or "much snow."
4. *Tung-che*, or "winter solstice."
5. *Siaou-han*, or "the temperature falls by degrees."
6. *Ta-han*, or "the temperature falls to the lowest point."

The Chinese almanac in some respects corresponds to our "Francis Moore" in England; and as some interesting features of this yearly book are given in "Household Words," under the heading of "Francis Moore in China," which the editor did me the honour to insert in his October number for 1854, I quote the following extracts:—

"It is an annual, regularly published and found in the hands of every person, and on the counter of the commonest tradesman. There are various forms and editions of it, some full, others abridged; sometimes pocket manuals, sometimes sheet almanacs. But the original, which is the largest and most complete edition, is that drawn up by the Astronomical Board of Peking, sanctioned by imperial authority, issued by government at the opening of the year, and sold at every huckster-stall at the small price of three farthings or one penny. It is a complete register of the months and days of the year according to the Chinese system, its various divisions, agricultural seasons, commercial terms, official sessions and adjournments, religious festivals, and the anniversaries of the emperors and empresses of the reigning family.

"Occasionally a few astronomical notations are put down; but generally the movements of the celestial bodies, and notices of solar and lunar eclipses are omitted. Silence on these points is maintained,—not that the members of the Astronomical Board are ignorant of them; for astral observations, accurate and minute, are regularly taken by that academy, and duly recorded for the premonition of the official courts through the country. In this work intended for the public, however, as little allusion is made as possible to such points, rather out of deference to the popular bondage to judicial astrology, it being the universal belief that sun, moon, stars, and comets—their motions, eclipses, and rotation—influence the destinies of mankind. Still further, while scarcely anything is said of the mysterious motions of the heavenly bodies, so much is explained of the prognostics that fall on each day as to allay the suspicions and quiet the anxieties of the populace. For this purpose, professed and skilful astrologers are consulted—men respected for their acquaintance with the science of interpreting astral movements, determining the magic power of the celestial orbs on human fate, and pronouncing what days are lucky or unlucky. According to the verdict of these men, the character of each day is set down, and transactions suitable for every day are named. Accordingly, this calendar is studied with no little curiosity by a great proportion of the masses in China, for positive information when they may or may not lave their persons, shave their heads, open shops, set sail, celebrate marriage, or perform any other act of life.

"As specimens of instructions of this nature, recorded in the imperial almanacs, we quote from the calendar for the last year, commencing with our February 8th, 1853,—the Chinese New Year's day. On the first day of the first moon—

"You may present your religious offerings (such as fowls or fish); you may send up representations to heaven (thanks, prayers, vows—by burning gilt paper, straw-made figures, or fireworks in infinite variety); you may put on full dress, fur caps, and elegant sashes; you must at noontide sit with your face towards the south; you can make up matrimonial matches, or pay calls on your friends, or get married; you may set out on a journey, get a new suit of clothes commenced, make repairs about house, &c., or lay the foundation of any building, or set up the wooden skeleton of it, or set sail, or enter on a business contract, or carry on commerce, or collect your accounts, or pound and grind, or plant and sow, or look after your flocks and herds

"In addition to the items specified as fit for the first day of the month, on the second (February 9th) you may likewise bury your dead.

"On the third—You may bathe yourself; sweep your houses and rooms; pull a dilapidated house down or any shattered wall.

"On the fourth—You may offer sacrifices, or bathe, or shave the head, or sweep the floor and house, or dig the ground, or bury the dead.

"On the fifth—You may not start upon a journey, nor change your quarters, nor plant nor sow.

"On the sixth—You may do everything specified as on the first.

"On the seventh—You must not go to school, nor enter on a tour, nor change lodgings, nor bathe, nor make house repairs, nor lay a foundation, nor set up a house-frame; nor purchase property in fields, houses, &c.; nor grind, nor plant, nor sow; nor give up time to your flocks.

"The eighth is looked upon as dubious. To-day nothing is specified as unlucky or lucky.

"On the ninth—You may offer your religious presents; visit your friends; call on tailors to prepare a new suit; make bargains; barter and trade; and collect your moneys.

"On the tenth—You may make your religious offerings; enter on a government office; make a matrimonial match; get married; visit friends; start on a journey; bathe, but it must be at five A.M.; shave the head; practise acupuncture* surgery; make contracts; barter and trade; sweep the house; and dig graves for the dead.

"On the eleventh—You can commence a journey; change your residence; acupuncture a patient, commission a tailor for a new suit; repair buildings; found a house; erect framework of it; set sail; open a contract; bargain; collect your accounts; look after your flocks; or bury your dead.

"On the thirteenth—You must at five A.M. sit facing the south-east.

"On the eighteenth—You ought to offer sacrifices, and take a thorough bath.

"On the nineteenth—You may go to school.

"On the twenty-first—Quite right to set up the framework of your house, or bury your dead.

"On the twenty-fifth—You can, among other things, enter upon your new government office; attire yourself in your best dresses, but sit facing the north-west.

"On the twenty-sixth—You ought not to work embroidery.

"Although the preceding is quite sufficient to indicate one of the methods adopted to gratify the vulgar taste, it is not to be presumed that among the millions of China, there are wanting sensible men, who despise all participation in such folly."

In 1843, as the term denoting "the commencement of spring" fell on the 5th of February, the official ceremony of "meeting spring" (*ying-ts'un*) was observed the day previous. The municipal authorities left their respective residences at an early hour and in procession went out at the east gate of the city;—that point of the compass being chosen from the prevalent notion that the spring comes from the east, summer from the south, autumn from the west, and winter from the north. The procession moved across the river to a large building in the suburbs, with an extensive area of open ground. The crowd that thronged to see the show was immense. The principal actor was the city provost. On one spot there sat "the god of spring," and hard by, a paper figure of an ox of many colours. Both having been officially welcomed into the neigh-

* An oriental practice of puncturing diseased parts of the body with fine needles.

bourhood with a number of childish ceremonies, the officers sat down to drink wine.

In other places there is a variety in this curious custom. For instance, there is in some districts a ceremony connected with it, called *p'ien-ts'un*, "whipping in the spring," when the presiding officer strikes the senseless figure with a switch, which farce signifies that the labours of the spring are to commence, and the ox must go to the plough. The act of whipping the paper effigy is a signal for the bystanders to rush in and tear the gossamer frame to pieces,—the man that carries home a shred of it believing that his own ox will be a fortunate animal for the year!

In other parts of China, the "spring ox" is made of mud, and of colossal dimensions. But in general a very rude representation is made of paper, pasted over a bamboo framework, about five feet long and three feet high. The head, horns, feet, and tail are black; the neck and belly blue; the legs white; and the back and sides, comprising the greater part of the surface of the body, yellow. These colours, it appears, are arranged from year to year, according to the book of ceremonies issued at Peking, and the paper ox is regarded as prognosticating the character of the coming year, by the relative quantity of each colour employed in its construction. The amount of black indicates the proportion of sickness and death; blue prognosticates winds; white, rains and floods; and red, fire. The yellow denotes the fruits of the earth, and if this colour predominates, the people expect a year of plenty. Not unusually, when the frail figure has been torn up, seeds of cotton, rice, beans, wheat, and other grains, having been beforehand placed in the cavity of its body, fall to the ground,—the relative abundance of the crop of each kind being foretold from the order of succession in which they fall out. There is also a great number of small clay figures of oxen in the same cavity. These are picked up by the attendants who may be able to get near enough to seize them.

Occasionally too, the idol of the "god of spring" is in the shape of a youth, reputed to be the deified son of one of the ancient emperors. This image is attired, it is believed by the populace, in a fashion truly prophetic of the fortunes of the year: for it to be bareheaded would predict cold weather, and a white robe augurs a dry year, &c.

In 1853, while I was at Shanghai, a "spring procession" occurred, far more ceremonious than that above specified. Preceding the mandarins in the procession, was a small junk decked with flags, borne by two men, designed to represent one of the emperor's tribute grain junks; next, a beggar, dressed up for the occasion, followed on foot, to personify the "spring mandarin," an officer of distinguished rank, who bore that title in ancient times; then, several coarsely-rigged tillers of the soil and eight fantastically attired fellows with painted faces. These sustained the dignified characters of genii. Next, were several square trays, the four corners of which supported small frames two or three feet high, from which were suspended miniature signboards, bearing the names of the various trades and handicrafts in the empire.

It is not at all improbable but all this parade is to be traced to a custom that prevailed, according to Chinese computation, about 4,000 years ago, during the *Hia* dynasty. The *Shooking* says of it, "In the first month of spring, an imperial messenger went hither and thither on the highway with a wooden rattle;"—the object of which practice was to awaken the attention of the agriculturists to the return of spring, and to call them to resume with renewed vigour their rustic labours.

A week after "whipping in the spring," there was commemorated a festival, perhaps the most popular of all in China, named "The Feast of Lanterns." It continued through five or six days, during which term, at eventide, every corner of the city was decorated with streamers and brightly illuminated. Spectators paraded the streets in crowds, letting off crackers, rockets, squibs, and ingenious fireworks of numberless variety. Generally this is called *Shangtung*, "the feast of elevated lanterns." But the gala night, which falls on the first full moon of the new year, is the *Saitung*, or "rival lantern" night, as it calls out public emulation in the display of festal lamps, &c. This feast is somehow connected with their worshipful respect for the manes of the departed. On such an occasion, of course the various temples had their share in the brilliant illuminations; but none so gay that night as was the Fuhkien temple.

That edifice lies close to the water's edge, outside the Ningpo walls, between the East and Bridge gates. It bears the name "Tienhowkung," "the palace of the Celestial Queen," and is dedicated to the pet idol of the Fuhkien sailors, Matsoopoo. The building was founded first at the close of the twelfth century. Up to 1680, it had been subject to many changes; but in that year, after having lain in ruins for nearly a century, the Fuhkien merchants thought to rebuild it. Previous to this date, some severe port restrictions had been introduced by the predecessors of the Emperor Kanghe, from fear of the pirates who had been infesting the coast. Those robbers and these restrictions had seriously checked the native trade between Ningpo and the south of China. But in the year above named, the Emperor Kanghe rescinded the port regulations, and the trade revived. A number of Fuhkien and Canton traders, taking advantage of the opening trade, sailed for Ningpo. During their voyage along the perilous coast, they had witnessed "great wonders in the deep." Out of gratitude for their miraculous deliverance, these men resolved to re-erect the temple in Ningpo, and for that object subscribed largely. In 1843, it was the most elegantly furnished building in the city; and although, during 1841 and 1842, it had been in the hands of the British troops, no plunder of its contents had been permitted, and it continued unscathed. To appreciate the taste in the ornaments and the finish of the internal structure, it must be visited, especially on the evening of the "rival lanterns." On that night the entire edifice glittered with lamps, lanterns, tapers, &c. The horn and glass lanterns suspended all around had the most curious devices and scenes delineated on them, in the richest and most vivid colours. The walls were hung with native drawings in all shades, and music (such as it was) rang through the decorated arches of the lofty roof; and life was given to the whole scene by the hum and gaiety of the thronging spectators.

But scarcely had the new year been inaugurated by its festivals of many days,—scarcely had the people recovered from the excesses of gaiety and merriment at such an auspicious time, when the star-gazers were startled at 7 P.M. of March 7, by observing the appearance of a comet to the south-west. This created some apprehension in the minds of the peaceably disposed citizens of the city; as a phenomenon like this is believed to be an infelicitous omen of warlike invasions from the quarter where it first appears. After their struggle with the British lion, not only a rumour, but any bellicose augury, seemed to strike the public heart with a panic throe.

It is worthy of notice how singularly minute the Chinese have been (probably from olden times) in recording in the topography of any place the several "wonders," celestial and terrestrial, that may have occurred there. Thus, in a topographical account now before me of Chihkiang province, one section is solely devoted to the *notabilia* of nature in this province, with astonishing preciseness naming the prodigies which have visited each district and the dates of their appearance; *e.g.* earthquakes, pestilences, excessive rains, severe droughts, locusts, famine, &c. &c. That Chinese work mentions fifty-five separate shocks of earthquake of unusual severity, having occurred in the province between A.D. 260 and 1660. One which occurred in A.D. 1342, "was attended with so terrible a storm of wind and such an overflowing of the sea at Wanchow, that houses were destroyed and inhabitants engulfed beyond all calculation."

From the same curious old relic, I extract the following notices of "comets and meteors" that have been visible in different parts of the province, from the opening of the Christian era down to A.D. 1700.*

A.D.	
3.	A vivid meteor.
78.	A comet without a tail.
82.	A comet with a tail.
118.	A comet without a tail.
	A comet with a tail.

* Upon this Humboldt writes,—"Whilst the so-called classical nations of the West, the Greeks and Romans, although they may occasionally have indicated the position in which a comet first appeared, never afford any information regarding its apparent path, the copious literature of the Chinese (who observed nature carefully and recorded with accuracy what they saw) contains circumstantial notices of the constellations through which each comet was observed to pass. These notices go back to more than 500 years before the Christian era, and many of them are still found to be of value in astronomical observations. The first comets of whose orbits we have any knowledge, and which were calculated from Chinese observations, are those of 240, 539, 565, 568, 574, 837, 1337, and 1385. Whilst the comet of 837 (which continued twenty-four hours within a distance of 2,000,000 miles of the earth) terrified Louis I. of France to that degree, that he busied himself in building churches and founding monastic buildings, in the hope of appeasing the evils threatened by its appearance, the Chinese astronomers made observations on the path of this cosmical body, whose tail extended over a space of 60°, appearing sometimes single, and sometimes multiple."—*Cosmos*, i. p. 84.

A.D.
132. A comet with a tail.
395. Very numerous shooting stars of a deep vermilion colour.
505. Comet with tail.
598. A vivid meteor.
819. Comet with tail.
880. Vivid meteor.
993. Venus visible at noonday.
994. A star visible at noontide, with a vermilion light more than ten feet in length.
1385. A vivid meteor.
1388. Comet with tail of a white colour, and a tail more than ten feet long.
1524. Meteoric stones fell at the city of Hangchow.
1539. }
1541. } Each year a vivid meteor.
1542. }
1545. Meteoric stones fell into the sea at Suingan.
1577. Meteoric stones fell at Ninghai town.
1620. Vivid meteors.

CHAPTER IV.

MARRIAGE PRELIMINARIES AND CONCLUDING CEREMONIES—MARRIED LIFE IN CHINA—REGARD FOR DECADES IN LIFE—RESPECT FOR AGE—BIRTHDAY FESTIVAL—THEATRICALS—ESCAPE FROM FIRE—CONFLAGRATIONS AND CONFUSION—WATCHMEN AND THEIR NOISES—CHINESE MODES OF KEEPING TIME.

In spite of the sudden and startling comet just alluded to, the opening of spring was not considered inappropriate or inauspicious for any couple to enter into wedded life. Numerous marriages occurred about this time; and of those witnessed by myself I offer a few gleanings.

Setting aside the peculiarities of betrothment, and the general seclusion of the engaged lady from her intended swain until the happy day of union, it is my decided conviction that, among the Chinese, "marriage is honourable." I claim this admission in favour of that people on the following considerations,—that their common law permits but *one* legal wife; that the *vox populi* compels a man to fulfil the marriage contract made on his behalf by parents or guardians; that both the day and the formalities of wedding are held in universal esteem; and that man and wife, on their elevation to their improved status, are the recipients of unanimous congratulations from all quarters.

The first step towards wedlock is the betrothal of the parties. Although the case is rare, I can cite that of a young man who, being without parents or guardians, was himself the prime mover in forming his alliance. Often the primary arrangements are made by the parents of the respective families; and even before the birth of their children, it is not uncommon for mothers and fathers to make contracts for them,—of course on the hypothesis of a difference of sex. But usually in such negotiations, the services of a match-maker are called in;—the part of a "mei-jin," or go-between, being by no means regarded as officious, nor in any other light than respectable. The performer, it is presumed, is of good character for judgment and veracity: otherwise his craft would be endangered. It is understood likewise that the mediator is well acquainted with the circumstances and reputation of both families; and reliance is placed in his honesty, as the contract-money is paid through his hands to the father of the girl. Preliminary to final arrangements, a serious item punctiliously examined is the horoscope of the two individuals;—the object being to ascertain on comparison that the *year, month, day,* and *hour* of their respective births involve nothing unlucky to the union. This has given rise to the colloquial phrase for a marriage engagement, *chuh-pah-tsze,* "passing the eight characters," or points; that is, that the four questions on either side above specified do tally. Under these circumstances the betrothment is to be sanctioned.

Although the age at which Chinese marry is not so early as has sometimes been represented in foreign books, it is not fixed or uniform. The actual day for the wedding depends on the *dictum* of a fortune-teller, or a fortune-telling book like the Imperial Almanac. But, presuming that all things are favourable to the union and the means of the intended husband suitable, the ceremonials at different steps of the negotiations are numerous and tiring.

A girl in her teens, or before she is deemed marriageable, is often seen with a knot of hair on one side of the head, and a slip or tuft flowing down either cheek. But on her betrothal, the custom still prevails, (probably of ancient date,) as thus described in a Chinese work,—"when a girl gets engaged, her hair is put up behind, and she wears the hair-pin of women in sign thereof;" and the celebration of the engagement is attended with endless ceremonies and feastings,—especially in the young lady's family. On the evening of ——, I stumbled into a friend's house, ignorant of there being a family gathering at the time for such an affair. There I found a large company in the midst of a merry feast, with a wondrous *exposé* of silks, ornaments, rings, fruits, &c. These were presents upon the betrothment of my host's sister; as the announcement of a nuptial engagement is a sure signal for the friends, particularly on the bridegroom's side, to express their satisfaction by gifts.

This crisis is of no mean import in the history of the Chinese couple; for hereafter both are virtually bound and pledged. Should the youth, however, lose his intended by death, he is under no tie whatever, and he may form a second engagement when he pleases. But it is the reverse with a young woman in parallel circumstances, who, to consult public opinion and to retain the respect of her own circle, will decline any other proposal, and choose to "live in weeds." When satisfactory recommendations can be offered of her virtuous and upright deportment through a life of widowhood, there is hope of government honours being lavished on her, *e. g.* public monuments of marble erected "*in memoriam.*" The Chinese cite instances of young women who have preferred suicide to disgracing themselves and dishonouring the departed by violating this rule of well-bred society. On this account, it is not uncommon for the bereaved maiden, on the death of her affianced, to submit to an abridged ceremony of leaving her father's house, for the purpose of placing herself under the shelter and control of her father-in-law. By this procedure she confirms the obligations of her widow state.

After the ratification of the matrimonial engagement, it is concluded that the young lady shall keep a strict seclusion. Perhaps it may be said with truth that this is a Chinese rule in high life. But that it is not universal in China scarcely admits of a question. Among the poorer classes, I have seen girls who had been taken immediately on betrothal to their mother-in-law's, to be maintained there and provided for until they became marriageable. Meantime they are employed as helps in the family. The circumstances of this class do not admit of seclusion, and the separation between the male and female branches of the household is ruled only by a sense of propriety and modesty. In a family not of the lower but the higher class, I have known a betrothed young woman to be many months resident there, and have frequently seen her and her intended conversing on the ordinary gossip of the family.

The seclusion of woman is insisted upon in families which can afford to shut up their wives and daughters in "inner apartments." Such a system limits the circle of acquaintance and intercourse to the narrow sphere of one's own relatives; and as a further consequence, a cold reserve is encouraged on visiting even these relatives; and in going out of the house close sedans are used, as if to shut out observation of men and things. Still, curiosity to know something of the outside world cannot entirely be extinguished. This often is awakened, excited, and fed by the maid-servants, female hairdressers, doctresses, and nurses, who superabound in the families of the rich.

The inquisitiveness of young ladies on this special point may not be so eager and prying in China as in western countries. But, with a lurking concern as to future prospects, it is not to be doubted that Chinese maidens, in spite of privacy and reserve, do "speer" about the young men allotted for them, and will take what opportunity they have to look at them even through a glass darkly. The same assuredly may be certified of the young men. Although perhaps they may not form any personal attachment, and are debarred from the bliss of a private assignation, they are clever enough to contrive many plans for getting a peep at the individual chosen as the future partner of their chances of life. It cannot be questioned that anxiety on the same score affects both sexes in every country and clime, and, among Chinese too, breathes out,—

> "We may not know,
> While life endures, whose lot is joy, whose woe;—
> Where is the sunlight, where shall be the shade."

In general, preparations for the happy union extend over a long period; but I am safe in asserting that, while the young gentleman may not be thoughtless, in all probability the juvenile bride is the more anxious of the two about the coming day. With some women, there is great painstaking to prepare their *trousseau*, especially pillows, coverlets, &c., on which embroidery can be worked. This forms part and parcel of the betrothment-money, being defrayed out of the affianced gentleman's pocket. As the memorable day approaches, the bride has to be arrayed in her best attire, which likewise she has to arrange, and in which she has more assistance from kind, perhaps officious, neighbours, than she needs or is thankful for. A young woman, at whose marriage I was a guest, had a day or two previous undergone the ceremony of "uncovering the face." Her maiden tresses were put up and the frontal hair was shaven off, so that the forehead assumed a peculiar openness, which has come to be a badge of the married woman in China. To this practice probably is to be traced the expression *kaimien*, or "uncovering the face." A parting feast was set out by the relatives. In her wedding habit the young woman sat at the head of the table occupied by the female guests. The men were feasting in another compartment. The bridegroom too, at his father's home, where there was a round of calls and feastings for several days in succession, had to undergo the ceremony of being "capped," which was performed by his father's hands as a preliminary essential to married life.

On the auspicious day itself, I hastened to witness the lady leave her mother's home, about seven o'clock in the evening. She was in the little room, to which her earliest associations had been confined, surrounded by women and matrons (her mother among them) weeping and wailing. She had trimmed herself, powdered her face, rouged her lips, musked her robes, and, as she could afford them, displayed her finest jewels. Had she been too poor to have jewellery by her, she could readily have supplied herself for the time at the nearest pawnbroker's. At last the bridal chair was at the door, with chair-bearers and musicians. A concourse of spectators stood outside, eager, if not impatient, to catch a glimpse of the *sin-niang, alias* "the new woman." After the procession was duly arranged, the bride was carried out of her room, as if *vi et armis*, by her brothers, and she was placed in her nuptial sedan seemingly in a helpless condition. When carried out of her father's house, she was lifted over a pan of lighted charcoal. This precaution was explained as necessary to prevent the lady carrying off with her all the good fortunes of the family! That is one interpretation, but there may be others equally absurd. The chair was capacious and elegant. The bride sat within, arrayed in a cloak fringed with tiny tinkling bells, and on her head she wore a singularly-shaped hat, with a veil of beads, &c., that almost completely covered her face. Every symbol of gaiety was exhibited, identified with their notions of a wedding occasion, when, according to their phraseology, "the phœnixes sing in harmony," and compatible with the bridegroom's finances. The whole retinue hurried on along winding streets lined with staring spectators, preceded by men and boys with torches and crackers. By this time a messenger had announced that the lady was "a-comin'," and all was astir at the bridegroom's, where the gates were opened to receive the gaudy banners, pink umbrellas, red boxes, and other pieces of baggage, which heralded the rapid approach of the bride. Presently the chair-bearers rushed in. Three heavy crackers intimated that the bridal sedan had actually come. This conveyance was attended by four bridesmaids on foot, in black dresses and with pink sashes; but they were old women! A singularly-dressed mistress of ceremonies came out to accost the young bride. As she stepped out of her chair, a horse-saddle was laid on the floor, over which she had to stride. Her four maids supported the lady in passing into the inner apartments. Here she met the bridegroom, who, by the way, had to be searched for and led out for introduction to his future companion, —a farce sometimes played at a Chinese wedding, as if to denote extreme modesty or timidity on the part of the husband in entering on his new *responsibilities.* The couple on meeting knelt down and paid their religious *devoirs* to "Heaven." Next, a document with the marriage contract was publicly and distinctly read. Worship was then paid at the ancestral tablets of the husband's family. After this, the pair were conducted into the bridal chamber, which immediately was crowded with friends and visitors. Here standing side by side, two cups of wine-syrup joined by a scarlet thread were exchanged between the couple. This part of the ceremony was concluded by what is called *sahchung*,* or throwing a plateful of various fruits, berries, and confections among the crowds of spectators, who were eager to pick up what they could. On this the bridegroom "came out of his chamber rejoicing." The bride was detained within to be unveiled and to change her upper dress, which by this time must have become excessively cumbersome.

I was much surprised to find the bridal chamber open to public gaze and scrutiny. And at this as at other weddings, two or three features forced themselves on me, as exceedingly *outré* to the notions of a Westerner. To any special visitor who entered, the bride was brought out for inspection, and at the interview he was at liberty to offer what remarks he might think *apropos*, about her lips, nose, eyes, eyebrows, feet, petticoats, &c. Evidently the remarks were stale and commonly current; for, when one experienced hand made his observations, they were responded to by appropriate sentences from another in the crowd. However outrageous all this was to me, a mere looker-on, it was amazing to mark the composure of the

* This custom (as their records state) was instituted above 1,900 years ago, by an emperor, who, at his own marriage, as he scattered a tray of five vari-coloured fruits, blessed the people in these words:— "As many of these berries as any one can catch, so many children may he have."

young bride through it all;—not a smile on her lips,—not a muscle moved,—not a blush in her face; and I was then informed that the reputation of a bride greatly depended on the gravity, calmness, and temper, with which she received the remarks of bystanders at such a time. If so, several ladies, at whose nuptials I have been present, must have earned a virtuous name by their collected demeanour during so trying a probation.

As usual, that evening closed with feasting,—men and women in separate apartments. In the female branch, the bride opened the supper by appearing at the top of the table, in the expressive parlance of some places, *doobi-no-no*,* acknowledging through one of her attendant maids, "Worthy matrons and young ladies, the bride desires to offer her respectful thanks to you all for your kindness and attention." She then for a while seated herself at the table, while the other ladies partook of the repast. When the men had taken their seats, the bridegroom came forward to pour wine into each guest's cup. The master of ceremonies now intimated that the bridegroom wished to express his obligations to the friends who had honoured him with their presence on the occasion. Supper being ended, the bride appeared in the gentlemen's supper-room to acknowledge the honour they had conferred on her. The feast concluded at a very late hour; and we left the nuptial pair to their honeymoon. But, a Chinese honeymoon,—how different an introduction to married life among these celestials, from a tour to the Continent, a trip to the Lakes, a visit to sundry watering-places! In some parts of the country, the Chinese bride is almost shut up to her own chamber for a full month.

What now about the altered condition of the Chinese

* "Stomach-rubbing," from the peculiar up-and-down-movement of her hands over the pit of the stomach in expressing her thanks.

woman on her marriage? Is it to be concluded that she must be unhappy, and that, on account of vexations arising out of novel and untried circumstances, if she could, she would be too glad to be released from her married lot? I think not.

In China, to be united in wedlock to some one or other is invariably set before the maiden, and anticipated by her, as her good fortune; whereas, not to be married stands more in the light of a mishap. No injustice is felt by her in having no voice in the selection of her partner;—indeed, this would be avoided by the young woman as a breach of propriety and decency. Nor are the responsibilities that now devolve on her in her married state altogether strange to her; for, under her mother's roof, she had been trained to housekeeping and other domestic duties. By discipline in her father's house, she had been prepared for the further steps of womanly experience of life; and, throughout her maidenhood, the status of woman had become familiar to her, as expressed in the common adage, that "Woman is subject to the following three conditions in life:—viz., at her father's house she is under her parents; on marriage she submits to her husband; and in widowhood she is under the guidance of her sons."

In some respects, then, it is not a great change for a young woman to be moved to a husband's house, nor is it always "for worse." Yet, in her new home, the young wife may find unexpected and unthought-of sources of trial. Possibly a mother-in-law is suspicious, jealous, domineering, and tyrannical; or, what may most unfortunately happen, the husband perhaps is unaffectionate, heartless, cruel, and a "wife-beater." Under either circumstance, the "unprotected female" finds it better and easier to submit with patience.

But the fault does not always lie at the door of the husband. Sometimes his life is one of intense misery, from the provocations and suspicions of a wife, her bitter revilings and revengeful freaks. A Chinese preceptor, with whom I was acquainted, so excited the jealousy of his young, handsome, and devoted wife, on a certain occasion, that she adopted a method for punishing him,—ingenious, amusing, and effective, as well as very annoying. One evening returning home late, he retired to rest without offering any explanation of his absence satisfactory to his wife. When he got up next morning to dress, he could nowhere find his habiliments, nor was he able to obtain any clue to the discovery. He was kept in suspense and without out-door clothing for a week; so that, in fact, he was confined to bed the whole time for want of clothes,—much to his discomfort, and not a little to my annoyance, as his services were just then required. At length, his "gude-wife," satisfied with the penalty she had inflicted, set him at liberty. She had taken all his clothes on that evening and concealed them in another part of the house for one entire week. This curious story I had from the man's own lips.

A word about *widows, widowers*, and *concubines*. I have met with widows that had married a second time, and others that had been engaged as secondary wives; but, in the eye of good society, neither is considered quite reputable. The support of a widow depends on her children, and the relatives especially of her husband's family; and the tribute offered by the nation, as has already been observed, in raising pillars of stone, &c., to commemorate the virtues of widows, must be a source of comfort and encouragement to her. But *widowers* are under no check in choosing a second partner or selecting the wedding-day.

As to the *extent of polygamy*, it is utterly impossible to guess at anything approaching statistics. Among the poorer classes, from their scanty circumstances, it is uncommon to find a man with more than one spouse.

The practice of taking concubines is confined to people in the higher ranks. Yet, whatever the number a man may choose, there is but one real legitimate wife. In public estimate, a concubine is inferior to her, and during the lifetime of the wife she cannot be introduced into the family with all the trumpery and paraphernalia of a proper marriage. By a parade of numerous concubines, a man may get a name for wealth, &c., among his neighbours; but the custom breeds interminable jealousies in the bosom of many Chinese families. To my knowledge, however, there are instances of wives among the natives who have consented to their husbands having concubines in a distant part of the country, where they were detained for some time on account of business; and Sir John Bowring, in his curious paper presented to the Statistical Society, names a similar ease, "that one of our female servants—a nominal Christian—expressed her earnest desire that her husband should have another wife in her absence, and seemed quite surprised that any one should suppose such an arrangement to be in any respect improper." It is possible too to cite cases in which some wives have encouraged their lords in this practice, out of an ambition for rule and authority which would be gratified by their having a larger household of handmaids and children to govern and manage.

To turn next to jottings of another page of social life among the Chinese. The 20th of March was the day selected by Dr. Chang to celebrate his "threescore years and ten." The 19th was his real birthday; but, as that happened to fall this year on a Sunday, which he knew to be my rule to keep sacred, it appeared that he deferred the observance till next day (Monday) to suit my convenience,—a mark of respectful deference which I could not overlook.

What I had frequently observed was, on this occasion, distinctly brought under notice,—the regard paid by the Chinese to every tenth year in their personal history. Each decade has a special designation applied to it. Thus, at ten, one is said to reach "the first degree of life;" at twenty, there is "youth-capping,"—a cap is placed on his head by his father, or a suitable representative of the family, to denote that, having passed the curriculum of boyhood and youth, he enters on the era and responsibilities of manhood. (In olden times, when a lad reached this age, the ceremony of *capping him* was attended with many peculiar rites. There were in addition other three grand ceremonials on which the thoughts and resources of ancient people were usually bent,—"marriage," "burial," and "the worship of the *manes* of the dead." Of these four ceremonies, the first, or "the capping," is the only one that has fallen into comparative disuse; or rather it has merged in the marriage service, when it is observed a day or two previous to the wedding.) At thirty, he is "strong and marriageable." It is presumed that at this epoch he has reached an age when he is competent for the general duties of a house and family; at forty, he is "fit to hold any official situation;" at fifty, quite able "to know his own failings;" at sixty, he has "completed one cycle;" at seventy, he is "a *rara avis* of antiquity;" at eighty, he has a rusty iron-coloured visage;" at ninety, "he is in his dotage;" at one hundred, "he comes to an extreme old age."

So much importance is attached specially to these advanced stages of human life, that, in the case even of deceased parents, the surviving children (if they can command the means) are often punctilious to celebrate the advancing decades of life, that would have marked their history had they continued in the land of the living. I have gained admission at different times to one or two of these posthumous celebrations; and the prominent feature in these "inferior occasions" (as they are called, to distinguish them from "the superior," or what are conducted during the lifetime of the parent), is, that they have more of a funereal cast, *e. g. white* colours substituted for *red, mourning* for *mirth,* and *wailing* for *congratulations.* On no anniversary has a man more respect and attention paid him than at the seventieth, which Dr. C. had now reached.

The sacred regard which Chinese pay to the claims of kindred, secures to the patriarchs of respectable families ample support in the advanced and helpless stage of their pilgrimage; and charity oftentimes relieves poor septuagenarians, whose relatives may be unable to provide them with comforts or necessaries at their mature age. In China, one's feelings are not harrowed with the sad spectacle of an aged parent discarded by his children and left to perish, unattended and unnursed, under a scorching sun or on the banks of a swelling river. But you will see the tottering senior, man or woman, who has not the means to hire a sedan, led through the alleys and streets by a son or a grandchild,—commanding the spontaneous respect of each passer-by, the homage of every junior. The deference of the *polloi* to the extreme sections of old age is manifest likewise from the tablets and monuments you may any day stumble upon, that have been erected by public subscription to the memory of octogenarians, nonagenarians, or centenarians. Nor is the government backward in encouraging this, but the reverse. Hence I have often seen very aged men and women in the streets arrayed in yellow robes, the gift of the emperor, in mark of honour and out of respect to their grey hairs.

The patriarchal type of the Chinese Executive requires that itself should pay marked attention to its long-lived subjects; and the laws and policy, of the reigning dynasty especially, have done much to sanction this common dictate of human nature so popular among the Chinese. Thus, the penal code of the present Tartar dynasty orders that "all destitute widows and widowers, the fatherless and childless, the helpless and infirm, shall receive sufficient maintenance and protection from the magistrates of their native city or district, whenever they have neither relations nor connections on whom they may depend for support; and any magistrate refusing such maintenance and protection shall be punished by sixty blows. Also, when any such are maintained and protected by the government, the superintending magistrate and his subordinates, if failing to afford them the legal allowance of food and raiment, shall be punished in proportion to the amount of the deficiency, according to the law against an embezzlement of government stores." It appears too the same code makes an exception, in criminal cases, of the aged: "Whoever is ascertained to be aged or infirm at the period of trial for any offence, shall be allowed the benefit of such plea, although he may not have attained the full age or laboured under the alleged infirmity at the time the offence was committed." An edict was issued in the year 1687, under the seal of the emperor Kanghe, "for regulating the aid given by government to people of the lower orders above seventy years of age. The septuagenarians were exempted from service and had food allotted them; those of eighty years had a piece of silk, a catty of cotton, a stone of rice, and ten catties of meat. Those of ninety double the rest." According to the official returns of the indigent aged who at the time came under the patronage of imperial favour, there were 184,086 who were seventy years and upwards, 169,850 who were eighty years and upwards, 9,996 who were ninety years and upwards, and twenty-one who were one hundred years and upwards. In 1722, in the sixtieth year of the reign of Kanghe, his majesty gave a feast to the old men of the empire; and his successor Kienlung, following the example of his predecessor, in the year 1785, also set on foot a jubilee of the same nature, a description of which is given in the memoirs of Father Ripa, who was present on the occasion. I extract one passage containing a brief summary of the proceedings:— "A vast number of aged but healthy men had been sent to Peking from all the provinces. They were in companies, bearing the banner of their respective provinces. They also carried various other symbols and trophies, and being symmetrically drawn up along the streets through which the emperor was to pass, they presented a very beautiful and uncommon appearance. Every one of these old men brought a present of some kind to the emperor, which generally consisted of vases and other articles in bronze. His Majesty gave to each of them a coin worth about five shillings, together with a gown of yellow silk, which is the imperial colour. They afterwards assembled all together in a place where the emperor went to see them; and it was found that this venerable company amounted to four thousand in number. His Majesty was highly gratified with this spectacle; he inquired the age of many, and treated them all with the greatest affability and condescension. He even invited them all to a banquet, at which he made them sit in his presence, and commanded his sons and grandsons to serve them with drink. After this, with his own hand, he presented every one of them with something; to one who was the most aged of the whole assembly, being nearly 111 years old, he gave a mandarin's suit complete, together with a staff, an inkstand, and other things."

The birthday anniversary of another aged gentleman occurred about this time too, that afforded me some additional instruction and interest, as it was on a higher scale than friend Chang's. It was that of Mr. Kiang, a resident at the West gate, a man of large property, good family, and extensive connections. He had attained the maximum of the "three felicities," which, in the Chinese estimate of man's chief end, consist of *high emolument, numerous children,* and *a good old age.*

It is not unusual for respectable families to own a private chapel, or rather a household temple, in which they lodge not idols but ancestral tablets. This is thrown open in times of family gatherings. Mr. K. arranged to entertain his surviving friends, and likewise the *manes* of the departed, in the small temple adjoining his own residence. On a birthday, at least on a *decade* of one's life, it being customary, with folks who can afford such things, to treat friends both with a feast of fat things and with theatrical amusements, Mr. K. was determined not to be slow or sparing in either. For several weeks previous to the auspicious day, his plans had been laid, and invitations distributed through a wide circle of acquaintances. To join the favoured party, I was only too happy to accept his polite request. His mansion itself was a perfect museum of curiosities. The old worthy had travelled much through his native land; but his hobby during his lifetime had been to collect foreign novelties and group them about his residence. Every room was ornamented with tables, mirrors, pictures, lamps, chandeliers, &c., of foreign workmanship. His garden was laid out with taste and at great expense;—elaborately set with artificial rocks, caverns, bridges, ponds, or adorned with a singular variety of trees, shrubs, plants, and flowers. Before the grand ceremonies of the evening opened, my host conducted me to the hall where the other guests were seated. On entering, I observed that a paling was thrown across the temple floor, to separate the mixed company from the *élite:* for, at a certain hour, the theatrical show was to be open to the public. The area allotted to the select party was nicely fitted up; chairs well cushioned and covered with scarlet serge tastefully embroidered, and teapoys* placed here and there laden with tea, cakes, sweetmeats, &c. The hall was flanked with specimens of fine marble, and on the walls there hung scrolls of exquisite pencilship. Overhead, glass lanterns were suspended, lit up with red tapers, and exhibiting on their panes amusing paintings, at times provokingly ludicrous; for some of the daubs were sketches of foreigners in ungainly postures, and with outrageous dresses, every one crowned with carroty hair! The hall itself presented a lively scene. All were on the *qui vive*. The gentlemen of the party were dressed out in their best, and attended by personal servants; and they conducted themselves according to the politest rules of Chinese etiquette. The contrast on the other side of the fence was striking,—a mass of "roughs," ill-dressed, noisy, and quarrelsome. Up in the latticed galleries I discerned female eyes, eager to peep at what they could, though secure from the vulgar gaze. They were the female branches of Mr. Kiang's family.

Perceiving that the evening amusements would not commence yet, I made myself at home and, each guest being at liberty to roam where he pleased, I strolled into a long narrow apartment. This I found to be the depository of half a dozen coffins. Some were empty, and each of very compact structure, great capacity, and formed of planks several inches thick. Upon inquiry, it appeared that one or two of them contained the remains of deceased relations, and the rest had been prepared by living members of the family, in anticipation of death. Mr. Kiang himself raised the lid of one, pointing to it with a smile of satisfaction that it was ready to receive him as soon as he should breathe his last. This offers a parallel to the conduct of many in

* Small convenient tables.

Christendom, of whom one has said justly, "They seem to have built their tombs, there to bury their thoughts of dying; never thinking thereof, but embracing the world with the greatest eagerness." In China, coffin preparation is not confined to the trade of the undertaker. To have coffins prepared for oneself and for one's relatives during lifetime, is not an unusual thing. As I penned these lines, there came to my recollection a foreign sketch which I met with some time previous, in which the writer, after relating a series of Chinese customs that were opposed to ours, concludes thus:— "Here comes a Chinese acquaintance accompanying a splendidly carved coffin. 'Who's dead?' said I. 'No man hab die,' replied the celestial in the Canton-English jargon,—'no man hab die, my maykee my olo fader cumsha. Him likee too muchee, countoo my numba one popa, spose he die can catchee.'" That is, in Queen's English, "No person is dead. It is a present from me to my aged father, with which he will be greatly pleased. It is a mark of great respect from me too; and the coffin will be at his service when needful." This is a description founded on fact.

Having satisfied myself with the contents of a spot so lugubrious, I returned to a scene in every respect the reverse. The play had begun. After the usual prostrations and incense-offering by the aged host, the actors mounted the stage, all of them young, none above sixteen, some under nine years of age. The dresses were gay and elegant, sometimes really splendid, and generally imitations of the court-dresses of the Ming dynasty. The acts were divided into different scenes and accompanied by music, which at last had become tolerable to me. Not being yet versed in the Mandarin language, the dialect of the stage, I was unable to follow the rapid enunciation of the actors, and was in the dark about the subject of performance. The female actors seemed to afford special satisfaction to the company. But, after I had been looking at handsome Chinese women on that stage, hearing their peculiarly whining tones that could never be mistaken, and watching their mincing gait and affected air in walking, with elegantly decked small feet,—what was my astonishment to find all to be a farce! At the end of the entertainment those very individuals came forward to me in their proper attire, mere boys that had been dressed up for the occasion in female habits! In China no theatrical show would be complete without parts representing women. Yet these are chiefly performed by men or boys, as in general it is considered a disgrace for woman herself to appear on the stage. It is tolerated only where dissipation is rife, as at Soochow.

At a late hour, the anniversary congratulations closed with a hearty "good night" to the host, already in his seventieth year, for whom (though we might wish it) we could scarcely hope that he would have many returns of the season.

While the subject is fresh on the mind, and suggested by the private performances just described, I will call attention for a little to *public* theatricals. As elsewhere, this is among the Chinese, too, the most popular means of entertainment.

There are no permanent erections under the name "theatres," that is, to say, buildings appropriated to this class of amusement. In the centre of their temples and "assembly halls," there is a fixed platform on which theatricals are performed, perhaps for a special festival, perhaps in honour of the presiding genius. Occasionally you meet with a shed of the rudest form, thrown up *pro tem.* for exhibitions under the open sky. Once I visited one of this sort erected at the bottom of a hill, at some distance from any village or temple. It was but a huge frame of wood and boards. The spectators numbered over 3,000. There were no seats. Most were standing, some squatting on the grass, and the rest mounted on trees hard by.

Theatricals intended for the public eye are got up not unfrequently by a wealthy family out of kindness to their neighbours, or from deference to a patron idol. If a mercantile house opens for the first time, or if a long-established concern wishes to commemorate its anniversary, or if a merchant has to signalize a successful stroke of speculation, theatricals are agog. Oftener, at the instigation of hungry and ravenous priests, a subscription paper is issued, which is headed with fine sounding phraseology about the gods and the fates, &c. This is circulated in the community. It announces that there is to be a performance to please certain members of the pantheon. Should the subscription list be large enough to secure competent performers (of course allowing a sufficient deduction of coppers for quieting the appetite of the craving *religieux*), an advertisement-sheet is next published, with a list of the subscribers and a programme of the *fête*. Exhibitions of this nature are chiefly in the daytime—rarely at night—and free to the public. Accordingly, it is not surprising to see the people of the vicinity all astir, even neglecting their own business to have a share in the pastime. The occasion is remarkably productive to those who let benches, sell confections, or keep gambling-tables. The actors, for the most part, are strolling players. These form companies, to travel about the country, under startling designations, such as "Splendid Exhibition Band," &c. The farces are chiefly pantomimic. I do not think I am rash in saying that the imitative acts are better understood than than the speaking; for the language usually is not in the local *patois*, and almost always is drowned by the hideous din of the orchestra and the applauding buzz of the audience. The scenic portion is simple, consisting of painted mats and boards, placed at the back and sides of the stage. On the platform, stools, chairs, and tables are arranged as required, their rude and clumsy forms concealed by silk or satin covers of embroidered work. The noisy choir sits on one side,—famous for grating fiddles, clanging gongs, and deafening drums. The robing-room is behind. From it start forth the performers, originally coarse and dirty wretches, arrayed in most gorgeous and brilliant specimens of the ancient costumes of China. The rapidity with which the players transform themselves, between the different acts, from one dress to another, from this to that character, is very great and remarkable. I have not so extensive and minute an acquaintance with the Chinese stage as could embolden me to give the decided verdict that its general tendency is low and debasing; but, I confess, I myself have witnessed what undoubtedly was calculated to pander to the depraved tastes of the eager and thronging spectators.

Some time previous to the new year, the religious ceremony called *paou-an*, "for securing quiet," had been observed. It took place in different parts of the city, its object being to conciliate the gods, and, as winter advanced, to insure their protection from fire or midnight disturbances. Generally this was a local affair, got up by tenants within certain divisions of the city, who subscribed towards a religious procession that lasted for a night or two. Free-will offerings were made by them of incense, candles, fruit, fish, pork, fowl, &c., and masquerades on a small scale went about after sunset. Although the ostensible aim was to "secure quiet," and to obtain from the gods a fire insurance during a season of indescribable risk from stoves and the random use of charcoal, the proceedings on this occasion by no means favoured either of these desirable results. The temerity with which I saw them dash fireworks about in the narrow lanes and purlieus made me stare with horror; and the deafening rattle of gongs and drums threw a burlesque on the *paou-an* ceremony for "securing quiet."

But the evening of our "April fool's day" was celebrated in Ningpo by an appalling scarefire which completely broke the spell of the tranquillizing ceremony above described. The whole city was in a hubbub in consequence. The fire broke out in the principal street, at a silversmith's shop. It raged for four hours on both sides of the street, threatening to envelope the entire vicinity in a general conflagration. At length, after destroying about one hundred houses, it ceased. As this public street was the chief place of business in Ningpo, on the first alarm of fire the clerks, apprentices, and partners of each establishment were on the spot. In an instant shop doors were bolted and warehouse-gates double-barred or guarded against gangs of rapacious volunteers,—vagabonds that beset every house, professing their readiness to render all needful assistance, while it was unmistakable that plunder was their object. At the different stores, goods and chattels were packed up by the inmates with the utmost expedition, and every package was arranged so as to admit of instantaneous removal, in case the devouring element approached. Although the soldiery and police were called out, unfortunately what aid they rendered was to make double confusion. The shopkeepers refused to intrust the military with their valuables, and, as they were carrying off their property on their own shoulders, it was curious to observe them flourishing a heavy bludgeon in one hand, as if to threaten a decided flagellation on any officious intruders.

In some Chinese towns they have a semblance to fire-engines, called "water-dragons." I could not ascertain that any such machines were within reach on the present occasion; but if at work they were truly inefficient. By the glare of the fire my eye detected a few servants on the neighbouring housetops, throwing buckets of water here and there. This, however, seemed to move the laughter or excite the wrath of the furious element. It raged on, ran its course, did its work, and stopped at its own pleasure.

Finding that the fire was making for my *séjour*, I had the baggage removed into a back garden, from which, in case of actual danger, it might readily be removed. No sooner done than I was informed that the wing of the building fronting my house was in flames. I happened at the time to be on a toploft watching the progress of the fire. Presently I overheard a shout beneath in Chinese, "Where's Meisiensang?—where's Meisiensang?" I hurried down. Instantly a hand grasped my arm. Despite all remonstrance, at the same time ignorant who was the captor, I was dragged, through the grounds behind, on to the top of the city walls. Then a voice exclaimed, "Now you are here, you shall stay by my side." It was my landlord. In fright lest I should suffer from fire, the good man had taken this summary proceeding, and determined that I should share the same protection with his own son who stood close by his side. On the ground of it being necessary to look after my luggage, I sought release; but he was too firm, and again seizing my arm with an iron hold, he drew me out of the range of risk, all the while brandishing his cudgel. We had not gone far before we met a group of spectators standing over the East gate. Bright buttons studded the company, and a large pink umbrella notified that the commander-in-chief was on the spot. His attendants, on observing me, informed his excellency that I had had a narrow escape, &c. His excellency invited me forward; but, being in dishabille, I begged off. He himself then advanced to condole with me on my misfortune. He kindly requested me to make his house my home, and, if need be, to use his wardrobe. At midnight, when apprised of the abatement of the conflagration, I returned to my lodgings, where to my agreeable surprise, I found the rooms in order, luggage rearranged, books reassorted, nothing damaged, thanks to my prompt and faithful Chinese servants.

All the following day the excitement in the city was great; and congratulations among those whose houses had escaped destruction were particularly noisy. Of these some hastened to the temples to vow various acts of public thanksgiving, which would in a measure depend on their means, such as theatrical shows for so many nights, or a recitation by the priests of a certain number of sections from Buddha's sacred hymns. At an early hour, the city walls were placarded over with huge and attractive advertisements of recitals, exhibitions, &c., to be conducted on such and such days and in such and such buildings. One mercantile establishment, for instance, bound itself over to "fast ten days." Another announced, that, "in consequence of having been protected by the gods during the conflagration of last night, the partners had humbly engaged to have forty-eight books of the *Fah-lien-hwa* sung before the idols." A third company promised to give a theatrical play, and, "upon selecting a propitious day, to notify it to the public."

Frequently, conflagrations in China are frightful in extent of destruction. Yet, knowing the extreme carelessness with which they use lamps and lights, the inflammable material of their houses, and the close compact style in which rows of dwellings are erected, it is a perfect phenomenon that so few fires occur. It is not unusual for a poor man's house to be burnt down over his head, by the reckless scattering of gilt paper which he has been offering by fire to his ancestors. Within my own recollection, a large fire broke out in Shanghai from a hatter burning a bundle of "gold paper" before his kitchen-god. He had left the flaming mass on the floor to smoulder out, while he attended to his shop. The unfortunate man paid a heavy franc for his superstition. The penalty is not the mere destruction of property by the furious element: if it be detected or suspected where and in whose premises the fire originated, the ashes and ruins of the surrounding buildings which may have fallen a prey to the conflagration, all are heaped upon that ill-fated site. Thus his neighbours have not the trouble of carting away the rubbish to a distance. They lay the entire *onus* on this unlucky landlord; and the re-erection of his house is necessarily delayed, sometimes long after the other dwellings around have been rebuilt and the business of their occupants has been revived.

Fines and degradation are threatened, sometimes inflicted with severity, on district officers for fires that occur within their jurisdiction. This makes the city authorities alert at such a time, and, with an effective police, they may manage both to keep off the interfering bands of pillagers, and to smother the burning pile by pulling down walls, &c.

Thieves and robbers of every stamp are the foremost on such an occasion to offer assistance; and the condition of the women and children is deplorable, especially when they fall into the hands of those ruthless vagabonds. But to rob during a conflagration is considererd by the people extreme cowardice, and a crime of the darkest dye. Hence, severely and summarily to punish those detected in the base act is deemed most necessary. I passed two such culprits one morning, who were encaged in a large case with open bars. The heads were tied by the tail .to the top of the cage. In this manner they were made to stand for four days, exposed to sun rain, wind, and public gaze, until they died. It was explained that the authorities had no power either to behead or banish, without special instructions from the Imperial cabinet; but they could inflict this mode of punishment as a warning to the public, without any avowed design to shorten life, but with the certainty that to keep a man in that position for three or four days without food, drink, and shelter, would rid the world of a scoundrel to be detested by all society.

At a conflagration in China as in England, there is a vast throng of spectators, who add their loud halloos to the crash of burning houses; yet not the least noisy are the police who hurry the rickety engines called "water-dragons," when they have them, along the rugged narrow lanes. In China the great want on such emergencies is an organized body of firemen, prompt in watching the flames, and expert in checking their progress, instead of shouting and roaring out to the mob.

In the principal street at Ningpo there were high walls, built so as, at certain distances on both sides, almost to overtop the shops and vault across the street. These were considered by the residents as successful in stopping the rage of conflagrations, and from this is derived the name "fire-walls."

In some of their philanthropic institutions provision is made for these terrible dilemmas, by having fire-engines, &c., on the spot. Yet the best are in wretched order if not entirely out of order. Some Chinese natives, who have visited Europe or America and seen our systems of fire-brigades, &c., have been in great admiration of them. One of them in 1853, after a violent fire which threw Shanghai into consternation for a whole night, wrote to the "North China Herald" on the subject, in the following strain, as translated by myself from the Chinese original:—

"TO THE EDITOR OF THE NORTH CHINA HERALD.

"RESPECTED SIR,—When I was in England lately, I had an opportunity of seeing some of the fire-engines there used, machines the structure and working of which exceed all praise, whether you speak of ingenuity or effect.

"It is true that, in this central empire of ours, there are fire engines, *alias* 'water-dragons' (several of which were at work last Monday evening at that disastrous fire in the city); still they are of little or no service during a conflagration, in securing the lives and property of our native population, crowded together, as it invariably is, in such thick masses, as in Shanghai for instance.

"I trust, therefore, you will not think it intruding in me, Sir, to suggest that some of your noble-minded and generous-hearted countrymen might set up an establishment here, with station-house, fire-engines, and brigade, for the purpose of aiding and abetting in the putting down the fearful fires that occur among us.

"This would certainly call forth a renewed expression of gratitude from our populace, and stimulate our princely merchants to follow your example; while, if I mistake not, it might provoke the close-fisted officials ('our fathers and mothers,' forsooth!) to be a little more prompt and liberal in providing means and measures for the benefit of these multitudes which, in their proclamations, they are fond of designating their 'little children.'

"Yours humbly and respectfully,

"INDIGENA."

Further to illustrate how "securing quiet" is carried out in this wonderful country,—in every Chinese town I visited, among the nuisances to "fright the night of its propriety," there was one in particular which, on my arrival at Ningpo for instance, I could not at first interpret: it was such a sonorous medley. At length the periodical regularity of the sounds, and their multiplication as daybreak advanced, suggested that it might be the *night patrol!* Precisely so. Whether at government expense or at that of private houses, or both, it matters not; but night watchmen were abundant. The vesper hours were not kept regularly, to be sure, but in general, at a signal from the drum-loft, the night watch was set at seven o'clock. The city gates were to be closed, bars put up at the ends of the alleys, and a patrol distributed through the wards. The watchmen were paired off two and two for each beat. But "the rule of contraries" seemed to be followed in this matter too; each watchman must have a blazing lantern by his side, and a noisy cylinder or clanking bamboo, just as if to warn the wary house-burglar when he might prepare to enter or to quit.

The noise which so disturbed my slumbers was made by striking the bamboo cylinder thrown over the policeman's arm, and pommelling the huge gong slung across a pole that was supported on the shoulders of himself and comrade. The gong-strokes told the watch hour of the night, one for the first and five for the fifth, the last watch.

At times the noise of these watchmen has been intolerably offensive to me; and so obstinately used they to persevere against rhyme, reason, and entreaty, that I have been able to silence them only by emptying on their heads the cold contents of water-basins. The truly animated *réveil* with which the patrol was wont to break up at five o'clock in the morning, announced not only the break of day, but the pleasure with which the Chinese "Charley" hailed a release from his nightly responsibilities. The setting of the patrol in the evening and its disbandment in the morning, were both notified by a gun-shot. Usually a second gun was fired at the close of the first watch, in accordance with certain rules at the principal offices, about the admission at the city gates, or the exit, of their clerks and secretaries. I have been told it by natives themselves as a sober fact, that watchmen, when sleepily disposed, keep *geese* to attend on them, these geese at the least disturbance cackling and waking them up; also that wealthy natives who have watchmen on the outer premises by night, couple with them fowls and monkeys to watch the interior!

I may now give a few hints of Chinese methods of calculating the hours of time. One whole day is divided into twelve parts, each consisting of two of our hours, and subdivided into eight of our quarters. Their modes for keeping time are odd and various, but for regularity and correctness not to compete with the European. Of these the following are what I have met with in different parts:—

1st. "The dripping brazen vessel," or the *clepsydra.* I understand a specimen may to the present day be found standing in some of the principal offices in the country. A native gives a brief but not perspicuous notice of it in these words: "It is made of six pots rising one above another, from which the water percolates. The lowermost vessel has a board over it, on which the water drips. On the face of this cover is an orifice into which an hour-index is inserted. As the vessel gets one degree full of water, the index floats up one quarter. The hours and watches of time are all noted in this fashion." One of this description in Canton city (to quote the words of the editor of the *Chinese Repository*)* "is placed in a separate room, under the supervision of a man who, besides his stipend and perquisites, obtains a livelihood by selling time-sticks. There are four covered copper jars standing on a brickwork stairway, the top of each of which is level with the bottom of the one above it. The largest measures 23 in. high and broad, and contains 97½ pints of water. The second is 22 in. high, and 22 in. broad. The third is 21 in. high, and 20 in. broad; and the lowest is 23 in. high, and 19 in. broad. Each is connected with the other by an open trough, along which the water trickles. The wooden index in the lowest jar is set every morning and afternoon at five o'clock, by placing the mark on it for these hours even with the cover, through which it rises and indicates the time. The water is dipped out and poured back into the top jar, when the index shows the completion of the half-day; and the water is renewed every quarter. Two large drums stand in the room, on which the watchmen strike the watches during the night."

2nd. *The dial,* possibly introduced by the Arabians, has now come to be used everywhere. It is very

* Chinese Repository, xx. 430.

simple,—consisting merely of a small string as the gnomon over a miniature compass. By placing the string to point to the north, its shadow is thrown upon the hour marked along the edge of the compass. There is also a dial upon the lid to denote the hours of the night by the shadow of the moon.

3rd. *The hourly incense-stick* is not uncommon—almost universal in their temples, and revives in our memory the story of Alfred the Great and his candles. This stick is notched at equidistances, and, when lighted, the progress of the slow combustion of the graduated match shows the waste of hours. It is a composition of sawdust mixed with glue, and evenly rolled into very thin cylinders two or three feet in length.

4th. *The revolution of the heavenly bodies* is their mode of reckoning time at sea.

5th. The use of *foreign watches* has now become quite fashionable among the natives; and the vanity of a dandy cannot be better satisfied than by displaying a pair of watches dangling from his gaudy belt, sometimes two pairs. The following are two legends from a native account of modes of keeping time: "For this purpose there are fishes which are taught each hour to take a leap to note the passing hour. So, likewise, fowls are trained to announce each hour by crowing once for the first, twice for the second, and so forth."

CHAPTER V.

RELIGIOUS WORSHIP TO THE DEAD—MILITARY AND LITERARY EXAMINATIONS—FAST-DAYS—CHOLERA—TRIP TO A LAKE, AND TO TWO LARGE TEMPLES IN THE COUNTRY—HISTORY OF FOREIGN INTERCOURSE AT NINGPO SINCE 1842.

THE third moon, or April, throughout was memorable for feasts and celebrations, set or movable.

It introduced the *Tsingming* term, commemorative of the dead, and most scrupulously observed by all classes in China,—in no way confined to the privileged. The season extended more or less from the end of the second to the beginning of the fourth moon, but was particularly lively between the fifth and tenth days of the third, when whole family groups proceeded, in neat attire and with marked decorum, to visit the family vaults in the country, which were set in order and duly arranged for the occasion. The names by which the festival is designated are various; *e. g. shang-fun*, "going up to the grave-mounds;" *saou-moo*, "sweeping the tombs;" *pae-shan*, "paying respect at the hills;" indicating the chief objects of the festival.

The willow-tree in Chinese estimation is emblematic of life and health, and there was, at this period, a prodigal use of its branches, twigs, sprigs, leaves, and buds; men, women, babes,—ay, domestic animals too,—being ornamented with this significant emblem. It was stuck in the hair, hung round the neck, put upon door-posts, slung over bedsteads, arranged round each apartment,—expressive, to be sure, that the desire which rules in the breasts of other people asking for "length of days," reigns also in Chinese bosoms.

But the special object of this ceremonial season is

(to tell the truth) to pay worshipful homage to their departed relatives. Some foreign writers, as Fortune, Davis, and Bowring, &c., have attempted to set it off merely as a series of "reverential services rendered to ancestors," and not religious homage. If so, what mean these trays laden with offerings of pork, fish, and fowl; these libations of wine, these bundles of candles and incense-stick; these holocausts of gilt paper, paper money, paper clothes, paper houses, paper furniture, and these numberless prostrations, ceremonies, and prayers offered up to departed ancestors and parents, with more earnestness, devoutness, order, and punctuality, than even before the shrines of the idols? "Reverential services and not religious worship to ancestors," forsooth! and yet so gross and palpable is this species of necrolatry, and so offensive to the religious sense of His Holiness of Rome, that even he, not always particularly nice on such points, has forbidden its observance amongst "the faithful" in China.

As any one in his right mind cannot help deploring that Chinese of every grade are given up to this form of superstition, it is likewise scarcely possible not to trace in it a feeble, misty, and imperfect recognition of the immortality of man's spirit and the existence of a future state. A man may not trouble himself much about the article of death during lifetime, yet "the quality of the coffin, the ceremonies of the funeral, the desire of a burial-place, and the spot where the grave is to be dug,—all this is matter of serious consideration."* But why?—because he has a lurking sense that he will not be happy in the world to come without these preliminaries. Progenitors are anxious to have descendants through whom a perpetual line of support shall be secured to their own departed manes; children feel bound to offer sacrifices to deceased

* Huc, ii. p. 216.

ancestors; the ghosts of the dead are supposed to be quieted by due ceremonials at their graves; neglected ghosts, it is believed, will haunt the houses of surviving relations to annoy and worry them, but, on the other hand, those whose vaults or tombs are well attended to, may exert a beneficial influence; the spirits of the departed must be provided with food and other comforts; gilt and silvered paper in the shape of copper money, dollars, and sycee bars, is set on fire, to pass through the smoke into the invisible world, where it is to be recoined into solid cash; and clothes, sedans, furniture, utensils, houses, buffaloes, and horses, made of paper or pasteboard, are transferred in the same mode to "Cloud-land," for the benefit of the dead. Surely all this indicates some notion of an immortality to be thought of and provided for! At the same time it exposes their woful lack of that divine revelation which hath come into our world, by Him who "hath brought life and immortality to light through the Gospel."

During the same month Ningpo was in more than usual bustle, not only from this Tsingming festival, but in consequence of an uncommon influx of strangers from the country, who had come to attend the military and literary examinations for honours, to be conducted by commissioners specially deputed under the seal of his Imperial Majesty.

The military examination occurred first, and was conducted in the open air. I embraced the opportunity of being present. The arena for the occasion was on a grand parade outside the city walls. Wind and weather favourable, there was a large concourse of spectators. It was probable many were drawn by curiosity to criticise the condition of the invincibles after their recent contact with the English soldiery and their sad repulses. Casting a cursory glance over that field of martial sport, I saw a large building at the upper end of it. The city provost (the president) sat there on a *dais*, surrounded by a coterie of buttoned gentry, smoking long pipes, trying to look dignified, and occasionally lording it over some intrusive native that pressed within the lines. The president was seated at a table with writing materials before him, taking notes on the conduct of the several competitors, and giving marks, good, bad, or indifferent. At the bottom of the steps that led up to his chair only twenty-two candidates for military honours appeared. These were robed in silks and satins of various hue and richness, wore ceremonial caps profusely tasselled with red floss-thread, and were armed with bows and arrows. The whole course extended over a space several hundred yards long, but only eight feet wide. On each side of it the spectators stood, all males and no women, eager to view the scene, nor by any means slow to express, by cheers or hoots, their sense of the success or the failure of the competitors. To keep order, several policemen were distributed along the course, who, however, served rather to excite the rage or provoke the ridicule of the mob. At the bottom of the course, opposite to the president's stage, there was the start for the mounted archers. As the proceedings commenced, a crier sallied out vociferating the title of each batch and the name of each candidate. These respectively answered to their names by kneeling on the right knee and making obeisance. The orders were then passed to every company as it came up.

The first trial was that of "the mounted archers," perhaps the most novel and interesting of all. They were sent to the other end of the course. There they mounted their horses. With one or two exceptions, the animals afforded a sorry specimen of *horseflesh* in China; they were miserably in want of forage as well as the brush and currycomb. They were fantastically caparisoned; saddles high and awkward, bridles heavy, rusty, and rough; stirrups clumsy, &c. On the candidate mounting his horse, two trumpeters sounded the signal for the start. It was not a race among the competitors, it was to test their skill in archery on mounted steeds. The course marked for them to run exceeded two hundred yards. To the right of it there were set up, at equal distances, three large cylinders of blackened sedge mat, each with three great red globes daubed on it. The bull's-eye was the middle red circle in each sedge cylinder, to hit which was the aim of the horseman flying down the horse-path. As he rushed on, a small flag was waved at the upper end to urge him on, and, if his arrow hit the mark, they beat a drum and smote the earth with a large banner. To race at the utmost speed, and to arrange bow and arrow as he passed from one sedge column to the other, required some management on the part of the candidate to keep on his horse without holding the bridge. But most of them proved tolerably good shots. Each one had to run the course thrice, and at each turn was summoned to the bar to receive the sentence of commendation, or disapproval.

Then came the archery practice on foot. The candidates were called up in companies of four. Each man shot six arrows at a distance of 100 yards. When he hit the bull's-eye, a billet was thrown down, to denote by the number of billets the skill of the bowman. The third exercise was to bend heavy bows, requiring a force ranging from 80 to 120 pounds. The fourth was the wielding of heavy swords. The fifth test of strength and skill, was to raise ponderous stones and heave weighty mallets. With this the examination closed for the day.

The literary trials also had attracted crowds of strangers to Ningpo. This examination extended over several days, under the direction of some leading officers at that time in the city. I was specially anxious to get a personal insight into the actual working of this contest for the *sewtsai* degree, the first stepping-stone to literary fame, and at several times asked admission into the examination-hall. The request, presumptuous perhaps, was invariably refused, though with great politeness.

This first degree which the aspirant scholar aims at, initiatory to honorary promotion of any importance, is named *sewtsai*, "elegant shoots." No limit is put to the number of candidates for the honour, provided their names appear under the certificates of individuals well known and duly qualified.

Yet there are exceptions. These generally embrace five classes; *e. g. brothel-keepers, play-actors, lictors, jailers,* and *domestic slaves,* with their children unto the third generation. Besides there is one class absolutely excluded from all hope,—root and branch cut off from rising up into literary "shoots" even. This unprivileged order seems to be confined to certain localities, though in some parts of the country it bears a large proportion to the bulk of the population. The designation under which it goes is that of *tse-min,* "degraded people," who are reputed to be the posterity of certain rebels that threatened the stability of the Sung dynasty, A.D. 960—1126. Those defeated rebels fell under the imperial ban, and, with their offspring, were consigned to perpetual infamy. Under the category of persons excluded from the privileges of striving for literary distinction, come also the *barbers, chair-bearers, watermen, musicians,* and their descendants. Now, notwithstanding the apparent encouragement given to all classes to seek for scholastic titles of distinction, and thereby to obtain a place among the rulers of the land, it must be evident, from the exceptions already named, how, by the standing decrees of the nation, an immense proportion of the *vulgus* is shut out from this law of privilege.

As to candidates whose applications are admitted, there appears to be an established rule, that no man can reap early laurels in literature except in his native province, and in the district to which his native place belongs. Accordingly, a man of the province of Chihkiang may not stand on the lists with the candidates in Canton province; and in the Chihkiang province, one of the district of Ningpo cannot compete with a native of the neighbouring district of Chinhai. This implies a degree of caution to preserve the honorary degree pure and unmixed, and to act with impartiality and fairness in its distribution. Yet such an arrangement must thwart the zeal and ambition of many young men who, having pursued their classical studies in other parts of the country, may be precluded by distance and other circumstances from revisiting their native places to undergo the necessary examinations.

By the laws of the empire, a fixed limit is assigned to the number of *successful competitors* in each place. This varies according to the population of the district,—not the number of candidates; and, it matters not how many or few offer themselves for examination, all go up to the contest, aware that of their number an overwhelming majority must return to their homes disappointed, and only a trifling minority carry the palm. For instance, 2,000 individuals had come up to Ningpo in the month of April, 1843, to compete for a prize that could be obtained only by twenty-five! Again, taking the six circuits belonging to the department of Ningpo,—5,000 candidates were enrolled, but no more than 139 could come off with flying colours! From native statistics at that time in my possession, I found that, by the triennal examinations for the degree of *sewtsai* held all over the empire, usually there are about 25,000 persons who can enter on this first step to literary honour, but of that number the province of Chihkiang, with a population of 26½ millions, could for its share every third year have only 1,845 individuals promoted to the rank and immunities of a Chinese B.A.

To secure justice to the ambitious aspirants, and to maintain the integrity of classical dignity, a Board of Guardians (some say twenty) is appointed of scholars that have already passed. Its commission is to ascertain the necessary qualifications of the several candidates. If satisfied with the claims of the applicant, the Board has authority to introduce him under its certificate. In registering his name on the chancellor's lists, care is taken to describe his person, age, features, residence, and lineage;—the object of this particularizing being to transmit the honorary degree without reproach through a line of virtuous and respectable characters. Fastidiousness like this leads to a rigid inquiry into the genealogical descent of the candidate. Although the competition is not free to all classes, there is no restriction as to *age*. A case is mentioned of an examination in the province of Canton, when a hoary-headed grandfather stood on the lists side by side with his son and grandson.

After the due preliminaries have been settled, the competitors meet after daybreak, and, as each enters the hall for trial, he takes with him his pencil, inkslab, stick of ink, and a little refreshment, but nothing else, —with a prospect before him of confinement within closed doors for fifteen or twenty hours. His pockets, his shoes, his wadded garments, are minutely searched, lest perchance keys to composition might be smuggled in. Detection leads to public degradation and perpetual exclusion from all future examinations. When they are quietly seated, the gates, wickets, doors, avenues, and windows are closed and guarded. The niches, crevices, and openings are pasted over with strips of paper containing these important words: "No sealed despatches for the presiding examiner can be handed in, as he is examining the essays. You must retire and keep out of the way." Of course, admittance to see a friend, to advise or assist him, is out of the question. Still, with all this array of espionage, they sometimes manage to deceive even the shrewdest and most wary bench of examiners. A native assured me—himself a thorough scholar—that he had assumed the name of an individual by whom he had been bribed to obtain the degree for him, and throughout personated him. He carried away the prize, which of course he transferred to the gentleman for whom he had acted, and by whom he was liberally rewarded.

Let us presume, however, that they are all "honourable men." There they are seated side by side at broad massive desks of pine, on long roomy benches, accurately numbered and classified, with paper, pencils, and ink before them. The examination-hall at Ningpo, which I visited when empty and unoccupied, was a fine spacious place. This filled or crammed with 2,000 anxious and gaily-dressed competitors must have presented a sight beyond description. The theme is given out,—generally a subject selected out of the "four books," and the "five classics." What is required of the competitors is to draw up an essay on the subject propounded, which is to be prepared with triteness and brevity, belaboured in a classical style, and with apposite quotations, all written in a clear, elegant hand. After several hours have passed, a signal-gun is fired, the closed doors are opened, and soon the hall is thinned.

The first and the last time of competition has come to many of these young men. Finding that really it is easier to read and recite books at their night-lamps than to write compositions *impromptu* in a public hall, with so many checks not only to the prompting of ready teachers, but to eating and drinking, scores of them vow to give up the strife for ever. And then, when the literary judge has scanned the various papers offered for inspection, he is soon able to reduce the number to a small company of picked men. These are called up to a second contest. The reduction of the list goes on in this way from one day to another, until the difference required is at last found. For this degree of *sewtsai*, there is a series of three examinations to be undergone;—the first under the eye of the district provost, the second under the prefect of the department, and the third under that of a chancellor appointed from the *Hanlin* college at Peking. The final decision rests with the last-named official, whose judgment doubtless is in a great measure influenced by the opinions of the examiners who precede him.

Unsuccessful candidates are at liberty to renew the contest as soon as the term returns. But the successful man at once acquires a name in his village, has a prospect of moving through the world in the higher circles of Chinese life, and is exempt from certain of the liabilities of his neighbours. Nor is he less free from fresh responsibilities and new duties. It is not thought enough merely to obtain your *B.A.* You must bear your honours well. Accordingly, there are two or three additional examinations, held at intervals during the following three years, to prove the fortunate competitor. The *sewtsai* licentiates are arranged in three classes, graduated according to the talents and attainments of the members. The lowest is named *fahsang*, the members of which just hold their degree, and that is all that can be said of them. The second class is the *tsiangsang*, a step higher than the former. But the *lingsang* is "at the top of the tree." For the separate and secondary distinctions, *sewtsais* recently created have to work hard for two or three years to come. Otherwise, they fall into the category of the indolent, and reap the reward of the slothful. Except by special permission, a man may not elude these crowning trials. To shun them, it is said, will even draw down the rod of chastisement on the naked back, when justice is severe; besides, it may be followed by expulsion from further share in the privileges that belong to "the elegant shoots."

So far I have noted the initiatory struggles of a Chinese bookworm, to attain the felicity of "roaming among the forest of pencils," as they dignify the highest point in their Parnassus. The other literary degrees are in the following order of succession:—*keujin*, "elevated men;" *tsinsze*, "advanced scholars;" and *hanlin*, "pencil forests;" each attainable only after severe trials. The examinations for these are not conducted either in district towns like Chinhai, Shanghai, or in departmental cities like Ningpo, Sungkiang, &c. The *keujin* examination comes off in provincial capitals, as Soochow, Hangchow, and Canton; and the other two are always conducted at Peking, the metropolis of the empire.

Of these literary contests, it is not too much to say that the one which thrills most families with interest and excitement is the first in the course already enlarged on. On this hangs the fate or fortune of myriads. According to some Chinese informants, who themselves had obtained it by such means, the degree often is purchased for several hundred dollars, with the entire sanction of the imperial government. By the purchase, the beneficiary is admitted to the privileges of the B.A. without the toil and anxiety of competition. He bears the name of *Kiensang*, and is entitled to wear the brass knob on his cap. But afterwards the man's own wits and industry must work his way to the higher degrees.

Besides periodical trials for the several honours in the literary world, the emperor himself may, under peculiar circumstances, decree *special* examinations. I find, for instance, that when the Emperor Taoukwang ascended the throne, and also subsequently, at the celebration of a grand era in his personal history, his majesty, to express marks of imperial favour, granted extraordinary powers for literary examinations in different parts of the country.

There has been an attempt on the part of the insurgents in China to cast on the Mantchoo-Chinese government also the stain and disgrace of not encouraging Chinese learning. Whereas the reverse is the real fact, well known and acknowledged, as by an educated native in these words:—"There has been as much consideration paid by the Mantchoos to the impoverished student in prosecuting his studies, as by the Ming family (the old Chinese dynasty of which the rebels profess to be the revivers). They also have built and supported academies, and favoured the poor scholar with midnight lamp-monies,"—referring to the allowances made by the present government for aiding poor students in pursuing their studies. Besides, the Mantchoo emperors themselves have done more than most of their predecessors to promote Chinese literature. "The Imperial Lexicon," and the still greater Thesaurus (viz. the Peiwanyuenfoo), which I may justly name "the Chinese Quotation Concordance," are two vast works compiled under the auspices of *Kanghe,* and are lasting memorials of the desire of the Tartar rulers to give stability to the pure classical form of the Chinese language. I may also mention "the Imperial Edition of the Thirteen Classics," "the Collection of Imperial Essays," "the Gleanings of Imperial Poems," "the Sacred Edict," besides many other classical works, published during the present dynasty and under the patronage of its rulers,—enough to disprove any allegation that the aim of the Tartar conquerors has been to alter or destroy the language, literature, or literary aspirations of their Chinese subjects.

The month of May was ushered in by the Chinese term *Lih-hia,*—in other words, "the opening of summer;" generally celebrated with a brief festival, attended, as all religious festivals in China are, with merriment, feasting, and theatrical shows, &c.

Previous to this there had been a great deficiency of "grain rains;" and, as the hopes of the agriculturists had been seriously disappointed about a rainy season, the first week of the term was appointed for "praying for rain." A public fast was proclaimed. At such a juncture, when all parties felt deep anxiety lest drought was about to threaten the staff of life, magistrates, priests, and people were seen repairing to the temples. In procession they paraded the gods of the land and grain,—the idols being dressed out very gaily, and the temples swept clean. In garbs of sackcloth, men of various classes were offering up long and repeated prayers that rain might not be withheld.

A fast of several days' duration was enjoined by official proclamation, in terms so strict that my cook had to smuggle in some animal food for me as long as it lasted; the use and slaughter of animals for the table being rigidly forbidden during these solemnities. At this time I had an invitation from a high officer to dine with him, which courtesy I accepted with a degree of curiosity, wondering how my host could feast a guest at a juncture when all kinds of *flesh* were interdicted and vegetable diet alone permissible. But, to my astonishment, his tables were laden with fish, fowl, mutton, &c., and the choicest niceties the Ningpo market could at any time supply.

Bad harvest, famine, and epidemics, the terrible consequences of frequent and severe droughts in China, have excited in the national heart a painful restlessness when there is scarcity of rain. Emperors are said to have offered themselves up to penance that rain might be given to the people. A Buddhist priest is celebrated for having plunged into a great water-jar up to his ears, and held himself there until the heavens were persuaded to open their water-treasures. In the city of Shanghai, during the month of July, 1853, because of a fearful drought, not only did the resident officials forbid the slaughter of sheep, pigs, oxen, and fowls, but Chinghwang, the city idol, was carried about the streets to propitiate the *dii majores* for rain upon the parched fields. The attendants of the patron saint bore umbrellas and wore straw sandals, expressive of hope that showers might deluge the streets. An immense jar of water was borne along, and, as the procession moved on, the acolytes dipped twigs of the willow-tree into the water and sprinkled the arid streets therewith. Two days after, while the heavens continued like brass, the provost himself went on foot to the city temple to plead for rain, and, as a mark of greater humiliation, paced the streets with queue unloosed and hair dishevelled.

Public forms of *kew-yu,* "prayer for rain," repeatedly are issued, some of them from the Imperial cabinet. The following is a specimen of an abridged form, written and offered up by the Emperor Taoukwang himself, during an excessive season of drought. "Alas, Imperial Heaven, were not the world subject to extraordinary afflictions, I would not dare to offer any special service. This present year the drought has been excessive; the summer is gone and the rain has not fallen. The fields have suffered as well as the field-worker; and even the brutes of the field, insects, herbs, and trees, are ceasing to live. I, the humble servant of Heaven, appointed to rule mankind and responsible for keeping the world in order and the people in comfort, find it impossible to sleep or eat. I am scorched with anxiety. Yet no showers descend to water our lands. A few days since I humbled myself, fasted and offered sacrifices to the gods of the land and of the grain, and was cheered by slight showers; but they did not suffice. * * * I feel compelled to examine myself and think of my errors, hoping that I may obtain forgiveness. In religious services have I been irreverent? Has there been any pride encouraged or concealed in my heart? In attending to government affairs, has there been any remissness, or has there been a deficiency of energy and diligence? Have I been ruled by justice and impartiality in conferring rewards and inflicting punishments? In erecting public works, mausoleums, gardens, &c., have I oppressed the people and wasted public property? In appointing officers, have I failed to choose fit persons, so as to avoid those that vex and annoy my subjects? * * * * * * Bowing my head, I humbly pray thee, Imperial Heaven, to hasten to confer a gracious favour, by timely and generous rain, to save the lives of my people. May the High Heaven mark these things, and be merciful to the people. On their account I am unutterably grieved, alarmed, and affrighted. Most humbly is this representation made!"

By the month of May the hot weather had set in; and even the Chinese felt the benefit of "the water system." Walking down an alley, I descried large characters on the side of a miserable-looking building, *Yuhtang*, "Bath-house." Having expressed a wish to inspect it, the doorkeeper admitted me and withheld no information. The Chinese have a horror of *cold water* in any form, for drink or lavation. Of course, then, this was a warm-water establishment. I was shown first into the dressing-room, a large chamber with compartments running along the wall, fitted up as wardrobes. In these the bathers suspended their vestments, each having one allotted to himself. Then came the bath-room. For an ordinary person a bath was charged but one farthing. As the door opened, a volume of vapour poured forth to envelop me. Being a foreign spectator, I was apprehensive that I might frighten the bathers by my sudden apparition. But the fog was so dense, that I could scarcely discern if there were any there. At last, through the steam-cloud, I spied out four stark-naked men, squatting opposite to each other in a tank, scrubbing themselves and splashing about. I am shocked to say, the water was detestably filthy. The keeper himself told me that he put the fresh water in only once a day, at an early hour every morning, and that the same element, whoever the bather, was used without change or admixture! Imagine the same liquid for one entire day, to cleanse and purify a multitude of filthy, itchy, diseased fellows! "Monstrum horrendum," &c. The odour generated and pent up in the confined chamber was overpowering; and, more than satisfied with my scrutiny, I beat a retreat and rushed for the door. At the back and under the bath-room, I was shown a large stove, in which a slow fire was fed by a stoker, to keep the water in the bath-room warm.

As the summer advanced, symptoms were becoming more manifest that the Chinese were great sufferers from the unhealthiness of the season,—doubtless aggravated by the want of public sanitary rules and arrangements. The most frequent forms of disease were dysentery and diarrhœa, intermittent and remittent fevers, and ague accompanied with obstinate diarrhœa. All this was promoted by want of free ventilation in their streets and houses; and the collection of stagnant water everywhere in pools, tanks, and ditches.

About this time one topic of inquiry with me was the existence of Asiatic cholera in China. It was suggested by several medical officers in her majesty's military service. The result of those inquiries, made both at Tinghai and Ningpo, led to the conclusion that Asiatic cholera had not unfrequently nor slightly, but often and with great severity, visited China. The heads of my inquiries were the following:—

Names.—There is a disease very commonly known among the Chinese, under the appellation of *hoh-lwan too-siay*. The first two characters denote *suddenness* and *confusion*, or we may say "sudden and violent;" the third signifies "to vomit," and the last "to purge." The translation of the entire phrase would be "sudden and violent vomiting and purging." Another name is given to this disease, which corresponds in meaning precisely to the former. It is *aou-siay hoh-lwan che-tsih*, "a sudden and violent attack of vomiting and purging." From minute inquiries it would appear that the two characters *hoh-lwan* are intended to express also the violent throes in retching which generally attend the attack. Hence, they mark out a distinct kind as the *kan-hoh-lwan*, or "dry retching," a case in which the patient retches violently, without being in the least relieved by vomiting. This type of cholera is attended also by writhing pains in the bowels, and by alternations of chills and fevers. Perhaps this is nothing else than simple cholic,—what is often called "English cholera."

There is, however, a species of cholera, which is spoken of by the natives of those provinces which it has visited, in terms that betoken their horror at it, while they regard it as entirely *sui generis* and utterly incurable. The names given to this type of cholera are not few.

Tiaou-kioh-sha.—The character *tiaou*, from the explanations of the native doctors, in this application conveys the idea of "bending up as a bow," a meaning it derives from the original signification it bears of "grasping a bow for the purpose of bending it." The second term stands for "the feet:" and the third is one purely medical, expressive of "violent pains and writhings in the bowels." The translation of this name, given to the disease, would therefore be "bending u[p] the feet and writhing of the bowels." *Kioh-kin-lwan.*— The first two characters mean "feet and tendons:" th[e] last, contraction or "tying up;" *i. e.*, "a contraction o[f] the feet and tendons." It is sometimes simply calle[d] *kin-lwan*, "a cramping of the sinews." *Kioh-kin-tiao[u]* is a name that signifies "a bending or curving up o[f] the feet and tendons;" *kioh-kin-chaou*, is a fifth repre sentation of the disease, meaning "a drawing up (vio lently) of the feet and tendons." The only remainin[g] appellation is *chun-kioh hoh-lwan*, or "a turning up —[a] rolling up of the feet suddenly and convulsively." In al[l] these names, it would appear as if the leading feature i[n] the Asiatic cholera were denoted, the extremely violen[t] cramping of the whole frame.

History of the Disease in China.—The first individua[l] that I met with, who could give any definite account o[f] the disease and its history was Dr. Chang. He wa[s] himself an acupuncturist of long standing, and ha[d] travelled not a little in his own country. From hi[s] account, the severe type of cholera broke out firs[t] in 1820, and had been transmitted by a Fukien jun[k] trading from Siam to Fukien, from which province i[t] travelled into Canton, and thence into Kiangse an[d] Chihkiang, taking a northerly direction until it reache[d] the province of Chihli, where, however, it did not commi[t] extensive ravages. The two provinces of Kiangse and Chihkiang were said to have suffered most from it[s] devastations. In its progress through the latter pro- vince, it reached the department and city of Ningpo in May, 1820; and it was calculated that, in that depart- ment alone, two thousand individuals fell victims to its rage during the first outbreak of the disease. It appeared again in the two following years, but with redoubled violence, and during the summers of these three years, 1820-21-22 (for it made its appearance always during the hot weather), ten thousand persons were supposed to have been carried off in the department of Ningpo. After a cessation of eight years, it again broke out in 1831, when it raged severely, but not so violently as in preceding years. In the year 1841, it appeared afresh in the city of Chinhai. Mr. Hoo, a merchant, confirmed the statements made by the aged doctor, adding that he was in the city of Ningpo at the time of the disease raging, and that while he walked the streets on his usual routine of business, he daily saw people suddenly drop down under its overwhelming attack. My teacher, a native of Hangchow, the capital of the province of Chihkiang, informed me that it raged there with the greatest severity during June, July, and August of 1821-22, when "people died like sheep," dropping down dead in the streets, apparently without a struggle; so that in Hangchow several myriads must have perished. Every person to whom I spoke on the subject answered in language most strongly expressive of dread, as if in recollection of past horrors and in despair of meeting with any antidote. As to the classes of men which had suffered most from its ravages, I could only learn that they were mostly the poorer, that they were under seventy years of age, that there was no particular class of labourers, and that death among males preponderated. Dr. Chang specified the priests and priestesses of the Buddhistic religion, as exempt from the attack of the epidemic, and attributed the exemption to the favour of the gods. If indeed exempt, it might be that their abstemious habits contributed not a little to it. Or, as that priesthood forms on the whole but a small proportion to the bulk of the people and might suffer correspondingly, the idea would get abroad that the priests were specially favoured; while the priests themselves would take advantage of the small proportion cut off by the malady, to impress the ignorant with the notion that they had been singularly favoured of the gods. In conversation with my informants, they pointed out a peculiar feature in the progress of the malady through the country,—its "leaping over" whole districts, and even departments. They instanced this case. As has already been remarked, it travelled from the province of Kiangse into the neighbouring province of Chihkiang. Having raged for some time in the district city of Yuhshan, which is on the border of the two provinces but belongs to the jurisdiction of the former, it suddenly broke out in Hangchow, the capital of the latter, having passed over a line of ground about two hundred miles in length, upon which—without reckoning innumerable townships, villages, and hamlets,—there are six considerable cities.

Cause.—On this point my friends did not presume to pass any conjectures, especially as healthy robust people were so suddenly cut off by it in the prime of their days. Dr. Chang, on being asked whether he had ever held any post-mortem examination to ascertain, if possible, the character of the malady, confessed that, so far from looking at a corpse, he was so frightened that at last he declined attending upon even the living, when his services were called for.

Symptoms were the following, as given in detail by the venerable acupuncturist, in reply to the simple question, "What peculiar and distinctive symptoms attended the attack?"—Sudden shaking of the limbs, vomiting, violent diarrhœa, pulse rapid before purging commenced, on purging pulse ceased, eyes dull and sunken after the diarrhœa commenced, persons delirious and afterwards insensible, nails black, lips corrugated and of a dark purple colour, nose blue, face black, drawing together of the whole body, the bowels greatly pained, no urine but all purging, convulsions before death.

Duration of the Disease.—The patient generally carried off in four or six hours. They spoke too of sudden deaths in the streets.

Favourable Signs.—The stoppage of purging and the recovery of sensitiveness in the limbs; motion of the eye.

Remedies.—Medicines taken internally of no use; *acupuncturing* the lower extremities and cauterizing, at a *very early* stage, sometimes successful,—perhaps in two cases out of ten.

The Tung-tseen Lake lies twenty miles south of Ningpo. In the end of May, in company with Captain (now Lieut.-Colonel) Kennedy, I made a venture to it. Two boats were engaged, one for ourselves, another for servants. We embarked at sunrise on the 23rd of May. Our starting-post was a wharf on the east bank of the main branch of the river, and our course up the canal lay east-by-south. For the first mile the left bank was lined with a range of shops and dwelling-houses. Although Ningpo had been held for many months by the British forces, and, since the restoration of peace and good order by the treaty of the preceding year, repeated visits had been made by subjects of different foreign countries, the curiosity of the people to see the face of the stranger seemed still to be insatiable. The canal was very bustling, in consequence of the large number of boats passing and repassing, the majority of which were passenger-boats, crowded with motley groups of all sizes, ages, and complexions. In such company we steered along for a mile or two, but at length, after crossing the suburban limits, we came in full view of lofty hills that skirted the extensive plain, in which our boats were tracked. Ahead there lay before us the T'ai-pih hills, in the direction of the Tung-tseen Lake.

While we were musing over the busy scenes we had left behind, the country suddenly burst upon us, and we found ourselves surrounded by the insignia of rural scenery. On every hand and at every interval, the eye met the implements and the employments of the husbandmen. Large farmyards struggled to push themselves into observation from behind closely-packed thickets of the tall wild-rose, or from the heart of groves of fir, that harped with the coo of pigeons, the notes of blackbirds, and the chatterings of magpies and minors. Farmyard boys and women were engaged in winnowing the grain for some time gathered in, talking, laughing, and singing as they laboured. In adjoining fields, stout sturdy men were sedulously occupied in clearing the soil of stones and weeds. These rice-fields were bearing the second crop for the current year. The paddy was growing in long parallel ranges, separated by a rut for the flow of the water poured into the field by the irrigating machines. That the rice alone might derive all the juices necessary to its proper nourishment, every weed and hidden root was sought out and torn up. To expedite this operation, the husbandman's sleeves and trowsers were tucked up, and the peasant crawled on all fours between the different beds of paddy, as he moved on working with his hands the moist earth around the roots of the rice-stalks. This task was rather laborious; and, as the poor fellows raised themselves to look at the passing strangers, we could see that their limbs had been much exposed to wounds from the sharp flints among which they crawled, as well as to severe bites from numerous leeches.

Withdrawing the eye from the farmyard to the bank of the canal, along which our boats were slowly dragged, it fell upon the irrigating implements. These were scattered throughout our line of journey, and at times were seen in such numbers, as plainly to indicate the extreme distress which the reigning drought threatened, and the intense anxiety felt by the farmers to water their grounds with sufficient and regular supplies.

In districts where there is neither a river nor a canal, wells are dug. Reservoirs too are filled up, to which water is conveyed by aqueducts and gutters from adjacent hills or some distant stream. At the mouth of the well or of the tank, a lever is raised, which at the one end bears a stone weight and at the other a swing bucket. This bucket is lowered, filled, and then raised again to empty its contents either directly into the field, or, should the patch of ground be upon a higher terrace, into a rut that lies on a level equal with that patch. But upon the banks of canals, rivers, or lakes, the following varieties of water-engines are in use—"the sitting-wheel," "the foot-wheel," "the hand-wheel," and "the buffalo-wheel." There is a trough that is carried down to the water's edge, and in it a chain-pump, or a set of wooden paddles linked together, is worked to raise the water over the bank. The power generally used to set the machines in motion is indicated by the names given. At one time you find a man at work seated and using his feet, from which it is called "the sitting-wheel." The second, or "the foot-wheel," requires the labourer to stand upon the machine, walking upon it as on a tread-mill, supporting his chest and arms upon a bamboo frame. The third, as its name indicates, is set in operation by the hand. The fourth is a more complicated machine, worked by the buffalo. The second and fourth were chiefly seen along the course our boats took. In working these, the energies of every household appeared taxed to the utmost vigour, as if each individual felt convinced of the necessity of his personal aid in securing a good and plentiful crop. I saw both old and young leaning on the same frame, treading the same wheel, and humming together their rustic song as they trod. Boys six years of age kept the step very well with men of fifty; and, if too small to mount the wheel, they were placed on the ground to work the paddles with their little hands; and women too, whose tiny or compressed feet disabled them from treading the mill, stood at the feet of the men keeping time with their hands. The wheel turned by the buffalo was more easily managed; but, in this instance too, activity was the order of the day, and, on the principle that he who did not work should not eat, the bulky animal was not suffered a moment's idleness. A man or a woman, a lad or a child, followed him in his routine, goading him on with a pike-staff and starting him into fresh vigour by an occasional shout. Yet, however anxious they might be to keep the docile creature sedulously at labour, his infirmities were not forgotten, and they took care to lighten his toil by suitable feeding, occasional rests, and other precautions, such as blindfolding his eyes to prevent giddiness from the incessant rotations of the engine. Here the division or share of labour was peculiarly marked, in the regularity with which the buffalo was kept in perpetual motion. Fathers, mothers, brothers, and sisters, all aided each other in watching the heavy but steady movements of the ponderous beast, or in leading him to green pastures and still waters.

None were indolent. There was no cessation; nor was there exemption from labour; and, while they fought amongst the thorns and thistles with which the ground had been cursed, and with the sweat of the brow under a blazing sun, sowed, weeded, and watered the earth, no murmurs were heard, save the undulating sound of the husbandman's song as it waved over the field. In our fatherland, as we used to look upon the smiling cottages and cheerful peasants, we fancied the rustic life a happy one; so, while we were sailing towards the lake, what from the homely appearance of the Chinese farm-houses, from the simple ornaments nature had thrown around to conceal their humble and rude appearance, from the warbling notes of the birds of heaven delighting and soothing the heart of the labourer, from the busy activity of the farm-servants, and from their smiling countenances and the bee-like hum which they kept up, we could conjecture that the Chinese peasant too was happy and contented.

After having been tracked about ten miles, with the wind right in our teeth, we struck into a canal that branched off to the southward; and at length heading south-west, we crept through a most fruitful valley, lying at the base of the *Luhshan*, a hill studded with young firs. Several extensive patches of wheat skirted this plain, some still green, the rest ripe for the sickle.

At four o'clock in the afternoon, we reached the borders of the Tung-tseen lake, and anchored at the bottom of a draw-sluice. Looking over the sluice, however, our disappointment was great to find that the sheet of water for which we had sailed, was converted into an extensive green "campo," the water of the lake, in consequence of the long continuance of dry weather, having been drawn off to supply the surrounding fields and canals. The only running stream discernible was a shallow canal running down from the southern head of the lake. At the upper boundary there was an artificial bank, which, from lining that edge of the lake for a mile and a half, is known as "the Five Le [one mile and a half] Bank." At either end of it, there is a beautifully arched bridge, named "the Bamboo Arch Bridge." The upper arch was perceptible from our position at the sluice; and we suspected that the running water in this narrow canal must pass under this opening from a basin further up. Upon ascending a neighbouring height to reconnoitre, our conjectures proved correct, for we discovered a sheet of water extending to the south-west as far as the eye could reach, and numerous boats of various sizes plying on it. On further inquiry, we found that the lake divided itself into two portions, the greater called *Tung hoo*, "the Eastern Lake," and sometimes *Tung-tseen hoo*, "the Eastern Cash Lake," the lesser *Mei hoo*, "The Plumb Lake." We happened to have reached only the latter; and we spent the rest of the day in endeavouring to make our way into the former. But, unfortunately, our boats were too large and bulky to be drawn over the lock or to float in the narrow canal, and there was no boat of smaller size immediately available. The only alternative left was either to scour the margin of the basin and seek for some other suitable conveyance among the numerous hamlets that skirt it, or to keep our own boat and enter some of the openings of the upper lake by a circuitous route. As the day was fast advancing, we chose the former. The walk in the cool of the afternoon occupied us until the shades of night began to cover in the surrounding scenery. But the stroll was very refreshing after the close confinement in our boats during so many sultry hours. We walked through various hamlets and villages, named after the families that are the tenants of the soil, as the "*Ling* family," the "*Woo* family," &c. The civility with which we were received was invariable, and the villagers seemed free from that awful dread which one was distressed to observe in the streets of Ningpo. The women flocked around to see our faces, examine our clothes, and watch our movements. Instead of flying from us as from hurtful beasts, the people escorted us out of their villages and conversed with us in words kind and friendly. The very dogs also seemed to have more civil tempers than their tribe generally. They would come at our call, wagging their tails with confidence and delight. All this formed a contrast to what I had seen in the early part of my stay at Ningpo. I could account for it only on the ground that they were removed from the seat of the late war, and out of reach of the numerous rumours so prejudicial to the interests and character of the English. Our search for a smaller boat having been unsuccessful, we had to return to the larger boats for the night.

Rising early next morning, we crossed a wide marsh,

and made for a singular stone-quarry to the left of the Mei-hoo lake. We reached it a little after sunrise. At the foot of an elevated hill, we passed a group of stone sheds, thrown up for the residence or shelter of the workmen. Winding our way upwards, a number of quarrymen met us, rolling clumsy wheelbarrows. After a fatiguing walk we reached the summit, where we found a large party of labourers at work, excavating, quarrying, and smoothing the stones. The tools were very rough. Powder was occasionally used for blasting, but the operation of detaching the blocks was effected principally by means of wedges. The stone slabs and columns were all cut and hewn out in the quarry. To transport them to the base of the hill there was an inclined plane along the full length of the hill-side; and the rapidity with which the pillars shot down the slope was truly frightful. The workmen treated us with much respect, giving us any information we wanted, and volunteering their services over the different parts of the quarry. In the centre of it there rose a lofty perpendicular rock about 160 feet high, from which we had a fine clear view of the city of Ningpo.

We returned to our boats and got under weigh about twelve o'clock, with a fine breeze,—our object being to take the nearest route to the Upper lake. As we glided along the smooth river, we espied a beautiful temple, peeping out from above a grotto. It was the Se-ting-miaou. Here we landed, and on our way up were met by the neighbours and a few of the priests, who received us with kindness. Christian tracts were readily accepted, and our conversation was untrammelled. The building is modern, only seventeen years old; it is built upon a rock, situate in the heart of a bamboo grove. There was little within the edifice to attract the attention, besides the carved ceilings and the images in process of manufacture. The latter formed a singular group of perfect and half-finished, ornate and unornate figures. Many of these had a shade put over the eyes to blindfold them. On inquiring the reason of this, I was informed that, if the idol should be already occupied by the divinity, the application of the bandage is supposed to exclude it, or to prevent the image being possessed. There is a superstition among the common people that causes them to apprehend the most condign punishment if they should touch, disturb, or anywise molest the image, without such a bandage over the idol's eyes; whereas, with a kind of bandage, they fear nothing. On this account the manufacturers of idols, in making or remodelling the images, generally adopt a precaution like that to save them from molestation in their handicraft. The popular notion is, that only to touch the idol will provoke infinite wrath and instant punishment. When the English, in 1841, landed at Chinhai, the troops, after the bombardment of the town, entered one of the large temples tenanted by many idols, and commenced to lay ruthless hands on the gilded semblances of deity. The Chinese spectators looked on in amazement, and watched in full expectation of seeing dire and fell vengeance inflicted on the rude intruders. They saw one dagon dethroned after another, but the sacrilegious barbarians remained untouched; and the natives retired from the scene exclaiming, "Well, *we fear poosah*, but *poosah* fears the British!"

Leaving the pretty site of the Se-ting temple, we traversed a well-watered plain, occasionally sailing on the canal, and sometimes walking on the banks. The curiosity of the peasantry, labouring in the fields, was intense; at the same time, their conduct was becoming. In no instance were we insulted, and we freely rambled among the fields, throughout escorted by a group of inquisitive and obliging boys. At length we reached the village Muh-che-yen, where we found the lock or sluice that protects the north-east entrance into the Tung-tseen lake. The village itself looked clean, and the people behaved with wonderful decorum. While arrangements were making to hoist our boats over the sluice, we mixed with the curious crowds, and walked about the village and its neighbourhood. The most interesting scene of the hour was the hauling up of the boats. There were two inclined planes upon the dam, extending across the outlet of the lake: one for *upheaving* boats from the canal below to the basin above, and the other for *launching* from the basin above down into the canal below. These planes were laid with fine stone slabs. The upheaving of the barge was effected by a thick rope, which embraced the boat astern, and was at both ends secured to a windlass. The windlasses, clumsy though they were, were set in motion by a number of men hired by the lock-keeper. By working the two windlasses, the one on this and the other on that side of the sluice, the boat was slowly raised to the top, whence it was launched into the basin. During the process, we had to lash every piece of furniture and baggage to prevent damage to our persons and our property; and holding on as tightly as we could, it taxed all our strength and vigilance to secure both from injury. In the launching of boats from the upper lake into the canal beneath, the operation was simply to work the boat round and round, gradually screwing it down the plane into the channel below.

When the final arrangements were completed, we proceeded. The channel, or the track for the passage of boats over the lake, was marked off by young trees being planted in the water to show where there was sufficient depth. Before the shades of evening had gathered round us, we anchored at the west end of the lake, by a village called Ying-kia-wan. Numerous visitors flocked about us; but soon the darkness shut us in. Late at night we called on the venerable headman of the village, aged eighty-seven years; but as early as possible next morning we left this anchorage, and, as our object was to cross the lake, the boat was poled along as the boatmen best could. Extreme difficulty arose from the shallowness of the water, which, in consequence of the prevailing drought, was often only two feet deep; the boat occasionally stuck fast in the mud, so that the boatmen had frequently to jump into the water to shove it off, a task which they performed rather reluctantly. As the lake deepened, we proceeded with more facility. At last a fine breeze sprung up to our assistance; but the boatmen began at once to take in sail, giving utterance to their fears, and pointing to the clouds that lowered in the west. They said a storm was coming on; but it was only a squall; yet the trepidation of these "fresh-water sailors" was great. One of them threw himself on his knees, begged for mercy, with uplifted eyes and hands implored the gods for help, and, on reaching port safely, he "knocked head" as an expression of his gratitude for their protection. On reaching our destination, the Hailing village, we were received by a multitude of spectators, some of whom waded up to their waists, or mounted the trees, to catch a glimpse of the strangers. Captain Kennedy and myself went to the principal temple, where we were entertained with tea, cakes, and sweetmeats, sent by the principal inhabitants, each presenting a separate tray. From this we walked into the village, a closely-packed and busy place. Returning to the boat late in the evening, we ascended a "tea-hill" that overhung the town, and was beautifully planted with the shrub, in terraces rising one above another.

On the following morning we made for the small village of Pihpoo-shan, to the westward of the lake. Our object in visiting this spot was to ascend the Peak of Pihpoo, or "Centipede Peak," which looked like a sharp needle shooting up into the very clouds. The hamlet looked insignificant, but prettily situated. As soon as we landed, the headman of the village obtained us the services of two lads to act as guides. We soon discovered several paths leading to the summit of the mountain. To the right a good road struck off, comfortably shaded by trees; but as it seemed circuitous, and we hoped another might be found nearer the centre of the mountain, we took a middle course, which turned out to be very romantic, though rough and little frequented. The ascent was toilsome. On reaching the summit, we named it "Discovery Peak," being the first Englishmen that had trod that height. The peak was narrow, barren, and rocky, and its sides, here and there, planted with young firs. The prospect from it was extensive and inspiriting. The entire department of Ningpo, with its mountain boundaries, large towns, numerous villages, and well-watered plains, lay at our feet; the distant parts of Chihkiang province invited our view to the north and north-west; while the east and south spread before us a "salt lake," and the sea broken by many a rocky islet.

Before descending, we determined to erect a monument on this peak in commemoration of the feat of the day. We collected heaps of stones, and, by dint of hard work, raised a pile, in the heart of which we lodged a bottle containing a written record of our achievement, with our autographs, dated on "Discovery Peak." Our descent was rapid, and our sail across the lake equally so. From various points we had taken a survey of the lake, and ascertained from native estimates that its circumference was about twenty-two miles. Its greatest depth was said to be only six feet, and the bottom all lined with a bluish clay. It had altogether six outlets, from each of which there was an open and clear water-passage to the city of Ningpo.

There were likewise seventy-two villages which encompassed the lake, all fertile and populous. From the numerous fishing and trading boats we saw plying about, there must be a very important traffic upon the waters of the lake. And we were told that, through its north-east opening and across the lake, a considerable trade is carried on between Ningpo and a village on the "salt lake," to the southward of Hailing.

After Captain Kennedy left me, I passed several days in visiting two renowned temples in the vicinity of Ningpo:—the one *Yuh-wang,* and the other *T'een-tung.* The first lies about seventeen or eighteen miles eastward of the city. The vicinity around the sacred grounds, as well as the site of the temple, offered some pleasing and curious objects. But the edifice itself, with the furniture and contents in general, corresponds so much with the descriptions of Buddhistic temples elsewhere given by me, that it appears needless to enter upon details, further than to remark, *en passant,* that the principal objects of curiosity in Yuh-wang temple were the following:—It is one of the sites chosen for erecting one of the 84,000 pagodas of which the Buddhist king Ayuh* is the reputed founder; hence the name of the building, "The Temple of King Yuh." On the edge of a rock in the grounds, an imprint of Buddha's foot was shown with much solemnity. When pointed out to me, I took the pains to measure it, — seven inches broad at the toes, and five at the heel. It was three inches deep in the rock. In evidence of its being genuine, a priest spat on it, to show how rapidly it would dry up. The spittle of the bonze somehow was too thick for the experiment, for it would not evaporate. In the estimation of priests and people that frequent this temple, nothing excels in sanctity

* This personage was king of Magaddha or Bahar, in Central India, and goes by the names Asoka, Ayeou, Azoke, Mokieto, Wooyuh, and Ayuh. His date is variously put from B.C. 1000 to 282.

and mystery one of the relics of Buddh deposited here,—an old tooth or splinter, that is said to have been discovered on a neighbouring mountain. It was locked up in a tiny wood box fourteen inches high and seven broad at the base. The priest who kept it told me that the casket itself was shown me as a mark of special favour. He informed me of the brilliant colours which the relic inclosed could flash forth to those of good faith and character,—only to such, and that the sort of colour depended on the state of a man's heart. With a show of ceremony I was invited to peer through an orifice in the reliquary. I did so, but saw nothing save what looked like a glass bead; however, it did not deign to shine at me, and the aperture was soon closed.*

My line of march to the sacerdotal halls of T'een-tung was partly by land, partly by water. During the land route, the aspect of the country differed much from that to which I had been accustomed. The ground rose in frequent undulations, and the road was remarkable for its ascents and descents, steep and rough. I passed through several villages, whose inhabitants had never seen "a white-faced foreigner." Yet villagers seemed to vie, not in the expression of their curiosity only, but in kind attentions to the stranger from a far country; and everywhere religious tracts were gratefully received.

When I reached the vicinity of the temple T'een-tung, the scenery was so grand that I dare not attempt to describe it. The site appeared as if it had been designed for some sacred spot. As far as the eye could reach, hill rose after hill, covered with trees of every

* In a paper on "Pagodas in China," introduced under the Fourth Part, I have dwelt at length on the Buddhist Shay-le, and will not here repeat my remarks on what cannot but be regarded as a singular vestige of the early transit of the Buddhist religion from India into the empire of China.

variety; and the temple lay concealed in the bosom of a circle of lofty hills. The avenue that led to the sacred edifice was one mile long, throughout shaded on both sides by a row of tall firs, growing at equidistances. Squirrels and pheasants were abundant. At the upper end of the avenue the temple suddenly burst upon the view, a novel and a noble sight, rising up the side of a hill, flight after flight, room upon room, hall within hall, corridor beyond corridor. But over my surprise there fell the gloom of sorrow, at the thought that I was now treading ground desecrated by idolatry, and occupied by one of the seats of paganism, a "school of prophets" themselves deceived and promoters of a delusion. A kind reception awaited me, and I was invited into "the visitors' room," where were laid out before me refreshments of every kind and quality admissible by the dietetic rules of the Buddhistic religion. The remainder of the day was spent in taking a view of the premises, from the cellars and store-rooms up to their *sanctum sanctorum.*

Although I was the first Englishman that had stepped within their precincts,. or come within their reach, still the priests, whenever they were able to offer explanations and unravel difficulties, did so without scruple and in the most polite and courteous manner. It would be tedious to drag the reader from this lobby into that cloister, and throughout the entire range of buildings; and it would prove equally desultory to detail all the incidents that came under my observation during the short sojourn under the roof of this noted temple.

Early in the afternoon the priests, whose number then did not exceed sixty, were called to their closing repast for the day. Not only is the quality and the quantity of the food regulated by their canon law, but the rules of monastic life, among the priests of Buddha, extend also to the times, courses, and frequency of daily food. Rice and other provisions are doled out with a most vigilant eye to the cooks by a comptroller appointed by the Order to look after the carnal things of the store-room and the kitchen; and it is fixed that at a certain hour the meals must be upon the table. The call for dinner is made by a succession of slow strokes upon a sonorous stone suspended at the door of the dining-hall; and the sound no sooner rang through the labyrinthic corridors than I saw the priests, of all ranks and ages, sally out to satisfy the cravings of hunger. A stanza or two was chanted, all standing up, and the dinner was devoured in solemn taciturnity.

I had heard previously in various quarters, that in this famous temple there were six or seven devotees who knew nothing of the world around them (for they had been so long and were now so completely absorbed in idolatries); also that they appeared always in the posture of devotion, that every man was seated in his own niche in the wall muttering conversation with Buddha, and that they were so much occupied with thoughts of their service that they had neither time nor inclination even to whisper a word or glance a look at a bystander. On approaching the hermitage, its few inmates were found engaged in their recitations. They looked filthy in their habits, and were far from prepossessing in their manners; but there was nothing approaching that external form of sanctity which I had been led to understand they assumed. The religious exercises on the occasion were marked with hurry, indifference, and levity; and no sooner over, than they approached me to handle my person and raiment. One of them, according to a practice frequent amongst them, had exscinded some of his fingers in order to fulfil a vow which he had made to his patron idol.

Comfortable apartments were provided for me for the night. At my request I was aroused at three in the morning to attend the early matins of the priesthood.

The "thunder-drum" and the "sounding-bell" both announced the call to prayers. The principal hall for worship was the most capacious and magnificent of the kind I had seen. The Buddhistic Triad stood in the centre, surrounded by the ordinary satellites, numerous demigods and genii. Before the centre altar-piece the priests stood in several rows of eight and ten, their flowing robes of grey adding to their sanctimonious cast. For a long time they remained motionless, slightly stooping and, with clasped hands and downcast eyes, humming a slow chant in low and measured tones. Time was kept by three priests, one beating a huge drum, another a brass vessel, and the third a large wooden ball in the shape of a skull. Each one had a mat before him, on which he bent the knee and knocked head before the massive image of Buddh. They repeatedly knelt, rose, faced each other, chanted, &c., the whole service lasting a full hour. The ringing of bells, the frequent bowing, the slow chanting, the smoke of incense, the use of the rosary, the shaven head, and the general garb of the priesthood that morning, struck me as bearing an unmistakable similitude to the ceremonies and paraphernalia of Popery.

At the conclusion of the service I was invited to breakfast with some of the priests; and shortly after re-embarked for Ningpo. Among some mournful reflections on "the idolatry in high places" which I witnessed at the two remarkable temples described above, one anticipation, suggested by the "sure word of prophecy," kindled up the bright hope that, when the glorious Gospel shall run its free course, these halls of superstition shall be consecrated to the service of the Divine Saviour, and shall be converted into colleges for Christian ministers and evangelists, who shall run to and fro as ambassadors for Christ.

* * * * * *

Before leaving Ningpo for another part of China, it

may not be out of place to add a short paragraph on the progress of foreign intercourse since the opening of this port under the Nanking treaty of 1842. So early as 1552, the Portuguese had set on foot commercial relations at the city of Ningpo; and to the present day a visitor on the spot may, by using his wits, find out "The Good Strangers' Club-house," a building situate near Bridge-gate, that was erected in 1528 for the accommodation of foreign traders. In the beginning of 1700, and subsequently too, the English attempted to open trade at the same place, but failed. This was attributable, in a measure, to the contempt and dislike of foreigners that had been engendered by the violence and rapacity of the Portuguese, who had been driven off the ground in less than a quarter of a century after establishing their factory. At the close of 1843 (four or five months after I quitted the place), with a view to carry out the negotiations of 1842, the British consulate was established at Ningpo under the able conduct of the late Mr. Thom, whose praise still lives among the Chinese, and whose name is known to many foreigners acquainted with his self-denying devotedness to the interests of that people. As Ningpo holds a prominent place among the cities on the coast,—as its traders are distinguished for skill and enterprise,—as its citizens are remarkable for general talent and industry,—and as the relations of the city with the interior of the country are of no mean importance, it was presumed that its port would be a point of attraction to foreign merchants. But this hope has not been realized. Although the distance to cities like Hangchow and Shauhing, &c., where trade and commerce are carried on to an amazing extent, is but short; the difficulty and delay *en route* to those places, occasioned by canals, locks, and fords, raise great obstacles to a free and easy traffic. This will account for the disappointment of expectations at first encouraged about Ningpo as being a first-rate port for foreign vessels. Occasionally a ship of foreign burthen visits it; yet the trade, if it is growing, is but tardy. By the *Hong-Kong Gazette* of March, 1856, the trade of Ningpo seems to continue very unimportant. The import trade for 1855 in British vessels is estimated at 231,618 dollars, and the exports at 398,328 dollars; the principal import being *sugar*, 79,454 dollars, and the principal export *rice*, 205,409 dollars; the whole consisting chiefly of coasting and Straits trade. Since 1850 the French, Americans, and Portuguese have nominated petty consuls at the port; but mercantile transactions here under a foreign flag are of no consequence to be detailed. As must have been already gathered from the preceding, Protestant missionaries were the first to secure a footing at Ningpo upon the ratification of the Nanking treaty. Soon after I left the city, two or three American missionary societies moved towards this promising field, and have ever since occupied it with honour and encouragement. The Church Missionary Society is the only English body of Christians that has laboured for any length of time there. In 1855 the Chinese Evangelization Society commenced its mission with a prospect of success, and bids fair to prosper at the place, if conducted with a due share of sagacity. By the most recent statistics of Protestant missions in China, there were in 1856 seventeen distinct missionary families in the following distribution:—Church Missionary Society, three; Chinese Evangelization Society, three; American Presbyterian Board, seven; American Baptists, four. Besides these, special and well-merited attention must be called to the devoted efforts of an English lady, Miss Aldersey, who, ever since an opening occurred at Ningpo, has been on the spot, consecrating her remarkable energy, as well as life and property, to the education and Christianizing of the women of Ningpo. By her zeal and devotion a large boarding-school of nearly fifty girls has been conducted for the last eight years. In this singular line of effort, in spite of numerous difficulties which she had to cope with almost single-handed, Miss Aldersey has proved remarkably successful. She has been instrumental in educating many female minds in useful principles. She has been blessed in converting some tender hearts to the reception of Gospel truth. She has succeeded in training up others, who, by their influence and instruction, will extend "truth and life" through many generations yet unborn. From what I know personally of the character, devotedness, and labours of this exemplary lady, no one more ardently wishes than myself that her objects should receive ample support from the sympathy of Christian ladies in Great Britain. Although, for prudential reasons, Miss A. has recently seen fit to place her school under the care of another English lady, her purpose still is to spend her remaining days in watching over its interests.

PART THIRD.

A GLANCE AT LIFE IN THE INTERIOR OF CHINA.

CHAPTER I.

NARRATIVE OF TRIP FROM NINGPO TO PIH-KWAN—FROM PIH-KWAN TO E-KIAOU.

THE preparations for an inland excursion having been completed by the 7th of July, 1843, it was arranged to embark at nine o'clock the same night.

The boat selected was a *pih-kwan* barge,* much like our coal-lighters, and one of a craft in general request for lightness and stowage. I chose as guide Woo, in whose fidelity I had sufficient reason for reliance as well as his acquaintance with the line of route to be followed. And besides, so far adopting a legitimate means of avoiding detection, I likewise took with me two lads, who had been for some time in my service and were intrusted with my secret.

After a late dinner, a hairdresser was called in, who shaved the fore part of the head and appended a queue one yard in length. Having undergone this operation, I exchanged my English suit for a Chinese summer dishabille. Previous to quitting my lodgings, the thought struck me that possibly the "tail" on which so much depended might be too loosely tied on. A slight tug proved the suggestion to be well-timed, for

* It derives its name from the village at the close of the first stage.

that appendage at once dropped off. When recalled, the barber was greatly disconcerted to find that his labour had been in vain. So, resuming his manipulations with more than redoubled diligence, he paid little heed to the pain inflicted on retacking it.

After this first trial of an adventurer's nerves, I left my lodging in company with my fellow-travellers, passed the porter's lodge at the east gate unobserved, walked through part of the suburbs under a bright moonlight, and, on reaching the eastern angle of the city wall, dropped into my boat to rest for the night.

At five o'clock next morning, we took the rising tide to enter the Tszeke river, running up to the north-west. We soon found ourselves in company with a large fleet of small boats, all ascending the stream with fair wind and tide. At one time I counted forty-seven of these native boats, most of them, as our own, called *pih-kwan* barges, manned by three men at least, and laden with cargo or passengers for Hangchow, the capital of the province (127 miles distant from Ningpo), or for the intermediate towns Tszeke, Yuyaou, and Shaouhing.

During this day's route, the first place of note was Kaoukiaou, a bridge five miles out of Ningpo, chiefly memorable for a repulse the Tartar hordes met with in A.D. 1130, from a band of native villagers headed by a hero of the name of Changtsiun. In the middle of the sixteenth century the Japanese appeared off this place, and committed great ravages in the vicinity.

A fine breeze brought us abreast of the Ta-ying-shan, a hill beautifully ornamented by nature with large shady trees, and decorated by art with family temples on its summit, family tombs on its slopes, and family residences at his base. Even here, "many a tale traditionary, and many a legend, peoples the dark woods." In olden times, amid the deep recesses of a retreat so peculiarly adapted to abstruse meditation, there resided a rustic poet and philosopher, Dr. Siay, who, being likewise far-famed for his skill in the art of Æsculapius, used in this lonely recess to make up his pharmaceutical preparations of a certain medicine that proved a universal antidote to old age and decay, sickness and death. Again, it is related that *Yu-he*, a man of note of the fourth century, took refuge in these blissful solitudes for the purpose of "communing with nature, at a distance from the low pursuits and the selfish malignity of ordinary mortals," and, although three times summoned by the reigning monarch to receive high honours, he preferred the romantic seclusion and primeval simplicity of his sombre hermitage to the pomp, glitter, and gaiety of an imperial court. No wonder the name given to the spot, "The hill of profound retirement!"

Five or six miles farther up we came to the ferry which derives its name from the hill on the right bank, about four miles to the south, called "the Chay-kew," or "Chariot-and-stable" hill, from the circumstance that Kaou-tseen, a martial chief of the Yueh state (which before the Christian era claimed all this territory), kept his cavalry there. The vestiges of those days may still be traced among the ruins that lie about the mountain. At the beginning of the Ming dynasty an aspirant to the throne started up, named Fang-kwoh-chin. Desirous of emulating the prince who had figured upon the hill 1,500 years before, he encamped on the same spot to guard and defend this part of the empire; but a general vested with an imperial commission outwitted the usurper by coming upon him at night and driving him from his fortress. As the tide failed us, we dropped anchor, and lay for four hours off this ferry. With the return of tide we moved up to Changting, a spot that appears to be selected by the rich gentry for the erection of some fine residences. As if to set these off by contrast, there stood a little farther on, on the same bank of the river, a large pottery, and numerous wretched straw huts tenanted by potters.

Before quitting this anchorage I must take notice of the Sze-ming-shan, a mountainous chain of the most irregular outline, which all day had been in full view. It lies eighteen miles to S.W. of Ningpo. Looking on it at this point, it presents to the eye of the traveller (as a native writer observes), "a distant and extended vista, marked with deep recesses and umbrageous shades. Massive rocks are seen to rise pile upon pile; castled promontories and lofty precipices start up before you: here, there meet you dark ravines and gaping chasms, and yonder you espy ample solitudes of unploughed and untrodden valleys." As you stand at different points of view, the range throws off various fantastic shapes, (again quoting a native work,) "to the east, frightful waves; to the west, scampering cattle; to the north, wriggling dragons; and to the south, driven goats." The natives say that a walk from its base to the highest summit measures 130,000 feet (between thirty and forty miles); and if you follow the range at its foot through all its windings, bendings, and twists, it measures 800 les, or 240 English miles. In its course it embraces territory belonging to the districts of Ningpo, Funghwa, Tszeke, Yuyaou, Shangyu, and Ninghai; and, if reliance may be placed on the same testimony for geological information, the vein of the whole bed may be traced fifty miles to the southwest as far as the T'ientai mountains. The Sze-ming-shan rank, in the Taouist books, as ninth in order of the thirty-six lofty mountains of China; and, on account of the bold fastnesses, bluff crags, and beetling cliffs which climb among the clouds,

"Those mighty hills, so shadowy, so sublime,"

are believed by the people to have been planted by

Heaven as "a guardian fortress" on the frontiers of Ningpo (which district, in native writings and official papers, is also called Szeming), to keep down calamity and pestilence. The rugged, rocky, and lonely recesses with which this mountain-range abounds, are said to be so unlike to the inhabitable parts of the earth as to be fit only for the residence of elves and fairies. The natives number no less than 280 peaks upon the chain, and give a name to each. The most remarkable of them is a clump of five, called by some the Wooyung, by others the Lienhwa, as their peculiar fancy may help them to trace a resemblance to the one or the other flower. These five stand apart at a distance of a mile and a half. On the middle one there is said to be a large square rock, marked with four perforations, like the windows of a house, from each of which you have a full and clear view of the sun, moon, and stars. Hence the name of the whole range, Sze-ming, that is, "four clear" openings; and upon this

> "Pile of simplest masonry,
> With narrow windows and vast buttresses,
> Built to endure the shocks of time and chance,"

are engraved in large text the four characters—

Sze-ming-shan-sin,

"The heart (or centre) of the Sze-ming mountains."

But, to return to my boat,—I found it, as I left it, at Changting, where the river changes its name, and onwards to its source is sometimes called the Yaou, and sometimes the Shun river, after the two patriarchal worthies bearing those names,—although generally known as the Yuyaou river, because, in the greater part of its course, it flows through the district of that designation. Having alluded to two of the fathers of the Chinese nation, I may observe that there are several other parts of the neighbouring country consecrated to the memory of the great Shun. On the Leihshan, not far from Yuyaou, he is said to have ploughed his fields with an elephant. His well is there too; and also his "stony bed," respecting which Chinese tradition has it, "he took of the stones of the place and put them for his bed, and lay down in that place to sleep."

Half an hour after leaving Changting, we entered the Yuyaou district,* by crossing the boundary-line between the departments of Ningpo and Shaouhing at Shuh-shan-too, twenty-three miles from the former city. As the river narrows much in this vicinity, the *loochuh* papyrus, that grows very rank on both sides of the river, was brought close under the eye. It measures from twelve to twenty feet long, and is turned to many accounts by the poorer natives. The root is used as a sweet, juicy cooling edible. The long waving leaf is particularly in request as a wrapper of small rice dumplings. The reed is useful for sails and awnings for boats, thatchings of roofs, partitions of rooms, floor-matting, and window-screens; and the root, the reed, and the leaf, when dried, are made use of by the lower orders for fuel. Sunset succeeding rapidly, we were quite shut in from everything far and near. This was followed by a tremendous thunderstorm, which drove us to the bank for shelter among its rushes, and there we anchored until midnight.

At two o'clock on the morning of the 9th, a sweeping tide carried us through Yuyaou, the capital of the district, and a town of some importance, occupying both sides of the river,—the site of the old town stand-

* This route was that taken by Captain McIntosh and a part of Lord Macartney's suite, when they separated from the embassy at Hangchow to go to Chusan, where the East-India Company's ship *Hindostan* was taking in cargo. It is the same also by which Père Le Comte and his company proceeded in the winter of 1687 from Ningpo, on their journey to Peking, to which they were ordered to repair by the Chinese sovereign.

ing on the north, that of the new on the south bank. It was by moonlight alone I was able to discern anything; and the only object at all seen to advantage was the bridge of three arches, which crosses the river about the centre of the town. It lies thirty paces from the south gate. Its entire length is given at 24 chang, or 240 English feet. The name, Hwuykiang, by which the river is designated at this part, is supposed to be derived from the *hwuy* tulip, which used to grow in profusion to the west of the bridge. The bridge itself is commonly called "the river bridge," though the inscription on it reads *Tung-tse-kiaou,* "the bridge of general thoroughfare." It is nearly 300 years old. Previous to its erection, the Japanese, during their invasion, received a terrible check at this point, and two years after, A.D. 1556, these three arches were thrown across to connect the old and new towns together, as a protective measure against future aggressions. In the year 1841, during the war with China, her Majesty's steamers *Nemesis* and *Phlegethon* moved up the river as far as this without hindrance or opposition.

By daybreak we had left the river, and pushed on to the Western Hwang-ho-pa, a very high dam, over which boats bound for Shaouhing or Hangchow have to be hoisted. This piece of workmanship is constructed of massive stones, in the form of a double glacis, perhaps with an inclination of forty-five degrees, and so built as to have two slopes, one on each side, uniting at the top in an acute angle, on which there is a crossbeam laid, or a rounded off piece of wood. The object of such engineering is to expedite the passage of boats between two canals which cannot form a junction, as their waters differ from seven to fourteen feet in their level. One cannot but observe with some astonishment the patience and perseverance of the Chinese in quietly submitting to public nuisances of this sort. It is no less surprising, too, that there are not more risks to life and property from such a contrivance. Although their keels are said to be made of the hardest and toughest material, yet the bottoms and sides of the boats must be severely chafed in being raised up these stony slopes. And as the boat rises to the summit of the triangular bank, where it is made to balance upon the sharp, narrow ridge, one naturally wonders that the barge does not split into halves. This is peculiarly awkward and hazardous for boats laden with cargo, so much so that not unfrequently they have to be emptied of their freight before they can be hauled up. Besides, there are other inconveniences arising from these clumsy barricades across an inland route, which will sufficiently appear from the following account of our day's sail to Pih-kwan, a distance of forty miles from Yuyaou.

As I have already said, we had by daybreak reached the *Hwangho* lock, if I may so designate it. Just outside of it, and at its foot, we found twenty boats already anchored, all lying in a watercouse wide enough for only two or three at a time. These boats had come in during the night, and were in waiting for the morning impressment of coolies to heave them up. As their boatmen had fallen asleep, ours managed to push their boat right to the bottom of the lock, where it took up its berth, snugly enough to be sure, first and foremost among the boats. But scarcely had the sun stepped over the horizon, when our position was discovered,—our presumption as interlopers was loudly denounced,—a war of words ensued, and then a trial of strength. The other boatmen united in a body to seize our craft and transfer it to the rear, which was soon and easily done. My guide; Woo, had gone ashore to purchase provisions for the day; but, on returning to the boat, great was his mortification at finding that it had been pushed back and behind those boats that had come in later than ourselves. Thereupon he called on our men to force their way up to their early station, hurling defiance at the crowd of stormy boatmen. The consequence was that bamboo poles and boat-hooks were instantly levelled at Woo, and prostrate he fell into the hold. On this, it was impossible for me longer to remain in seclusion, and out I burst from my cabin to his rescue. Finding they had silenced Woo's insolence, the victors walked off shouting "What! suppose a foreigner were in that boat, we would not care a fig for him!" So "here could I sit alone, unseen of any." After a detention of two or three hours, it fell to our turn to have the boat hauled up, by a process almost similar to what has already been described in a former part.* For this purpose a stout halser was laid round her stern. Each end of it was lashed to a rude capstan that stood on either side of the sluice. The two windlasses were worked by twenty or thirty coolies, who put arms and shoulders to work, all the while roaring and bellowing as if they were under the cat. This was to haul us up the slope on the one side. As they were heaving us up this inclined plane, every hand inside the boat had to hold on, to keep persons and baggage from going adrift. After half an hour of tugging and screaming, our barge reached the top of the embankment, from which by its own gravity it was launched down the second slope into the stream on the other side. Here, too, they attempted to lay on us what was considered a heavy impost, and created no little jarring. We got off, however, with the usual charge of what to an English ear does not sound too large—twelve cash, nearly two farthings, for "despatch boats,"—the levy on cargo boats and passenger craft being usually 170 cash, or almost sixpence.

At length, about 10 A.M., we began to move on from that bar, congratulating ourselves that we had not been

* At page 205.

detained two or three days, as many boats are during the busiest terms. Fear of long detention, and anxiety to avoid detection, had shut me up in my cabin during the last few hours; but when we had got fairly upon the upper canal, breathing-time was gained for looking round on the fine landscape that stretched out to the right and left. The waters that run across to the foot of this sluice mostly come from the Maou-shan lagoon, a mile and a half distant. Blue hills skirted our view, while the plain on this side was beautifully carpeted with young rice-sprouts. Men were at work in the fields; romping children sporting in the water; and women everywhere busy at something or other, most of them with the foot unbound and of the natural size. Among other novelties, there frequently passed before me the *Kioh-wa chuen*, "foot-oared boat,"—a sort of light canoe, on the stern of which the boatman sits working the paddles with his feet instead of his hands.

Three miles further on we come to Changpa, a second dyke, lower than the first and attended also with many difficulties. Men's shoulders alone were called into requisition here in elevating the boat. There was no windlass in use. But, to meet the case, first of all the boat was lightened by moving on shore the chattels and the boat-gear; and then the boat itself was actually shoved up by the united force of hands, arms, and shoulders,—along with the invariable accompaniments of braying and howling. Quiet once more restored, I caught sight of a variety in the fashions of the fair sex of this neighbourhood, especially their head-dress. At Ningpo they have what they call "the Ningpo helmet;" here, however, the Shaouhing fashion obtains, or the "*yuan-paou* form," from its resemblance to the figure of the bar of Sycee silver.*

* There are other varieties of style in which the ladies put up the hair of their heads,—each fashion prevalent in peculiar localities

A wide channel brought us to Yih-ting, beyond which the canal lessens in width and depth. Here, however, a third bar awaited to intercept, detain, and annoy us. It must occur to every one, in the course of his travels through this part of the country, that, not improbably, one reason why Ningpo offers so little encouragement to foreign trade is that the native merchant meets with so many inconveniences *en route* to and from the interior. He is so often and so long locked up or locked out by these canal dykes; and at every other interval, barriers of the same sort are thrown up and impediments meet him such as are unknown at Shanghai or Canton. But, should one remove those dams, or break down the sluices, and open a direct line of communication between the Ningpo river and Pihkwan or Shaouhing, there can be little question as to the prospect of a successful trade with a city like Ningpo, which holds daily intercourse with Hangchow, the great capital of a vast province, as well as with all the other inland and central provinces of the empire.

After we had submitted to the usual amount of delay and pother, they managed to get our boat across the barrier at Yih-ting on to a wide stream running six miles direct to Pihkwan. Hereabouts, and in several other parts, there were noticed those fluvial lagoons which are frequently found in China on the borders of rivers and canals, where the land in the vicinity, being lower than the bank, becomes inundated by the overflowing of the river-beds, or where, there being no drainage or outlet, the rains collect and form great stagnant pools. These reservoirs, however detrimental in general to the health of the natives, are of immense service in time of drought, especially for purposes of irrigation.

The women of Canton province adopt a style different from the Chihkiang ladies. There is another called the "Kwanyin helmet," &c.

As I sat at the window of my boat looking out on the country around, some passers-by, pointing at me, expressed their admiration of "the snowy whiteness of that man's face;" yet they offered no interruption, nor did they behave rudely,—imagining, I suppose, that I was a visitor from the northern parts of the empire returning homewards.

However, the test of my Chinese disguise awaited me at Pihkwan, which we reached at 3 P.M. My traps were landed first, and then I set about attiring myself in the cabin in the summer costume of the country,—a broad-brimmed straw hat, a grass-cloth jacket, calico trowsers, bran-new sash, gay blue garters, light straw shoes, a fan in one hand, and umbrella in the other, and a rough handkerchief up the sleeve. Thus accoutred I landed. But I had scarcely set my foot on the bank when a voice near me shouted out in the *patois* of the place, "Hie-ya! here's an Englishman!" Out there started a score from the boats in the anchorage, looking here, there, and everywhere for the intruder. Fortunately I had presence of mind to take no notice of them, and set to work arranging my baggage and giving orders to servants and coolies,—seeing which, they all threw themselves down into their boats, saying, "Although his face is whiter than ours, he's no Englishman." This was trial the first at Pihkwan.

I sent my luggage on before to the inn at the other end of the village, where travellers generally put up to make arrangements for prosecuting their journey. I myself leisurely followed my guide through the village, which was about three quarters of a mile in extent; but, in doing so, I had some difficulty in steering clear of the villagers, many of whom sat at their doors fanning themselves after their day's toil. Although in gait and swagger I acted the Chinaman pretty well, at least as well as I could, yet many an eye was cast at me as if I seemed some odd specimen of a native-born, and not unfrequently I had to offer a laconic apology for awkwardly jolting against a foot-passenger, which he received with remarkable courtesy.

That (I may call it my second) trial at Pihkwan, ended on my walking into the Wang-maou-chay inn, where my servants were waiting for me. I myself was ushered into an inner room, and Woo stepped aside into the office to make arrangements for a passage to Shaouhing. The innkeeper offered a seat, tea, and pipes, &c. There were several other travellers in the same apartment, some lying asleep on the lockers; while outside the din was stunning,—what with passengers coming to and fro, the landlord shouting and waiters repeating his orders, and a crowd of idlers sauntering about brawling or laughing. How thankful did I feel to be able to take refuge in a quiet back room! For the last half-hour I had been somewhat an object of curiosity, and I knew not but suspicion had been created;—perhaps detection by spies might follow, then detention by the police, and possibly desertion by my servants. With my mind full of surmises and apprehensions like these, I seated myself under the open window of the traveller's room, hoping that I might, by a short rest and a little quiet, recover from the excitement into which I had been thrown on landing. On entering the room, I kept my straw hat on my head, and, in case any one might again indulge suspicions about me, I also drew my queue over my right shoulder, as a precautionary measure,—the advantage of which will presently appear. I had not taken my seat many minutes when a fellow walked in (I presume) from the police-station right in front of the booking-office. The intruder looked sternly at me, and in an under-tone asked one of them in waiting, "Who is that there?" The man replied, "I really don't know. He has just come from Ningpo, and must be a merchant bound for the interior." The boor then came up, and, placing himself before me, demanded, "Take off that hat of yours." I made no reply. He repeated his demand. I could no longer keep silence and answered, "Don't you see, my friend, that I am very warm; and, as there is a draught over-head, I cannot take it off till I am a little cooler? If you will, however, quietly sit down and bide my pleasure, I shall take it off by-and-by." I was a little disconcerted at his instantly squatting on the opposite bench. Next, he commenced to catechize me on the following points:—"What's your surname? name? Where do you come from? What are you about here? Where are you going to?" These questions he couched in rude and uncivil language. Perceiving this, I mustered the usual polite style adopted by his countrymen in their intercourse with strangers, and taking courage (for I felt sure of vanquishing him by politeness and etiquette), I replied to his successive queries in the following manner. "My vulgar surname is ——" (giving the surname I had adopted for my travels). "My trifling name is ——. The low and humble place from which I have come is ——," &c. When he had exhausted his stock of interrogatories and found that I could give him such pat replies, he evidently began to feel rather uncomfortable at having intruded himself. Detecting the advantage I had already gained over my unpolite inquisitor, and, as according to custom it was my turn now to interrogate, I commenced in the complimentary phraseology of the country:—"And pray, sir, what may be your excellent surname? honourable name? famous native place?" &c.; to all which the fellow gave replies in a tone somewhat subdued and in language more humble. He looked uneasy, and as I eyed him fixedly he grew very sheepish. I had observed that, from the time of his entering, he watched my "tail" with a deal of earnestness; and, probably, suspecting it to be false or only for an occasion tacked on to my straw hat, he had, with a view of proving its genuineness, required me to take off the hat. Having promised to comply with his wish when I felt cooler, and now perceiving that the opportunity of confounding him had come, I gently raised the straw bonnet without saying a word, and with a handkerchief wiped the perspiration off my forehead. But the tail over my right shoulder did not move! "Paul Pry" saw this and felt outwitted. So he rose from his chair, bowed humbly, walked off, and no more appeared. Thus much for my third trial in this village.

In half an hour after reaching the inn, preparations were completed for crossing the Tsaou-ngo river, and we moved down to the ferry. Two or three men and women rushed to the water's edge to stare at the new-comer, of whom it was pretty clear whispers of a dubious character had gone abroad. As, however, the ferrymen themselves had no suspicions of the sort, they could not wait long enough to satisfy the curiosity of the handful of idlers on the banks, and in a few minutes we were out of reach and safe on the opposite side, where I must stand a while with my readers to say a few words about the river.

The small establishment at the ferry being set on foot and supported by the gentry and merchants of the Ningpo and Shaouhing departments, the passage across is free, and no impost whatever is permitted,—a thing which my cicerone assured me, with all possible gravity, was not looked upon in his country "as disgraceful or undignified." By this means, communication between the two departments is greatly expedited, and passengers and goods of every variety are carried over. In the eye of the government and of the people, this place is considered a point of some importance, as is evident from the means adopted by the latter to render the passage across as open and easy as possible, and from the names that, at different periods, have been given to it by the former. During the Yuen dynasty, early in the fourteenth century, it was made the Pihkwan-yih, "the postal town of 100 officers." In the beginning of the succeeding Ming dynasty, its name was slightly varied to Tsaou-ngo-yih, "the governmental stage on the banks of the Tsaou-ngo river." At present it is commonly known as Pihkwan-too, "the passage for 100 officers," indicating it as the place across which and from which all official communications are carried to and fro between the capital and the northern and eastern parts of the Chihkiang province.

The river is sometimes spoken of as the Shang-yu river, though it bears that name only as far as it skirts the western limits of the Shangyu district. Even there, however, its popular name is "the Tsaou-ngo." It itself is but one of the branches of the Poo-yang, whose principal source lies in the Kinhwa department, 150 miles to the south-west. The original branch goes under that name for 100 miles, till it reaches the north-west of the Shaouhing county. There it divides into two streams, the one the Tseentsing-kiang, emptying itself into the great estuary at Hangchow: the other stream turns to the north-east of Shaouhing, and takes a serpentine course from north-east to north, in its circuit both watering and draining the two districts Ching and Shangyu. In the latter district it makes a north-west bend, and, about twenty miles from where we now stand, disembogues into the Yellow Sea. From the angle where it leaves the principal artery, the Pooyang river, it is variously named; in the upper parts of the stream called "the Siaou-shun," or "the Tung-siaou," and in the lower "the Shang-yu," or "the Tsaou-ngo."

The name Tsaou-ngo is founded on the following story, the truth of which is universally credited by the people, and its particulars have been minutely put on record in one of their topographical works. In the second year of Ngan-te, of the Han family, A.D. 109, there lived a priest of the Taouist religion, a native of the Shang-yu district, who had won great repute for his skill in magic. On the fifth day of the fifth moon of that year, at the festival known to foreigners as "the feast of the dragon boats," this priest went to sport in the river in honour of his gods (still a custom prevalent throughout some parts of the empire), by swimming against the tide, or playing somersaults in the stream, or racing the dragon boats. Whether in swimming or rowing up the river it is not accurately known, but the priest was drowned, and his body nowhere could be found. His dutiful daughter,* Tsaou-ngo, a girl fourteen years of age, felt her sudden bereavement deeply, and wandered along the banks of the river for seventeen days and nights, weeping and wailing over her loss. At last she threw a large melon into the river, putting up the prayer, "May this melon sink wherever the body of my father lieth!" With a most anxious eye she watched the gourd as it floated on the surface of the stream, until it stopped at a certain spot, where it sank. The poor damsel, frantic with grief, rushed to the place and plunged after it. She too perished. But five days afterwards her lifeless trunk rose to the surface, with her father's body in her embrace. Both were buried on the river bank; and, in commemoration of the incident, the name of the girl has been given to the river, and a temple has been erected also to her name.

* Her father was not a priest in full orders. In the Taouist sect there are two orders,—the one bound to perpetual celibacy, the other not. The latter, being looked upon as mere assistants and not as ordained to the work, reside in their own dwellings, and dress in the ordinary style of the country. Of course they are debarred the use of the canonical cap, head-dress, and gown, &c. They are called the *Ho-keu-taou*; but those in full orders are styled the *Taou-sze*, reside in their temples and monasteries, and are entitled to the mitre and gaudy attire of the class.

But having lingered long enough on the banks of this river, we must again set our faces westward to prosecute the rest of this day's journey. On the foot-road, two miles in length, I met with numerous travellers, going and coming, some on foot like myself, others in sedans. The luggage was carried either on men's shoulders or in one-wheeled barrows. About six o'clock, a little before sunset, I reached the *Pih-sha* hamlet, where, at the *Taoukiun-chung* inn, my bearers had already lodged my traps. At this place I met with another half-hour's detention, till the boat (that had been engaged at Pihkwan to take me sixty miles inland, as far as E-kiaou) should be got ready. It was evident, from their side-whispers and sharp glances, that I was an object of curiosity to the occupants of this little village too. Most probably the rumour of suspicion had travelled across with me. And although I sat quietly in the tea-shop, with a cup of plain tea and a plate of ripe fruit and sponge-cake before me, smoking my long pipe, and talking to my servants at my side, yet, after what had happened at Pihkwan, I felt not quite comfortable, for I knew not but I might have to undergo a fourth examination, and, as it was rather late in the afternoon, I could not wear the straw hat any longer. Well, so it was. A little while after, when my boat had been put in order and I had got into the cabin, two respectable-looking men walked to the door and peeped in. I rose, and accosted them in a friendly manner. They at once dropped their arms by their side, as foreign soldiers in obedience to the word "attention," or Chinese servants in the presence of their *taoutai* receiving orders. Then, with due politeness, I inquired about their names, residences, occupations, and the object of their visiting me, to all which they gave replies in a style totally different from that with which I had been entertained an hour or two previously. These gentlemen returned my civility by inquiring about my "honourable surname, lofty residence," &c. As they continued to loiter about, I invited them to enter and sit down with me. They said they really could not think of such a thing, and withdrew one step from the cabin-door. Again I requested them to come in and take a cup of tea. "Oh, we cannot hear of this," said they, and retreated two more steps. It appeared that politeness alone could drive my friends away, so I advanced towards them, and asked if they could not just for a moment or two seat themselves "in my worthless berth." Even this they humbly declined, and, wishing me a "favourable breeze," they respectfully bowed and disappeared. So ended the four trying encounters of the day.

At seven o'clock in the evening we were under weigh. The boat I found in every respect an improvement on the clumsy barge which I had left in the afternoon, and in which I had been couped up for the first thirty-six hours. The new boat was of the class peculiar to the city of Shaouhing, much used by the merchants in their journeys by water. Its name, *woo-pung*, "dark-awning boat," is derived from its cover of bamboo being painted black. It was calculated by the boatmen that this class could carry as much as eighteen tons of goods besides passengers. The accommodations were really good. Three cabins were at my service, which I disposed of by reserving the front one for myself, and giving up the middle one to my teacher, and the one abaft to the servants. All the luggage was stowed away in the hold, so as to be got at when required.

A cool breeze having sprung up, we very quietly moved down the Shaouhing river. While we were passing several villages I witnessed a pleasant sight, (by no means uncommon, and the like of which one has the opportunity of seeing every now and then in China,) villagers, with their wives and children, all seated together under a wide-spreading tree, taking their supper upon the river-bank. A great number of boats, some very large indeed, were plying up and down,—most of them laden with goods, and bound for the "Tung-kwan," a custom-house about five miles from Pihsha, our starting-point. At ten P.M., under moonlight, we reached that "Eastern Barrier," and there anchored for the night.

On July 10th, very early, the boat got under weigh, and hurrying past various unimportant places mentioned in a native itinerary I had with me, brought us at 8 A.M. to Shaouhing, in N. lat. 30° 6′, E. long. 120° 29′.

Nearly 2,000 years ago, the capital of the Yueh state stood here, which, during its most flourishing era, comprised all the territory now included between the Canton and Kiangnan provinces. At present this is the chief city of a department extending E. to W. 90 miles, N. to S. 130, embracing within its limits and jurisdiction the eight districts, Shan-yin, Kwai-ke, Siaou-shan, Yu-yaou, Shang-yu, Ching, Choo-ke, and Sin-chang. The city itself lies 40 miles east of Hang-chow, 12 south of the sea-coast, and 87 west of Ningpo. Du Halde says "that it is situated in one of the most beautiful plains in the world; there are canals in every street, and no city so much resembles Venice as this, though it is vastly preferable to that, because the canals are filled with very clear running water." I must scruple to assent to the former of these statements, as it is exaggerated; and, although I have never visited Venice, yet, from what I have seen of Shaouhing and heard of Venice, I cannot believe the latter.

Pursuing a south-west course, we crept along the bank of the river, with the city and suburbs on our left. At the north gate there was witnessed a lively scene of civil citizens passing to and fro, and

> "Poor mechanic porters crowding in
> Their heavy burdens at the narrow gate."

Upon the river too all was life and bustle. Boats of every description were afloat,—some of them measuring forty, fifty, and seventy feet in length, chiefly used for cargo. It seemed to be quite a high day among the river-craft. Gay streamers were flying over dragon-boats and pleasure-barges, and a gorgeous procession passed through the fleet in celebration of the birthday of their god Kwan-te. Immense crowds of spectators were out upon the banks and on the river,—men, women, and children mingling together to witness the idolatrous spectacle.

As, however, time and tide wait for no man, I could not linger long to gaze on the scene. Proceeding onwards, the city walls still kept in view. Upon inquiry, I found these were reputed among the natives to measure (forty-five les) nearly thirteen English miles, though certainly they did not look more than four or five, in circuit. They measure 17½ ft. high, 15 broad along the top, 27 ft. broad at the base, with a parapet, or, as the natives call it, "the woman's wall," running right round five feet high. The population of the city and suburbs has been put down at 250,000 inhabitants; but within its walls alone there is a mass of human beings amounting to at least 60,000, whose character (as that indeed of the whole department) is gazetted in the Redbook every quarter of the year as "diligent, frugal, fond of learning, and by no means dependent on trade merely,"—that is, willing and ready for the sake of subsistence, to turn the hand to the loom, the hammer, or the plough. They have many learned men among them; and I have been assured by competent authorities that some natives of Shaouhing are to be found in almost every mandarin court throughout the empire.

Of the sundry buildings, erections, or establishments about the city, there are two or three that deserve special notice,—both on account of their singular form and objects, and because, being placed either on the river-bank or in a commanding position, they cannot fail to attract the eye of a foreign traveller.

On approaching the city, and indeed throughout the whole line of this day's sail, there were military posts erected at every interval of three miles:* and on each side of the guard-houses there were "smoke-hillocks," as they are designated. These are hollow cones built of brick and in the shape of a sugarloaf, six or seven feet in height, whitewashed outside and marked with a daub of red in the centre. They are intended for making telegraph signals of smoke by day and fire by night, specially to give notice of the advance or the retreat of an enemy. In times of active service, it is required that they be kept full of wood, hay, and stubble, so that at a moment's notice they may be fired. At this time, however, they seemed to be deserted or left in the keeping of old women and beggars. When placed on prominent situations, as the top of a hill or rising ground, they serve well for beacons to give warning of any military movements. They are also called "wolf-smoke beacons," because (as described by natives) "in making signals, the dry dung of the wolf mixed with gunpowder and made into large balls is thrown on the fuel in the pyramidal cavity, and the entire mass is set on fire;—then, there rises up a pillar of smoke which no wind can agitate or disturb!"

In our sail past the city it was not necessary to be told that we were in the neighbourhood of distilleries and wine-vaults. Of the Shaouhing wine every one in China has heard, how rich its flavour and intoxicating the beverage. The tables of the great and opulent

* The original arrangement in laying down the military positions of the country was that "at every 5th le (one le being ⅓ of a foreign mile), there must be a set of telegraph hillocks; at every 10th le a guard house; and at every 60th le a military station, where men and horses are stationed for the carriage of despatches," &c.

cannot be without this liqueur; and, as at their usual feasts "every man at the beginning doth set forth the good wine," in China it must be the far-famed cordial of Shaouhing. This forms part of the trade of the city, and is said to be its principal traffic.

I must now call attention to the monumental erections around Shaouhing, particularly those south of the city and along the river-banks;—many of them being architectural ornaments by no means disagreeable to the eye. They are generally composed of two large square pillars, standing erect and at a distance of six or eight feet from one another, joined by a cross-piece at the top, looking somewhat like immense gateways without doors. These stone slabs are carved with figures and inscriptions, and not unfrequently there are huge ornaments perched upon the top. They have been called, though most inappropriately, "triumphal arches,"—but only by foreigners (as Abel, in his narrative of the embassy to the court of China) who could not have been aware of their use and objects. The majority of them are erected to commemorate the virtues of *young widows*, who, having unfortunately lost their intended husbands, had, without contracting a second marriage, remained in widowhood maintaining their reputation unblemished to the end of their days, or who, also after the decease of their husbands, had continued to honour, revere, and nourish their parents-in-law as they would their own fathers and mothers. In Western countries there are not a few who, without disguise, express their abhorrence at seeing a widow marrying a second time. Chinese moralists too are strong in condemning such conduct, and carry their prejudices yet further, in binding by the vow of perpetual virginity the girl who has been betrothed at an early age, and has been bereft of her intended by death before the nuptials could be consummated. The Hindoos at one time entertained so severe an opinion of the marriage of widows being indecorous, that, as long as Hindooism swayed its sceptre, the widow, no matter of what age or rank, was compelled to sacrifice herself on the funeral pile of her husband, and, in most cases, a close to her conjugal career like that was regarded and sought for by the sorrowing wife as the only praiseworthy, virtuous, and honourable. As to the Chinese, however, although one may greatly differ from their view of young widows marrying a second time, we must say that their policy is wise and merciful as compared to the diabolical precept of Hindooism, in providing suitable and respectable occupation for widowhood,—for the aged widows, that they bring up their grandchildren, and for the younger ones, even those who have lost their plighted partners before wedlock, that they serve and take care of their husband's parents. Then, the names of these heroines are heralded forth as examples of conjugal fidelity and filial respect; and in order that such patterns of virtue may secure a prominent place of honour, their names, their lineage, and their excellences are engraven on tables of stone, which are supported on upright pillars, as above described, and set up on the "king's highways," or the most frequented thoroughfares. Many receive these honours during lifetime, and many more after death, in which case their commemorative tablets are generally to be found in the vicinity of their graves. According to the statutes of the empire, any woman who, in widow's weeds, has conducted herself in a manner so as to win the esteem and confidence of all around her, may be reported to the magistrates of her native province. She is by those officials recommended to the attention of the Board of Rites, which, on representing her case to the Emperor, is empowered by his Majesty to make a grant in her behalf of twenty-four liangs, or thirty-five dollars, towards the erection of a monument by the officers of her native district; and upon this erection it is required that her graces and virtues shall be blazoned forth. These ornamental arches or gateways are everywhere stumbled upon; but I have not met with so many in one place as around the city and throughout the department of Shaouhing. The reason alleged is, that the "younger widows" of Shaouhing are reputed to be far superior to their countrywomen in avoiding second marriages, keeping at home, and cultivating the graces that adorn the female sex.

Although the scenery around Shaouhing and in its vicinity is pleasant and pretty, the line of journey for ten miles out of that city was through a flat country, with red hills in the distance, fields under water, and tallow-trees constantly before the eye. The tide had all day been high, very high, so that, at three bridges, the bamboo awning and cover of the boat, with framework, &c., had to be removed, to enable it to pass under them. The heat was excessive, so that the furniture of the cabins was annoying to the touch, and to lie down on the floor-matting was intolerable. In the villages and hamlets upon the river-bank little children were going about quite naked. Men at their work in the fields were in a state of perfect nudity, and the boatmen were seen diving into the river to cool themselves. Between the Ho-kiaou and Tseen-tsing, the temperature at mid-day was so intense and overpowering that the boat had to be anchored for an hour or two. Early in the afternoon we reached the last-mentioned place, from which a small branch strikes off to the north-west, leading direct to the capital of Hangchow, at a distance of only sixty les, or eighteen miles. The river that runs by this market-town is of the same name. It is a branch of the great Pooyang river, of which mention has already been made.

In passing through this market-town, it may be worth while to relate a singular story, on which is founded the origin of its name, Tseen-tsing. About 1,700 years ago, when Yen-he occupied the throne of the Eastern Han dynasty, Lin-Tsung, the magistrate of the canton in which the town lies, on leaving office, was waited upon by the gentry and elders. They strongly urged him to accept of a large sum of money, in token of their respect for him and as a memorial of the opinion which they held regarding the straightforward and honourable policy he had pursued during his term of office. The magistrate politely declined; but, on being most earnestly begged by the people to take something, he took only *one cash*. Hence the name of the spot, Tseen-tsing, "cash uncorrupted,"—one among millions in China!

At sunset we passed the Lo-shan Buddhist monastery, situate on the brow of a hill that derives its name, "Screw-shell Hill," from being supposed to resemble a screw-shell. As we passed under the bridge close to the monastery, one of the brotherhood was stationed on the top chanting his beggar's song, and lowering his basket to receive alms of the numerous passenger and cargo boats that were going to and fro. Around the monastery there were several tombstones, over the graves of Buddhist priests. The style is singular, and obtains only among this sacred order. Buddhist priests and nuns, on their decease, are interred in a sort of miniature pagoda. There are two modes of burial. Any one remarkable for devotion and virtue who dies at a good old age, is buried in a sitting posture, just as priests usually sit in the presence of their idol reciting prayers, with their legs drawn under them, the hands clasped, and the head drooping on the breast. The deceased is in this position put into a large earthen jar, with another jar placed over the head. The two are hermetically sealed, and built all round with brick and mortar, in the shape of a pagoda, about ten feet in height. Occasionally they take the bodies of devoted Buddhists, commit them to the flames, and search for a relic called *shayle*. On finding this, they lodge it in a casement like a small pagoda. The ordinary class of priests and priestesses are not so highly honoured on leaving the world. Their remains, bones or (if burnt) ashes, are cast into a hollow pagoda. These cases are carefully lodged about the monastery and grounds.

CHAPTER II.

TRIP THROUGH CHIHKIANG PROVINCE CONTINUED—FROM E-KIAOU TO CHANG-SHAN—FROM CHANG-SHAN TO THE BOUNDARY-POST BETWEEN CHIHKIANG AND KIANGSE.

JULY 11.—Overnight entering a small creek, by day-break we reached E-kiaou, a place that lies about fifty miles south-west of Shaouhing, and of importance only as affording conveyance for goods and passengers direct from that city to the central branch of the Chihkiang river. This obviates the necessity of making a circuit by Hangchow. A distance of eighteen miles is in this manner curtailed; and, what may be considered a greater advantage, the custom-house at that capital is avoided, which for its strict surveillance is notorious throughout the empire,—it being reported in one of the native itineraries to be "the only custom-house in the world where search is so severe and rigorous."

Our boat had no sooner reached the wharf here, than we were visited by the agents of five or six "conveying-houses," proffering their ready assistance to the new arrivals. This post-town contains about 1,400 families, and has at least twenty "conveying-companies," whose chief business is to provide accommodation for passengers and secure the transit of goods to and from the interior. We selected the firm of Kia-wan-shing, which at once engaged to let us have one of their boats.

For this purpose they sent coolies down to remove our luggage, and expedite arrangements for prosecuting our trip as far as Changshan, 186 miles farther inland, up the great river Chihkiang.

At 8 A.M., the head of the house came to pay his respects, and informed us that our boat was in readiness. Upon landing, we walked through the small town, and, having crossed the strip of land that divides the two creeks from each other, were soon comfortably seated in the new boat.* This was a variety of the Kientih class, in every way superior to either of the boats which I had been occupying during the last three days. Its accommodations were roomy. Between the prow, where the rowers squatted, and the stern, where the helmsman and family, cook, crew, and all put up, there were three large cabins furnished with beds, lockers, tables, chairs, &c., and in the hold six or seven distinct compartments for freight and luggage. There were on board six hands, besides an old woman and her daughter not yet out of her teens. These were employed to steer, row, and drag the barge, as necessity might require, and they expected at the close of the trip to receive each one his own perquisite, namely, "wine money" for the helmsman and boatmen, "tea money" for the old dame cook, and "head-dress money" for the daughter in waiting.

Before starting from this place, I posted a letter for Mr. Lockhart, medical missionary then resident at Chusan. It was sent under cover to a native hong at Ningpo, and subsequently I learned, with satisfaction, that it safely reached its destination.

By nine o'clock that morning a light breeze rose and helped us to creep slowly down the E-kiaou stream, which widened as we advanced, until it emptied itself (not

* Not to speak of the larger craft at this station, the smaller style is divided into two classes, named after the places where they are built, the E woo and the Kien-tih boats, each set of a different model.

more than three miles from our starting-point) into its recipient, the lower part of the great Chihkiang, known in this locality under the name of the Tseentang river. At ten o'clock we were afloat in the middle of that vast stream, whose channel opposite the village, called in the native tongue Yu-poo-kaou, measures more than one mile in width. From hence the main river flows north and north-east towards the capital of the province, Hangchow, only sixteen miles distant. As our course lay south-west towards Changshan, the head of the boat was immediately turned to stem the rushing current. We now fell into the same route along which Lord McArtney proceeded from Hangchow towards the south of the empire.

The shore on both sides was lined with white sand of a peculiarly fine texture; and embankments of stone and pebbles, sand and mud, extended for a good distance along the northern and southern margins. These artificial banks, unfortunately for the country around, being easily carried away by the overflowing river and its rapid tides, constantly require repair. Turning the eye to the right of the boat, or the north, the hills were distant and irregular, and little was seen but extensive paddy-fields. But looking over the south bank, the adjacent hills at once gratified one's view, some of them high, most of them rich in soil and thickly planted with various kinds of trees and shrubs. Among these mountains there rose one called the *Hoochaou*, "the tiger's paw," a rambling pile of rugged rocky peaks, well suited for a den of robbers, by whom, indeed, it is said to be actually frequented. It is closely linked to the neighbouring hills, and, by a rapid slope, descends into the Chihkiang. It is estimated by the natives as one of the most important and advantageous natural defences, rising up in the centre of the four principalities of Hangchow, Shauhing, Yenchow, and Kinhwa.

Near this neighbourhood, on either side of the river, whether in the plains or on the hill-sides, numerous and large mulberry plantations were growing. On inquiry, I found that at this time the second crop of leaves was ready for gathering. By the testimony of the natives, the tree here produces three yearly crops of leaves; the first, during the third and fourth moons, reputed as productive of silk of the best quality; the second, taken in during the fifth and sixth moons for second-rate silk; and the third, ready by the seventh moon; but only silk of the lowest quality can be expected from the worm fed on it. In winter the fallen and dried leaves are used to feed goats with. Among the Chinese the mulberry-tree is often kept merely as an ornament about a family mansion, or a fruit-tree in an orchard; but the use of its leaves for the silkworm renders its cultivation an important and lucrative branch of labour, chiefly in this province, which, as well as Kiangnan, Hoopih, and Szechuen, produces the finest silk in the empire. The raw material is sent from the country to the large cities, where it is wrought and made into every form of fabric one can well imagine. The stuffs of Hangchow are peculiarly fashionable, and perhaps the most eagerly sought for. The principal branch of trade in the Chihkiang province consists in silk stuffs.

At noon the weather set in very squally. There were heavy puffs blew over us, carrying clouds of sand and dust from the river-banks. This threw the boatmen into considerable fright, who had to anchor often; and in consequence of these interruptions, our progress all day was slow. Anxious to reach Fooyang for the night anchorage, every exertion was made before sunset, and at length they succeeded.

About one-third of a mile from that walled town we came to a hill with a solitary peak on its summit, upon which, during the reign of the three kingdoms, about

A.D. 200, a Taouist temple was erected; hence its name *Kwan-shan*, "Temple-hill." To the south of it, on a small rising ground, there was a seven-storied "dragon-boat pagoda," or *lung-chuan-t'ah*.

Sweeping round the foot of the hill, we suddenly came in full sight of the town, hitherto quite concealed from view. The town itself looked well at a distance, and the scenery in the neighbourhood particularly fine, as if pictures of groves and gardens had been hung up to relieve the vision. At 7 P.M., after a day's sail of only twenty miles, we dropped anchor off the south-east side of the town.

Fooyang stands on the north bank of the river, built upon a rocky foundation, with a low, dilapidated wall, measuring in circuit but one mile and a third, and having its south portion resting on Kwanshan, named above. The population of the suburbs is much scattered. Although this is the chief town of the district of the same name, it seems to be a quiet place, with little stir and bustle, except early in the morning and at sunset. It lies in the department of Hangchow, and is the indigo market for the surrounding country, whose hills produce it in great abundance.

The tide-wave ascends no farther than this town, fifty miles from the sea. There is besides a "quiet tide" observable some way farther up the river, which is caused by the outpouring waters of the river being impeded in their downward flow by the ascending tidal wave, and forced back to some distance. To that remoter distance, then, the tide is said really to ascend, though the water is fresh. "The Bore" is a phenomenon of frequent occurrence on this river. In the estuary before the great city Hangchow, where the Chihkiang disembogues itself, the tide at certain periods ascends with a prodigious noise, in one vast wave rising from five to thirty feet above the natural level, and rolling up with a foaming head, upsetting all it meets with until, exhausted by resistance, it sinks into a feeble undulation. Of this peculiar phenomenon this is the only instance of the sort mentioned by the Chinese as known in the empire. In one of their topographics they say of it, "The surge thereof rises like a hill, and the wave like a house; it roars like thunder, and as it comes on, it appears about to swallow the heavens and bathe the sun." The seasons at which it occurs are (according to native calculation) in the second and eighth moons particularly, as well as monthly at the change and full of moon, at the spring-tides. The tide-wave always is high, especially at these periods, when it rises twenty or thirty feet. It stretches across the Tseentang estuary, which, ten miles south of Chapoo, from side to side, measures full fifteen miles wide. The boat population around the city of Hangchow is perpetually on the look out for the occurrence. Its approach is sufficiently indicated by its noise: and of course it occasions great alarm. Chinese vessels inward bound wait for it first to rise, and then, drifting in with the tide that succeeds, they escape damage. Among the sailing directions published by Captain Collinson, of H.M.'s naval service, he warns all sailors navigating through the Bay of Hangchow to pay attention to the tide up this bay. He remarks, "Particularly on account of this tide, the bay cannot and ought not to be navigated at night." During the survey of the said bay, taken by H.B.M.'s naval officers in 1842, they found that, off the town of Chapoo, "at the spring-tides the velocity of the tide is 5 knots, and the rise and fall 25 feet. Seven miles south-west of Chapoo, and towards Hangchow, during a stay of three days, the night tide rose 30 feet, and its velocity was 7½ knots; while at the Fog Islands, 10 miles to the south-eastward, the rise and fall was 17 feet, and the velocity 4½ knots; showing a rapid increase in rise and velocity as you enter the estuary of Tseentang river, leading to Hangchow."

When Captain Collinson went, in the steamer *Phlegethon*, to reconnoitre the approaches to the city of Hang-chow, before the termination of hostilities with China, he found there a tide of 11½ knots an hour; and although the steamer had one anchor down with a whole cable, (having previously lost an anchor with a cable when she tried to bring up,) and was under full power of steam with sails set, still she was driving. On a second trial, at the dead of neap, the *Phlegethon* had a tide running 5½ knots nearly at the same place. The rapidity of the flood setting into this bay was probably the cause of the loss of the *Kite* transport, in 1840.

During the whole of July 12th, we were sailing along a deep broad channel, both sides lined with a border of fine sand, in some places abundant. On the banks there was a beaten path for boatmen engaged in dragging their boats. For the firstt welve miles, high hills arose upon the right, forming precipitous banks, in some places sloping down to the water's edge. At the bottom of the hills there stood military stations with sign-posts, notifying the distances of various places *en route*. Not unusually one finds that, under the influence of the scorching sun, nature around puts on a dumb-struck aspect, when everything seems lifeless, and the elements inert. The heat to-day was of this over-powering intensity, and both man and beast felt glad to be still. Yet, so grand and attractive was the scenery which every now and then burst upon the view, that it was impossible to refrain from taking a frequent, eager, long look around.

On the Luhshan, in full view of which we passed, there was no point that did not offer some attraction. It is singular that the natives have given it two names, the one a contrast to the other, the Luh or the Lung-shan; the former intended to describe its general form, which is thought to resemble "the deer;" the latter intimating it to be the residence of "dragons." There obtains here a popular legend that, for a long time, a crowd of dragons dwelt in the caverns of the mount, and, by exhausting the canals and streams in the vicinity, brought drought and dearth on the country. Fortunately, a skilful priest by his recitals of sacred incantations charmed those monsters away, and so put an end to the disasters that for a long period had been inflicted on the people.

But, whatever may be the origin of these designations, each may be interpreted as descriptive of different views which the mountain presents to the eye of the spectator. In some places it frowns with dark rugged rocks, or towers up with steep precipitous cliffs, or yawns at you with wide dismal chasms, (to a Chinese fancy) like "a retreat of dragons." Then, in other places one may imagine it to be "the resort of the deer," specially where it is ornamented with green swards running up the slopes, and with rocks broken into fanciful shapes or scattered over the hill-sides. Everywhere there stand numerous tallow-trees displaying their beautiful autumnal purple leaf, and huge thick camphor-trees spreading out massive branches, clothed with glittering leaves.

To pass on, however: in the course of the afternoon, we sailed by two "river-bed islands," lying in the middle of the channel,—the one "the five-le islet," the other "the extensive isle." The former lies about nineteen miles from Fooyang, our starting-place in the morning. It measures ten miles in circumference, and is covered with mulberry plantations. The latter is four miles further up the river and only six miles in circuit, given up to paddy cultivation. At six o'clock in the evening, I took a stroll on the river-bank, and kept up with the boat for three miles until the evening meal was announced, for which I had acquired a keen appetite by the pedestrian exercise.

As I returned to the boat, the Tungkiun-shan hove

in sight on the north bank, a mountain standing forth in a most conspicuous manner, towering up over the river with a remarkably precipitous crest, (to borrow the native description) "like a thirsty whale about to bounce into the water." About a mile from its western fort is situate the chief town in the district of Tungloo. We anchored for the night abreast of that town, which formed an exception to other district towns that I had passed through, as it was unwalled. Its population was very scarce, "few and far between," and the walls of the houses were whitewashed!

Next day, starting at daybreak from Tungloo, we made for the chief city in the Yenchow department, at a distance of twenty-four miles, or with fair wind half a day's sail at Chinese rate. Unfortunately, what with foul wind and strong rapids, we could average only a mile and a half per hour, sometimes not more than a quarter of a mile, sometimes less. The boat had for the greater part of the way to be pushed on by poles, or tracked along the banks by ropes, which made it a laborious and tedious day to the entire crew. To the passenger, however, there was full compensation for the delay in the sublime and splendid scenery everywhere bursting upon his view. One of their poets has justly observed, "Though this department may be unimportant in other respects, in mountain and water scenery it is *nonpareil.*"

To be particular:—When the boat got under weigh with its head S.S.W., it crept along the right, or northern bank of the Chihkiang. The banks on both sides gradually rose up until, in some parts, they overtopped, and appeared to overhang the boat. At breakfast-time we were approaching the Lewkiang rapid. The river here was only one-third of a mile in width, and, as the whole volume of water from the upper channel poured down this narrow bed, the rush was violent. At certain spots the fall was quite shallow.

The bed was paved with white pebbles and round boulders. The boat was hauled along the bank, and, as neither the length of the rapid nor its declivity was great, we soon effected the ascent, and in half an hour reached a point where scenery of the finest order awaited us. The next three miles the river was wide, deep, and perfectly limpid, presenting the rich tint of the bright blue sky. The current was sometimes smooth, frequently rapid, and then again broken into whirls and eddies. On both banks the mountains towered up, covered from the base to the summit with rank vegetation, spontaneous or cultivated. The banks were exceedingly high; in some parts formed of abrupt rocks rising precipitously from the foot of the hills, and often intersected by ravines, gullies, and torrent-beds. Those deep, rugged beds, as we passed them to-day, were quite dry; but I was informed by the boatmen that a small shower soon occasions immense torrents. While the boat was dragged along the northern bank, the towing-path was a shelf beaten or cut out of the mountain-side. In one place the track-road was so narrow that I could not but tremble to watch the men tramping "the dizzy step," and straining every muscle as they towed the clumsy boat. Each man had the tow-line thrown around his waist, and it was fearful to think of the consequences that might befall the whole of the tugging party, should one of them take a false step, or lose his hold, or beat out of time. Fortunately, at one of the most critical places, they got within a rail of stone, which had been put up by some benevolent gentry in the neighbourhood to prevent a repetition of the dreadful accidents that had previously occurred from want of such precautions. The mountain scenery about this is perfectly wild and romantic, with its rifted cliffs, deep dells, rocks piled up like lofty pillars, and

"The rocky pass half hung with shaggy wood."

Often I could descry sheltered cabins peeping out of the corners of the small green vales, which were described as the straw huts of woodcutters, who roam upon the hills gathering brushwood and dry sticks for sale as fuel. Before we left this attractive spot we were enchanted by the dropping of a beautiful cascade, that, in its descent of several hundred feet, leapt from rock to rock, until it bounded among the dark blocks with which the precipice bristled, when, in a sheet of foaming water, it boiled over and fell tumultuously into the river beneath.

The *shay-yu* is a native of these waters, a fish remarkable for its rich delicious flavour. That and some other valuable fishes make this part of the river a large and lucrative fishery. It appears also that frequent piracies are committed upon the little fishing craft floating about; on which account the native "itinerary" in my hands lays down, as a precaution to travellers approaching the spot, "The fishing-boats here are particularly on their watch against lawless freebooters."

By noon we reached the Tiaou-tai, a lofty hill on the right bank, remarkable for three prominent observatories, perched on three separate peaks, each several hundred feet high, rising the one above the other, built of stone, covered over with tangled creepers, screened by groves of trees, and fit only for "monks unlettered and unknown." The two higher ones especially looked as if they were each "a castled cliff and brown monastic shade."

In the annals of the place, a story is given which agrees with the above description. Some time in the first century, when the Han dynasty held the reins of government, there flourished a man named Yenkwang, who, by his close intimacy with the then reigning emperor, brought no small renown on his native place, Yuyaou (spoken of at p. 221). In his boyhood he had been at school along with Kwangwoo, the heir expectant to the throne, and during that time the warmest friendship was formed between the two lads. As they grew up, these class-mates were separated and lost sight of each other. However, when Kwangwoo ascended the throne, he thought to do honour to his early comrade, and sent through his dominions to seek him out. After some delay, the messengers got information that he was living a hermit's life in this romantic rookery, dressed in sheep-skins, and gaining subsistence by fishing in the river. The emperor at once sent a fine chariot, with presents of silks and satins; but, it was only after three distinct invitations from his majesty, that Yenkwang was prevailed on to leave his lonely life and enter the whirl of court dissipation. The emperor, on meeting him, found that their friendship had not diminished, and, as a mark of the highest honour and confidence, made him share the same bed with him. Such is one of the legends of the Tiaoutai, or "fishing platform."

The only other incident during the day's sail was stemming the *Woo-shih t'an*, a "black-pebble rapid," about three miles from last night's anchorage. Its name denotes one of its peculiarities, it being bedded with jet-black stones, generally as large as a good-sized loaf, and called "loaf-like boulders." The margins of the rapid were lined with white sand. The rapid itself was very deep, though not more than one-sixth of a mile in width; the declivity in the bed was sudden; the channel interspersed with huge blocks, and the velocity of the rush was fearful, at the lowest calculation exceeding thirty miles an hour. The labour in stemming the current here was excessive; for often the master and servant, husband and wife, helmsman, crew, and old dame together, had to wade into the stream up to the waist, and to give "a strong pull, a long pull, and a pull altogether." But sometimes it was almost labour lost, and, as if giving it up in despair, they had to lie by for five minutes at a time to recruit exhausted strength. Two or three hours of tug and toil effected the ascent of this rapid, and at the top of the fall, it was the source of some musing to look back on what mere manual labour had done in raising a boat of such magnitude and bulk against a current of apparently irresistible velocity, up an acclivity whose perpendicular fall must at the least have been eight or ten feet.

After this it was plain sailing along numerous serpentine bends, until we anchored off Tungkwan.

July 14.—On getting up this morning, I found the boat had left its moorings and was crosing the mouth of the Sin-ngan-kiang, one of the chief affluents of the Chihkiang.

Here it will not be unsuitable to insert a few hints about the principal tributaries of the Chihkiang, especially as they unite in one channel at this place. There are three of them. The one we had now come upon was the western tributary, rising from the hills of the Nganhwuy province, some distance to the west of Yenchow city. The second, or the south-east tributary, is that into which we shall enter after sailing across the mouth of the western stream. It goes by the name Tungyang, and flows out of the mountains of Kinhwa. Thethird affluent is "the south-western supply," the highest sources of which rise at a distance of 250 miles. As I have already said, the grand junction, generally known as the Chihkiang, is formed here at the Sin-ngan-kiang. Its name is derived from the bends, twists, and twirls the river takes along its course from its various sources, through the centre of numerous departments, until, passing Hangchow, the capital of the province, it disembogues itself into the sea about twenty miles below.

Sweeping round from Tungkwan, where we had

anchored during the night, and reaching midway across the mouth of the western tributary, we came in full view of Kientih, the chief city in the department of Yenchow (N. lat. 29° 37′, E. long. 110° 30′), upon the north-east bank of the stream, a little more than a mile off. On either bank, margining the entrance, there rose a seven-storied pagoda, each built upon the slope of a grotesque hill. The channel of Sin-ngan-kiang being one of the principal water-communications between the centre of the Chihkiang province and the upper parts of Nganhwuy, a boat may sail up for 100 miles to the north-west of Kientih as far as Hewhing, a market-town of the Hwuychow country.

We soon had to leave this tributary river to our right, with its picturesque amphitheatre of hills around the walled town Kientih, and enter on the waters of the south-east affluent, the river Tungyang. During the rest of the day the sail was on a wide stream flowing between high banks. The course was towards the town of Lan-ke, about twenty-five miles distant. We had several rapids to ascend. Of these the most remarkable was that which lies close to the boundary-line of the two departments Yenchow and Kinhwa. The difficulties that were encountered here were extreme, in the ascent at least, arising chiefly from the strong current which at times rushed like a torrent over massive blocks, strown over the bed, most of them as large and sonorous as the huge water-jars in common use.

Before crossing the boundary of Yenchow, we fell in with a convoy of mandarin boats. They were conducting the notorious Tartar, Tahunga, on his recall from Formosa, where, as commander-in-chief, he had ordered the massacre of the unfortunate crew of the *Nerbudda*, whom he had reported as being taken in battle. Strong remonstrances had been sent in by H.M.'s Plenipotentiary, Sir H. Pottinger, against such barbarities.

Accordingly, the monster had been ordered up to the Imperial metropolis, ostensibly to be called to account for his inhumanities. I saw him seated at the door of his cabin, smoking his hookah. What would he not have given to know that at this time there was "a barbarian" passing his prow!

Very soon we came within the department of Kinhwa, and suddenly found ourselves at the foot of the Tung-tsze-shan rapid. Here, upon the left hand, there rises a high precipitous rock, called the Tsiang-keun, or "Commander-in-Chief Cliff," presenting to the traveller an aspect, wild, strange, and frowning. For a while I had an opportunity of watching a couple of fishermen, engaged in fishing by cormorants. It has been reported by some foreigners that these are not used *in summer;* but here, on the 14th of July, they were at work with them in this river. The boat was small, with two men in it and some twenty of these aquatics. There is nothing remarkable in their appearance or figure: they look like a large duck, or rather a pelican, with a brown back, a tinge of white beneath on the crop, yellow and hooked bill, and web feet. The marvellous thing about them is their docility,—in which they quite equal the hounds, spaniels, and hawks of Europe; each being at the bid and beck of the boatman. Several were perched on the edge of the boat looking as if satisfied they had done a day's work, yet watching the eye of their master to dash into the river at his signal. The others were dispersed across the breadth of the river, diving about in search of prey and working indefatigably, either till they succeeded or till they were called in by the well-known voice of the keeper. Many had not to dive long before they caught large or small fish, which they immediately brought in their bills to the master. One or two, although as obedient to orders as the rest, were observed to be not so trusty as their messmates. The fisherman, who kept a sharp look-out on his charge, perceiving that these had on the sly swallowed the fish they seized, by a stroke of his guiding-rod on the water and a shout of his voice, brought them up to the side of the skiff. He at once caught them by the neck, and made them disgorge the fishy contents of their stomachs,—whole and undigested fishes of no mean dimensions. He then dismissed them to do double work. I could find neither ring nor cord about the necks of any of them to prevent the swallowing of fish. Wherever the boat moved they followed, as quick at interpreting the pointing of the fisherman's rod as they did the variations of his voice. They are well fed on eels, fish refuse, bean-curd, &c.; but are sent a-fishing before feeding-time, or only when very hungry.

As I have already said, during this day we frequently came upon rapids of great slope. These occasioned much annoyance to the boatmen, who were obliged to go into the water to drag or shove the boat along. The approach to a rapid is the sure and invariable signal for a war of words. They commence to roar at each other; and bawl, scold, rail, and fight,—but for which they might accomplish their work in half the time. Nevertheless, it cannot be blinked that the difficulty, especially in getting up a rapid, is well-nigh insuperable, particularly in midsummer, or during a heavy drought. Fortunately for our boat to-day, it at length reached the crest of one of the rapids, where we saw seven boats fast and immovable, in the act of unloading before they could be got off.

July 15.—We did not reach Lan-ke last night, as expected, but at eight o'clock this morning. This chief town, in the district of the same name, stands on the eastern bank of the river, in a beautiful valley of hills and vales covered with tallow and camphor trees, and, with its newly whitewashed huge walls, looked rather better than other places hitherto visited by me along the route. Boats of every description skirted both sides of the river; and the bustle of business was great. The Lanke hams, wine, dates, and soy, have universal repute, and may be had very cheap here:—the dates peculiarly delicious. The relation of Lanke with Kinhwa, the principal city in the department, is of some importance, and the traffic between the two places is by no means small.

At the southern end of the suburbs the river divides into two branches,—the one to the left, or south-east, leading direct to Kinhwa, and farther on to the departments of T'aichow and Wanchow, adjoining the Fuhkien province; the other bends to the right, south-west, running towards Kiangse. These are the second and third tributaries to the Chihkiang, of which mention has been made already. Of course, as they divided at this point, our boat dropped into the south-west branch, where, after a few hours' anchorage before the town, it got under weigh about noon.

At 3 P.M. a heavy squall from the south-west came down upon us, drifting before it clouds of white sand. The terror among the boatmen in the crafts sailing up and down was excessive. All made for the bank, dropped anchor, and kept as snugly together as they possibly could. On our left bank there were large accumulations of exceedingly fine sand, and all around the marked traces of extensive ravages occasioned by severe inundations were too perceptible. A little before sunset we sailed between three or four water-mills, turned by the rapid stream, for grinding wheat and paddy.

July 16.—Yesterday we made only seventeen miles, and early came to anchor at Yangkiang, the boundary-line of the Kinhwa and Keuchow departments. Refreshed by a good night's rest, the men began to stir at daybreak. After passing vast piles of rocks heaped together along the right bank of the river, especially at

Hoochin, after spying many temples, stained not as usual with red or yellow, but whitewashed like plain cottages, and after admiring the tidy and clean appearance of the women in the villages, where they were meeting in large numbers to wash their clothes in the bed of the river,—at 10 A.M. we stopped for refreshment at the Ts'ihtoo pagoda.

The mid-stream there was shooting down at a fearful rate. It was with some degree of anxiety I watched a small boat flying along the rapid under the management of two youths working the scull. While I looked on in breathless suspense, apprehensive of a misfortune, a shriek of despair rent the air, as one of the lads lost his hold and fell into the middle of the stream. All screamed for help. Our boat was immovable, for it was at anchor. The only one at liberty was that of a poor fisherman at a short distance. On perceiving the case of distress, he left his net, and, with the aid of his wife and boy of seven years of age, rowed as fast as he could to the rescue of the drowning youth, all the while shouting out to him, "Fear not, fear not; keep your courage up." Had there been the delay of half a minute, rescue would have been too late. But the lad was saved,—the gloom that hung over every countenance was suddenly broken,—all felt relieved and thankful. I called the fisherman alongside, and astonished him by giving him one dollar for his pains. The master of the young apprentice who had been delivered from a watery grave, on being informed of the gift, came aboard, and went through various prostrations in expression of his gratitude to the stranger (little thinking he was a foreigner) for his unexpected kindness.

At mid-day we came in sight of the chief town in the district of Lung-yew, lying at the base of a hill on the eastern bank of the river. The approach to it is denoted by a pagoda upon a sandy plain, the Chang-yuen-t'ah.

The town is very insignificant, though walled. The number of its inhabitants does not exceed 5,000; and the chief article of produce for which it has any note is the common paper made from bamboo. Our sail to the night's anchorage at Pofang-tan did not exceed twelve miles. The greater part of the route was lined on both sides with large shady trees, chiefly the camphor and tallow. As to difficulties in sailing, however, we had never experienced greater than to-day, — what with shallows, rapids, mill-ponds, rugged rocks, and incessant hauling, bawling, and railing. During the latter part of the day no less than twelve people, men and women, were working the boat, nine dragging the tug-rope, two poling it along, and one at the rudder; while all kept shouting to each other, and venting forth torrents of ill-nature and abuse.

On July 17th, we made only twenty-one miles of progress, the weather continuing intensely hot, and the passage up the river more than ever impeded by a series of rapids, shallows, &c. The route between last night's anchorage and the city of Keuchow, where we rested a little after mid-day, lies through a flat, level country. The monotony of the course was occasionally relieved by a few striking objects along the river-banks,—on the right hand by gigantic rocks, on the left by remarkable mounds of white sand, or here and there by a solitary pagoda rising up as a watch-tower over the surrounding plains. While the boat is making for Keuchow, let me impose on the reader's patience for a few minutes in looking at my present whereabouts in the heart of the Chinese empire. I have just passed a pagoda,—the boat creeping up against a rapid stream, nothing serving but the steady tug and haul of the men upon the river-bank. What I would give to have the luck of those people whose boats are swiftly gliding by, borne down by the favourable currents from above! In many of those boats I see passengers lounging about idle and indolent, some of the merchants returning home with goods gotten at Canton, various specimens of which foreign purchases I can detect arranged on their decks. The sight of these articles,—how it touches one up as he is travelling, a lonely Englishman in the interior of China! What thoughts and feelings arise about "auld lang syne," such as could not be suggested in his own native land,—such as meet with no response amid the throngs around! But the reverie into which one falls about the "homes and hearths of England," is broken in upon by the approach of several large mandarin barges, conveying the officials of this department into that, flying broad banners emblazoned with the rank and titles of the official personages. There sits his worship at the cabin door, fanning himself and smoking his pipe. He is eyeing me,—is struck with something un-Chinese about my face, yet suspects not for an instant that I am a native of that notorious country that has recently humbled the pride of the Imperial Crown. Yet why should he suspect me? I am in a boat almost as good as his. I too am fanning myself, drinking my tea, using my chopsticks, and smoking my pipe, and withal have the rag-tag and bob-tail of a genuine son of Han. So he passes me with a look of indifference, as no longer worthy of notice; for I am only of the common herd. But what next? What is this coming down the river? —a floating isle with huts and human beings upon it. It is a large raft of wood transported from the interior forests, requiring great care, time, and labour in its navigation. Then, looking out ahead for the city of Keuchow, which the boatmen are exceedingly anxious to reach for an hour's rest, one cannot help again remarking how low the surface of the country stretches beyond the banks of the river. At the same time, you must admire the remarkable fringe of mountain-tops that bounds the amphitheatre. Nothing but peaks are peeping over the distant horizon, and pinnacles of all shapes and dimensions. To the right, westward, there are the mountains of Nganhwuy; ahead, or south of us, those of Kiangse; but the most striking, to the south-east, the heights of the Fuhkien ranges.

At length we came within hail of the chief town of Keuchow department, a few hundred paces from the river-side on the east bank, a very high bank. It had a wall around about seven yards in height. We could but see its western wall running direct for half a mile from north to south. At the north corner of this face it had a curiosity in the shape of a pagoda, miniature in size, of seven stories, and of solid iron: and at the very opposite end there was peering over the wall a dilapidated pagoda of brickwork. This city, with a population of 50,000 inhabitants, is chiefly important as the official seat of a *Taoutai* of three departments, which will account for the large number of clumsy barges and government boats along the river's edge.

When we had come abreast of the city we were interrupted by a floating bridge, thrown over the entire breadth of the stream. It consisted of boats anchored fast, chained together, and boarded with planks for passengers and burden-bearers to cross. On paying the usual toll of two cash (7½ cash equal to one farthing), a passage was made for the boat, which is done by unloosing one of the linked barges. We sailed on till we dropped anchor at 1 P.M., to give the boatmen rest and shelter after half a day of extreme toil under a furious blazing sun. They had a respite till three o'clock, by which time they appeared refreshed and prepared to get under weigh again. But the first difficulty they met with was at the south end of the city, where a most rapid shallow awaited to test the temper and patience of all parties.

A mile farther on we came to a fork of the river, in the vicinity of which is the *Tungtsien-ling*, famous in the records of the Tartar dynasty for a three years encampment of the then surviving forces enlisted in support of the Ming rule, and for their final overthrow in the year 1676, since which the conquerors have till of late enjoyed undisturbed security and quiet. At the point specified, the river divided into two streams;—the one on our left, the principal watercourse from the interior of China through the Fuhkien province, having its rise in the Kiaoushan mountains of that province. But the other channel, which trended to the south-west, was that we had to take. This branch, still called the Chihkiang, may be considered the grand highway between Hangchow, Nanking, and the southern and south-western parts of the empire, as its waters pass directly through, or have direct communications with the Chihkiang, Kiangse, Nganhwuy, Kwangse, Canton, Szechuen, Kweichow, and Yunnan provinces. The region, a little above the fork I have pointed out, is famous for its oranges,—orange-groves being seen everywhere upon the river-banks. I happened in the evening to land for a quiet stroll, while they dragged the boat up the river, but lost myself in one of these orange-yards. This threw the faithful, trusty servants into some dismay. Ere long, however, I recovered the track, and relieved my domestics of suspense.

At sundown, the boat anchored for the night at Ts'an-tsze-poo, the usual anchorage for passage-boats.

July 18.—To-day we expected by sunset to reach the next landing-place, at Changshan; but what with a tearing squall that drove us to the bank for two hours, and numerous shallows, we could make only eighteen miles, and, much to our mortification, had to come to for the night five miles below that station. It was another day of struggling up difficult and narrow rapids. There was one that especially proved the irritability and tried the nerves of the men. The channel of the river was mostly dried up except in the middle, where there was a passage, but with room enough for only one boat at a time to ascend or descend. To descend was easy. Our lot was to ascend—terrible work, to be sure, under a scorching sun, and the galling fire of abuse from every side. Well, how can this be tolerated, even in China? With so large an inland trade upon one of her principal highways, how can the government—how can the merchants of China tolerate the perpetuation of such difficulties? Why not open, and keep open, wide and deep channels in spots so crammed with obstacles and impediments?

Of the several places we touched at to-day, it was impossible to obtain any information from the boatmen; indeed, but for the "Itinerary" in my possession, I should have slipped by without a knowledge of their names. Whether boatmen or passengers that frequent these parts, you seldom meet with men who can tell you more than the names of the places from which they started, and whither they are bound: scarcely anything else. Sometimes they cannot name the places.

July 19.—The boat got under weigh before cock-crow, and by five o'clock in the morning was sheared along the Sanlot'an bank, the landing-place of the Changshan town. The town itself lies about one mile from the wharf. There are in it several companies established for transporting goods and passengers into the Kiangse province, or across a land-passage of twenty-four miles to Yuhshan, the next stage. These houses have their respective agents at the anchorage, who look out for traffic and passengers. My slumbers were early disturbed by the voices of many candidates for employ. The firm Wang-luy-sien secured our patronage on engaging to supply us with two covered chairs for self and guide, and two uncovered ones for cook and boy, besides five bearers for the luggage.

Having arranged our traps and equipped ourselves with food and clothing for an overland route of eight hours, we were stepping out of the boat, which, during the last eight days, had carried us on 200 miles of our trip, when the boatmen assailed us for donations additional to the bill of fare, perquisites, &c., settled at Ekiaou. Each one demanded something more for himself—one for being captain, another as boatman, a third for looking after the baggage in the hold, &c., like boots or butlers in an English hotel. At length we got rid of these suppliants, and by 9 A.M. were ensconced in shabby, hard-bottomed sedans. In half an hour we reached the suburbs close to the east gate of Changshan.

In passing along I counted no less than twenty "transit-company offices," in connection with which there were inns where any disposed to tarry a while might have board and lodging. We stopped a short time at the Wang-luy-sien office, where we completed arrangements for the transit of party and chattels. The building where this company holds its office, &c., is large and commodious. From what I heard, the firm is in good repute; and from the treatment I received in their house, I myself can bear witness of their kind, honest, and obliging conduct.

Entering the east gate, we passed the provost's official residence, went down the principal market-street, a long, busy thoroughfare, caught sight of numerous "salt-depositories," and got out at the west gate, where fine rural scenery met the eye.

Having mentioned salt-depôts, I may remark that these are let out by government on purchase by private individuals. At Changshan they are numerous, as the salt used by the inhabitants of Kiangse passes chiefly from the coast of Chihkiang, and must cross over through Changshan. The entire salt monopoly of the empire is under the control of the Imperial government, which maintains on this service a large suite of officers and excisemen. The common salt used by the myriads in China is procured along the maritime coasts east and south of the empire. The plan pursued in the manufacture of it, as I have had the opportunity frequently of observing, is to level the ground along the margin of the sea, or the banks of rivers running close to the ocean, and at high-tide to draw sluices so as to let sea-water in sufficient to cover the face of the levelled ground. The dams are then stopped up, and after an interim, the water being all evaporated by the heat of the sun, a thickish crust is left upon the surface of the field, which white coat, on being scraped together, is laid up in stacks. This is the property of government, by whom it is farmed out to merchants, who alone hold the monopoly, and thereby make immense profits. Accordingly, no salt may legally be removed out of the maritime provinces without a distinct permit; still, there is a most extensive smuggling-trade of this article carried on.

In a short time I was fairly on the road to Yuhshan, the chair-coolies carrying my sedan firmly, and trudging at a steady pace,--lofty mountains in the distance, high hills in the neighbourhood, and a great deal of rising ground dotted with graves, or covered with a blue slate-rock. These graves are of a construction different from what I had seen in Canton, &c.—built on the ground, shaped like small houses, with open windows, and capable of holding three, four, and five coffins. Along the entire highway from Changshan to Yuhshan, twenty-four miles, there was a good beaten path, fourteen feet in width, mostly laid with a kind of flint-stone, and frequently shaded with magnificent tallow-trees. The road throughout had two unbroken trains of coolies, the one going, the other coming, carrying sedans, passengers, goods, and burdens. Stone pillars stood on the roadside with four characters engraven on them, to say "this is the highway (from Chihkiang) to eight provinces," viz.—Kiangse, Hoonan, Hoopih, Kwangse, Kwangtung, Yunnan, Szechuen, and Kweichow. As travelling here is kept up through the night too, light-beacons are stuck up along the road-sides. Every third mile had its caravansary, chiefly kept by old women, where the chair-bearers could whiff their pipes, drink tea (such horrible stuff, too, for the *land of tea!*), and take a short nap. The half-way house for dinner was at Ts'aoufang, which we reached at 1 P.M. Here we had a quarrel with the coolies about the chop-house to be patronized.

As for the cooly-hire upon this thoroughfare, it may not be useless to remark that, from inquiries I have made, the system of porterage appears to be pretty regular. The charges do not vary much during the year, except from the fifth to the eighth moon, when the people are principally engaged in field-work, at which time the fare rises. For instance, for eight months in the year covered sedans from Changshan direct to Yuhshan, inclusive of cooly-hire, cost but half a dollar each; but during the season above specified (under the provisions of which I had to fall on this the 19th of July), the charge is one dollar. Thus, the highest rate does not exceed five shillings for twenty-four miles! The bearers invariably expect something extra at the end of the journey for "wine-money." The luggage-carriers rank under four classes. The best and most expeditious are allowed to carry no more than 100 pounds per load, and engage to carry it to Yuhshan within eight or ten hours, at the rate of seven cash, or a farthing per pound. This I give from my own "pocket experience." The luggage-train is attended by a security, or a trusty man in the employment of the transit-company.

En route we came upon a prominent pass that lies across the public road. We had already passed one about seven miles out of Changshan. This second one was seven miles farther on, called the Pingfung-kwan, or the "Folding-screen Pass," that had been repaired in the fourteenth year of Taou-kwang. It is formed of a ledge of massive rocks right across the path, like a screen to separate one part of a building from another. To this notion it owes its name. Besides, it is considered the grand boundary between the two provinces,—Chihkiang, which we are on the point of leaving behind us, and Kiangse, which we are about to enter. The security of this pass has always been deemed of first importance, especially to keep the province of Kiangse from all incursions from the north-east. At the breaking up of the Ming dynasty, the Tartars found this to be one of the most difficult passages in their career of conquest. And hitherto, in order to keep the overland route between Chihkiang and Kiangse free from the depredations of prowling banditti, a military guard has been constantly stationed here. In a native work, there is one section on "the dangerous routes of Chihkiang province," of which "there are said to be three,—one by sea and along the coast, another upon its rivers and lakes, and a third over the mountains. On the first you are in danger of attacks from piratical craft. The second swarms with all sorts of smugglers. The last route is frequented by bands of mountain robbers." The Changshan pass is mentioned as belonging to the third description. The paragraph concludes with these words:—"Ah! the load of anxiety that must lie upon the mind of the viceroy of Chihkiang! What with setting a coast-guard to free our waters from pirates who damage our junk-trade, and with appointing a police to keep a strict surveillance over the smugglers of prohibited goods, and with putting down the lawless banditti on the frontiers of the province, his Excellency surely cannot have an easy life of it! If one should say, 'He need not be a man of great intelligence or much tact,' we have only to reply, 'How can this be?'"

While lingering at the Folding-screen Pass, reluctant to quit the province of Chihkiang, on whose highway I had during the last eleven days travelled 360 miles, crossed six of its shires, passed through thirteen of its boroughs, and visited nine of its walled towns, kind reader, indulge me with a parting look at the opulent and populous region behind, one of the finest of the eighteen provinces of China.

Chihkiang, laid down on European maps, comprises four degrees of latitude, and nearly four of longitude,—extending in north latitude from 27° 30′ to 31° 15′, and in longitude from 118° to 121° 50′ east of Greenwich; its greatest breadth measuring (by Chinese calculation) 260 English miles from east to west, and its extreme length, north and south, about 380. By its geographical position it is bounded on the north by Kiangsoo, the chief province in the empire and the most famed for its wealth, luxury, and products; on the south by the province of Fuhkien, peopled by an ambitious race; on the east by a wild rugged coast; and on the west by the provinces of Nganhwuy and Kiangse, the natives of which latter are for the most part poor, lowly, and unpretending. The area of Chihkiang (over which we take this rapid glance) is large enough to afford room for our Emerald Isle to float in it, or Scotland, with all her islets, could, without any inconvenience, be set down within its limits; or, still to vary the comparison, it is equal to the entire territory of Portugal, or twice the size of the kingdom of Denmark. In short, it embraces land almost sufficient to contribute one acre to each individual in its population, which, by the last census, exceeds twenty-six millions of souls.

To take a bird's-eye view, you find this not a petty kingdom; marked off as it is into seventy-seven cantons or districts, which again are distributed among eleven counties or departments, chiefly watered by the river we have sailed upon, and its large tributaries. These separate divisions have their own corps of municipal officers, under the rule of a governor, who, with his *suite*, including members of the financial, judicial, military, and civil boards, resides at the provincial capital, Hangchow. The climate being mild, the face of the country well watered, and the soil fertile, the products of the province are rich and abundant, especially its silk, in the quality and quantity of which it competes with its neighbour Kiangnan; and the manufacturers being rather expert and skilful, the workmanship is fine,—especially the silks, damasks, and *senshaws*, which are unsurpassed. The maritime trade is limited, but the internal traffic very large.

Of the character of the people, all we are prepared to say is, that the northern departments (approaching as they do Soochow, the seat of Chinese literature, fashion, and dissipation) can, for wealth, learning, and refinement, vie with any other part of the empire; but the southern counties, bounded by the rugged coast or bordering on the wild lands which separate the province from Fuhkien and Kiangse, descend in the scale of respectability and polish. Perhaps a tolerably correct view of the people's character may be had from the opinion recorded in the official Red Book that is published every quarter. Take, for instance, the six departments we have traversed the last eleven days, begining with our starting-point, Ningpo, and travelling southward to where we now stand, and let us see what this official document says:—"The natives in the Ningpo department are given to the culture either of fields or of letters. Their most profitable business is in fisheries, or in salt-works. The people of Shaouhing-foo are diligent, frugal, fond of learning, and by no means dependent on trade alone. Its neighbour county, Hangchow, is famous for having all the greatest as well as the dearest curiosities of the world: merchants from all quarters flock hither. The manners of the people are polished, and their education of the first stamp: it has crowds of *literati* in its population." Then, coming southward, we read of the department of Yenchow, that "its scholars are fond of their books, while the lower classes are active in agriculture." The people of Kinhwa are said to be of two distinct orders: the educated classes, guileless and sincere; and the commonalty, eager in pursuit of husbandry. The natives of Keuchow, the last of the six departments I have visited, are described as "trusty and faithful, though rather rough and unpolished in manners."

Chihkiang province has, from olden times, been the theatre upon which some of the principal acts in Chinese history have been performed. For example, the modern traveller is informed, as he is passing the city of Shaouhing, that at no great distance there is a spot which tradition has rendered famous, and yearly donations from the Imperial family have hallowed, as the tomb of the patriarch King Yaou, who drained off the waters of the Deluge. Again, during the division of the country into the "three kingdoms," the Woo state occupied this whole province, and within its territories carried on its fiercest contests; and not long ago the greatest power of the West, Britain, in her war with China, transferred the seat of contest to this same province; by which means its islands and strongest positions all fell into the hands of the foreign foe. By the treaty of 1842, one of its chief ports, Ningpo, was opened to all foreigners; and may we not hope that that friendly alliance with foreign powers may be perpetuated, free intercourse with the various parts of this large province gradually secured, and thus an entrance gained for Christianity and her handmaids?

CHAPTER III.

TRIP THROUGH KIANGSE AND CANTON PROVINCES—FROM THE BOUNDARY BETWEEN CHIHKIANG AND KIANGSE TO YUHSHAN—FROM YUSHAN TO THE CAPITAL OF KIANGSE, THE CITY OF NANCH'ANG—FROM THE CITY OF NANCH'ANG TO THE TOWN OF NANK'ANG—THE OVERLAND ROUTE ACROSS THE MEILING PASS—FROM MEILING PASS TO NANHIUNG—FROM NANHIUNG TO CANTON AND HONG-KONG.

JULY 19.—To resume the thread of travel:—At five in the afternoon the city of Yuhshan hove in sight upon the brow of a hill,—proof positive we had got fairly into the province of Kiangse. It was no little relief to see myself near the close of the day's ride; particularly as the bamboo sedan was one easy only for the carrier, but not for the carried during an eight hours' session, and after the bursting of a thunderstorm over-head, which, in a tremendous splash of rain, entirely swept off the chair-cover.

Yuhshan has a wall measuring one mile and a quarter in circumference (first erected three hundred years ago). The town looks as if built of red sandstone, and is decorated with famous large trees that cast a delightful shade on the houses underneath. Within an hour we were in the heart of the suburbs. We crossed the Tung-tsin bridge. Originally this was a floating bridge, but so often carried away by inundations, that the authorities hit on the economical expedient of throwing up a stone bridge. It is the finest specimen of the kind in China that had hitherto fallen under my eye, with wide and lofty arches built of massive stone, probably of recent construction. We took the east gate, that opened into a pretty, neat, clean town. Yuhshan was perhaps the nicest-looking town I had yet passed along the tour, and, being an intermediate *entrepôt* between the southern and south-west provinces, and the north and north-east of the empire, its great population was in active employment from sunrise to sunset. Riding past the mayor's office, we kept on the chief street for more than half a mile. By sunset we got to the west gate, outside of which is the *Lo-min-wang* establishment, the house where we had engaged to lodge for the night. I believe this is the most respectable hotel in the place, and carries on an extensive business in the transit line. We supped here; but, having been furnished with a boat to take us six or seven hundred miles farther on to Nan-ngan-foo, we immediately embarked, as we preferred sleeping on board the boat.

July 20.—On waking up I found the boat still lying at the back door of the hotel. Like the rest of the passenger-craft at the place, it did not look so well nor did it afford such accommodation as the junk we had lately quitted. Its roof-matting was frail, slight, and porous, promising little shelter from rain and sun. Nevertheless we must put up with it, though we had about seven hundred miles before us, or twenty-eight successive stages, till we should enter the province of Canton. When we were on the point of starting at noon, I was greatly mortified at finding the small tributary stream leading out of Yuh-shan quite shallow, in some places dried up. On this account we were under the necessity of unloading the boat for the purpose of shifting the luggage into a smaller craft, which should take it to Ho-k'ow, about fifty miles ahead.

At last we managed to start by twelve o'clock. For the first three miles the boat got aground on three distinct sand-banks, each of which could afford a narrow passage of only three yards' width. The sight of stark-naked men working their boats to and fro under the blazing sun, without a rag to cover their shame, arrested and disgusted the eye. The drought of the season being severe, the farmers were most busily engaged in irrigating their fields out of the passing river. This of course made the river shallower. The ordinary water-wheel was everywhere upon the banks, worked either by the hand or the foot, the workmen cautious enough during this terrible scorching to spread an awning overhead. Where the fields were lying in terraces one above another, the higher terraces were watered by working the water up from a lower shelf of land already supplied from the river. After this fashion, land three, four, or five terraces high, was irrigated by half a dozen water-wheels placed at some elevation the one above the other. The most novel spectacle of the sort was that of huge wheels, 20 ft. in diameter, turned by the passing current. To the several paddles of these tremendous wheels small buckets were lashed, which, as the wheels revolved, got filled with water down below, and then rising up to the top, emptied their contents into a trough above, or an aqueduct leading to a neighbouring field, perhaps two or three thousand feet distant.

July 21.—Having to follow the Yuhshan stream, called the Shang-yaou-kiang, we made more way than usual, and came to anchor by nightfall at the well-known mart, Ho-k'ow.

To journalize the notes of the day:—On starting early, we kept south-west for Shang-yaou, the chief town of Kwang-sin-fu. We first glided down the "sandy brook" named Sha-ke, that comes from a hill-summit, fifteen miles north, famous for producing the fine soft stone of which their best ink-slabs are made. As I stood on the prow of the boat, looking on the surrounding land, the eye roamed over an uninteresting level country, and espied a few peaks and hill-tops in the distance. On the whole, perhaps it may be said, the description given by a native topographer respecting the figuration of this shire is pretty accurate: "The mountains are lofty; the water is clear; east and south particularly there are commanding positions." Of these mountains two in particular were attractive; the one to the north-west of Shang-yaou city, "the Ling-shan;" the other behind us, a range of irregular and curious heights, "the Nan-ping," or "the southern screen." In the latter range there is a remarkable peak, called "the Wolf's Tusk." The former is considered one of the citadels of the Kiangse province, and, in the catalogue of "the lions of China," marked off by the Taouist religionists, this range of heights stands No. 33. It has seventy-two pinnacles on it, the loftiest of which has a walk from its foot measuring 70,000 feet in length, and the entire extent of the range is about thirty miles. Upon the loftiest elevation of said range a wonderful lagoon is reported to exist, famous for strange wood, curious weeds, and splendid crystals to be found in it, of which last they used, during the Sung dynasty (A.D. 900—1200), to send a yearly tribute to the court of ten vases made of it.

Shang-yaou is a city built close to the northern edge of the river,—a large, fine-looking place; its wall is thirty feet high, three miles in circumference, and appears to have been lately repaired with two rows of materials, the lower of red rock, the upper of blue brick. The annals of the locality mention several instances of the destruction of the city by inundations. There cannot be much bustle among the people, who, in their ways and manners, give you the notion that they are a "take-it-easy" race; large-footed young women walking about at pleasure, and old matrons riding in one-wheeled barrows moved by young men. The river opposite the town is 400 feet wide. There is a floating bridge of forty boats linked together, boarded over, and lying across the whole width for the accommodation of foot-passengers. After leaving the city, we passed a large boat anchored near the middle of the stream, matted over like a cottage, and with wheels working on both sides of it, like a small steamboat: it was a flour-mill. The wheels, being moved by the current of the river, set the inside machinery a-going, for pounding grain.

A little onwards, three miles from Shang-yaou, on the same side of the river, there is a seven-storied octagonal pagoda, from each corner of whose separate stories there are bells hanging which ring with every passing breeze.

Along the day's route, especially between Shang-yaou and Ho-k'ow, the mountain soil appeared to be of a reddish hue, and the rocks sandstone. The fluvial deposit on both sides of the river was remarkable: embankments of fine dust rose on all hands. The high rocks were of a singular figure; being of exceedingly soft material, they had been rubbed or washed down by frequent and violent inundations into the most fantastic shapes, called by the natives "burnt or scorched rocks." The low hills, all day in sight, were generally covered with rocks, sometimes with trees or brushwood, though not unfrequently bare of all vegetation, and drilled throughout into caves and caverns, usually tenanted by gipsies and houseless wanderers.

July 22.—Ho-k'ow, named so from being "the point where several rivers meet," has by its local position gained a great repute. It lies north latitude 28° 27′, east longitude 118° 6′. South-east from it there is a land route 120 miles in extent, leading to the black-tea districts of Fuhkien, on which account it has become a grand depôt for all black teas destined either for the Canton or the northern marts. There is a large crockery business here also. All this accounted for the thousands of boats that lay here when I visited the mart,—boats of every size and shape, evidently from various parts of the country, with crowds of merchants who had flocked hither from the four points of the compass. There was every sign of a flourishing trade. While immense cargoes of tea, &c., were shipped for Canton, an equal number of boats were returning laden with foreign goods. Most of the warehouses were old, capacious, and lofty, some of them of five stories. The native products of the place, that are sold in large quantities, are hemp, cane, tobacco, tea, paper, "white-lily seeds" and flour from the root of the same, grass-cloth, the finest edible bamboo-shoots, and flours from various grains. The "Red Book" says of the people, "The educated part of the community is marked for temperance and charity, and the lower classes are faithful and trustworthy." At this place I made various purchases of provisions for the rest of the journey, which were got at a moderate price. I bought 460 pieces of fine porcelain, cups and saucers, plates, bowls, vases, &c., for only thirty-six dollars. I had my head shaved by one of the town barbers, who felt much pity for me when he found my tail come off! The Taiping rebels are said recently to have taken possession of this place and its neighbourhood.

Being anxious to reach Canton by the middle of August, I stipulated with the boatmen, and, by an additional fee of twenty dollars, secured five more workmen, who engaged to work day and night. We set sail at mid-day.

A little after leaving Ho-k'ow, there were on the opposite shore nine extraordinary-looking rocks, which it was impossible not to remark. They stood detached, of a deep black colour, of enormous size, and of the shape of a huge bowl turned upside-down. Seen at a distance, they are supposed by natives to resemble the great stone lions that figure at the court gates of the higher officials; and the name given to the group is "The Nine Lions fording the River." This part of the river itself is called "The Lion River."

Before we proceed further, it will not be amiss to

allude to Kingtih-chin, a large market-town, which communicates directly with Ho-k'ow, and contributes greatly to its business and traffic. It is one of four famous interior marts of the empire, lies thirty-five miles north-west of Ho-k'ow, and is far famed for being the chief manufactory of porcelain. It is situated north latitude 29° 16′, east longitude 117° 14′, in the department of Jaouchow (which we are just about to sail across), and within the jurisdiction of its district Fowliang. It is described by those that have visited the place as an immense village, or unwalled town rather, stretching three miles along a beautiful river, and flanked by a semicircle of fine mountains, from which much of the earth required for the ware is brought. A native writer observes, "The earth and water of the vicinity are very suitable for making pottery." The same authority enters into minute details of the great mart, and says it first came into notice 850 years ago,* when the Sung dynasty occupied the throne, and in the reign of Kingtih, who established it as a porcelain mart, and gave his own name to it, "the market-town of Kingtih." Of course, the capabilities of the place for the manufacture and merchandise of the ware had been tested long before his Majesty condescended to honour such a spot with his royal favour and letters patent. During the next five centuries, the credit and reputation of the place grew by degrees until about A.D. 1510, when the eleventh ruler of the Ming line set on foot a particular manufactory for the making of crockery for the Imperial service. This was the very glorification of Kingtih-chin. After this, separate works were erected for the manufacture of official ware and crockery for the common people. If rumour is to be relied on, there are at least 500 kilns constantly at work, "on the fire of which," say they, "the workmen wait as anxiously

* For Fowliang annals say since the sixth century of our era.

as men do for rain in the time of drought." The population of the place, though given out to be quite one million, may be nearer the truth if set down at half a million, which is borne out by the common saying, "At King-tih they daily consume 10,000 piculs of rice and 1,000 pigs." The peculiar ware of this manufacturing town is remarkable for its pureness and glaze. It is made chiefly for native supply. There is not much prepared for the foreign markets, as their limited demand is met out of Canton and Fuhkien, each of which provinces has its own porcelain manufactory. Neither the Canton nor the Fuhkien ware, however, can compete with the Kingtih porcelain, although they are obliged to hire their best workmen from this mart. The material and mode of manufacture are minutely described in a native work of four volumes, copious extracts from which are given in "Duhalde," vol. ii. pp. 311—351, and abridgments thereof in Davis, Grosier, Abel, and other modern writers.

I have above stated that Kingtih is one of "the four marts in China:" The seaports are of course excepted, their commerce being almost confined to foreign exports and imports; as well as the small local markets, which, though numberless, have only the sales and purchases of their immediate neighbourhood. But "the four markets" particularly referred to are spoken of among the natives themselves as the four most important and convenient for commerce in the interior of the Chinese empire, having intercommunications, and affording facilities for transit between every division of country through the eighteen provinces of China within the Great Wall, and in the colonial territories without.

Having entered into a few particulars of Kingtih, one of these interior markets, it remains to mention the other three. One is Choo-sien, of the Honan province, twelve miles south of its capital, K'aifung, in

N. lat. 34° 10′, E. long. 114° 23′. The native writers say: "Here is the point where travellers and merchants meet in passing to all parts of the empire, whether by land or water, and ships from the south, cars from the north, assemble here, and from this diverge to their separate destinations." Next, there is Fuh-shan, twelve miles from Canton, which we shall touch at on our way to that city. And then there is Hank'ow, in the province of Hoopih, which is situate in N. lat. 30° 34′, E. long. 114° 10′, on the south bank of the "Ocean-child," 250 miles from Nanking, and 500 from the mouth of the Yangtsze-kiang. Though a little below the city of Hanyang, to which department it belongs, it is contiguous and stretches along the river-bank right opposite to Woochang, the capital of Hoopih, both banks of the river being separated by a breadth of three miles. According to native statements, the concourse of people and the commerce carried on here must be enormous, which is corroborated by some foreign travellers that have visited the spot in disguise. It is matter of regret, though not of surprise, that these four marts have recently been visited, and it is to be feared devastated, by the marauding mobs under the Taiping flag.

To return from my long digression:—before sunset we reached another district town, Yih-yang; but, unlike the rest we had visited, its walls were crumbled and had fallen, the place itself mean-looking, and the people few and poor. On approaching the spot, I could not but observe a massive rock rising up, close to the water's edge, perhaps ten yards high, in shape like a huge store, and called Tseentsang, "the cash-store." It owes its notoriety to a tradition, dated from the fifth century, about a poor fisherman who went on a day's work early in the morning, and, on looking into a gaping fissure in the rock, to his no small delight he found a bag of money. And, although one did not see "the stone house" (as another curiosity in the neighbourhood is called), yet, from the character of the place one might almost credit a story given of a native of the town, who, to shun society (somewhat like the cynic philosopher of Sinope that lived in a tub), cut a cavity out of a great rock, and made it a sort of circular granary in which to conceal himself, shutting himself in from all intercourse with his fellow-creatures and rejecting every offer of official promotion.

July 23.—This was an unusually fine day, though devoid of incident. As for scenery, there was scarcely one hand's breadth of rising ground in sight to relieve the flat level on both sides of the river. The first part of the description given in the topography of the country was verified by the observations of the day, "that its plains are extensive and its streams very large;" but I cannot confirm the latter part of the sketch given in that work, that "it lies as a sort of cap, or fine and elegant ornament, upon the southern borders of the provinces of Kiangnan and Hoopih!" The only breaks upon the monotony of the day were:—First, on sweeping past the walled town Kweike, we looked, but looked in vain, for a spot mentioned in the Chinese itinerary, as "the Kweikuh hill," chiefly celebrated for an "immense cavern, measuring a mile or two in area, capable of holding several thousand people, but having the light so excluded that you are obliged in entering to carry torches with you." Second, a cormorant-fishery carried on as in other places above specified. And third, a salt-guard station, which we passed at Shihkang, or three miles above the town Nganjin. The yellow Imperial standard flying over the guard-house, could be seen a good way off, with the three characters inscribed on it, *Fung-che-sze*, "under Imperial orders to check smuggling." The object ostensibly is to prevent all kinds of smuggling of salt from the sea-coast of Chihkiang into Kiangse. When our boat had come abreast of the station, we had to lie to for one of the detective force who boarded us, and rummaged among our goods and chattels, but went away empty-handed.

Here we enter a new tract of country, of old known by several names, but latterly adopting what is considered more appropriate to its fertility and productiveness, the name "Jaou county." Of its people they say, "Their habits and temper are remarkable for openness and generosity, as the soil is for its productiveness, and the higher classes are educated and refined." At midday we passed Nganjin, a borough town, which when first built was unwalled. About three hundred years ago, when a notorious bandit, Yaouyuen, made fearful depredations, it was deemed prudent to defend it. They accordingly ran up a mud wall round it, capped with stones and bricks. Still, judging from the general aspect of the place, with its low buildings, dilapidated walls, and scanty population, the dreary conclusion is forced on a traveller, that it must be wretched and poor in the extreme. To-day my teachers and servants got on with some difficulty in communications with the boatmen, the majority of whom smattered a strange Canton-Kiangse gibberish.

July 24.—We encountered a fearful thunder-storm last night, and a second edition this morning; after which the boatmen got the boat under weigh. Fortunately wind and current favoured us in hurrying out of a district which, begging "the Red Book's" pardon, is the most flat and uninteresting, perhaps, that I have had to cross. For the first part of the day, along thirty miles we sailed over, the banks were low, country level, fields nothing but millet, cotton, or rice, mountains remote, villages scattered, human beings scarce, birds and beasts scanty. The peculiar products of the neighbourhood were pottery of various kinds, tea, a peculiar fine fish called "silver-fish," and a singular material named "plum-cloth." A little after noon we managed to reach a small harbour, on the north-east edge of the Poyang lake, into which the river, that has brought us with rapidity from Ho-k'ow, empties itself. But we were unable to purchase any provisions whatever at this place. The point at which we entered the lake was Kwantang, on the east limb of the Poyang, about six miles from the last-mentioned station. Here the water was by no means shallow, close to the brink measuring fifteen feet deep. We took a westerly course, intending to sail across a distance of twelve miles, to get into the stream that leads from the south-west edge to Nanch'ang, the capital of the province. A light breeze, however, swept us up to the northward, towards a high mountain lying in the centre of the lake. On the western shore chains of high mountains rose up in the distance. The face of the lake was sprinkled over with islets, and dotted with little hills. It was not a little enlivening to watch numerous boats, and occasionally a large junk, sailing about upon this inland sea. By native measurements the Poyang lake is 140 miles in circumference, —its greatest width, east to west, twelve miles, and length, north to south, ninety miles. Four different counties meet in the centre, and the waters of three provinces flow into its basin,—the streams from Keu-chowfoo, in Chihkiang; from Jaouchow, in Kiangse; and from Hwuychow, in Nganhwuy; and at the upper or northern end, the lake pours its contents into the great Yang-tsze-kiang.

As night-shades fell rapidly upon us, we were kept from pursuing further observations. Occasionally ducks were to be seen floating about on the surface of the waters. The lake abounds in capital fish. Upon the banks, there is a deep chocolate-coloured mud, used for making a peculiar kind of pottery exported in large quantities from these parts. The vicinity of the lake is also said to abound with granite rocks, which supply some of the *matériel* for their porcelain manufactories.

July 25 opened with a dusky, drizzling morn. During the whole day we were travelling in the Nanchang department, which native writers portray as being remarkable for the rivers that roll through its territories. The great Poyang lake stretches along its north-east bounds, and the eastern border of the Hoopih province fringes its western. It is commanded by the city of Nanchang, the south-east capital of the empire. This city, according to the most recent observations, lies north latitude 28° 37′ 12″, and east longitude 115°48′ 17″, or 855 miles south-west of Peking. By 9 A.M. we had evidence sufficient that we were approaching the capital, which, being 600 miles on our trip, was our half-way house to Canton. At Kiang-kow, a few miles out of Nanchang, there were two novelties *en passant* : the one, a man sailing in a tub across the river, a mile in width ; the other, a spectacle of two droves of horned cattle, fifty a drove.

At 3 P.M. we were off one of the principal *mattoes* of Nanchang city ; where there were lying junks of enormous magnitude, for the carriage chiefly of grain and tribute to Peking, and equally large pleasure-boats to be let out on hire.

The suburbs of this provincial city are extensive, though rather disappointing to one who had heard marvellous things of Nanchang capital. Large portions of the extramural buildings were in complete ruin, showing traces of some recent devastation by flood ; old houses, government granaries, &c., were scattered about the outer suburbs. The city itself was an irregular polygon, with six gates, the larger side towards the river, and the circuit of the walls about 5½ miles.

At the earliest convenience we laid in a stock of provisions, and, having but a short time to spare, I hired two covered sedans to espy the city in company with my old guide. The city is situated upon the east bank of the Chang river. Entering in by the west gate, whose designation was tastefully put over it, "The Chang-kiang Gate," *i. e.* "the gate on the banks of the river Chang," we passed through the principal thoroughfares. The streets were broader than usual in Chinese towns, and the shops looked fine, large, and clean. As it was raining, the bazaars were not crowded, though they were amply supplied with various kinds of goods. The people seemed generally well dressed, and the few women that ventured out remarkably good-looking. We made for the east gate, and passed by the several offices of the city mayor, the chief judge, and the provincial viceroy, each one having a massive showy gateway thrown up in front. The high officers resident here are the lieutenant-governor, literary chancellor, a colonel, a treasurer, a judge, a grain and a salt commissioner. This is the chief seat of civil administration, courts of law, and various departments of public business for a population almost equal to the last census of Great Britain. The capital, though an entrepôt rather than a manufacturing city, is the centre of education, fashion, conveniences, and luxuries, from which at least seventy-six country towns of fourteen counties are supplied.

We intended taking a round in the Pih-hwa-chow, "the islet of all kinds of flowers," extensive pleasure-grounds near the east gate; but the rain, as well as the rapid approach of the hour for departure, debarred us a ramble through these gardens. Here every visitor is pointed to a tablet, upon which there is inscribed what is considered a remarkable saying of General Changching, of the Sung dynasty (the eleventh century), who laid out a lagoon in these grounds for boat-racing, and proclaimed to his countrymen his firm opinion, that "before one talks of military affairs, he must first of all be skilled in naval tactics." Returning by the south gate, we observed a small pagoda with an exceedingly bright steeple. Not far from it is a famous "iron pillar," cast by a native a long time since, and set up over the mouth of a well for the benevolent object of checking the noxious influences supposed to issue from beneath out of "the cavern of dragons." The pillar is now inclosed within the precincts of a temple.

By sunset we found ourselves at the west gate again. Just outside we passed the Tangwang hall, one of the oldest and the most reputed buildings in Nanchang. It was originally erected in the middle of the seventeenth century by Kaoutsung, of the Tang dynasty, "in memoriam" of the elevation of one of his sons to the governorship of the principality. The base of the building is adorned with trees and flowers most tastefully arranged. Besides smaller tablets stuck up in various parts of the hall, its central wall is covered with poetic effusions and original scraps. There is one literary piece in particular, the narrative of which production is related by the natives with great zest. It appears that some time ago a governor, who had repaired the edifice, opened it with due pomp and ceremony, and appointed a feast to be held within the walls that was to last for nine days. Being anxious to embrace this as an occasion for the display of his son-in-law's scholastic attainments, he got a fine literary article stealthily prepared to commemorate the opening of the hall, which he wished should be produced at the height of the festal season by his son-in-law, as an extempore effusion, to startle the guests and draw forth their applause. Of the *literati* invited to the feast there was a young man of poor parentage, who, previous to the festival, was under the necessity of going home to visit his father two hundred miles away from the provincial capital. However, after reaching his father's domicile, a water elf came to him in a dream upon the night previous to the grand festival, and assured him that, if he would start instantly, she would aid him with fair wind and tide to reach Nanchang by next morning. He consented, followed her advice, and returned in time to meet the jovial crowd. After all had been regaled with wine, the noble host called on each of the learned guests by name to write off a piece in commemoration of the event to celebrate which they were then assembled. Considering the imposing pomp of the spectacle, the number of scholars present, and the high character of their host, each guest in turn declined, until this youth's name was called out, when, to the amazement of the governor, he answered the challenge, and began to write off-hand a paper as required. The host, trembling for the fame of his own son-in-law, set a servant to stand behind the essayist and telegraph each sentence as he wrote it. When he came to the middle of the piece, his excellency could not help exclaiming, "Ah, this is celestial talent!" Upon this, his son-in-law retired from the contest, ashamed and confounded. Such is the story of the writing ordered to be inscribed upon the middle wall of Tangwang hall.

July 26.—We left Nanchang at seven o'clock last night. By nine we were sailing over legendary ground, where, among other things, it is related that, a long time ago, as a poor fisherman was engaged at his daily toil, he threw a handful of rice, still in the husk, as a bait for the finny tribe, and himself dived into the depths below in search of his prey. Suddenly he came upon a rocky gate at the mouth of a cave, where one of the white-bearded genii accosted him somewhat abruptly with the speech, "This is a spot whither you have no business to come." This so frightened the rude native, that he made his way as fast as he could to the bank, and declared to his family that it seemed as if he had been three days and three nights under water. That stupid story has nominated these "the raw-rice depths." Having kept up sail the whole night, we made about twenty-four miles, and by five o'clock in the morning were at She-ch'ah. The greater part of the morning's route lay through extensive plantations of indigo, found to be a more profitable speculation in this neighbourhood than any of the grains.

In the vicinity of Fungching the river widens considerably, from having three or four tributaries flowing into it. Hereabouts we passed under several embankments, erected for the purpose of keeping the river within its channel, one in particular at Hwang-fow-hiung, of immense masses of granite, extending a mile or two along the river-side.

All day long several enormous rafts floated by, with cottages built on them, and woodmen at work flaying timber. There was one in particular, of which I could not but take notes. It measured nearly a mile in length, rising about four feet above water, and nine feet broad. The entire train was a junction of smaller rafts, the separate rafts being of the same length (perhaps fifteen or twenty feet), as they were of the same height and width. The logs and trunks of trees on each raft were lashed together by willow-twigs and rattans, and the separate rafts were fastened one behind the other. By this method of connecting the distinct parts of the train, the whole float moved easily round the windings, and yielded to the crooks of the river as pliably as the links of a massive chain. Several men were stationed at the front part of the raft to direct its course with their sweeps, and a few others walked along its edge to push it off the river-bank. In one or two parts there were short masts and tiny sails set. Huts were erected on it for lodging, booths for cooking, also small cots for the stowage of different articles picked up on private speculation *en route* from the interior of the country; *e. g.*, medicinal herbs, vegetables, birds, squirrels, monkeys, &c. Small kitchen-gardens were growing here and there on the float to serve for the trip. It was unmistakable too that there was a child's nursery upon the moving mass, along with nursing mothers. The rafts contained all sorts of timber-trees, cut down far inland, or probably on the mountains of Hoonan, and destined for the midland and northern provinces.

July 27.—At midnight we entered the Linkiang shire, and passed Changshoo, described as a great "medicine market," where all the herbs of the Chinese pharmacopœia may be had. The river here becomes wider, the sand white, and the soil around very rich. The native topographer appears to give a tolerably accurate account in his descriptive geography of this county:—"The rocks look blue, the water clear, and the soil is fine and fertile." Medical herbs and coals are the special products of the neighbourhood. While mother-earth is lauded for her fatness and fertility, the official Directory gazettes "the scholars as eminent, and the commonalty good-natured."

In Kiangse, cattle of the bovine class abound more than in Chihkiang. Pork-flesh (it is said) is not much eaten in this province. Candles of animal tallow are extensively used, save in idol-worship. For this latter purpose, it being profane to employ anything but vegetable productions, tea-oil or vegetable moulds and dips are in great request.

July 28.—At 5 A.M. I was called up to look at the singularly-walled town of Kiah-kiang, on our right hand, built upon the bank of the river, inclosing one half of a hill, the town wall running for a quarter of a mile along the ridge of the hill.

At sunrise next morning we were abreast of the chief town of Keih-ngan department, apparently well fortified with a fine white wall. Its wall measures seven yards high, is in books said to have at one time had nine gates, and originally six, though now only three miles in circumference. The sight was new, and took me rather by surprise, after the numerous small towns and petty cities, &c., I had recently passed. The population was dense, and apparently bustling. The eastern face of the city is full one mile along the western bank of the river, and its eastern corner is remarkable for a pagoda, snow-white and dazzling in the sunshine. The heart of the city includes some large, lofty, and commanding buildings. Among these there is one far-famed as the Tsinsze ti-yih-tang, "the chief hall of the Tsinsze scholars," erected in memory of a celebrated native of the city, a dux of the Tsinsze literary degree, who flourished in the eleventh century. On his promotion, he wrote out the character *kw'ei*, "head, chief, foremost,"—used in designating the high scholastic attainments he had reached. The peculiarity in this instance was that, on having fully written it out, the character alone measured upwards of ten feet square. To commemorate this feat of penmanship, an exact copy thereof was engraved upon a large stone of proportionate dimensions, which was lodged in the above hall, where it remains to this day. The river abreast of the city is wide, deep, and rapid; and we slipped by under a fair wind, leaving the city to our right, with some regret that we could not wait a while to roam about the precincts of a place unusually attractive.

The 30th was dreadfully barren of incident, except that, outdone in our calculations of obtaining provisions, we had nothing for food all day but plain rice and hard-boiled eggs. The stock of vegetables and meat had all been consumed; and, wherever we touched in search of something substantial, we could meet with nothing they could spare to supply our lack, except in one village, where we had to refuse "canine flesh" that was offered for sale. As far as one might judge from casual observation on a trip like this, the greater proportion of the country people of Kiangse must be deplorably poor,—in general wearing the coarsest hempen cloth, and eating the loathsome bean-curd with rice. That impression was confirmed from the further observations of the next day; in the earlier part of which we were carried through a territory certainly most forbidding, with villagers and tenantry as miserable as one can imagine the peasantry of the most unfortunate country on the face of the earth to be. Here and there whitewashed pagodas, of various stories, rose up to relieve the sad monotony; and if really there be any geomantic charm in such erections to improve an inhospitable neighbourhood, (which is the belief of the people with respect to pagodas,) most undoubtedly we may hope, from the number of these towering buildings about this district, that in due time the soil will fatten, and the territory improve, in a region of such dearth and dreariness.

In the afternoon we came to the town of Wan-ngan, a wretched-looking place, to be sure, although we managed to lay in a stock of food and fuel for a few days to come. Quitting this station, our course lay direct south. Following the upward course of the river, we by-and-by found ourselves upon the threshold of a mountainous range. Before nightfall we got encircled by wooded banks, and hills conical, abrupt, and bleak. In sight of these we anchored, and found a pleasant retreat for the night, after the dull and dreary monotony of the last week.

August 1.—The reason given by the boatmen for anchoring last night a little above the town of Wan-ngan was, that they wished to refresh themselves by a night's sound sleep for the eighteen rapids (commonly called twenty-four) that awaited them during the next two stages. Among other preparatory measures, I saw they took care to propitiate the favour of the spirits which they believe preside over the rivers, and haunt the mountain crags in the neighbourhood. At daybreak we moved, and by sunset had ascended eleven rapids. None of these were by any means so difficult as those already described along our route up the Chihkiang river.

The romantic scenery and mountain grandeur of this day's journey well repaid the patience and forbearance called forth during the last ten days' travel upon the uninteresting flats of Kiangse. Lofty hills all round, near and far,—everywhere showing a deep red soil, sometimes patched with verdant spots, or dotted with trees, but oftener bleak, rugged, and laid with large blocks of dark granite. The river-bank, on either side, rises high, and frequently is cut through by torrents pouring down the steep ribs of the mountains aloft. The river itself was more like a mountain stream, fitful and capricious, in some places expanding wide and broad, and running smooth without any obstacles, but more often interrupted by rugged rocks, over which its waters splashed and foamed in wild fury. The rapids were remarkable at times for their shallowness, and always for the enormous and curious blocks strewed along their beds, shaped like spires, pinnacles, &c., or, as the native topographer describes them, "jutting up like sharp iron spikes, or with sharp corners and broken faces." In many places the channel looked as if it had been worked out by the water's flow, or dug through the rocky foundations of the steep banks; and though it was scarcely six feet wide, through that narrow channel the great volume of water leaped, flashed, and rushed, with the roar of a magnificent fall. Numerous examples came under the eye, along the beds of these rapids, of huge solid rocks, either considerably worn down by the abrasion of the rushing water, or wrought into most grotesque shapes.

August 2.—All day fine hills in view, with goats grazing on the slopes; numerous tombs of the horseshoe shape, the Canton style; extensive fields of sugar-cane cultivated in the plain; lofty trees ornamenting the river-banks; more people than usual at work; numerous women, with large aprons, unbound feet, and straw hats, labouring in the fields, or carrying loads, &c. By 4 P.M. the men craved a "cumshaw" for their skill and expertness in mounting the last of the eighteen rapids. At this point we were boarded by a party of the river-police belonging to the branch custom-house stationed here. Their object was to inspect boats south-ward bound, and to give due notice of the contents thereof to the head establishment. This provision has been instituted to prevent the smuggling of goods and merchandise to the south along the innumerable small branches into which the river divides itself a mile or two farther on. Before sunset we reached K'anchow. Since we left the Poyang lake, our course had been up what is usually called the K'an river, though along its flow it picks up a great variety of local names. From the city of K'anchow down to the Poyang, into which it empties itself, the K'an river measures nearly 300 miles. It has two chief tributaries, the *Chang* and the *Kung*. The grand river divides at the city of K'anchow into two streams; the one to the east running direct up to its source, 110 miles off in the Sienloo mountains, upon the western border of Fuhkien province; the other to the west, if traced up to its fountain-head, carries us at once to the Wangking range, on the southern boundary of Hoonan, about 186 miles distant. The above two tributaries meet together at the city of K'anchow, until their united waters pass Nanchang and pour into the Poyang lake, running altogether a course of 486 miles down from their highest springs. At K'anchow we found a number of boats lying together. Their tonnage being too large for the draught of water in either of the above streams, it was found necessary to send their cargoes on to Canton or Fuhkien by smaller craft.

Our boat being small enough to admit of steering along in safety, we were by 7 P.M. at anchor. There are two custom-houses here; the eastern for Fuhkien boats, the western for Canton traders. We of course chose the latter anchorage. The city itself is large and strongly built.

August 3.—At sunrise we secured passports at the custom-house, purchased provisions for the next hundred miles, (the last part of the journey through Kiangse to Canton,) and after breakfast were again under sail. The chief part of the day's journey (only twenty-five miles) lay close to the bank of the river, lined with immense bodies of timber-rafts on their way to the midland or northern parts of the empire.

The bamboos of this department are particularly elegant and valuable,—of every variety, chiefly the speckled. Large groves of them were everywhere met with: also fields of the sugar-cane, of which (what the natives call) "the sand-sugar" is made in large quantities. We found immense fields of this article cultivated here. Indeed, it is one of the principal products and exports of the province. The raw cane is often cut into small pieces fit for chewing,—a practice very common among the people in their leisure hours. For granulation and crystallization it is first pressed in the mill, when the juice is boiled and refined. At one time this coarse brown sugar used to be bought very largely for India. The candy sugar continues to be still a favourite with foreigners.

Nothing else came under the eye during the day worthy of observation, except huge waterwheels. These were frequently seen at work on the banks, turned by the flowing river, and with the utmost regularity conveying water up to reservoirs in the heights above, for the purpose of irrigating the inland fields. Some of the wheels measured forty feet in diameter; whose paddles consisted of large bamboo or rattan buckets, inserted with pivots upon the outer rim of the circumference. Lest the axletree should catch fire from the severe friction, a contrivance was adopted by which the wheel was supplied at that very point (where there was so much friction) with a constant stream of water trickling from above.

The products of the Kanchow department, besides those above mentioned, are grass-cloth, tea, tea-oil, olives, and hemp. In the neighbourhood the most beautiful varnish of China is obtained, distilled from the tree called Ts'ihshoo. The grass-cloth is made of hemp, grown most extensively in this and the neighbouring provinces. This cloth is a native substitute for linen,—a cool, glossy, summer cloth, made into what they call "perspiration-jackets," to be worn next the skin. Of the varieties of hemp, the most common in the Kiangse province is the *choo-ma,* miserably mispronounced by some foreigners, *chuh-ma,* as if made from bamboo, of which kind of cloth, indeed, there is no specimen whatever in all the eighteen provinces of China. The Government Directory remarks of the people in the Kanchow department, which we are on the point of leaving:—"They are fine-looking, the scholars good-tempered, and the *plebs* in general upright and honest."

During the 4th and 5th of August we were dragging a slow and weary course towards the chief town of Nan-ngan, the department of Kiangse most contiguous to the province of Canton. In this wearisome part of the excursion, a little relief was afforded to the vision by the novel appearance of the river-bank, in some parts shelved with (what looked like) dark-coloured coal-slate, occasionally ornamented by thick-set bamboo groves, or shaded by wide-spreading camphor-trees. There seemed to be engaged in field-work quite as many female as male labourers; at least, the former appeared to be equally busy and energetic, if one might judge from their noise and singing. The women were particularly noticeable for their short outer dresses, long pantalettes, and bonnets of circular shape, made of straw, and fringed with blue cloth or blue threads round the edge, with an opening exactly on the crown, through which the tuft of hair might be pushed. We passed but few villages—indeed, no place of consequence, except the walled town of Nank'ang, on the western bank. This place was neither large nor bustling, yet neat, with many fine, well-built houses. The traveller's attention cannot fail to be taken here by the large Confucian temple, which rises high and commanding, with four characters emblazoned over its principal gateway, "Tih-p'ei-t'ien-te," signifying, "Virtue compeers with heaven and earth."

August 6.—Until mid-day we were working our way to the terminus of our journey in Kiangse. While our progress was intolerably slow, from early dawn to 1 P.M. making not more than nine miles, the weather was fine, and the scenery agreeable, affording a pleasant change to the scenes that had passed before us during the last week or two. All nature looked picturesque and lovely, along a crooked, winding river, with steep banks rising into high hills, whose sides were grooved by innumerable mountain streamlets, studded with immense trees and massive blocks, or ornamented by pretty glens and shadowy dells.

Among other sights, one particularly riveted the attention,—a few miles above Nan-ngan, upon our right hand, an exquisitely fine waterfall, dropping down the side of the hill right into the river, in a narrow, long, silver-white stream. * * * * At last, sweeping round the base of a hill, we came suddenly, to our no little relief, in sight of the long-looked-for town of Nan-ngan, and by one o'clock dropped anchor at its mart, remarkable chiefly as "the go-between" of Canton and the northern provinces.

The terminus here looked well, with the numerous junks ranged in complete order on both sides of the river, and large hotels, caravansaries, &c., upon the left or eastern shore. On reaching the wharf, we took the first opportunity to engage the services of the "Choo" hong agents, who undertook to expedite our trip by an overland transit of several miles, principally across the well-known Meiling pass.

* * * * * *

Before moving forward, let me take a rapid glance back on the province of Kiangse, in which I have spent the last twenty days in only one boat. I have got over about seven hundred miles of circuitous route, passing through seven counties out of fourteen into which the province is parted, and touching at fifteen walled cities, one the great capital Nanchang. The wide amphitheatre presents a face mostly flat, sometimes uneven; three parts of its circle being bounded by mountain-ranges, on the east, south, and west, separating Kiangse from Nganhwuy, Chihkiang, Fuhkien, Canton, and Hoonan; and its northern limit consisting to a great extent of the province of Hoopih and partly the river Yangtsze, which runs eighty miles along that frontier. The soil is uncertain, in some places remarkably rich, in others exceedingly sterile. Of its twenty-three million inhabitants, the common people are on the whole poor, often deplorably wretched, though industrious and hardworking at crockery-manufacture and weaving of hemp cloth, besides boat-navigation, fishery, field labour, and carriage of goods. As to literary attainments, the scholars do not compete in number or eminence with those of the neighbouring provinces. The situation of the province renders it of peculiar importance to the Chinese empire. It commands the thoroughfare between the northern and southern parts of the interior, supporting a line of land and water communication that measures full seven hundred miles in length. In other words, it is the key-province between Canton and the inland provinces. A native surveyor observes particularly, that "Kiangse has five gateways into different parts of the empire. Suppose," says he, "there is a rebellion in Hoopih, you can enter that province from Kiangse by the department of Kewkiang, which lies on the north of Kiangse; if any trouble in Chihkiang and Fuhkien, there is Kwangsinfoo to the north-east, through which you can pour down on the troubled districts; or let there be a commotion in Canton, why you have K'anchowfoo at command; or imagine that a disturbance breaks out in Hoonan, we can at once enter to quell it by crossing from the department of Nan-ngan."

* * * * * *

As for the narrative of my passage across the Meiling mountain:—By one o'clock we had moved our traps on shore and committed them to the custody of bearers in the employ of the "Choo" hong. Four chairs were hired for my party,—that for myself a large, ponderous, clumsy concern, which required four men to carry it. Without delay we stepped into our conveyances, and commenced the journey across an isthmus reported to be nearly thirty miles in length. Generally eighteen hours are allowed for accomplishing the transit.

Passing out along the suburbs of Nan-ngan, we avoided traversing the narrow dirty streets of the walled town on a dry sultry afternoon; and shortly we were led out into the open conntry, when, taking a south-west course, we came in full view of the Meiling pass, the foot of which lay five miles off. Thither there stretched an even, well-paved, or, I should say, a compactly pebbled road. On this highway there were two continuous and almost unbroken trunk-lines of carriers, the one coming, the other going. These porters were generally in couples, with a pole-end resting on the shoulder of each, on which pole there swung travellers' baggage or merchants' goods. The larger number of the carriers I met were evidently intrusted with the transport of foreign ware and manufactures from Canton into the interior. It is said that fifty thousand persons gain their livelihood by being employed on this high road as porters for carrying packages, passengers, and merchandise over the pass. As I looked at them, they presented a most amusing sight,—walking with a quick measured pace, and, as they trudged, singing, chanting, and responding to each other, though in a strain and style altogether novel, and quite different from the cooly shouting and yelling that meets one in every street of the "cinque ports" of China. What added to the curiosity of the scene was the sight of women turning burden-bearers, often yoked with one of their own sex, not rarely paired off with one of the other, more frequently in groups of ten and twelve of various ages, and in every instance carrying as heavy loads as the males.

With regard to the defile ahead of us: from the native authorities who have written on this frontier pass—or, as they nominate it, "the throat of the north and south of China"—it appears that Meiling is the most eastern ridge of a range of five mountains in Canton province. It is variously named,—in books the Tay-yu, in common language the Meiling. The latter is derived from the *prunus*, a species of wild cherry, growing over its northern and southern faces;—of which the singularity is noticed, "that the shrubs on the north face begin to blossom just when those on the southern drop their flowers." Several attempts have been made to open across its summit a road passable for troops, traders, and travellers. Both public engineers and private contractors have summoned their wits and united their energies on the achievement of the grand feat. A thousand years ago, under the reign of Yuentsing, of the Tang dynasty, some officials set to work clearing the mountain-sides, and laying down a kind of rough footpath. Four centuries after, a fine consolidated pathway was laid, with bricks made from the clay taken from the hill-sides. But a later result, with some very recent repairs, is the present footpath. According to a native document on "Repairing Mountain Roads," it seems that not quite four hundred years ago, when the Ming family was on the throne, the road was repaired in the following mode:—"Immense rocks, having had large fires burnt over them, were broken by huge mallets: streams of water were turned off by opening new gutters; collections of mud and stones were beaten down flat; and thus a spiral staircase was in course of time formed up the hill-side." This was probably the original of the improved highway which I was now in the act of mounting.

The northern face of the pass presented a prospect to the eye pleasing beyond description. The vast mountain-side, from the base to the crest of the ridge, was one carpet of verdure and luxuriance, relieved by stern, rocky cliffs, and the sombre foliage of huge, expansive pine-trees. Up through the heart of the picturesque landscape,—which, to a person confined so long in boats, looked like a hanging garden,—I was able to trace a beaten path, about twelve feet wide, worked by man's hand through rugged rocks and thick jungles, forming something of the staircare fashion, by which a footpath ascends and descends mountain acclivities, running zigzag up to the top of the *sierra*. This was "the spiral ladder" above alluded to.

Sitting in my sedan, while it was borne up this staircase on the shoulders of four men, I took the opportunity of looking on the scenery above and below. From top to bottom the fertility of the ground was remarkable; right and left there was almost one green expanse. After proceeding for some time amid rich, exuberant vegetation, I rose to an elevation from which a wide and strangely varied prospect of mountain and champaign scenery in China met the eye. Below and behind there opened out the cultivated country of Kiangse,—a valley at this season almost stripped of its harvest, a province looking as lonely as a waste of waters, a far-extended and monotonous plain, upon whose boundaries, in the distant horizon, there rose up some few and sparse hills, that seemed like small rounded eminences. Drawing the eye from the plain beneath up to the *sierra*, computed by some to be 1,000 feet above the level below, I observed that on the acclivities which I had been ascending there were splintered and projecting crags, dark and ragged ravines, steep slopes, with numerous rocky masses, tall cliffs, and stony mounds, grouped together in wild disorder. Through openings in the nearer ridges, there could be detected a wilderness of high mounds, stunted hills, &c., the one rising above the other; while here and there, also, a ridge shot up, rugged and angular, full of dusky glens, narrow gorges, shivering summits, and broken crests. But this is an imperfect description of the Meiling pass on the Kiangse side of the ascent.

Having reached the very summit of the pass, the bearer set my chair down for a short respite; and here, once more looking down on the scenery behind, which inclosed not one but many provinces and ancient kingdoms, all comprehended within the sweep of vision from this mountain-top,—it was impossible to forbid the rush of thought on what may have been their past history, changes, convulsions, overthrows, calamities; or on their present state, population, agriculture, manufacture, idolatry, and ignorance; and likewise on their future destiny, improvements in civilization, arts, and sciences, and the introduction, struggles, and triumphs of Christ's religion. The wondrous grandeur of the lavishments of nature, as well as the serious reflections created by the whole scene, alike contributed to leave the deepest impression, and to draw forth the earnest ejaculation, "How long, Lord?—Give this people to Thy Son for His inheritance, and these parts of the earth for His possession."

By the time we got to the Meikwan, (the highest point in the pass which was to be reached in order to commence the descent on the south side of the mountain,) the sun had begun to set. The distance from our starting-place to this "plum pass" was but six miles and a half. Eighteen miles more stretched before, towards Nanhiung, our first station in Canton province. The distances, on the road were indicated by milestones and handposts, set up at intervals of four or five miles. The top pass itself was a gap, cut through the mountain-crest to the depth of twenty or thirty feet, fifty feet long and twenty broad, and fortified on each side by a towering buttress of limestone rock; where, in ludicrous contrast, there lay an awkward squad of Chinese soldiers stationed to guard the passage.

In the native history of the southern provinces of China this pass is regarded as a sentry-post of first importance; and, in a native description of Canton province, it is put down as "always having been the world's struggling-place," or "the Thermopylæ of the world." In passing through it, I felt as if "I entered where a key unlocks a kingdom," it being the territorial line between the two provinces Kiangse and Canton.

On coming to the southern slope of the Meiling, a fine view presented itself of a country covered with green fields and wooded hills; and while the "mind's eye" is gazing down upon the Canton province, it may not be out of order to say a few words of its geographical position and relations. It lies between 18° and 25° N. lat., stretches in E. long. from 107° to 120°; and, according to native reckoning, measures 750 miles from east to west, and 540 miles from north to south. The capital is 2,400 miles from Peking. The province is hemmed in on the S.S.E. and S.W. by "the great sea," to the N. and N.W by Kwangse, N. by Hoonan, N.E. by Kiangse, and E. by Fuhkien. It is partitioned off into fifteen *foos* or counties, and boasts of a population exceeding nineteen millions. The ground is fruitful; and the face of the land, with its fine rising hills and pretty low valleys, combines the scenery of the two provinces already skimmed over in the early part of the route. Its people are aptly portrayed in one of their own books to be, what every foreigner can fully attest, "active in trade, pushing in business, and clever at anything; their *literati* are eminent and shining, and the *vulgus* extravagant and showy."

At the foot of the mountain, on the Canton side, we came to the head-quarters of the colonel in charge of the soldiery set to protect the pass, and found a large village in the vicinity, with innumerable eating-houses for passengers and burden-bearers, of whom there was a large gathering this evening, all bustling and boisterous. After nightfall we pursued our journey till near midnight, when we stopped for supper at what was named "the central station." From "plum pass" above, to this halfway house, the greater part of the road was well laid, and on it we passed through numerous villages, some of them overshadowed by beautiful, umbrageous, and lofty trees rising up on both sides; which sight becomes the more remarkable on a summer's night, from crowds of insects singing or screeching upon the branches, and clouds of fireflies illuminating the shades beneath. Greatly tired with the first part of the overland carriage, I felt glad to enter this village for a short reprieve: where also a warm fresh diet was served up, during which the waiters paid the most assiduous attention,—not knowing all the while that they had caught a "red-haired devil."

Upon taking a due portion of rest, it was with difficulty the chair-bearers could be made to move. They complained of the darkness of the night, particularly as they had no lanterns with them. It was stipulated, however, that as the moon was still shining overhead, they should prosecute their journey until she should set, when they might rest again for a little. The men, relieved with this hope, proceeded until within five miles of the city Nanhiung (N. lat. 25° 11′, E. long. 113° 55′), the goal of the day's weary trip, when, determined that I should keep my part of the bargain about the setting of the moon, they dropped the chair down and would not stir a peg farther. Having been roused again at daybreak of the 7th of August, they resumed their tramp, and hastened to the town beyond, whose gates were just being opened. The suburbs were extensive. We made for the east gate, walked along the central market-place (then empty and very quiet), passed by two or three public offices, went out at the south gate, crossed the Taiping bridge of seven arches, and put up at the magnificent *hong* of Yang-san-ho.

August 7.—After breakfast a passage-boat was hired, at the heavy charge of fifty dollars,—on condition, however, that we should be taken to the city of Canton in six days at the utmost, a distance of 1,315 les, or 390 English miles. The river which we entered at Nanhiung was throughout easy of navigation down to Canton. There were several interruptions, from its narrowness and shallowness; yet the run was rapid, compared with the up-stream work of the previous three weeks, and the scenery upon the banks was a decided improvement on the flatness and monotony of Kiangse.

On the evening of the 8th we brought up at Shaouchow, a consequential city, as evident from the immense fleet of boats lying before it, and the planting of a custom-house, where we had to anchor for the night. A bribe of a few dollars might have procured an imme-

"A TEMPLE IN THE CLEFTS OF THE ROCK

diate release; but, short of the needful, I was under the necessity of putting up with the rest of the fleet till the morn. There was here also a bridge of boats across the river, affording a clear communication between the two banks for foot-passengers; and what is very usual, there was but one opening for the passage of boats, which was closed at night by a massive iron chain hung athwart. But when day broke, three guns were fired at the custom-house, and the office-gates were opened; then, that iron chain was dropped, and officers were sent on board to search the boats. So, on the morning of the 9th, two of the river police boarded us, examined our boat, and handed us the passports.

Early that morning we passed along the foot of a curious rock, which rose upon our right, in the midst of the stream, to an elevation estimated by Sir G. Staunton at 600 feet, though, to my eye, it certainly did not exceed eighty. Along the face of the rock, hanging over the rushing waters beneath, there was a range of rooms dedicated to the service of Kwanyin, the reputed goddess of mercy. The temple, or rather this approach to the temple within, has been largely, and in some cases elegantly, described in the reports of the embassies of Macartney and Amherst, &c. The priests here located are popular, and exert a great amount of influence on the native travellers and merchants passing up and down,—at least in securing donations from them, or levying a sort of idolatry-mail to support the rock-temple establishment.

The only thing to enliven the 10th of August awaited us at Yingtih in the evening. This, though unimportant as a town, has some lovely landscapes in the neighbourhood, two pagodas, one on either side of the river, and several extraordinary fantastic-shaped hills.

The stream we had hitherto been sailing upon flows out of the Meiling range. At Yingtih town it receives a large accession to its waters out of the Hoonan province, and from this point the united stream flows southward, under the title of the "Northern River." At Tsing-yuen, about fifty-five miles above Canton, and forty from Fuhshan, we came next day to the junction of the northern with the branch trunk, called "the Western River," that takes its rise far west in the Yunnan province, and passes through Kwangse. These two, the north and the west rivers, flow together in one volume past the city of Canton, when, not far from Whampoa, the waters of the eastern parts of the province descending from the mountains of the south-eastern regions of Kiangse and Fuhkien, mingle with them. Thus is formed, by the conjunction of three rivers,—the north, west, and east,—what is commonly called by the natives, and is now well known to foreigners, "the Pearl river," and this flows out due east from Canton city a distance of sixty miles into the open ocean.

The appellation, "Pearl river," given to this grand junction of the three rivers (each of which in its own channel takes names from the separate localities through which it flows), is derived, according to a story narrated by the Chinese topographer, from a misfortune that befell a merchant sailing up the river several centuries since with a bundle of oceanic pearls under his arm. On a sudden the packet tumbled out of his grasp and sunk in the stream. Near that spot, it is said, there now rises a rock or crag, upon which there is a building called *Hai-choo-sze*, "a sea-pearl temple." At one time that same place was the scene of a fight between the Tartars and Chinese, six hundred years ago; and more recently, being ranked among the Bogue forts and registered as "Dutch Folly," it has been seized by the British.

In continuing the sail down "the west branch,"—the country was fine to the view, and rich, as proved by the variety of land produce brought under the eye of any traveller,—nankeen, cotton, mulberry, and sugar-cane plantations, &c. The traffic upon the channel was immense, chiefly in boats inward bound : and the whole population appeared exceedingly active,—particularly the women, whom I saw dragging the boats shoulder to shoulder with the men.

But of all places along this inland journey, Fuhshan (Fatsan), which I passed through on the 12th of August, was perhaps the most remarkable for the exhibition of universal energy in business of every form. It may be named "the Birmingham of China." It lies twelve miles W. by S. of Canton city; is a large town without walls; reputed to contain 1,000,000 inhabitants. Both the canal and river through the town were crammed with boats; each side of the river thickly populated and built up with dwellings, shops, godowns, factories, and hongs. My boat rapidly flitted by wood-stores of Kiangse timber, boat-building establishments, iron-foundries, brick-kilns, and manufactories, and, before I was aware of it, was hurried to Hwate, where, meeting with a strong flood tide, it had to drop anchor.

Here, to my no small surprise, I found myself only nine miles from Canton, having sailed 330 miles during the last six days, and passed through three large departments, Nanhiung, Shaouchow, and Kwanchow, in which latter the provincial capital is situated. At 6 P.M. the ebb began to drop; and in an hour or two the boat was abreast of the foreign factories. As I did not think it expedient to land here, I hired a boat to start forthwith for Hong-Kong. By nine o'clock P.M. I left the anchorage at the foreign factories.

It remains for me to add, that in two days I reached Hong-Kong, and with great satisfaction, found myself once more safe and sound among my countrymen. Still retaining my *incog.* habiliments, I joined a party of them then assembled on Morrison Hill, and at the time engaged in the act of united prayer around the footstool of Heaven's Majesty. I associated with them in heartily giving thanks to the Guardian of my life for His gracious protection throughout a journey of thirty-eight days, during which I had passed unmolested through three provinces of China Proper — crossing sixteen counties, and touching at two capitals, twenty-eight walled cities, and seventeen unwalled towns, besides villages innumerable, along a route measuring fully 1,300 miles in length.

PART FOURTH.

SHANGHAI.

CHAPTER I.

SHANGHAI—GROWTH IN IMPORTANCE—GEOGRAPHICAL POSITION—VARIETY OF NAMES—WALKS ABOUT THE CITY AND SUBURBS—TIDES—BUBBLING WELL—EGG-HATCHING—DEAD-HOUSES—FRUITS OF THE EARTH—CLIMATE—NATIVE THEORIES OF NATURAL PHENOMENA—FALL OF DUST—CHARACTER OF POPULATION.

BEFORE the last twelve or fourteen years, how many persons in well-informed circles had ever heard of Shanghai? Or who of those that were present at the signing of the Nanking treaty, could have prophesied that this newly opened port would have become of such importance as it is now?

During 1844, the first year of its occupation for purposes of commerce by foreigners, Shanghai statistics gave only 44 foreign merchant-ships, 23 foreign residents and families, 1 consular flag, 11 mercantile houses, and 2 Protestant missionaries. But, by the Shanghai Directory for 1856, it appears that, at the beginning of that year, there were upwards of 330 foreign residents (besides their families), 8 consular flags, 70 mercantile houses, and 36 Protestant missionaries. Perhaps the most significant evidence of the growth and importance of the port is in the return of foreign shipping at Shanghai, from 1st July to 31st December, 1855, published by the Office of Maritime Customs there. Shipping:—British, 249; American, 57; Danish, 7; Hamburg, 11; Dutch, 11; Swedish, 9;

Spanish, 6; Portuguese, 5; Peruvian, 3; Siamese, 4; Bremen, 2;—total ships, 364. The return of tea exported from Shanghai during that half-year, was 38,277,923 pounds; and of silk, 30,207 bales. The "returns" for the whole year, 1855, give of arrivals, 434 ships of all countries, amounting to 154,000 tons; departures, 437; tea exports, 76,711,659 pounds; silk, 55,537 bales.

At last, how soon we have become familiar with the name Shanghai! and indeed there is so much of interest and consequence about the place, that a traveller or a merchant would blush to leave China without a visit to this greatest emporium on its eastern coast. And now a word to begin with on the name of the place, the pronunciation of which has been wofully mutilated by some people. It has been written variously, Çanhay, Changhay, Xanghay, Zonghae, Shanhae, Shanghay, Shanghae, Shanghai. To represent it in Roman characters the last is decidedly the best, but in pronouncing the final syllable, let it be sounded as our English "high," and not "hay," *alias* grass cut and dried.

Sailing towards the north of China, keeping perhaps fifty or sixty miles off the coast, as the ship enters the thirtieth parallel, a stranger is startled some fine morning by coming on what looks like a shoal,—perhaps a sand-bank, a reef,—he knows not what. It is an expanse of coloured water stretching out as far as the eye can reach, east, north, and west, and entirely distinct from the deep-blue sea which hitherto the vessel had been ploughing. In course, he finds that it is "the Yellow Sea;" a sea so yellow, turbid, and thick, certainly, that you might think all the pease-soup in creation, and a great deal more, had been emptied into one monster cistern.

Between the thirtieth degree of north latitude, where the Choosan group begins, and the promontory of Shantung in the thirty-seventh degree, this muddy sea ranges; and into this extraordinary reservoir three great rivers pour their tawny liquid contents,—the Tseen-tang, the Yangtsze-kiang, and the Hwang-ho,—which draw their resources from distant, immense, and populous regions in the north and south of the empire, and flow more or less through one half of the eighteen provinces. The greatest of these three rivers is the Yangtsze, about midway between the others, the one that affords access to the port of Shanghai.

Beyond the northernmost islands of the Choosan group, slightly to the north-westward, is the mouth of the *embouchure* of the Yangtsze-kiang. As you enter, the mainland forms a low bank to the river from north-west to south-east. Forty-five miles further up, cutting this line of coast nearly at right angles, there is a tributary flowing into the main stream; and turning southerly into this branch, you reach the Woosung anchorage, in lat. 31° 25′ N., long. 121°. 1′ 30″ E. Ascend that rapid and coloured stream; pass by Woosung village, which has grown surprisingly within the last few years as the anchorage for the opium receiving-ships; take hurried notes of the hamlets and farm-steads over the bank, the flat fields and marshy grounds below the river level; and suddenly you come upon Shanghai, on the right or west bank. In a direct line nearly due south, *i. e.* by footpath, Shanghai is not more than seven miles from Woosung; but by the river, which almost midway between Woosung and Shanghai makes a wide bend eastward, the distance must be twelve or fourteen miles.

Quite three-quarters of a mile from the walls of the native city, the river you had been stemming divides into two. The branch to the west, called "the Woosung river," flows past Soochow, seventy-three miles up in the interior. The other branch, "the Whangpoo" (Whampoa), runs along the eastern face of Shanghai, in a broad channel, often 650 yards wide and thirteen fathoms deep, at its head receiving the waters that flow out of the departments of Hangchow and Kiahing, in the adjoining province of Chihkiang.

At that fork, where the two separate branches blend their streams, the British consulate stands, with its spacious premises, buildings, and noble flag. The settlement ceded to the British extends above half a mile from this corner to a wide ditch, the Yang-king-pang, which forms the southern boundary of the English grounds. The eastern boundary is the bank of the Whang-poo, where the foreign shipping lies. The western limit is a mile or two in-shore. Within these bounds, foreign residents have erected godowns, mansions, a church, &c.; live in ease, comfort, and luxury, as well as "in ceiled houses;" and are carrying on an enormous and lucrative commerce with Chinese merchants.

Leaving the foreign for the native settlement, both which are accurately sketched off in the accompanying map,—I must premise a remark, that certainly no country under the sun has kept records so voluminous, regular, and calculated to elucidate the condition of the empire, as China. For instance we have, in the first place, a general account of the country, compiled by the present dynasty, in two or three hundred volumes. It contains minutiæ of the extent, divisions, and population of the country; its rivers, mountains, products, and revenue; defences, walls, cities, temples, schools of learning, examination-halls, and other private buildings; notices of wondrous objects, marvellous legends, prodigies in every form, and eminent men and women. Then, in addition to the general survey of the country, there exist separate topographies of each province, department, and district; each work entering elaborately into the history of a province, or a department, or a district. Thus, of the eighteen provinces, we have a general view of Kiansoo; of the divisions of this province we have a full and detailed account of the Sungkiang prefecture; and then of the minor partitions of this prefecture (each having its own and separate topography), we have a description of Shanghai alone in twenty large volumes. Much that is recorded in these works would not be very interesting to us; yet there is a vast deal of matter in this department of their literature, to exhibit the interior of China as it has been for ages past, and to gratify the most ardent curiosity of any archæologist. In these native works you are invariably supplied with a large number of maps and woodcuts to describe the boundaries, watercourses, bridges, streets, walls, public buildings, and a variety of curious objects.

Anciently, and still in the records of the city, as well as in many of their public papers, Shanghai goes by the name Hoo. The origin of the appellation is to be traced as follows:—In early times (as in some places at the present day too) they used this curious method for catching fish. Rows of bamboo stakes were stuck in the stream, and joined together by cords. These rows opened out into two wings towards the shore. As the tide flowed, the stakes were covered by it; at its ebb they became visible. Fish borne along with the flow and ebb got entangled among the stakes, so that they could not escape. This mode of fishing was called *hoo.* At one time the neighbourhood of Shanghai was famed for its fishing-stakes, from which circumstance it gained the name of "the Hoo city." During the last 900 years, the district has passed under other designations, with which it were more than needless to trouble the reader. The general designation under which it now goes is Shanghai, the more likely explanation of which is "the upper sea," to distinguish it from another watery region known as "the lower sea."

The city was built in its present irregular form just three centuries ago, and encircled by a wall which, according to English measurement, is three miles and three-quarters in circumference, fifteen feet broad, and twenty-four high,—the good people of the city having at different times freely made large contributions towards the erection of it. The original object of so clumsy a piece of engineering was the defence of the inhabitants, hitherto constantly exposed to the depredations of freebooters and pirates, who infested the country. Upon that wall there is a superabundance of "loop-holes," "arrow-towers," "terraces in stories," and "military observatories." It is perforated by six gates, that open and shut by rule, whose grandiloquent designations are bombastic enough, though ludicrously inappropriate. For instance, the north gate, "calm-sea gate," (of all places "calm!") the great east gate is the gate of "paying obeisance to the honourable ones;" the little east is the "precious girdle gate;" the great south is the gate for "riding the dragon;" little south is the gate that "looks towards the south;" and the west gate is "the pattern phœnix."

After the description of buildings, &c. in the city of Ningpo, that has been given in a former part, it would be superfluous even to point out the leading edifices in Shanghai; for, in general, they correspond to those in the former, although much inferior, and peculiarly insignificant. Besides, it is to be hoped that, in consequence of the recent ransack to which Shanghai has been subjected both under rebels and imperialists, many of the old buildings, already far gone, have been by this time quite removed, or, if rebuilt, remodelled with improvements in style and architecture; although, even on this score, there is scarcely encouragement to ejaculate, "*Nil desperandum.*"

What cannot fail to arrest the attention of any common observer at Shanghai are its tides, remarkable for rise, regularity, and rapidity,—especially the neap and spring tides at new and full moon, which are very high and very low every spring and autumn. The tide before the city is about three-quarters of an hour later than at Woosung anchorage; and when the north-east wind blows, the tide (as it comes in from that quarter) is earlier, but later when the opposite wind prevails. The tide is felt thirty miles above Shanghai. The natives keep tide-tables, which in general may be relied on as correct. The inundations occasioned by the high tides of autumn are sometimes alarming and disastrous,—fields, gardens, and the ground-floors of the houses being covered with the dirty flood.*

Of the river water at Shanghai, which after undergoing a few filtrations is the beverage here, a better description cannot be given than in the graphic language of Lady S. Wortley respecting the Mississippi river:—"I cannot bestow any praise on the colour of its turbid, thick, muddy-looking water. It is reckoned very wholesome, however, to drink, repulsive as it looks; and certainly it ought to be so for one reason: it looks marvellously like an enormous running stream

* The native theory of the ocean tides is very singular, as, in a short extract from the "Chinese Miscellany" (No. iv, p. 83) a native work says, "When the moon is full, the ocean wave prevails in a westerly direction; when the moon is in the wane, it rises in an easterly direction." Another says, "The advancing or retiring of the tidal wave corresponds to the waxing or waning of the moon. The morning tide comes on in the early, and the evening tide in the later part of the day. The moon is said by astrologers to produce water; hence when the moon is full the tides are high, because they follow their like. On the day of the first decade of each moon, and on the night following, the sun and moon are a little distant from each other; the moon differing rather more than thirteen degrees, and the sun being about that much behind the moon; hence it is that the tides do not keep pace with the revolving seasons. Every evening and morning, there are early and later tides; every new and full moon, there are neap and spring tides; and every spring and autumn season, there are high and low tides; for sublunary things correspond to the motions of the heavenly bodies, still maintaining the discrepancy of thirteen degrees. Heat and cold depend upon the revolving seasons, hence the exact periods of the sun arriving at the extreme point are fixed to midnight and noon, while the extremes of heat and cold occur generally about two hours afterwards. The moon in her revolutions, likewise, comes to her extremes at the new and full, while the early and later tides come on at the quarters. With regard to the early and later

of apothecary's stuff, a very strong decoction of mahogany-coloured bark, with a slight dash of port-wine, to deepen its hue; it is a mulatto-complexioned river, there is no doubt of that, and wears the deep-tanned livery of the burnished sun."

Within and without the walls, the city is cut up by innumerable ditches and moats. These water-channels, if kept constantly clear by the flow of the river and the tidal wave, might contribute greatly to the convenience and health of the inhabitants. But from want of care and management in their commissioners of public works, they get filled, clogged, and stagnant; they become intolerable nuisances, and, no doubt, add much during the dog-days to the pestilent vapours that generate in the neighbouring marshes. I remember when, at midsummer, the city magistrates occasionally undertook to delve out the mud and offal from the reservoirs, not only did they stir up these sinks from the very bottom, but, instead of carrying off their horrible contents to some remote fields which they might have enriched, the offensive and polluting ingredients were poured forth on the ditch-sides, to waste and evaporate the most detestable effluvia, not into "desert air," but into the atmosphere to be consumed by crowds of human beings swarming along the banks.

tides, it may be observed, that their periods during each day may be reckoned from the time when the sun is in the centre, which during the darkness is as the day declines to midnight, and during the light is as the day advances towards noon; with respect to the tides at the new and full moons, it may be observed, that their periods during each month may be reckoned from the time when the moon is at her two extremes; which during approaching brightness is from her beginning to wax, and during darkness is from her beginning to wane. With respect to the high and low tides occurring annually, it may be observed, that their periods during each year may be reckoned from the position of the milky way; which during the approaching heat is from the time when the branch of the galaxy rises to the zenith, and during approaching cold is from the time when the main body thereof advances to the ascendant."

In our daily walks about Shanghai, it was a special annoyance to foreigners to encounter "dung-boats," "dung-tanks," "dung-buckets," "dung-carriers," and "cabinets d'aisance." Of the last-named, though some consisted merely of a huge jar, with a trellis-work around of common hedge, or convolvulus, or honeysuckle, others stood in by-streets and on the highways,—looking like sentry-boxes, built of mud and brick; numbers of them having paintings of flowers on their whitewashed walls, or a window often shaped like a fan, a vine-leaf, or a flowerpot. But as for the other named nuisances, they had no disguise whatever, and for offensiveness exceed all description. Throughout China human ordure is collected and treasured up, as a native said one day, "like precious jewels;" and is used in agriculture with a most jealous economy,—being valued by them as the best manure;—in which, perhaps, they offer a lesson to people in other parts of the world.

Among the few curiosities about Shanghai, casually mentioned among visitors from the South and the West, there is an insignificant "gurgling well," at a walk of three miles in a westerly direction. It adjoins the Tsing-yen, a Buddhist temple. They say that people used to bathe in this well in former days, and found the water below the surface pleasantly warm. Although the gas emitted from this bubbling spring ignites, it is very odd that, in an early number of the *North China Herald*, and in one number of the *Chinese Miscellany*, published about 1850, it was announced, in sober English, that the well emitted "carbonic acid gas!!" The following brief notice of it was given in one of Dr. Lockhart's medical reports: "About three miles to the westward of the hospital, at the village called Tsing-yen, there is, in front of a temple, a pit or well, about eight feet square and ten or twelve feet deep, faced with blocks of limestone and inclosed by a good substantial paling; there are about three feet of water in this well, and from the bottom bubbles up a large quantity of gas, so that the appearance is as if a large volume of water was being constantly thrown up: the people call it Hai-yen, or 'Eye of the Sea,' and say that the water neither increases nor diminishes, nor ever runs out: the fact is, the water that is in the well is merely drainage, and the gas rises through it. On descending by means of a ladder to the water, and holding a light over the agitated surface, the bubbles explode with a light-blue flame, which continues all the time light is applied. The gas may easily be collected by means of a bell-glass and bladder; the water has a slightly brackish taste, but small fish are noticed swimming about in it; the gas is no doubt carburetted hydrogen, and probably emanates from a layer of peat or coal at some distance below the surface. The villagers make no use of the water for any purpose, and appeared to be much surprised when the gas was ignited; they did not seem to be at all aware of its inflammable nature."

Not the least interesting object in the vicinity of Shanghai was "an egg-hatching establishment," at the south-west corner of the settlement. Possibly under the new *régime,* adopted since the Shanghai disturbances have been put down, this native building may have been removed. But a notice of it will elucidate the artificial mode of egg-hatching popular in China, particularly as my notes were taken on the spot. Ordinarily the establishment was in full operation not more than five months in the year, beginning with the Tsingming term, about the end of March. Goose, duck, and fowl eggs were taken in. Hen-eggs were hatched for customers at a halfpenny each, and if to be hatched for the firm were bought up at a farthing. Duck-eggs were only taken in for the latter object, and purchased at sixpence each. Goose-eggs were only hatched for customers, and at twopence-halfpenny. As soon as the eggs were brought in, they were examined, and marked in ink with the name of the owner. This helped to fix the owners of the addled eggs, or of the chickens when hatched. To ascertain if the shells were cracked, I observed the examiners take the eggs up one by one, and gently tap them, the peculiar sound revealing to their experienced ears whether or not the shells were perfect. Broken or cracked, the egg was wrapped round with common paper, and sometimes inclosed in an empty shell. After these due preliminaries, the first process was to expose the eggs to an oven heat of about 100° Fahrenheit. In this establishment I counted twenty-six ovens, with large exterior, small interior, built of mud mixed with straw, and having a thick straw-mat cover. The fuel consisted of fine charcoal; and when lighted, the oven-doors were closed to prevent a draught. Upon the top of every oven a large, thick, covered basket was laid, over the bottom of which the eggs were spread. To distribute the heat equally, the eggs were turned over and over five times a day. They remained a certain number of days on the ovens for the purpose of proving them. To detect the productive ones, for goose-eggs six days were needed, fowl-eggs four, and duck-eggs only two. The mode of detection was the following:—Having been over the oven the number of days required, each was carefully taken out, and exposed to a strong light. But those in which no dark interior speck was seen were pronounced barren, and returned to the owners. To secure a strong light for this purpose, the following easy and natural mode was adopted; as the interior of the hatchery was necessarily gloomy and dingy, otherwise it could not have answered its objects, a hole was pierced through the wall, large enough to place an egg in; and through this orifice it was examined, with the aid of the sun-blaze outside. I was told by the heads of the company that, of hen-eggs, they found that only four in ten would hatch by this artificial method, and in general they hatched 700,000 chickens a year on the establishment. If pronounced good, the eggs were replaced in the oven-baskets, and, after another term of days, were transferred to shelves nicely matted with straw, cotton, &c. The workmen arranged them on these with great regularity, and it was surprising to see the expertness with which they shuffled them about without injuring them. They were covered over with cotton quilts. There was no fire underneath; but the warm temperature of this cavernous kitchen was uniformly kept up at a certain point by the stoves already mentioned. The eggs opened to the very day,—almost to the hour. The time needed for hatching was given thus:—for goose-eggs 32½ days, or 16 days on the oven and 16½ days in bed; for duck-eggs 28 days, or 14 days on the oven and 14 days in bed; and fowl-eggs 22 days, or 12 days on the oven and 10 days in bed. Each time I visited this "poultry nursery," I was amused to hear in every direction the chirrup of a little creature within its shell, or to listen to one as in impatience it pecked at the walls of its prison-house. Nor was it less entertaining to watch one poking out its funny head with a look of strangeness, eyeing the new world into which it was coming; another half-fledged, leaping on its "marble dome," exulting in its liberty; and a third eating its own shell to satisfy the first cravings of hunger. As soon as hatched, the tiny creatures are taken away by the owners, or sold to poulterers. I was told by natives that hen-hatched chickens were preferred, and that "the fire-hatched ones cannot drink cold water, but die immediately after sipping it, which is not the case with others." I was informed likewise that pigeons and partridges were forced in a similar mode, though not at this place. The artificial hatching is extensively practised in Canton province, where "duck-boats" abound, in which ducklings are thus raised, to be reared along the low muddy bank of the "Pearl river."

There is this curious notice on the subject in an old Chinese cyclopædia:—"It is a common saying among us, that 'in the south we have fire-hatched fowls; and in the north, lambs, that have sprung up from the sowing of sheep-bones.' Now, of the former (says the writer), I can bear testimony from having myself seen them. By this means it is unnecessary to trouble the hen. The eggs are merely put into a sort of basket with a slow fire underneath, and to a day they will hatch, exactly in the same way. But, as for lambs produced from bones, I have only heard of such a *lusus naturæ*. I have likewise read an account of it in some ancient work in these words:—'Take a sheep's bones and pound them; as the winter advances, bury the powder in the ground; and at spring-time young lambs will sprout out from the field.' But (adds the cyclopædist), although I have in all directions made inquiry on this curious point, I am assured that it is impossible. So that I believe it is a hoax imposed on many people (by a conundrum which, with its interpretation, is annexed). Some lambs are small in size, but have large and heavy bones; in speaking of which they say, 'their bones are weighty;' but the characters in Chinese with a slight variation, may be written and pronounced as the phrase 'bone-seeds.' Hence the puzzle reads 'bone-sown lambs.'"

Around Shanghai there are several club-houses, "Hwuy-kwans," or assembly-halls, similar to those described in a former part,—built and supported by resident merchants or frequent visitors,—for the purpose of encouraging social intercourse with countrymen from the same locality of the empire. Some of these erections are extensive, and fitted up with temples, theatrical platforms, apartments for travellers, porter's lodge, &c.

Instead of re-entering into particulars about these, there was at Shanghai "the Ningpo guild-house," outside the city walls, between the north and west gates, to whose "depository for the dead" I wish to call the reader's attention. As the name indicates, that club-house belonged to merchants, &c. of the six districts within the prefecture of Ningpo. Its general objects were to offer every available convenience to natives of those districts who at any time visited Ningpo on mercantile and other pursuits. But it was the special object of the founders that their dead should not lie forgotten. To provide for them, there were two parts of the premises set apart:—one large space within the walls of the spacious building, consecrated solely as a depository for unburied dead; and another, a cemetery, which consisted of a plot of ground outside for burial.

The object of the "dead-house" was two-fold:—first, that friends who desired to remove the remains of a deceased relative for burial in his own native spot and family ground, but did not find it convenient to do so at once, might have a place at hand in which for a time to lodge the encoffined with a degree of security and confidence. The coffins were provided either by the relatives or by the deceased himself before death. Generally these were large and strongly made; some singularly varnished and decorated. There is a special compartment on this flight for the rich and opulent, the lodgment-fee being one dollar. But for ordinary admissions into the depository it was only 200 cash, or *7d.*, per coffin. As I was quitting the spot one morning, I met a Ningpo native of the middle class, bringing the coffin of a dead child along with him; and I saw him deposit his valued treasure there with that moderate entry-fee.

A second object of the dead-house was, that the bodies of the Ningpoites who died at Shanghai poor, friendless, or unrecognised, might be taken in and kept until acknowledged and removed by their respective families. With this view coffins were provided out of the funds of the institution, all of one style and perfectly plain. The names of each individual, if known, or their supposed name and district, &c., were carefully marked on the shell. This expedited recognition. Such were the two objects of that curious depository. Subsequently, on repeating my visits, I found it was divided into two separate apartments, for males and for females. The women, no matter to what place they belong by birth, in burial belong to their husbands' native place. In the former I counted one day 900 coffins, in the latter 400. The apartments consisted of a series of sheds, running parallel, with a separate roof over each shed. In this manner the "dead-house" was neither exposed nor confined. Each roof was well raised and supported on pillars; the floors laid in some places with cement or bricks; the coffins arranged upon benches, and not on the bare ground. The foot-walks between the coffin-rows were slabbed; and, as the distinct roofs were not connected together, there was a gutter under the various eaves to carry off the rain. Although there was a very large collection of dead in coffins in the separate rooms, I could detect nothing offensive. This arose doubtless from the deceased, when laid out, being covered with chalk and lime, &c., and their coffins being closely cemented. The provision that the coffin should remain three years is the same both with rich and poor. During that time, friends may remove their dead; but, at its expiration, if unremoved or unrecognised, they are buried in the cemetery hard by, which I have mentioned. In that burial-ground I observed the coffins were buried underground, each with a small rising mound and headstone. Relatives may, if they like, subsequently transfer them from this plot of ground, but at their own expense;—to aid which friendly act, the gravestones have inscribed on them the names &c. of the entombed as on their coffins.

In this depôt for the dead, there were curious emblems of mourning on some of the coffins, which either had been laid there by disconsolate friends themselves, or sent from a distance for that purpose; *e. g.* mourning-caps of hemp and unspun cotton, wisps of straw, bundles of silvered paper, and "tablets to the spirits of the departed." If I might judge from the specimens I saw here, mourning husbands appeared to have been specially fastidious in marking the names and titles of their wives upon their coffins.

I inquired of the resident manager, whether he would show me his registry-book. He did so; and in it I found that the entry of males in twenty-three years (between 1830 and 1853) had amounted to 3,083; but of women *in four years* (between 1849 and 1853) there had been 1,118;—a strange disproportion this, which so struck me at the time that I noted down the particulars on the spot. Possibly it may be explained on the hypothesis that Ningpo citizens who had married Shanghai women were travelling merchants, and may have been unable to return in time to remove their deceased wives, or may themselves have died in distant parts of the empire; but as their wives, although by birth natives of Shanghai, by marriage belonged to the husbands' native places, on their decease their coffins were placed here to await removal to the real family vaults at Ningpo.

As to the fruits of the earth at Shanghai, of the various grains, rice of every species is abundantly cultivated, also wheat, millet, and pulse of different kinds. But Shanghai is famous chiefly for its cotton. The fields are extensively cultivated with it,—alternately with rice, or during two summers with cotton, and every third year with rice. The cloth manufactured from it by the native families is plentiful in the markets, and the working of cotton in the field, the shop, or at the loom, gives large employ especially to the young people and women. Kitchen vegetables are prolific and of endless variety,—greens, spinach, onions, radishes, parsley, mushrooms, taro, yams, cucumbers, water-melons, &c. "The Chinese potato" (as it has been designated in England) is indigenous here, and probably the recent recommendations given at the horticultural meeting on its introduction into this country will be advantageous for English and Irish.

And of the products of fruit-trees, we have an abundant supply of persimmons, cherries, plums, oranges, citrons, pomegranates, figs, and last, but not least in size or flavour, most delicious peaches; so that, for a strict vegetarian visiting this native city, there is every prospect of a good supply and great variety; nor will there be any lack to those of the opposite school, who prefer beef, mutton, and pork, fish, fowl, game, shrimps, or frogs. There is no fear, then, of any Westerner starving at Shanghai, for, at any foreign resident's table, he will meet with little change of diet from what he has been accustomed to in his own country.

But his greatest suffering and his hazard, if he be a new comer, is from the severe excesses of temperature throughout the year, the rapid changes in spring and autumn, and the malarious gases from the marshy lands in his vicinity.

The first year or two foreigners settled here, the maximum heat was 100° Fahr. and the minimum cold 15°. In summer, the average heat ranges between 80° and 95° by day, 60° and 75° by night; and in winter, the thermometer varies from 45° to 60° by day, and from 24° by night. The following table may give some idea of the temperature at Shanghai. It was carefully drawn up by Dr. Lockhart from daily observations throughout the year 1855, and, being published by himself, may be relied on for accuracy :—

ABSTRACT OF OBSERVATIONS made by the thermometer, in the open air, in a shady situation, with a southern exposure; the maximum by day, and the minimum by night, taken by a self-registering thermometer.

1855.	Maxm. by day	Minm. by day	Maxm. by night	Minm. by night	Average by day	Average by night	Rainy days	Rain table
January..	52	33	40	18	44	25	4	1½ in.
February.	68	35	45	18	51	30	5	¾
March ..	72	36	57	30	55	41	11	5¼
April....	82	52	67	37	63	51	15	11½
May	90	60	73	50	74	63	18	8½
June	90	73	79	56	79	70	7	5
July	94	82	82	73	89	78	8	5
August ..	99	83	81	75	87	78	12	7½
September	88	70	78	58	81	70	8	4¼
October..	80	65	69	45	73	58	3	1¾
November	78	55	62	33	62	49	11	4
December	73	40	43	22	60	36	0	0

In such a climate (not to speak of musquitoes in clouds, flying beetles, and other disagreeables) "rainy seasons" are abundant, especially in March, April, May. From the table given, it appears that in 1855 there were 102 days of rain; in May alone there were eighteen rainy days; and throughout the year four feet seven inches of rain had fallen. "The monsoons," thought to be regular, are at times excessively fitful and lazy; and dry seasons are not wanting. Thunder and lightning, sometimes appalling beyond description, are really indispensable; and Shanghai is visited also by earthquakes, not very frequent nor periodical, but in such short, sharp shocks, as to startle the foreign residents at this new settlement, and to shake the nerves of the most stout-hearted,—the instinctive impulse of each one (if not paralyzed for the moment) being to make for the door.

Alluding to earthquakes, it may not be uninteresting or unamusing to retail sundry theories and explanations given me by natives about various phenomena in nature; *e. g.* "earth-tremor," lightning, and eclipses

Of earthquakes which occurred during my residence in this part of the country, sometimes the prognostics were a highly electric state of the atmosphere, a long drought, excessive heat, and what seemed a stagnation of all nature. At the critical moment of the commotion the earth began to rock, the beams and walls cracked like the timbers of a ship under sail, and a nausea came over one, a sea-sickness really horrible. At times, for a second or two previous to the vibration, there was heard a subterraneous growl, a noise as of a rushing mighty wind whirling about under ground. As might be expected, the effect on the natives was to strike with excessive alarm, especially if the quake happened at night. Upon this there suddenly burst out a mass of confused sounds from the native town, —"Zah-tsze, zah-tsze!" "Kew ming, kew ming!"— "Thief, thief!" "Save your lives, save your lives!" &c. Dogs added their savage yell to the medley, and the bang of gongs and tomtoms. Next day there ran through the Chinese community exhaustless gossip about a profusion of tiny hairs having been scattered on the surface of the earth by the earthquake, plots of ground sinking, cavities filled with water, flames issuing from the hill-sides, and ashes cast about the country, &c. &c.

From personal inquiries, I ascertained that the Chinese ideas about the origin of this phenomenon are unformed, obscure, and over-superstitious. Some said, that, as the earth was too hot, it had to relieve itself and gain its equilibrium by a shake; or that it was changing its place for another part of the universe; or that, as so much ground in the locality of Shanghai had been recently turned up and its configuration altered, the ground would readily be agitated; or that the Supreme One, to bring transgressors to their senses, thought to startle them by a quivering of the earth; or that, when people grew careless in rashly throwing grains of rice about and profanely using lettered paper, mother earth could no longer brook it, and shook herself to frighten them, &c. But the notion most common among the *vulgus* is, that there are six huge sea-monsters which support the earth, and, if any one of these move, the earth accordingly is agitated. In Kanghe's Imperial Lexicon, it is gravely said that a certain king, who lived long before the deluge, cut off the feet of one of these monsters and set them up for the pillars of the earth. On this account, the earth has ever since been unsteady. But superstition is rife in ascribing these earth-shakings chiefly to the remissness of the priesthood. There is in almost every temple a *muh-yu*, "wooden fish," a typical figure of the scaly prodigy just alluded to, suspended near the altar-piece, and, among the duties of the priests, it is rigidly prescribed that they keep up an incessant and everlasting tapping on this fish. If, however, they should become lax at the rite, it is certain that the foresaid "*Ngaou* fishes," on which the earth rests, will wriggle and shake to awaken the drowsy priests to their drumming duties.

The following is another explanation of the *te-chin*, propounded to me by a learned native, after one such commotion in December, 1852:—"Under the thick coat of the earth there is an immense cavity filled with a sort of ether, the breath of the *yang* and *yin* principles, which is capable of expansion and collapse. This immense volume of air, as it rushes about underneath the surface of the earth seeking vent, strikes against the earth's crust and agitates it. From this come the earthquakes."

But is it not singular that, although the Chinese have derived aid from Europeans in astronomy, &c.,

they appear so closely to stick to superstitions like the above, against every form of evidence, and make no struggle to rise above such paltry and childish notions?

So it is with eclipses too. They are able to calculate these with tolerable accuracy; yet the men who are acquainted with this part of astronomical science, do not seem to have extended the fruits of their knowledge even among the higher and intellectual classes.

During solar and lunar eclipses visible at Shanghai, the curiosity of the people was remarkable. Sometimes they peered at the object through smoked glasses,—which they had copied from foreigners;—or, they would of their own accord use red card-papers pierced with a pin, a nail, or an awl. Sometimes they watched the progress of the *umbra* on the face of a full tank, cistern, jar, or a basin of water.

It is a prevalent notion that an eclipse is occasioned by some monster "dragon," attempting to swallow up the sun or the moon: accordingly, an eclipse is called, not only by the lower orders, but by all ranks, and in their books and proclamations, "the moon-eating," or "the sun-eating." One of the characters to represent an eclipse is the verb to "eat," and "a worm or insect;" as if the object were being gradually eaten and wormed out. The result of such absurdity is that, during an eclipse, there is an incessant din of gongs, drums, horns, cymbals, pipes, fifes, &c., along with the letting off of crackers and popguns; all this hurly-burly being kept up to frighten away the devouring beast. They likewise shoot arrows at the sun or moon. At the temples the idols are brought out and seated on large chairs; and tables are set before them, with burning red candles and incense-sticks. Buffets are arranged, on which the idols are supposed to kneel and entreat the monster to desist from his "sun-eating" pranks. The priests are particularly religious on the occasion, and go throw all the ceremony of bowing, kneeling, chanting, &c.; and in their private residences the people are observing a similar farce, imploring the animal to pity their dilemma and spare the greater and lesser lights. When the eclipse is over they believe they have been successful in their entreaties. The government authorities uniformly lend their aid to all this nonsense, at their official residences. Several days beforehand, they issue proclamations to inform the public of a notice received from the Astronomical Board that on such and such a day, hour, and minute, there will be a "sun-eating," &c., and they command that the underlings of office "shall all meet at their several offices at the said hour, to rescue and protect the sun or moon."

To mention one other crudity,—that when lightning strikes a building, that edifice must be infested with snakes and other reptiles. In the month of August, 1853, a severe bolt struck a foreign residence not far from my own. The natives were amazed at the occurrence, as the house was quite new, and they could not imagine it could already be haunted by such odious creatures. I requested a native scholar to inform me what was the nature of this fable so current among his townsmen, and he wrote out the following:—"When lightning strikes the ridge of a house, you may be sure it is because, in the heart of that building, there are poisonous serpents, &c., lurking. In olden times there was a family mansion thus struck, yet no apparent injury was done. However, in course of half a month, the roof began to leak without intermission. At last it was discovered that an enormous toad-like monster, partly in the shape of a child, lay sleeping under the tiles. So, likewise, in the year 1802, the god of thunder went through China to destroy all reptiles, venomous creatures, &c. The result was that, when the destroying angel came to the Nanking pagoda, its steeple was instantly struck, and it fell for no other reason than that a brood of nasty insects and snakes was concealed somewhere in it."

After dilating on such clumsily devised fables, let us come to a meteorological fact that frequently appears at Shanghai,—*a fall of dust.* This happens once a year, sometimes twice, and occasionally with an interval of two or three years. In 1852 it fell in the month of December. But more commonly it occurs in the month of March; which agrees with the Chinese observation, "It usually descends during the second moon." It comes with the wind veering between north-east and north-west, continues for a day or two, and varies in intensity. It is an infinitesimally fine powder,—sometimes black, ordinarily yellow. Though no real fog or mist obscures the sun or moon, they are scarcely visible during the sand-shower, and, if visible, only as seen through a darkened glass. The deposit of this exquisite powder is found to be a quarter of an inch thick in some places, after a fall of a day or two: it can penetrate the closest venetians; it overspreads every article of furniture in the house; it finds its way into the most secluded apartments; it blows into the tightest wardrobe. In walking abroad, one's clothes are covered with dust,—the face gets dirty, the mouth and throat parched up, the teeth grate, the eyes become irritable, the ears tickle, the nostrils feel itchy; and it is to be feared that for ophthalmic and pulmonary patients these showers are far from beneficial. The fall used at times to extend as far as Ningpo,—also 200 miles out to sea, and (it has been said) inland over the midland provinces Honan and Kiangse.

In explanation of it, the Chinese themselves say it comes from the northern provinces Shantung and Chihli. Supposing this to be an approach to the real source of it, it may be conjectured that the fine dust is blown down upon the plains of China from the elevated steppes of Mongolia, after having been wafted by typhoons into the upper regions, as it has been ascertained is the case in Africa with the sands of Sahara, which are deposited 1,200 miles away from their original bed.

In 1850 I sent to England a packet of the dust which happened to fall that same year (of which I have still a good sample by me). It was submitted to a naturalist, who observed in reply:—"Its particles sink slowly in water, and are so light that they might be carried up into the atmosphere by a tornado, or by evaporation, for much earthy matter, in a state of minute pulverization, is carried up by evaporation; or they might be projected from a volcano. I do not, however, think that the dust is of volcanic origin; nor do I think it is star-dust, or that it has emanated from any of the heavenly bodies. The fact of its having fallen or settled from the atmosphere appears to be well established; but, in order to form a correct opinion as to the source whence it came, many other particulars must be known."

Some have said that it was of volcanic origin, to be traced probably to one of the Japanese volcanoes, frequently subject to eruptions. In the report of the Shanghai Hospital for 1852, after remarking that on December 16th of that year there had been two smart earthquakes, it is observed,—"The day but one after the earthquake, the atmosphere was filled for two or three days with impalpable dust or sand, which gave to the atmosphere a very misty appearance, and was deposited on the ground in all directions. The wind was northwest at the time. It is impossible to say what is the cause of this sand-rain, or where it comes from. May it not be volcanic sand projected high into the air from some distant volcano in eruption, and carried about by the upper currents of wind, till at last it falls on the earth?" On this point I may quote the opinion of

Mr. Piddington, the curator of Economic Geology of India, who, having examined a sample of the dust, gave an official report thereon :—" We have seen that it is not in the least volcanic, its animal nature putting this entirely out of the question, and all the volcanic dusts upon record are for the most part fusible and pulverurent (like pumice or obisidian), while the residuum of ours is perfectly infusible, for the little globules are properly the only fusible parts, being alkaline concretions. . . . We are assured, moreover, that our dust must have come from the land, by its semi-animal constituents, and that it must have come therefore originally from some quarter to the westward of the meridian of Ningpo and Shanghai, for to the eastward is the ocean; and, as it was brought down by a north-easterly current, below that, it must have come from the northward. The north-west, then, seems the most probable direction to suppose it was originally carried into the atmosphere; and it is improbable it could have come from Corea or Japan." This seems to encourage the hypothesis of its having been brought down from the high land to the north of China.

In bidding adieu to the city and walks of Shanghai, let me give a parting word about its population. A rough estimate of the inhabitants in the city and suburbs would give from 350,000 to 400,000. But no accurate statistics have been yet taken on which a correct census could be drawn. The multitudes here are composed, in a great measure, of migratory people, traders, merchants, &c., from every part of the empire, bent on commerce or gain of some sort;—and yearly the mass is growing. Crowds are begetting crowds; for there is a stream of vultures, in China as elsewhere, flying in the direction of the carcass. But it is easy to detect that this mixed medley is truly Chinese,—physically, intellectually, morally. As for the indigenous part of the community, it is plain they are not even on a par with men of Soochow, Shantung, Ningpo, Amoy, or Canton, for independence, energy, vivacity; yet it cannot be denied that the Shanghai people are equal to all others in industry, perhaps superior to them for gentleness and docility. The following description of the people is translated from a native work, and perhaps, on the whole, depicts justly the state of the Shanghai natives when the work was written, about the beginning of the present century:*—"Generally speaking, the scholars of the district are polished, but rather superficial, and the husbandmen are sincere, but approaching to vulgarity. The common people are poor, and the merchants wealthy; sometimes, however, while they have a deficiency at home, they display abundance abroad. The citizens aim to imitate the manners of the inhabitants of Soo-chow and Yang-chow, but it ill becomes the insignificance of their district; though an elegant appearance is presented to the gaze of the multitude, yet they have not the means wherewith to maintain it long; for in order to perpetuate the grandeur to distant generations, the source from which it sprang should be of an ancient date."

That is an olden portraiture of Shanghai people and poverty,—in some respects too true at the present day. There is little doubt, however, that the opening of the port has wrought beneficially on all classes; intercourse with foreigners of every country being calculated to spur them up, as well as contact with more of the intelligent and enterprising of their own fellow-countrymen, who have recently been flocking to that foreign mart. The men and the women make good servants, tractable and trusty; and it is scarcely to be feared but, after a fair trial, the Shanghai natives will prove themselves in other points as active, clever, and successful as their countrymen in other parts.

* Chinese Miscellany.

I am aware that the character of the people, not only of Shanghai but of all China, has been sadly depreciated by some, who, I believe, if they had not given so much bridle to their pens, would have secured more confidence in their accounts, and a better name for fairness and moderation. Some American, of the name of Bayard Taylor, after a flying visit to Shanghai (where I acted as his cicerone for half a day), and perhaps to one or two other ports in China, records his estimate of Chinese morality thus, in one of his last works:—" It is my deliberate opinion that the Chinese are morally the most debased people on the face of the earth. Forms of vice, which in other countries are barely named, are in China so common that they excite no comment among the natives. They constitute the surface-level, and below them there are deeps on deeps of depravity so shocking and horrible that their character cannot even be hinted. There are some dark shadows in human nature which we naturally shrink from penetrating, and I made no attempt to collect information of this kind; but there was enough in the things which I could not avoid seeing and hearing,—which are brought almost daily to the notice of every foreign resident,—to inspire me with a powerful aversion to the Chinese race. Their touch is pollution, and, harsh as the opinion may seem, justice to our own race demands that they should not be allowed to settle on our soil. Science may have lost something, but mankind has gained by the exclusive policy which has governed China during the past centuries." I know this shallow observer of human nature has been skimming nearly over every part of the globe; but, with all deference to him, I only enter a flat contradiction, that it " is my deliberate opinion that the Chinese are morally *not* the most debased people on the face of the earth."

CHAPTER II.

COLONY OF HEBREWS IN THE INTERIOR—MOHAMMEDANISM AMONG THE CHINESE—INFLUENCE OF BUDDHISM, AND STRIKING SIMILARITY TO POPERY.

MANY topics for curious inquiry occurred during my long residence at Shanghai, which it were superfluous to recite here. It will be sufficient to assure any reader who may be fond of investigation, that, in the pages which follow, it will be my object to bring within due compass, and in as interesting a manner as I can, the result of researches made by me on the spot, on such subjects as the existence of a colony of Hebrews in the interior, as well as of Mohammedans; Buddhism, and its effects; the nature and history of Pagodas; and the working of Popery and Protestantism in China.

With these preliminary remarks, let me bespeak the reader's attention to a

Brief Narrative of the Discovery of a Hebrew Colony in China.

The most recent information we have had regarding the existence of any remnant of the Hebrew race in China, was published in 1851, at the London Mission Press, in Shanghai, in "The Narrative of a Mission of Inquiry to the Jewish Synagogue at Kaifung." That mission of inquiry was promoted the preceding year, at the instance of the London Society for Christianizing Jews, to whose funds a lady of great liberality had bequeathed a large sum, for the purpose of instituting definite researches on this very point,—the existence of Jews in China. Dr. Smith, the Bishop of Hong-Kong, on leaving England for his diocese, promised his assistance in pursuing this inquiry; and, on reaching Hong-

Kong, in 1850, as the Church Missionary Society's Mission in China was but in its infancy, his lordship communicated with the representatives of the London Missionary Society at Shanghai, requesting our aid and counsel, which was readily afforded. As we had two intelligent Chinese converts, whom we could recommend as qualified to enter on the work, their services were accepted, and we despatched them on the 25th of November, 1850.

After an absence of a few months (Kaifung lying at a distance of six hundred miles from Shanghai), our messengers returned. They brought with them two Chinese Jews, with whom I had frequent interviews, as they resided in our mission during their sojourn at Shanghai. Neither of them had a Hebrew name. The one was forty years old, the other about forty-five. They had both submitted to the rite of circumcision in infancy. One of them had a remarkably Jewish cast of countenance. But in nothing were they distinguishable from the surrounding masses, except in religious profession; for they talked the Chinese language, dressed in the Chinese style, and had the usual Chinese manners and customs.

But not the least interesting proofs brought by our messengers of inquiry were eight MSS., containing portions of the Old Testament Scriptures *in Hebrew*. These were Exod. i.—vi.; xxxviii.—xl.; Lev. xix., xx.; Numb. xii.—xv.; Deut. xi.—xvi., xxxii.; and the remaining two MSS. contained selections from the Pentateuch, Psalms, Hagiographia, perhaps parts of a Liturgy. These MSS. were chiefly on large scrolls, a few of them in a smaller book-form written on thick paper, and some on sheepskin. One or two were of considerable antiquity. The writing in most was clear and distinct, with vowel-points. On comparing the MSS. of Exod. i.—vi. with the editions in general use at the present day, I found a remarkable agreement.

These MSS., lying imbedded in the interior of China for centuries, may be of service to those engaged in the collation of ancient Hebrew Scriptures.

The narrative of this mission of inquiry is full of important particulars of this journey and residence at Kaifungfoo: and, from the statements made by these individuals and their companions, the two Chinese Jews, I give the following summary of the colony of Jews in that city and of their synagogue.

In all probability this sect took refuge here about the third century of the present era, but not later,—coming from India across the north-western boundary of China. At first they numbered seventy clans, but at present not more than one tenth of this number exists, and of these seven families not above 200 individuals survive. They are chiefly located in the centre of Kaifung city and in the vicinity of their synagogue. A few are shop-keepers, some are peasants; but the majority are sunk in poverty and misery, almost destitute of raiment and shelter,—so poor indeed, that some of the materials of the synagogue premises have been sold by the professors to supply the wants of their families. Still they retain their distinctness from the surrounding masses of Mohammedans and Pagans, although by the mere name of their religion. Originally they were called followers of the *Tienchuh* religion, that is "the Indian religion;"—*Tienchuh* being the Chinese name for India, from which country this sect is reported to have come. But, instead of that appellation, they now go by the name *T'iau-kin-kiau*,—"cutting-the-sinew sect,—because everything that we eat, mutton, beef or fowl, must have the sinews taken out." The rite of circumcision is still practised on males, within one month after birth. Of festivals, one is "for perambulating round the Scriptures;" this is the twenty-fourth of the eighth month. Their Sabbath is the European Saturday. They intermarry only among themselves, not with pagans or Mohammedans.

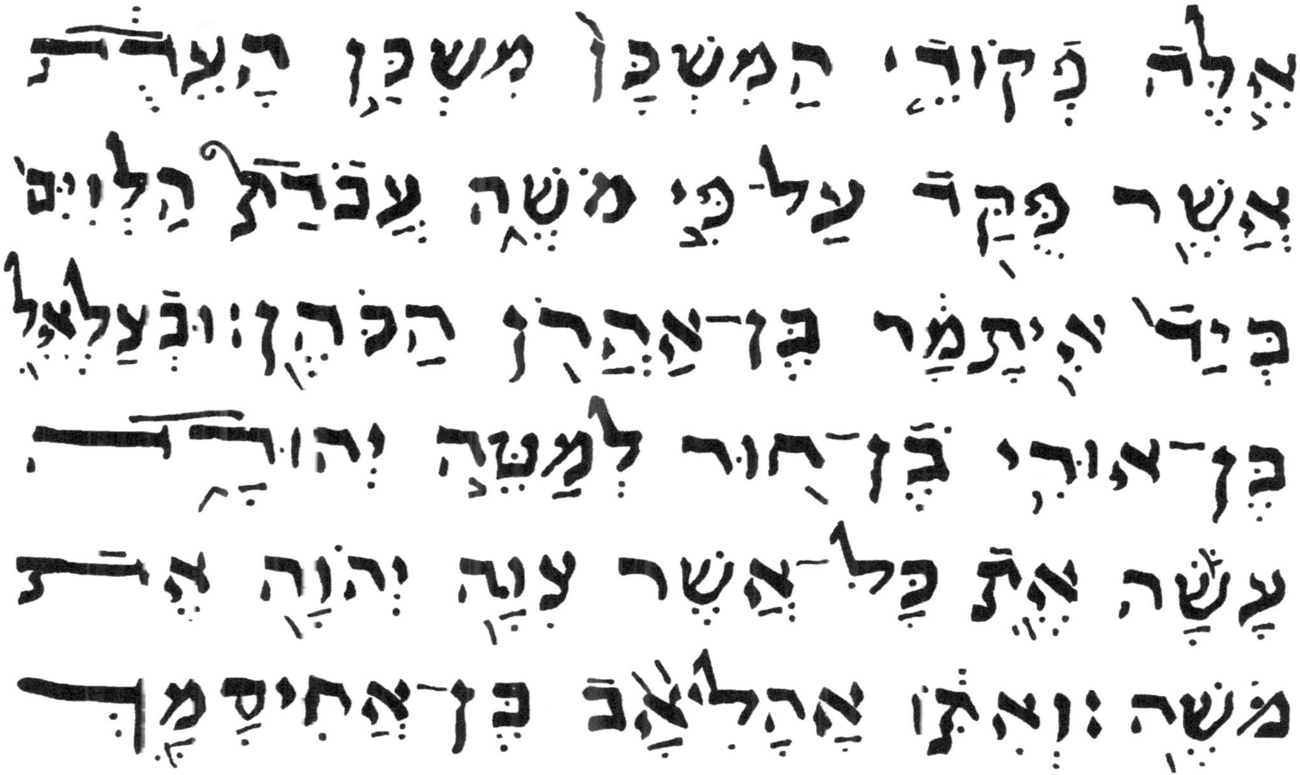
אלה פקודי המשכן משכן העדת
אשר פקד על־פי משה עבדת הלוים
ביד איתמר בן־אהרן הכהן׃ ובצלאל
בן־אורי בן־חור למטה יהודה
עשה את כל־אשר צוה יהוה את
משה׃ ואתו אהליאב בן־אחיסמך

FACSIMILE OF THREE VERSES OF A HEBREW [illegible] FOUND AT KAI FUNG. Exodus xxxviii. 21–23

Nor is it permitted to marry two wives. They are forbidden to eat pork. In the observance of Divine service, they have to wash their bodies before entering the synagogue; and, for this purpose, on each side of the holy place there is a bath. During service they face the west, in the direction of Jerusalem, or, rather, as near that direction as they know. In the performance of sacred worship, the priest at one time used to wear a blue head-dress and blue shoes: hence the name by which Jews have gone in China, "the blue-bonnet Moslems." The people are not permitted to enter the temple with their shoes on their feet; nor the women with napkins on their heads,—the common head-dress among the Chinese females of Honan province. However, the expectation of the Messiah seems to have been entirely lost. The elder of the two Chinese Jews informed us, that he remembered people talking of Hebrew teachers, at Kaifung, who had died a little before he was born, or about fifty years since. The Rabbi was called "*Mwanlah*," that is *Mullah*. Besides him, there are two officers,—the one "the sinew-extractor," the other "the preacher of doctrines." At this time, there seems to be none able to decipher Hebrew writings. Indeed, they have begun recently to amalgamate themselves with the myriad pagans and Mohammedans in the vast population of Kaifung, which must amount at least to one million.

Although the Jews must have entered China so early in the Christian era, it appears that their synagogue was not built here before the close of the twelfth century, or nearly 1,000 years after their entrance. Jewish professors used to call this building "the temple of *Yih-sze-lo-hi-nieh*," in which possibly there is an attempt at expressing the name *Israel* phonetically;—but the inscription at present over the door is "The true and pure temple." According to the accounts brought by the Chinese investigators, the synagogue itself stands within a third inclosure. Here there is one large hall, eighty feet deep, and forty feet wide, the roof of which is covered with green tiles. In this stands a seat, "Moses' seat," about a foot above a wooden floor; where, on grand festive seasons, the Rabbi took his seat under a large red satin umbrella held overhead, which is still preserved in the building. Here too was a cell for depositing "the twelve tubes containing Heaven's records," or the copies of Hebrew scriptures already spoken of.

During their researches, our messengers copied many inscriptions within the synagogue and on its various pillars,—some in Chinese, a few in Hebrew characters. I transcribe one or two of the latter from their journal, exactly as they are given by the transcribers themselves, without vouching for their accuracy or making any correction. Over a tablet in Chinese,—similar to what is found in Mohammedan mosques or Buddhist temples,—with the customary formula, "May His Imperial Majesty live for ever," &c., there is this Hebrew inscription:—

שמע ישראל יהוה אלהינו יהוה אחד
ברוך שם כביר מלכיתו לעלם ועד

"Hear, O Israel! Jehovah our God is one Jehovah. Blessed be the name of his glorious kingdom for ever and ever." These sentences are repeated in another part. Close to the cell for containing the scriptures we have this sentence:—

ביכי שמו כיהוה אלהי האלאים

"Ineffable is his name, for Jehovah is the God of gods." Of the Chinese inscriptions, which are very numerous, the following couplet is singular:—

"The sacred scriptures consist of fifty-three sections; these we recite by mouth, and meditate on, praying that the imperial sway may be firmly established."

"The letters of the sacred alphabet are twenty-seven; these are taught in our households, in hope that the interests of the country may prosper."

In our common Hebrew Bibles, the Pentateuch is divided into fifty-four sections; but it appears that among Indian and Persian Jews their division gives only fifty-three; and as to the number of Hebrew letters, by making the final forms of *kaph*, *mem*, *nun*, *pe*, and *tsaddi*, separate and distinct letters,—the same Jews make up twenty-seven, instead of twenty-two, as usually given.

From two long Chinese tablets outside the gateway of the synagogue, I make the following extracts, and with them conclude this notice of "the peculiar people," who have for 1,500 years resided in the very centre of China, the unconscious witnesses of departed glory and unknown treasurers of the oracles of God:—

"From the beginning of the world our first father Adam handed down the doctrine to Abraham; Abraham handed it down to Isaac; Isaac handed it down to Jacob; Jacob handed it down to the twelve patriarchs; and the twelve patriarchs handed it down to Moses; Moses handed it down to Aaron; Aaron handed it down to Joshua; and Joshua handed it down to Ezra; by whom the doctrines of the holy religion were first sent abroad, and the letters of the Jewish religion first made plain"

"The founder of this religion is Abraham, who is considered the first teacher of it. Then came Moses, who established the law, and handed down the sacred writings. After his time, during the Han dynasty, this religion entered China." [The Han dynasty arose two centuries before and endured two centuries after the opening of the Christian era, so that the introduction of Judaism into China must, according to this, have been between B C. 200 and A.D. 200.]

"Moses was intelligent from his birth, pure and disinterested, endowed with benevolence and righteousness, wisdom and virtue, all complete. He sought and obtained the sacred writings on the top of Sinai's hill, where he fasted forty days and nights, repressing his carnal desires, refraining even from sleep, and spending his time in sincere devotion. The sacred writings (that is of the Pentateuch), amounting to fifty-three sections, were thus obtained. Their contents are deep and mysterious, their promises calculated to influence men's good feelings, and their threatenings to repress their corrupt imaginations. The doctrines were again handed down to the time of the reformer of our religion Ezra, whose descent was reckoned from the founder of our religion.

"Thus our religion has been handed down from one to another. It came originally from India. Those who introduced it in obedience to God's commands were seventy clans. [The names are given.]

About 1166, Yen-toolah built the synagogue in Kai-fung capital. But as this temple required some one to look after its concerns, there were appointed certain men [who are named], themselves upright, intelligent, and able to admonish others. They had the title of Mwan-lah [Mullah]. So that up to this time [*i. e.* when the tablet was written, A.D. 1489], the sacred vestments, ceremonies, and music, are all maintained according to the prescribed pattern. . . . . Yen-toolah fixed the foundation, and commenced the work, towards the completion of which all the Jewish families contributed. In this manner were provided the sacred implements and furniture, with the cells for depositing the sacred writings."

Above is a summary of the valuable information brought by the two Chinese messengers, who left the mission at Shanghai in search of the Israelites in Kaifung. Their narrative, translated by Dr. Medhurst, and prefaced by the Bishop of Victoria, has already been published, though, I regret to find, little known in this country. It deserves republication, for it contains a mass of information, adding to, as well as corroborative of, the particulars to be found in the duodecimo published twelve years since by Mr. Finn, entitled "The Jews in China."

Another subject of investigation somewhat novel and important was the growth and progress of "*the religion of the Prophet,*" among the professed followers of Confucius.

The name by which Moslemism goes in China is the *Hwuy-Hwuy* religion. Judaism also has the name *Hwuy-Hwuy koo-kiaou,* or "the *Hwuy-Hwuy* ancient religion." The characters *Hwuy-Hwuy* convey no meaning in this appellation, as it is an attempt to transfer a foreign name. I have met with no satisfactory explanation of the origin of that name. And the only attempt at a solution, that I have seen somewhere, is that, as a large proportion of subsidiaries in the service of the Chinese emperor in A.D. 750 were Mohammedans of the *Ouigar* tribes, the Chinese have since that time denominated them and their creed by the first syllable of their name, *Oui, Hwuy,* and *Hwuy-Hwuy.*

It has been supposed by some that the Mohammedans entered China first by land; but a native cyclopædia before me observes, as to the question how and when the *Hwuy* people visited China:—"The *Hwuy* nations lie above 1,000 miles beyond the frontiers of Northern Tartary, called the *Yuhmun* boundary, in 53° N. lat. It is the peculiar custom of that people to worship Heaven alone. At the beginning of the *Tang* dynasty, A.D. 750, they came by ship [from India, Persia, or Arabia] to the Canton province, where they erected a place of worship. After Kublai mounted the Chinese throne, this sect spread very widely throughout the empire. Wherever they went they formed close alliances amongst themselves and settled down." Another native account fixes the introduction of the Moslem religion into China, about A.D. 633. At the latest, however, its entrance must have been at or near the year 130 of the Hegira. It has been remarked by some foreign residents at Canton, that they have been struck with the strongly-marked Arab faces of many natives there. Upon inquiry of the origin and creed of these people, it has been ascertained from themselves that their ancestors had settled at Canton several centuries ago, and that they themselves were Mohammedans in religion. This appears to second the account of the first appearance of this people at Canton.

From the beginning, the sole object of the followers of the Prophet in entering the middle kingdom seems to have been commerce; nor do they at any time appear to have taken pains to proselytize the Chinese. If they have increased in numbers, it has been by marriage and offspring.

Except in strictly maintaining their religious sectarianism, they differ not from the surrounding myriads in dress, language, and manners. Instances occur in which superstition works remarkably among them; of which the following is a singular case that occurred at the city of Canton in 1835:—One evening, a follower of the false Prophet, contrary to his creed, accidentally ate a piece of pork and lay down to sleep. In his dreams a man appeared before him, inquired the reason of his violating the laws of the Prophet, and forthwith dragged him away. Frightened, he raised his voice and awoke, and after telling his family what he had done and seen, immediately expired. His neighbours believed this story to be true, and that his death was a punishment inflicted on him for not adhering to the faith in which he was born.

At present, the Moslem sect is to be found in all the provinces of China, but fewer in the south than in the north-west. I am not prepared to give even their probable census at the present date. Early in the eighteenth century it was put down at half a million. That part of Little Bokhara under the government of the Chinese to the west of China Proper is called in our geographies "Eastern Turkistan," but by the Chinese themselves "the territory of the eight Mohammedan cities." There the professors of Mohammedanism are divided into three classes, differing in the shape and colour of their head-dresses,—the red, the white, and the common Arab turban.

Through ignorance, the Jews in China, as already stated above, are also designated by the name under which Mohammedans go, probably owing to a similarity in some of their tenets; but they are distinguished not only as belonging to "*the ancient*" form of the Moslem faith, they are also sometimes called "the Blue-bonnet Mohammedans," from wearing the blue turban.

At different times I have been introduced to members of the Mohammedan profession, officers that had passed the regular examinations for promotion. In an ancient account of China, by two Mohammedan travellers that visited that empire in the ninth century, they state (what I have been unable to ascertain as existing at the present day) that "there is a Mohammedan appointed judge over those of his religion by the authority of the Emperor of China, and that he is judge of all the Mohammedans who resort to those parts. Upon festival days he performs the public services with the Mohammedans, and pronounces the sermon or *kotbat*, which he concludes, in the usual form, with prayers for the Sultan of the Moslems. The merchants of Irak who trade hither are no ways dissatisfied with his conduct or his administration in the post he is invested with, because his actions and the judgments he gives are just and equitable, and conformable to the Koran, and according to the Mohammedan jurisprudence."

When the Imperial forces came down upon Shanghai, in the autumn of 1853, to expel the pirates then in possession of that city, I visited their encampment, and found crowds of soldiers from Kansuh and Shense who were of the Moslem creed, distinguished from their comrades in arms as "men who have no idols, and would not eat swine's flesh." They professed likewise to adore "Allah," to follow "Moohamihtih," and to abstain from wine.

A native writer, speaking of their religious views, observes:—"Although the Mohammedan territory borders on India, the customs of this people differ greatly; for they do not worship Buddha, they do not pray to the dead, nor sacrifice to spirits. What they reverently honour is what we represent by one character, *T'ien*, or heaven." The native messengers, who, in 1850, were sent by the Protestant mission at Shanghai in search of the Jews at Kaifung, informed us on their return that the Mohammedans there are numerous, and that over a wine-jar, painted upon their signboards in the market-places, they have written two characters, "pure and true," implying their sincerity and constancy in abstinence from all intoxicating drinks. In various parts of the country they have erected mosques, principally in the larger cities, often with this Arabic inscription over the gateway,—"A temple for Mohammedans who desire to consult the Koran." In the city of Canton there is the *Kwang-t'ah*, or "bright pagoda," lofty and prominent, erected about 1,000 years since by the resident Mohammedans, and around its base they have their mosque. Beyond the city walls there is a Mohammedan burying-ground, known among the natives by the name *Hiang-fun*, "Echoing Cemetery;" for, say they, "when people enter it, their words and steps re-echo, moving for a time and then stopping."

From the Mohammedan teacher (my interview with whom I have mentioned at page 80) I obtained a pictorial sheet almanac for the year 1843, prepared for the use of the Mohammedans. It purported to have been issued from Hangchow, the principal seat of their religion in China, and published with the sanction of the Imperial Cabinet, containing directions to the followers of the Prophet for the observance of set days of rest, fasting, and other festivals. The upper portion of a temple is depicted on it, with two maxims in large characters, viz., "In receiving instructions be serious and reverential," and "Strictly keep fast-days and worship-days." A few short notes line the margin of the table-almanac, such as "Whenever the new moon is observed on the first day of the week, it is of prime importance not to attend to ordinary business on that day. Let business be anticipated the day before; should the moon appear on the third day, let business be put off till the next day." The table contains a list of the Sabbaths and "pure, true fast and feast days."* The year of the publication is given as

* To their mosques and services, as well as signboards, they attach the description "pure and true," the same which the Jews appropriate to their synagogue and services.

"the 23rd of Taoukwang," also "the 1249th year of the exalted and sacred parting with the world [that is, the decease] of Moohamihtih of the West." Each month has the Arabic name given in Chinese pronunciation as follows:—

Month.	*Chinese Pronunciation of the Arabic Names.*	
1st.—Mei-hoh-lan.	......	Moharram. (1)
2nd.—Sih-fei-lih.	......	Safar. (2)
3rd.—Leih-ngan-wei-lih.	......	Robuland. (3)
4th.—Leh pi-au-lih-hah-lih.	......	Robusanny.
5th.—Che-ma-tuh-lih-o-wah-lih.	......	Jumadelavil. (4)
6th.—Che-ma-tuh-lih-o-hah-lih.	......	Jumdiassany. (5)
7th.—Lih-chih-puh.	......	Rajeb.
8th—Shay-ur-pa-nah.	......	Shabaun. (6)
9th.—Lih-mah-shah-nah.	......	Ramyan. (7)
10th.—Shau-wa-lih.	......	Shawal. (8)
11th.—Tsuh-lih-kah-ur-tih.	......	Dhulkaada.
12th.—Tsuh-lih-hau-chih.	......	Dhulhujja. (9)
13th.—Mei-hoh-lan.	......	Moharram. (10)*

I have heard, but I cannot recall my authority, that yearly there is a band of Chinese pilgrims for Mecca. I am disposed to doubt it. The only instance of the kind is mentioned in a number of the "Chinese Repository" for 1834, of a man of the province of Chihli, a Chinese Mohammedan, who returned to Canton from his pilgrimage that same year:—"This poor and ignorant man, three years ago, came down to Canton, and

* Special days to be observed in each month :—

(1) Twelfth-day of *Ashuholih* (Achurry), the appointed time for liberality to the poor.

(2) During this entire month all business must be attended with special care and circumspection.

(3) The third day is the anniversary of the Prophet's sickness ; the fourteenth is the day of his death ; both to be kept as fasts.

(4) The second day is the birthday of the great sage *Ur-li-ali.*

(5) The fifth day is the first commemoration of the death of the holy woman *Fatima.*

(6) This is an intercalary month.

(7) Keep one month's fasting.

(8) The whole month is a festival of congratulation.

(9) The twelfth day must be observed as the *Kur-purh* feast.

(10) A day of liberality to the poor as in the first month.

obtained a passage in a country ship to Bombay, whence he found his way to the tomb of the Prophet. In the same way he has now effected his return, bringing with him a large store of Arabic books. Though altogether unable to make himself understood either by his fellow-countrymen on board the ship, or by the Mohammedan lascars, he was, on account of his pilgrimage, treated with respect and attention by the latter. At Canton he joined the society of his religious associates, from whom the sanctity of his character would insure to him support, and the means (which he did not possess) of returning to his native province."

Buddhism in China.

As you mount to the summit of any of the idolatrous towers called pagodas, and view the landscape o'er, studded with similar erections, temples, monasteries, and other monuments, there is this inquiry which you cannot but study with some degree of interest:—"What has Buddhism done for the Chinese—for education, morality, and religion among the Chinese?"

Deserting its Indian nursery at the opening of the Christian era, as a refugee it sought protection in "the central country," and, with its Indian deities and missionaries, Indian tenets and language, Indian ritual and canonicals, it found favour with a people already dissatisfied with their own religionless systems, and prepared to admit any new form that might work more effectually on their feelings of devotion. Making the heart of the empire its first station, with a handful of priests, and with loads of tracts and books (the silent and most effective messengers of every religion), Buddhism branched forth in all directions, and crept over the breadth of the empire, erecting monuments of its ascendancy, such as pagodas and temples. From being unassuming at first and unpretending, it worked itself into public favour, till it obtained the finest, richest, and most prominent grounds for sites of monasteries, &c.; and has hitherto fed itself on the fat of these lands.

Although the speculative and intellectual discourses of the Confucian school were so much simpler and purer than those of the Buddhist, without any of its farce and nonsense, and although there are several of the common tenets of Buddhism the tendency of which is entirely repugnant to the Chinese sense of propriety (such as celibacy enforced on its followers, which, of course, results in deadening all filial regard for parents), yet, in the census of its adherents,—it has been able to count some emperors, ministers of state, and literati, and a majority of the middle and lower ranks, especially the most sensitive and impressible class in society, the daughters of China. This can readily be accounted for. Taouism, an indigenous religion of China, had already encouraged the appetite for the marvellous and mysterious by magic, alchemy, and sorcery.* But Buddhism, rife with superstition of every form, when it entered China at once adapted itself, with its ritual performances, &c., to the popular tendency of the lower and uneducated classes in particular, became the favourite religion in the empire; and the result has been, as Dr. Morrison has remarked, "Buddhism in China was decried by the learned, laughed at by the profligate, and followed by all."

What the Chinese know of rules for human conduct existed long before in the writings of Confucius and his compeers; and for what they know of morality they will thank the Confucian school. Buddhism, it is true, is a religion, but it is not "the religion of common life." It aims at making a man entirely separate himself from his fellow-men, but not at fitting him to associate with his kind. It requires every one to "retire from the world," in Buddhist phrase, but it does not train him to be "diligent in business and fervent in spirit." It blunts the common feelings of human nature, and has nothing to cultivate the best, the noblest risings of the heart. Added to this, it has not tended to prepare the Chinese mind for the worship of the one living and true God; but, by adding to their pantheon an endless catalogue of idols, by ingrafting into the saint-calendar whatever genii in China it saw fit, and by adopting the popular superstitions of the country, *e. g.* the worship of the manes of the dead, homage to superior and mystic powers, passion for charms, magic, aud invocations, &c. (all which was quite compatible with Buddhism), it has made the Chinese more idolatrous than ever. In its religious tenets there is not a hint that mankind is involved in guilt; but it rather mourns over man as involved in misery. Its motive for the prohibition of vice and the practice of virtue is only the obligation of mitigating human distress and promoting happiness. Instead of humbling the anxious inquirer after truth, or any way fitting the oppressed heart to cast itself on the provision of Divine mercy, it fosters one's native conceit, establishes a system of self-righteousness, and insists on rules of self-salvation. To quiet the curiosity of the mind about the future state, it is satisfied to conjure up a creed of fables,—on the one hand, cheering the good with the hope, after death, of migrating into extraordinary forms, or into the bodies of other men, or becoming gods, or (what is its *summum bonum*) reverting into nihility; and on the other hand, warning the wicked by threats of being changed at death into hungry ghosts or unclean beasts and reptiles.

What is there in a vapid system like this to elevate the Chinese mind, or to change the natives of this empire into really honest, amiable, and virtuous men? It has deluded them more than ever. It has widened and deepened the current of idolatry among them. Its influence has been to destroy those rational principles that are inculcated in the writings of the learned. It has introduced a mass of gross and endless absurdities. It has thrown a denser fog about the path of the immortal pilgrim, and deserted him in his dreary wanderings. It has carried the Chinese nation further off from the fountain of life than it was before.

In a paraphrase on one of the celebrated maxims* of the Emperor Kanghe, there is a lengthy paragraph which gives a description of the character and influence of Buddhism, from the pen of a learned Chinese, who flourished one hundred years since. The text on which the comment is made is the seventh maxim :—" Have nothing to do with strange notions, but give all due importance to orthodox doctrines." I give the following quotation :—" The whole talk of the priests of Buddh is about becoming demi-gods, like Buddh, their founder; and when a son leaves the family to become a priest, they say that all the members of his family are sure of ascending up to heaven. . . . . It is very true that the superiors of the priests of this sect, who reside in the pearl monasteries of the famed hills, and well understand how to deliver their doctrines, sum up all in one word, *the heart*. Yet, to steal away to those solitary abodes, where there is not even the smoke of human habitations, and sit cross-legged in profound silence, is completely to root up and destroy the obligations of relative life. Do but observe these austere priests of Buddh, who, for no advantage whatever, break up all the relations of human life; they are not worth the down of a feather to society! . . . . From them has arisen a class of men who, void of any source of dependence and a settled place where they can get food, throw themselves on the monasteries, and take up their rest in the temples. They borrow the name of Buddh, and of immortal spirits, and invent a multitude

* There were sixteen maxims.—See Milne's Sacred Edict, pp. 134—147.

of idle stories about celestial temples, subterraneous prisons, transmigrations, and retributions. According to them, the most honourable of all things is to feed the priests and be liberal to the gods. This (say they) is to sow the field of bliss! They say, 'Always give, and you will always have.' And lest people should not believe them, they say, 'Only contemn the priests, revile Buddh, discredit the canons; on seeing the gods, refuse to worship; meeting with riches, give none away; then, you are sure to be cast down to hell; either the thunderbolt will strike you, or the lightning consume you!' All sorts of marvellous and fictitious tales they tell in order to frighten people to believe, submit to, and support them. At first they only cheat people out of their money, that they themselves may obtain and use it. By degrees then they proceed to the utmost excess of irregularity; collecting (what shall I call them) dragon-adorning assemblies, flowerpot assemblies, orphan-pardoning assemblies, where they beat drums, ring bells, explain doctrines, deliver laws, and have promiscuous mixtures of men and women, who separate not day or night. It is said, that it is for good purposes that people go thither; but every one knows that it is precisely to do evil. You, simple people, know not how to discriminate. For, even according to what the books of Buddh say, he was the first-born son of the king Fan; but, retiring from the world, he fled away alone to the top of the Snowy Mountains, in order to cultivate virtue. If he regarded not his own father, mother, wife, and children, are you such fools as to suppose that he regards the multitude of the living, or would deliver his doctrines to you? If he rejected the imperial residence, the palace of queens, the royal throne, &c., is it not marvellous to suppose that he should delight in monasteries, nunneries, temples, and religious houses, which you can build? . . . All those nonsensical tales about keeping fasts, collecting assemblies, building temples, and fashioning images, are feigned, by those sauntering worthless priests, to deceive you. Still you believe them, and not only go yourselves to worship and burn incense in the temples, but also suffer your wives and daughters to go, with their hair oiled, their faces painted; dressed in scarlet, trimmed with green, they go to burn incense in the temples; associating themselves with those priests of Buddh, touching shoulders, rubbing arms, and pressed in the moving crowd. I see not where the good they talk of doing is; on the contrary, they do many shameful things, that create vexation, and give people occasion for laughter and ridicule. Further, there are some persons who, fearing that their good boys and girls may not live till they attain age, take them and give them up to temples to become priests and priestesses; supposing that, after having removed them from their own houses and placed them at the foot of the patriarch Buddh, they are then sure of prolonging life! Again, there is another extremely stupid class of persons, who, because their parents are sick, pledge their own persons by a vow before the gods, that if their parents be restored to health, they will go to worship and burn incense on the hills; prostrating themselves at every step, till they arrive at the summit, whence they will dash themselves down! If they lose not their lives, they are sure to break a leg or an arm. They say, 'To give up our own lives in order to save those of our parents is the highest display of filial piety.' By-standers also praise them as very dutiful. But they do not consider that in this manner to slight their own bodies, which they have received from their parents, discovers an extreme want of filial piety. Moreover, you say, that your serving Buddh is a very profitable service; that, if you burn paper money, present offerings, and keep fasts before your god, he will dissipate calamities, blot out your sins, increase your happiness, and prolong your age! Now, just reflect;—from old it has been said, 'The gods are intelligent and just.' Were your god Buddh of this description, how could he avariciously desire your gilt-paper, and your offerings to engage him to afford you protection? If you do not burn gilt-paper to him, and spread offerings on his altar, the god Buddh will be displeased with you! Then, your god Buddh is a scoundrel! Let us take, for example, your district officer; should you never go to compliment and flatter him, yet, if you be good people and attend to your duty, he will pay you a marked attention. But, if you transgress the law, commit violence, and usurp the rights of others, though you should use a thousand ways and means to flatter him, he will still be displeased with you, and will, without fail, remove the pests from your society. . . . As to charms in the books of Buddh, they are all in the brogue of Buddh's country. Well, the priests take that country brogue of Buddh, and say it contains the charms of Buddh, the deliverer; and, while repeating them, they make foolish and magical motions with the fingers. . . . The sum of the whole is, these licentious priests are indolent; they will neither go to labour in the fields nor buy and sell in the markets: thus, being without food and clothing, they set to work and invent means of deceiving the people."

But, the spell of Buddhism in China has been broken; its glass has evidently run out; and often, as I have watched the tumbling ruins of its numerous pagodas, &c., it was impossible not to interpret the handwriting on the system of Buddha to be—"God hath numbered thy kingdom and finished it. Thou art weighed in the balances and found wanting." What the author of "Saturday Evening," some twenty years ago, noted of China, was at that time just, and is still more appropriate at the present crisis. "In truth it must hardly be said that there is anything of religion in China, if we deduct on the one hand what is purely an instrument of civil polity, a pomp of government; and, on the other, what is mere domestic usage, or immemorial *decoration* of the home economy. Ages have passed away since mind, or feeling, or passion, animated the religion of China. The religion of China is now a thing not only as absurdly gay, but as dead at heart as an Egyptian mummy. It is fit only to rest where it has lain two thousand years; touch it—shake it—it crumbles to dust. Let but the civil institutions of China be broken up, and we might look about in vain for its religion."

Buddhism is falling,—is falling! Still, there is one aspect in that sensual and scheming system that must awaken some concern in the promoters of Bible Christianity,—I mean the striking features of resemblance in it to Popery. In its *pantheon*, there is the image of a woman with a child in her arms, "the goddess of mercy," and a host of canonized personages, pictures and images of whom abound. In its *buildings*, "The Buddhist monasteries," says Huc, himself a Catholic priest, "are similar in many respects to our own,"* where the hermits and priests may shut themselves up from the wide world, and from all the charities of life; and there is the nunnery too for the woman ascetic, who has vowed (and by shaving off all her hair has confirmed her vow) never to marry, but to spend a lifetime in the worship of her idol, and devote herself as a sister of charity to acts of benevolence. In the *priests*, you have the clean shaving of the head, the use of long flowing and many-coloured robes, vowing celibacy, living in secluded abodes, frequently fasting, making long pilgrimages and severe penances, and constantly abstaining from rich food, amusement, and the most innocent socialities of life. In *sacred furniture*, there is

* Huc's Travels, vol. ii. p. 56.

the altar-piece, with candles, incense, holy water, bells, relics, and offerings. In *worship*, there is the use of the rosary, chanting prayers, offerings in behalf of the dead, the use of a foreign language, numberless repetitions, bowing the body, and bending the knee without end. In Huc's Travels, I find the Romanist padre writes with an amount of satisfaction, on "les nombreuses et frappantes analogies qui existent entre les rites Lamanesques et le culte Catholique." He says,— "Upon the most superficial examination of the reforms and innovations introduced into the Lamanesque (Buddhist) worship in Tartary and Thibet, one must be struck with their affinity to Catholicism. The cross, the mitre, the dalmatica, the cope, which the Grand Lamas wear on their journeys, or when they are performing some ceremony out of the temple; the service with double choirs, the psalmody, the exorcisms, the censer suspended from five chains, and which you can open or close at pleasure; the benedictions given by the Lamas by extending the right hand over the heads of the faithful; the chaplet, ecclesiastical celibacy, spiritual retirement, the worship of the saints, the fasts, the processions, the litanies, the holy water, all these are analogies between the Buddhists and ourselves. There exists at Lha-sa a very touching custom, and which we felt a sort of jealousy at finding among infidels. In the evening, just as the day is verging on its decline, all the Thibetians stay business and meet together, men, women, and children, according to their sex and age, in the principal parts of the town and in the public squares. As soon as groups are formed, every one kneels down, and they begin slowly and in undertones to chant prayers."

With points of similarity so marked in this form of priestcraft, is it unlikely—is it not indeed certain, that the Romish Church will take advantage of them to establish its own ground for reverence and adhesion in the minds of the natives of the empire? "Such, we know, was continually the policy of that Church in its early days of corruption.* Such is still the practice of Rome, adopting, as she does, on the one hand, the music of India,—on the other, the fantastic dresses of the sun-worshipping Peruvians into her religious feasts."

CHAPTER III.

PAGODAS IN CHINA—A GENERAL DESCRIPTION OF THESE EDIFICES—A DISCUSSION TO SHOW THAT PAGODAS IN CHINA ORIGINALLY WERE INTRODUCED BY INDIAN RELIGIONISTS.

THE subject discussed in this chapter was laid before the China Branch of the Royal Asiatic Society three years ago, and published at Hong-Kong in the Transactions of that Branch. In a remodelled and corrected form it is now presented to the public, with a hope that a little information may be contributed to the stock of those who feel an interest in Asiatic archæology. For the sake of convenience, I divide the paper into two sections.†

* The Island of Saints, p. 211.

† The principal works consulted by me during this inquiry were, of *native* authorities —Kanghe's "Imperial Lexicon;" the "Peiwan-yuen Foo;" three Chinese "Encyclopædias," and a full account of Buddhism, its rites, buildings, &c., prepared by a priest of that religion who flourished in the eighth century of the present epoch, and of which work Julien says, it is "la Grande Encyclopédie;"—and of *foreign* works the chief were Stanislas Julien's "Histoire de la Vie de Hiouen Tsang et de ses Voyages dans l'Inde, depuis l'an 629 jusqu'au 645:"—(Published by Julien, 1853.) A revision and continuation, by Klaproth and Laudnerge, of Rémusat's Translation and Commentary on the Chinese work entitled "Fuh Kwohke," or "Relation des Royaumes Bouddhesques, par Fahhien:" and Sykes's "Notes on the Religious, Moral, and Political State of India, before the Mohammedan Invasion, chiefly founded on the Travels of the Chinese Buddhist Priest Fahh'en, in A.D. 399," as given in Art. xiv., of No. xii., in "Journal of Royal Asiatic Society."

Sect. I.—*A General Description of the Pagodas in China.*

The word "pagoda" has travelled into the English nomenclature from the Hindustani or Persian language, the former pronouncing it *bootkuda*, the latter *poutkhoda* or *bootkhoda*, both being a corruption of the Sanscrit *bhagavati*. The interpretation of the three forms (Persian, Hindustani, and Sanscrit) is one and the same; either "the house of idols," "the abode of god," or "holy house." *

According to the original use of the word in India, it is a name given to the various buildings where they worship idols.† Some writers on China have used the term in the same indiscriminate manner for every variety of religious edifice,‡ sometimes distinguishing the very lofty by calling them "towers," as "the Porcelain Tower of Nanking." The majority of modern writers on China, however, have more conveniently confined the application of the name "pagoda" to a peculiar class of buildings, that rise several stories high in the form of a narrow and polygonal obelisk, whether tenanted by idols or not. It is in this restricted sense the term in the present chapter is used, as a translation

* Vide Webster's "Dictionary," under the word; also "Encyclopædia Britannica," and "Chinese Repository," vol. xix. p. 535. It may be as well, however, to give the following extract from the glossary at the end of Hamilton's "East India Gazetteer:"—"Pagoda—This is a name applied by Europeans to Hindoo temples and places of worship, but not by the Hindoos themselves, who have no such appellation. It is the name also of a gold coin, principally current in the south of India, called *varaha* by the Hindoos, and *hoon* by the Mohammedans."

† In the description of Orissa by Andrew Sterling, Esq., and in the chapter on "the Religion, Antiquities, and Temples of Orissa," the word is used in this general application.

‡ Especially the continental writers; see Du Halde's "Memoirs," also De Guignes' "Voyages à Pekin."

of *T'ah*, the designation universally given to the building throughout the Chinese empire.*

As I shall attempt to show in the second section, the pagoda in China is a style of structure borrowed from India after the opening of the Christian era.† Since that date, however, the form or figure of the erection has become altogether popular to the Chinese taste.

Probably it is not averring too much to say, that there are few spots in China the surrounding scenery of which is complete without a full-sized or a miniature pagoda. That this form of structure is a favourite with the people, is evident from their invariable propensity to draw it off in pictures and paintings, or delineate it on works of porcelain, or cut it out on all kinds of ornamental slab and stone, or carve it upon wood of every variety. The pastrycook stamps it on cakes and buns; the artist paints it on fans and screens; the weaver weaves it on silks and satins; and the embroiderer works it on pillow-cases, cushions, coverlets, and curtains. The "toy-pagoda" stands for sale in the toyshop, or among the house-ornaments of the furniture-warehouse. In a rich man's garden, probably the first object that strikes your attention is a dwarf pagoda of stone rising out of a labyrinthic rockery, or, in a poor man's yard, some small tree trained into the pagoda-shape, which he calls the *Pih-shoo-t'ah*,

* The following are some synonyms not uncommonly used by the Chinese:—*Paou-t'ah*, "gem-pagoda;" *Fan-t'ah*, "foreign-pagoda;" and *Fow-too* and *Ts'ah*.

† There is an old Pharos in England, a relic of the ancient Romans, that seems to have some resemblance to an obsolete pagoda, though used for different purposes. The one I allude to "is within the precincts of Dover Castle. It is about forty feet high, octagonal externally, tapering from below upwards, and built with narrow courses of brick and much wider courses of stone in alternate proportions. The space within the tower is square, the sides of the octagon without and of the square within being equal, viz., each fifteen Roman feet. The door is at the bottom."—Smith's "Dictionary of Antiquities," word Pharos.

or the *Hwang-yang-t'ah,* "the cypress," or "the box-wood pagoda." Wandering through China, one sometimes espies perched on a city wall a little pagoda, not above twenty or thirty feet high, built of bricks, or of stone, or of cast-iron; he will also note that there are few cities of eminence without at least one such structure, and some with two or three;* and he may likewise remark, that a large pagoda is not unusually to be found upon a rising ground or the top of a hill in unfrequented and sequestered spots. In the inland tour which (as already described) the writer took during the summer of 1843 from Ningpo to Canton, a line extending about 1,300 miles, chiefly by water, he passed twenty-five pagodas, several standing close to the bank of the river.† It is reported that the largest number of pagodas, as well as the finest buildings of this order, are to be met with in the middle provinces of China, at least in the two Kiang provinces. This is not unlikely, as "the first pagoda" was that at Nanking; and when the celebrated traveller Fah-hien returned from India to his native country, A.D. 414, he lodged the Buddhist relics and scriptures in that city, and, with the aid of other priests, greatly promoted the Buddhist faith in the country round about. There is little question, too, that the pagodas of Nanking and Soochow are the most famous in the empire.‡ The pagoda structure is considered by the natives to be the largest style of building in China: hence the phrase *Tan-ta t'un fan-t'ah,* "Your daring is so great that you can swallow a foreign pagoda."

Of those now extant, the most are of a very antique build, or upon an ancient foundation, and few have

* Canton has two within the city; and Soochow has five or six pagodas within and without the walls.

† In this enumeration I do not include those that were inclosed within city walls, or out of my route, though in sight.

‡ Of the Nanking pagoda it is now to be written, "It is no more." During 1856, it was blown up with gunpowder by the Taiping rebels!

recently undergone repair. The Nanking pagoda was probably first founded in the middle of the third century of this epoch. The *Hwa-t'ah*, "flower pagoda," at Canton, was built more than thirteen hundred years ago. The *T'ien-fung* pagoda of Ningpo has stood for more than 1,000 years. A vast majority of the pagodas are at present either out of repair or in ruins.

Within the present century, some efforts have been made by men of wealth and property at Soochow and Canton to restore the dilapidated *t'ahs* in their neighbourhood, in the belief that the presence or the perpetuity of such structures is of the first importance to the destinies of their localities. But although I made during my stay at Shanghai most strict inquiries whether any new pagodas had been erected in that or any other part of the empire during the last fifty years, or within their recollection, or as far as they had learned in their own travels, researches, and intercourse with natives of other provinces, I was unable to obtain a more definite reply than what was given by an experienced traveller among them, who, to word his evidence as cautiously as he could, observed, "If new ones have been built anywhere, they must be extremely few and scarce." Perhaps one of the most recently-built pagodas is the *Wan-show-t'ah*, in the suburbs of the walled city Tsing-poo, about twenty miles westward of Shanghai, erected by public subscription in the eighth year of Kien-lung, or 110 years since. An attempt was made at Macao, in 1821, to erect a pagoda; but, although the Portuguese magistrate lent his aid to "such foolery" (as Sir John Davis calls it *) by contributing the sum of 100 dollars towards its erection, it does not appear ever to have been built.

In the time of the Sung dynasty, or under T'ai-tsung, A.D. 980, there seem to have existed pagodas of a square

* See Davis's "China," vol. ii. p. 138.

figure.* The remains of Buddhist priests are deposited in small pagodas (spoken of at p. 242), some of which are to be met with of a square figure. Hence the author of a Buddhistic work says, "*T'ah* is sometimes called *T'ah-po*, which means a square mound or grave." On Mr. Fortune's return from Poo-too Island (August, 1853), he obligingly showed me a picture, taken on the spot, of a square pagoda-looking building in ruins. Four stories were still remaining. Each face of the separate stories had a prettily-carved figure of Buddh on it. On referring to the official account of Poo-too, published in the beginning of Kienlung's reign, I find the following description of a square pagoda, most probably the same as that of which Mr. Fortune had taken the above-mentioned sketch:—"The *T'ai-tsze* pagoda lies to the south of the Poo-too monastery. In the middle of the reign of Shun, the last Emperor of the Yuen dynasty, one of his grandsons, named Siuen-Jang, presented 1,000 pieces of silver to erect this pagoda, in token of his high estimate of an eminent Buddhist doctor, Fow-chung. It is ninety-six feet high, and built entirely of fine marble from the lake T'ai-hoo. It is strongly built, and the carving on it is very good. It has five stories, each story has four faces (*i. e.* it is square), and each face has a figure of Buddh cut on it. There does not appear to be one whit of alteration on anything. The forms of the figures are very handsome; their eyebrows, eyes, and looks are like those of a living being. The side balustrades are erect; all the carved-work of hovering angels, lions, water-lilies, &c., is of first-rate workmanship: and down to this date (1740) there has been no part overgrown with weeds and moss."

But the figure of the larger pagodas, now generally

* In the official description of the city of Soochow, § 40, leaf 8th, we read—"In the monastery built by the Emperor T'ai-tsung, there was a square pagoda that has fallen to total ruin."

found, is hexagonal or octagonal in the exterior, yet probably of a different shape within; for, in the Nanking tower (polygonal as Mr. Taylor remarked during his visit in 1852), "after the first or ground story, all the others were quadrangular in the inside, instead of conforming to the octagonal exterior."

Kanghe's Imperial Dictionary observes that the pagoda ranges in elevation "from seven to nine stories, but no higher." The small pagodas often met with, in which the remains or bones of Buddhist priests and nuns are deposited, are generally of two stories. There are also low buildings of a similar shape that rise three stories high, called *Koh*, "pavilion," or *Wan-t'ah*, "literary tower," and used for varions purposes, religious, literary, theatrical, or ornamental. Kanghe's Dictionary adds,—"Those of five stories are commonly called *Ch'uy-tsze*, or awls." Those of this sort are not unfrequently met with. There is one in the village Foo-le, about twelve miles south-west of Soochow, and one on the northern wall* of the city of Canton. Pagodas of eleven stories are scarce. De Guignes in his travels visited one of this height at Kan-tang-chow, in Shan-tung province.† The native account of Soochow, speaking of a fine pagoda in the city, called the *Pih-she-t'ah*, states it was originally eleven stories high. Little, if any, information regarding those of thirteen stories can be had, beyond what Kanghe's Dictionary says, that "they do not rise above this dimension."‡ A native of Shen-se and of the district of Se-ngan-foo assured the writer that the remarkable Yent'ah pagoda in. that capital is a thirteen-storied building, and not

* The geomancers say—"Canton is like a junk; the two large pagodas within the west gate are her masts, and the five-storied one on the northern wall her stern-sheets."

† This place lies N. lat. 36° 32', E. long. 116° 17'.

‡ Klaproth says in his note on the word *T'ah*, "This is a construction of seven, nine, and even *thirteen* stages."

called so merely to designate its height and renown. There is another at Soochow that is said likewise to have been originally built of this elevation.* However, it must be remarked, that the most famous pagodas are, in common parlance, denominated "the thirteen-storied pagodas," while really they are but of seven or nine floors. For instance, the one at Nanking numbered only nine, but was invariably spoken of by the surrounding inhabitants as "the pagoda of thirteen lofts," and it was believed to be so by natives at a distance who never visited the spot.

The most usual height of a pagoda is either seven or nine stories. It has been conjectured by a writer on China,† that the preference for pagodas of one or other of these dimensions is, the one "to convey a mystical allusion to the seven Buddhas who are said to have existed at different periods," the other to represent "the ninth incarnation of Vishnu." There is reason, however, for believing that Buddhism was introduced into China before Vishnu‡ was worshipped in India. Besides, the Imperial Lexicon does not specify the buildings of seven and nine stories as the

* It is a pagoda connected with the Shuy-kwang monastery, inside one of the city gates; at first a famous depository of a relic of Buddh, or a *Shay-le.*—See "Native Description of Soochow."

† Davis's "China," vol. ii. p. 84.

‡ Buddhism was officially introduced into China during the first century of this epoch, and its pagodas probably in the third. But Colonel Sykes, in his "Notes on the Religious State, &c., of Ancient India" (Journal of Royal Asiatic Society, No. xii. p. 271), remarks,—"One fact is sufficiently remarkable, that, in the minute and multiplied details (given by the two Chinese travellers Fah-hien and Hiung-tsang) of the heresies of the followers of Buddha or Brahma, no mention whatever is made, directly or indirectly, of the worship of the Linga, the votaries of which divide the Hindu world with the Vaishnavas, or the followers of Vishnu. Neither Fah-hien in the fourth, nor Hiun-tsang in the seventh, speak of this worship." And Professor Wilson says, in his preface to "Vishnu Purana,"—"It is highly probable that, of the present popular forms of the Hindu religion, none assumed their actual state earlier than . . . . . the eighth or ninth century of this era."

only ones in existence. It states that the height of the building varies from seven to thirteen, and it takes notice too of "five-storied pagodas." It must also be remembered, that one with eleven floors has been visited by the foreigner De Guignes, and one of the same elevation is reported to have been originally built at Soochow. Authority has already been given for believing that there are pagodas that have been built of thirteen stories; and, though their plans may have been defeated, there is ground for entertaining the idea that the aim of the founders of the highest pagodas was to make a tower that might reach the thirteenth story, but fright or want of funds deterred them from rising so high. Having questioned an educated Chinaman "why, with such ample resources at command as they must have had in erecting the celebrated pagodas of Nanking and Soochow, the builders did not raise them higher?" he replied,—"Buildings of that elevation would interrupt the path of the clouds, or might easily be overturned by a hurricane or struck by a thunderbolt. The original intention in building the Nanking *t'ah* was to make it of thirteen stories, hence it goes by that name; but, for the reasons I have stated, it was deemed prudent to desist at the ninth." From these considerations, there appears no ground for the conjecture of Sir John Davis as to the Chinese preference of the seventh and ninth story, because these odd numbers convey a mystic allusion to the manifestations of Buddh. It may be observed that there is no large pagoda that has an *even* number of stories.* The reason of this is that the Buddhists consider the *odd* numbers to be the most religious and propitious.

Of pagodas in China there are two classes, that derive their distinctive names from the interior being

* The "Imperial Lexicon," already quoted, mentions five, seven, nine, eleven, and thirteen stories—all odd numbers.

penetrable or not. There are the *solid* and the *hollow* pagodas, or, in Chinese, the *Shih*, "the substantial, or compact," and the *Heu*, "the empty, or cavernous." The former is nothing but an impenetrable mass of brick-work to the very summit of the structure, called also *Tsang*, as if a receptacle or store crammed with valuables.* Those named "hollow" are open through the interior, and supplied with either a spiral or zigzag staircase up to the top; as the Nanking tower, which counted 190 steps. There are none of them that carry a screw staircase winding round the outside of the building. In the pagodas furnished with staircases inside, there is generally on each story a landing-place at the top of the flight leading to it, with two or three window-like openings that afford an agreeable survey of the surrounding country. Sometimes these lead out to a small balcony with a balustrade running outside and round the building, which gallery is overshaded by a jutting-out roof, that, if kept in repair, might add not a little to the beauty of the whole structure. In a few of the much-frequented pagodas, as the *Lung-hwa* pagoda near Shanghai and the *Pih-she-t'ah* at Soochow, it is safe for a few to venture out on the balconies outside, as they are protected by an outer railing. The gallery on the highest story of the *Lung-hwa* pagoda is almost invariably mounted by foreign visitants who resort to that village for a day's stroll out of Shanghai. According to Mr. Taylor's notes on the Nanking pagoda, which he visited in 1852, "On each face [of the floors] there is an arched opening, in which one can stand and look out upon the surrounding scenery; but a wooden grating prevents you from stepping out upon the galleries, which are not provided with balustrades." Outside and over each floor of some of the pagodas

* There is one such in the walled town Kw'an-shan, about sixty miles west of Shanghai. It is situated on *Ma-an-shan*, or "Saddle-hill," within the town walls.

there is a short, pithy, and proverbial text put up, generally extracted from Buddhist works.

With regard to the dimensions of the pagoda, generally speaking, the thickness of the wall is great, particularly at the base of the building. The one at Hangchow, examined by De Guignes, was eighteen feet thick. The Nanking pagoda, Le Compte computed to be twelve feet thick at the bottom and eight and a half at the highest loft. The *Pih-she-t'ah* at Soochow measures from eight to ten feet in thickness. The average height of the loftiest pagodas is about 170 feet. The Nanking pagoda, according to its original plan, was to be 329 feet high in Chinese measurement, but it was said by the latest foreign visitors to measure only 261 English feet. They all decrease proportionably in width from the foot to the top, but the various divisions or stories are nearly of equal height throughout. The most famous one in Soochow, which I have often named, the *Pih-she-t'ah*, is nearly 300 feet in circumference at the bottom, or about 100 feet in diameter, and its ninth or uppermost story is about one-third of that in circumference. The Nanking pagoda was computed by Mr. Taylor to measure more than 300 feet round the base, each side being about forty feet, and the diameter of it was ninety-six feet ten inches, as taken by Lieutenant Fitzjames, who visited it in the British expedition of 1842.

Some pagodas have a huge and lofty mast running up the centre, to form a sort of shaft for the whole structure.

The tops of the pagodas at present vary much, according to the state of repair or ruin in which they are. Several that were passed by the writer during his route through the provinces of Chihkiang and Kiangse in 1843 were headless and truncated. Those in good order look, at a distance, as if mounted with a large Chinese cap and button, or, as the natives say, " a big-bottle-gourd." The spire of the Nanking pagoda was computed to rise thirty feet above the roof of the highest story, and carried on its apex a massive gilded ball. In the Buddhist description of this pagoda (procurable on the spot), it is stated that "nine iron hoops were put on its pinnacle, the largest measuring sixty-three feet in circumference, and the smallest twenty-four feet, altogether weighing 3,600 catties," or 4,800 English pounds. To ward off noxious influences, there were also deposited there "one night-illuminating gem,* one gem for averting damages occasioned by rain, a third as a fire-escape pearl, a fourth for protecting against wind, and a fifth precious stone as a guard against dust." Besides which, there were placed here with the same object "a bar of gold that weighed more than 53 lbs., a chest of tea exceeding 133 lbs., and a lump of silver above 133 lbs. in weight, along with a piece of orpiment weighing 133½ lbs., one precious pearl, 1,000 strings of cash of the Emperor Yungloh's coinage (each string having 1,000 cash on it), two pieces of yellow satin, and four sets of the Buddhist classics." †

In Soochow, at its south-east corner, an attractive spectacle rises before the view of the visitor in what is called the *Shwang-she-t'ah*, or "twin pagodas,"—two such buildings having been erected only twenty feet apart from each other, nearly nine hundred years since, or in the time of T'ai-tsung, the second emperor of the Sung dynasty.

* Something corresponding to this is described as on the top of an Indian pagoda seen by Hiuu-tsang in his travels through India in the seventh century. To give it in Julien's words,—"A deux cents lieues au sud de Sin-hala, toutes les nuits quand le ciel est pur et sans nuages, le diamant précieux placé au haut du Stoûper de la dent du Bouddha projette une lumière éclatante, qu'on aperçoit de loin, et, par sa forme radieuse, il ressemble à une planète suspendue au milieu des airs."

† According to native description:—One set of the Te-tsang Scriptures; one set of the books of Omi'to-fuh; one set of those of Shih-kia-fuh; and one set of those of Tsieh-yin-fuh.

Generally pagodas have a religious temple or monastery of the Buddhistic order at their base; or, if much frequented by visitors, they are in charge of the priests in the neighbourhood, who look for a gratuity from the hands of the benevolent. The Nanking pagoda stood in the centre of monastery grounds that extended about three miles in circuit. It is sometimes the case, however, that being removed from all buildings and unguarded by any priesthood, they are given up to the moles and the bats. Generally they are not inhabited by human beings, as they were not built for any such object. The most popular ones have idols ensconced in the different niches of the interior, or on the several landings of the staircases, and have pictures of their famous genii painted upon their inner walls. Mr. Taylor, in his notes on the Nanking pagoda, observed: "The inner walls of each story are formed of black polished tiles, a foot square, on each of which an image of Buddha is moulded in bas-relief, and is richly gilt. There are, on an average, more than two hundred of these images in each story, giving an aggregate of nearly two thousand in all." It has been calculated that in the *Pih-she-t'ah* of Soochow "the whole number of idols cannot be far from five hundred."

As may be presumed, from what has been said above, the original purpose in erecting these pagodas in China was entirely religious. In some places they are still kept in repair, also with some religious object in view. In large, populous, and wealthy cities, like Soochow, where funds may easily be obtained to keep them in good order, these towering structures become resorts for the idle or the curious, particularly as the openings on the several floors offer them an extensive view of the scenery and country around. At some of the pagodas there are yearly gatherings, professedly to commemorate the birthday of the presiding deity, or celebrate a religious festival. The day, however, is spent in frolic and gaiety. Immense masses are collected, and the scene is more like a Scottish tryste than anything else. At the village of Lung-hwa, about five miles from Shanghai, in which a pagoda stands, there is an annual celebration on the fifteenth day of the third moon. On one such occasion, when the writer visited the spot, the pagoda presented altogether a most lively scene, from the thousands of spectators around the foot of the building, and the crowds that had mounted the structure. With the interest excited by the spectacle there was, however, no little anxiety in watching the crowds that were crushing the gallery on each story, and leaning over balustrades that at the best are weak and brittle.

Many pagodas have bells hung at the corners of the various roofs that project over the balconies. These keep up a perpetual jingle as the wind sweeps by. According to the native account of the Nanking pagoda, "From its pinnacle there hung eight chains of iron, with seventy-two bells; besides, there were eighty bells suspended from the corners of the separate lofts up and down; so that, on the whole, there were 150 bells on this edifice." Not unfrequently these buildings are also ornamented with lamps or lanterns at each window, or hung from each corner of the several stories. The Nanking pagoda had 140 lamps in all:—"Outside the nine stories there were 128 lanterns, and in the lower floor twelve glass lamps, which in one night altogether consumed 85½ lbs. of oil." Sometimes, when a rich man, living in the vicinity of a structure like this, is overtaken with a fit of showing forth good works, he subscribes a certain sum to have the lamps in it lighted up on such and such a night. In the department of Shaouking, of the Canton province, "there is a pagoda situated on the Ting-hoo hill, to which many people repair and give a sum of money, from six to one hundred dollars, in order to illuminate it. In doing this, there is said to be great merit."* Speaking of the lamps and lanterns in the Nanking tower, the native writer already quoted observes, "When lit up, they illumine the thirty-three heavens, and detect the good and evil among men, as well as for ever ward off human miseries." The effect of a spectacle such as these buildings present, when illuminated on a dark night, is truly novel, and rather enlivening to any class of spectators. A foreigner, on witnessing the sight, thought at once of the "Pharoi" of olden times, and of the "lighthouses" of Europe.

As to the object of the illuminations, I may give the following extract from the Chinese account of one of the pagodas in the city of Soochow:—"It is a tale handed down from time immemorial, that, when the lanterns on the *Shuy-kwang-shen* pagoda are lit up, their glare is cast upon the Taihoo lake, in consequence of which the fishermen there can catch nothing. The lake is thirty le, or about ten miles, off." A Chinese teacher, who had not seen this quotation and was not aware of its existence, but who was thoroughly acquainted with the views and superstitions of his countrymen, on being interrogated as to the object of the pagoda-illuminations, stated that it was to save the lives of fishes, and to carry out the injunctions of Buddhism to abstain from destroying animal life. "On a pagoda, lanterns are often lighted," said he, "but, at the sight thereof, the fresh-water fishes that come up to the surface in the darkness of the night will immediately submerge: thus, the fishermen that toil in the night cannot catch their fish. This is what may be called a *life-preserving idea*."

There is a ceremony called *Shaou fan-t'ah*, or "burning foreign pagodas," that is observed on the 30th of the 7th moon."† It is kept in celebration of

* See Morrison's "Dictionary," part i. vol. i., under the character *T'ah*.

† Not as Morrison says in his "Dictionary,"—"the fifteenth of the

the birthday of the Te-tsang Buddha. Children club together to build a small pagoda of brickwork, filling the interior with wood, hay, stubble, oil, resin, powder, and other combustible stuff; and when all is ready, they set the pile on fire amidst shouting, laughing, huzzaing, and clapping of hands.

Pagodas, if ornamented, as they often are, with variegated bricks, tiles, flags, bells, and lanterns, present a picturesque scene, especially when they stand on a rising mount surrounded by a flat plain, or are lighted up on a dark evening. On this account, some Chinese have asserted that the term *Fow-too*, often given to this form of structure, denotes that it is a kind of "floating or aërial picture;" but, as will be shown hereafter, this is merely an Indian name transferred into the Chinese language and applied to a pagoda.

The cost of these erections in each case must have been very great. "The entire building of Nanking cost the Imperial treasury upwards of £600,000 sterling." The mere repairing of the great *Pih-she* pagoda at Soochow during the early part of Taoukwang's reign, or since 1821, cost above 26,000 dollars.

The consumption of time in erecting some of them has also been enormous. It is said that the one at Soochow, just named, required more than sixty years.* The rebuilding of the Nanking pagoda in the beginning of the fifteenth century occupied nineteen years. In the year 1801, three of its nine stories were demolished in a fearful storm, and it required four months to repair them.

The material used for such construction is generally

eighth moon," which is merely illuminating the pagodas and burning incense, and indeed properly named the fête of "burning heaven's incense."

* Reports on the spot tell that three different individuals had to undertake the completion of the work in succession,—one was a Viceroy; the second a wealthy gentleman, who spent all his property on it till he was reduced to beggary; and the third, who finished the work, was a prince of the Loo-choo islands.

brick and stone. Besides the usual method of laying the foundation, a native has informed me that "there are several thousand hundredweight of coal-dust laid on the foundation of a pagoda to make it secure and solid, as there is some apprehension that the ground may sink from the height and weight of the structure. This at least," adds he, "is a tradition from olden times, and not a figment of my own imagination." The Nanking pagoda stood upon an elevated platform of brickwork ten feet high, up which a flight of ten steps all round the base led into the tower. Of the "Porcelain Tower of Nanking" (as it used to be called in the list of "the wonders of the world"), most of the present generation of foreigners have formed the idea that it must have been as white as the China-ware of their breakfast-table. Its real name, *Lew-le paou-t'ah*, "the vitreous precious stone pagoda," in other words, "the crystal palace," figuratively describes the material of which it was built, or rather the impression made on any one who saw it for the first time as to the nature of the material. The Rev. Mr. Taylor, the last foreign visitor at the pagoda, writes of it thus: "A comparatively small portion of it is white. Green is the predominant colour, from the fact that the curved tiles of its projecting roofs are all of this colour, while the woodwork supporting these roofs is of the most substantial character, and, in the peculiar style of Chinese architecture, curiously wrought and richly painted in various colours. The body of the edifice is built of large well-burnt bricks, which on the external surface are green, yellow, red, or white. The bricks and tiles are of very fine clay and highly glazed, so that the tower presents a most gay and beautiful appearance, that is greatly heightened when seen in the reflected sunlight."

There are to be found in China "cast-iron pagodas" likewise. In the year 1843, when the writer passed the walled town Keu-chow, in Chihkiang province, he saw a small structure of this sort on the city walls built of iron.* In the neighbourhood of Chihkiang, there is a hill on which also stands an iron pagoda. Of this Mr. Taylor gives the following description:—"It is nine-storied, and some forty or fifty feet in height, built of cast iron. The octagonal pieces forming the walls are each single castings; so also are the horizontal plates forming the roofs of the several stories. The whole of this curious structure, including the base and the spire, was cast in twenty pieces. Originally perpendicular, it now has an inclination of two or three degrees towards the south. It is about eight feet in diameter at the base, each side of the octagon being nearly three feet; and its interior is entirely filled up with brick masonry, so that it is impossible to ascend it. It is evidently of great antiquity, but bears no inscription from which its age could be determined."

I have already intimated the original object of erecting the pagodas in China to be religious. They were built to preserve relics, or to store up valuable books and documents belonging to the Buddhist sect; and, from what I have shown above, they are still kept in repair for similar objects.

It has been repeatedly pointed out by me that Buddhist priests and nuns often are buried in miniature forms of pagoda. These tiny monuments are named *Kwuh-t'ah*, "pagoda for bones," or *Kien-kwuh-t'ah*, "a pagoda for selected bones." The name *Ts'ah* is also given it, which is described in Kang-he "as a term given to the pillars over the graves of Buddhists, in which are deposited precious relics." They are sometimes square, called *Fang-fun*, "square grave-hillocks;" and are also hexagonal, of two stories in height or more. There was one of an hexagonal shape, which,

* Vide page 262.

before the late disturbances in the city, used to stand outside the north gate of Shanghai, between that and the west gate, at the back of a nunnery called the *Kwei-hiang-yen;* and, according to the tablet inscribed on it, one of the inmates of this convent died in the 19th year of Taoukwang, or A.D. 1839, leaving behind her a good name for devotedness to her service during a long lifetime. She was buried here (as above described in page 241), in two huge jars, the one above the other. The pagoda is only ten feet high, and of two stories. In the official History of Pootoo (published a century ago), there are mentioned thirty-five such pagodas of celebrated dead men's bones, or of men connected with famous monasteries on the island.*

I will now speak of the more common notions afloat among the Chinese as to the uses, influence, or objects of pagodas, besides those above specified. From the records of the Tang dynasty (A.D. 810), it appears that the original high-sounding aims of the pagoda-builders had even at that time begun to be perverted by mean low fellows, who assumed them with a view to aggrandize themselves by working on the minds of the people. And an Imperial mandate was issued by Hien-tsung, in the beginning of the ninth century, "forbidding the priests of Buddha and others erecting pagodas within his dominions, because by lying and beggary they make gain, and rob the poor people of their property."

Some natives have supposed that they were at first intended as "watch-towers" in time of war, so distributed and arranged throughout the country as to be convenient for making telegraphs and signals. Though they could be turned to this service, it does not appear to have been one of the prime purposes aimed at in their erection under the Buddhist religion. Neverthe-

* In the following section something is said of the resemblance between these buildings designed for the remains of Buddhist priests in China, and the old Chatyas in ancient India for the relics of Buddhist patriarchs.—(See pages 241, 382.)

less, there is some ground for the conjecture just given, from the following fact recorded in Chinese history:— "During the reign of Chin-tsung, of the Sung dynasty, A.D. 1020, a certain officer of the name of Le-yun-tsih, in charge of the Hiung district, in Chihli province, was found laying out the Imperial funds on the erection of a pagoda. Upon the representation of one of the censors, his Majesty sent a messenger with secret instructions to the officer: but Le-yun-tsih replied,—'It is not from any regard to the Buddhist religion that I am engaged in this building, but only that I may erect an observatory for watching the country around.'"

There is a popular saying also, that the pagoda is a monument erected in token of one's estimate of the character of a great man,* or principally to perpetuate the remembrance of the virtues of one's father or mother. This idea is probably derived from the motive that is said to have led Yung-loh, the third emperor of the Ming line, to rebuild the ruined pagoda of Nanking four hundred years ago. On removing the court from that capital to the north, in A.D. 1410, his Imperial Majesty, in order to recompense the great favour of his august mother, commenced to re-erect this structure, which had been destroyed by fire nearly a century before. It was a magnificent tribute of the gratitude of a son for his mother's love. This object, indeed, was fully denoted by the name it bore, the *Paou-ngan-she-t'ah,* "the pagoda of the recompensing favour temple;" or, as it reads at greater length on the native description of the pagoda,—the *Paou-ngan-she lew-le-t'ah,* "the crystal pagoda of the recompensing favour temple."†

* I have already mentioned a square pagoda of five stories having been built on Pootoo by one of the Yuen family, at or near the close of the fourteenth century, "in token of his high estimate of the eminent Buddhist, Dr. Fow-chung."—(See page 362.)

† The pagoda at Nanking has had (through its history of at least 1,600 years) a variety of names, of which these are a few—the "Oyuh

On examining the notions of the Chinese regarding the uses and objects of these pagodas, however singular and subordinate may be some of their opinions, that which may be said to be predominant and universal among all ranks and classes of society is, that they have a serious and important connection with the "wind and water" fortunes of the locality in which they are situated. The presence of a structure like this in any place is believed by the people to exert an influence for good or evil on the destinies of the neighbourhood.* The raising of a pagoda anywhere is supposed not only to secure and perpetuate to the vicinity the protection and good-will of Heaven, but likewise to repress any evil influences that hitherto may have haunted the region, and to act like an electric tractor in drawing down from above every felicitous omen; so that, as they say, "the five elements (fire, water, wood, earth, and metal) should be at the service of the people, the soil productive, trade prosperous, and the natives submissive and happy." Effects like these will be ascribed to the pagoda by the people that live in its neighbourhood; and such too is the repute in which a building of this structure is held among their countrymen at a distance, whose locality may be destitute of pagoda-patronage. In the plan proposed in 1821 for the erection of a pagoda at Macao (to which I have alluded at p. 361), the above objects were distinctly mentioned in the following words:—"The Chinese and foreign merchants have hitherto been prosperous, their wealth abounding, and the destinies of the place altogether felicitous. Of late, however, its fortunes have waxed lean and the influence of the atmosphere has

pagoda," and the "Chang-kan pagoda." It is in common parlance called Paou-ngan-t'ah or Lew-le-t'ah.

* On building the Baptist chapel in Shanghai a few years since, with its high, thick, and massive steeple, there were many forebodings among the populace as to the influence it would have upon the vicinity.

been unlucky, so that the acquisition of riches has become less certain. A proposal is accordingly made to erect a pagoda, in order to renovate and improve the commercial fortunes of the island on which Macao lies. [After alluding to the architect, it proceeds,]—He declares that a high pagoda should be built on the eastern arm of Monkey Island, and affirms that prosperity and riches will be the result, so that both Chinese and foreigners at Macao will share in the felicity." The same belief in the geomantic charms of the pagoda is professed in another subscription-paper, that was circulated among the literati, gentry, and merchants of Canton early in the year 1837, for the purpose of collecting funds for the restoration of the dilapidated pagodas of their district; as this extract from that appeal will show:—"Fellow-countrymen,—The region of the country, south-east of the provincial city of Canton, has an important influence on the fortunes of the inhabitants. All the pagodas there have had a most salutary influence on everything around, causing the literati to be very numerous, and the productions of the soil most abundant. Their appearance at present is unsightly. Therefore, to secure the return of happy and prosperous times, they ought to be repaired."

Sect. II:—*The Chinese Pagoda an Indian Building.*

That is, *the pagoda style was introduced into China from India between the third and ninth centuries of the present era by Buddhists, to serve the purposes of their religion.*

It may not be out of place to remark in the outset, how there has existed in various parts of the world a style of structure of an extremely antique date, or form of building like a tower, an erection with a heaven-pointing spire, rather approximating what we nowadays call a pagoda, and originally consecrated to religious purposes. The style of architecture spoken of is a square, a circular, or a polygonal tower, rising above-ground—diminishing in diameter as it ascends—hollow or solid throughout—either breaking into several stories in its upward elevation, or supplied with a flight of steps straight, spiral, or zigzag, outside or inside the building, leading up to the top—at the summit truncated, rounded, or tapering—and appropriated to sacred objects, *e. g.*, the hoarding of images, the lodgment of sacred writings, the conservation of holy relics, the repository of the dead, the worship of idols, the offering of sacrifices, the giving of thanks, the making of vows, the commemorating of important eras, events, or acts, &c. This form of structure ranks among the archæological curiosities of our age almost all over the globe; *e. g.* the Temple of Belus at Babylon; the Pyramids of Egypt; the pyramidal mounds of Mexico; and, in all probability, the "round towers" of Ireland.

But, as the heading of this chapter leads attention particularly to the religious towers in India, let us turn to India in search of pagoda-like structures.

In Central India there exist two forms of what we call pagodas,—in other words, towers connected with religious objects. There is the ancient style and the modern.

Of the modern pagoda-architecture of India I must make the following summary of quotations from different writers. This architectural form is principally connected with Hindooism or the Brahminical faith, that arose in India about the seventh century, and superseded Buddhism. There are specimens of this structure in various parts of India, especially in the southern division. At Tanjore and Medura there are two of the most splendid. The one at Tanjore is greatly celebrated, rising from the ground by twelve successive stages, and is considered the finest specimen of this kind of architecture in India.

In Orissa there are three eminent structures of this order, minutely described by Andrew Sterling, Esq.* Of the great pagoda at Bhobanaser he remarks, that "local tradition as well as the histories of the country concur in fixing the date of its completion at A.D. 657." The tower of the temple of Juggernaut, he says, "was completed A.D. 1198;" and "the Black Pagoda" near the site of the old village of Canarah, "it is well known, was built A.D. 1241." At Conjeveran there is a "celebrated Hindoo pagoda to Mahadeva as the Linga," which was not erected in the middle of the seventh century, when the place was visited by the Chinese traveller Heuen-tsang. "This one," as described by a European traveller, "in the most elevated part of the building consists of fifteen stories or stages; the floor of the lowest of these was covered with boards somewhat decayed, and was about twenty feet square, having much the appearance of the belfry of a country church in England. A ladder of fifteen rounds conducted us to the next stage, and so on from story to story until we reached the top, each stage or floor diminishing gradually in size to the summit. Here our labour was most amply repaid, for never had I witnessed so sublime a prospect. It surpassed every idea I had or could have formed of its grandeur and effect, that I was almost entranced in its contemplation. I forgot all the world beside, and felt as if I could have continued on this elevated spot for ever."†

In Central India, however, there is traced a more antique style of pagoda, built during the predominance of the Buddhist religion, which prevailed there at least from B.C. 600 to A.D. 700.‡ As Colonel Sykes, in his "Notes

* Vide Pegg's "Orissa Mission," chap. iv. The first part of the work contains an account of "Orissa, its Geography, Statistics, History, Religion, and Antiquities," by Mr. Sterling, late Persian Secretary to the Bengal Government.

† Extracted from Nathen's "Voyage to Madras."

‡ Sykes, p. 334, where, in a note, it is stated that the Buddhist re-

on the Religious State of Ancient India," remarks (p. 359),—"At the time of Alexander's invasion, Buddhism must have been in the palmy days of its power, judging from . . . . . the topes, ... the obelisks, and other works of art, most of which are referrible to the period between the first and sixth centuries before Christ, and more particularly to the period when Azoko reigned, or B.C. 319 to B.C. 282." Here topes are mentioned, which are towers, pillars, tumuli, or in the original tongue of that part of India, "sthûpas," a name given in the Buddhist vocabulary also to the pagodas that are at present found in China.

On carefully comparing Lieutenant-Colonel Sykes's "Notes" with Klaproth's "Commentary on the Fuh-kwoh-ke," and Julien's "Histoire," I have ascertained the following particulars respecting these religious erections in India called "sthûpas." They must have existed as early as 600 years before the Christian era: the whole surface of India was then dotted all over with these eminences. Azoko, the king of Central India (who lived B.C. 319—282), was a most devoted Buddhist, and famous for repairing old ones and erecting new; and, according to some, this king raised 8,000 such pagodas, according to others 84,000. (See p. 208 of the present work.) They generally stood alone, or connected with temples and monasteries. The object was altogether religious, and chiefly for the purpose of commemorating epochs in Buddha's history, or to preserve his teeth, bones, and hair as holy relics, or to contain the remains of his most eminent disciples. Thus, when Fahhien, a noted Chinese traveller, visited India during the fourth century of the present era, he found in Peshawur, "with one exception, the most splendid tope in all India, 400 feet high, which contained the begging-pot of Buddh;" and "he abso-

ligion held predominance "from the eleventh century B.C., according to the Chinese, Japanese, and the Buddhists of Central Asia."

lutely describes a great tower in Oude which contained the entire bones of the third Buddha;" then he describes the spot where Buddha accomplished the law, &c.

Allied to this large style of pagoda, I may, in passing, refer to a smaller model which obtained under ancient Buddhism. It is called in the Pali tongue *Chaitya*, and is to be found on Buddhist ancient coins. It is more of the monumental style (though pagoda-shaped), for burial of Buddhist worthies. It is singular that we find the name of this sort of pagoda transferred into Chinese as *Che-te*.—(See pp. 191, 375, 383.)

To show the Indian and Buddhist original of the Chinese pagoda, I will now proceed to two or three illustrative evidences. Possibly one or two might alone have sufficed; but, as numerous interesting features of Buddhism in China have come to light during my inquiry, I am reluctant to abridge any portion of the investigation.

1. *Examine, for instance, the Chinese Nomenclature for Pagoda.*

1st. The name by which the pagoda structure is designated in China is *t'ah*. Some have suggested that this is merely the last syllable of the Indian word "poutkho*da*" expressed in Chinese sound. But, as we have no evidence that this form of erection was called *poutkhoda* in India itself during the early history of Buddhism, or when Buddhism entered China, such an hypothesis cannot be entertained.

Of the Chinese form or character *t'ah*, which represents a pagoda, the very ancient Chinese writings seem quite destitute. After the middle of the third century, a dynasty was established under which numerous new words were coined and characters added to the native lexicon. And, as Buddhists began to raise buildings of this order just about that time, it is presumed by those qualified to judge, that it is more than probable that the written term for *t'ah* was introduced then. This idiograph is explained in Kanghe's Lexicon to be "piled-up earth, a heap or mound, a tumulus, an agger," which no doubt was an appropriate designation for the form of building as originally introduced into the country. Then, the learned lexicon which I have just quoted adds, "The Indian term *suhtoopo* (*i. e.* sthûpa) means in the Chinese language *t'ah.*"

2nd. The Chinese themselves speak of these eminences as *fan-t'ah,* "foreign tumuli;" *e. g.*, in the phrases "burning foreign pagodas," "swallowing foreign pagodas," &c., in which they refer distinctly and alone to these sacred structures common among them.

3rd. There are various Indian terms for this style of building, that have crept into the Chinese vocabulary, and which have to be explained to the native students. For instance, *t'ahpo,* "which is a square mound or grave;" *tansowpo,* "that is, a building for perpetuating praise;" *fowtoo,* "which is the name of the religion of Fuh,—its temples and high buildings are also called by this name." But the most distinct transference of Indian names for the pagoda into Chinese orthography are *che-te* and *suh-too-po. Che-te,* explained by a Chinese work on Buddhism, is a Buddhist "place for ridding oneself of evil and cultivating good." It is probably an equivalent to the *chaitya* in India, which Sykes explains to be "a tower," and, according to Klaproth, existed in former days in Hindostan, as "depositories for relics of Buddha and the patriarchs of the sect." This form may now be traced out among the ancient ruins of Buddhism in India, and copies of it are to be found among ancient Buddhist emblems and coins. In Sykes's "Notes," he gives a pictorial sketch of a row of "different forms of the Buddhist *chaitya,* or temple of relics."

Of the name *Suh-too-po,* the native writers say, "a building for preserving the remembrance of any occasion of grief is expressed in the Buddhist language by the word *Suh-too-po* (*i. e.* Stoupa or Sthupa), which is a temple of elegant appearance and form." Upon the transference of this Indian word into Chinese, I may give the following quotation:—Julien, speaking of the word *Suh-too-po,* observes, "Constructions bouddhiques connues dans l'Inde supérieure sous le nom *Stoupas,* les topes des modernes." Klaproth remarks, the Chinese word "*T'ah* répond au terme Sanscrit *Stoupa,* qui signifie tumulus, pile of earth, chapelle, couvent." Sykes, in reference to Fahhien's visit at Khotan, says, "The people all built towers, or pillars, or *tumuli, that is, Sthupas;*" and Kanghe's Chinese Imperial Lexicon, under the character *t'ah* for pagoda, reads, "The Indian name *Suh-too-po* means in the Chinese *t'ah.*"

There is a pagoda in Shense, the name of which is "Wildgoose Pagoda." The explanation of it is thus given in Kanghe's Dictionary:—"The Indian word *Tsangpo* means in Chinese *Yen,* or 'Wildgoose.' The origin of this appellation is as follows:—The primitive Buddhists of India, not under strict rules of diet, were at liberty to use three kinds of clean meat,—veal, venison, and goose-flesh. It happened that, on a certain day, as a party of priests was seated in the open air, a brace of wild geese was observed flying overhead. The priests suddenly exclaimed, 'Our wish is that these fowls would *moko-sa-to.*' This phrase *moko-sa-to* means 'do a benevolent act.' Upon this one of the geese instantly dropped down dead. Seeing this, however, the sacerdotal fraternity cried out, 'This goose brings down a prohibition to abstain from flesh. We must commemorate its meritorious act.' They accordingly erected a building over the remains of the devoted goose, which they called *Tsangpo* pagoda. Our term, *Yen-t'ah,* is a translation of the Indian name." (At page 386 a different account is given of the foundation of this pagoda by another Chinese writer.)

2. *In further illustration of the Indian Original of the Chinese Pagoda, consider its invariable connection from the first with Buddhism.*

The cradle and seat of this religion was India. There it flourished from B.C. 950 to A.D. 800; although, as Col. Sykes remarks, "its final overthrow in India did not take place until the twelfth or fourteenth century." Regarding the introduction of the Buddhist sect into China, a native writer has recorded:—"From the western regions there came a priest of this order. The Emperor Muh, who reigned from B.C. 936 to 928, was residing at the time on the Chung-nan mountain, in the province of Shense. His Majesty erected a very high platform and paid him homage. But 700 years after, when another Buddhist priest and his company visited the empire, the emperor on the throne, supposing him to be a sort of monster, imprisoned him. Then, overnight, a good-looking person opened the prison-door and let him out; on which his Majesty at once believed and paid him all due respect." It does not appear, however, that Buddhism obtained a firm footing in the empire, before the middle of the first century of the Christian era; and, as far as I have been able to investigate the question, the pagoda-architecture did not exist in China for some time after that date. That it has uniformly been connected with Buddhism, may be deduced from the following suggestions:—Among the Chinese themselves it is a common saying, "In pagodas they save and preserve the family of Buddha!" Usually priests of this order are in charge of the pagoda, and sit at the doors of the most famous and frequented, to receive gratuities from visitors. Pagodas are situated generally on Buddhist lands, and there are in their vicinity, or around their base, temples or monasteries for Buddhist priests. Within pagodas that are at all in a state of preservation, Buddhist idols, relics, pictures, and books are deposited. The histories of these buildings throughout the empire, at least the earliest of them, are crammed with Buddhist tales and fictions.

But properly none of these erections belong to the native systems of Confucius or Taouism, or any other religious sect in the empire.

An exception may be taken to this by some who may have heard of "the Bright Pagoda," in the city of Canton, and of which it has been said that it belongs to the Mohammedans of that city. One writer has remarked,—"This pagoda is remarkable, as it shows the wealth and power of the Mohammedans in Canton at the time it was erected, about one thousand years ago. The Mohammedans still reside in its neighbourhood, and there stands also a mosque for their religious services, which surrounds the base of the pagoda, rising like a minaret from the centre." On minute investigation, however, it appears as more than probable that this pagoda was built by the first Mussulman merchants who visited Canton, with a view to conciliate the favour of the sect of the Buddhists, which was at that time gaining the ascendant in China.

The following is one story of the origin of one of the first pagodas ever built in the country, the far-famed "Wildgoose Pagoda" of Se-nganfoo, the capital of Shense province, N. lat. 34° 16′, E. long. 108° 57′ (see different account at page 384):—"Nearly six hundred years after Buddhism had been officially patronized, Heuen-tsang, a priest of this sect, was sent to India to collect and translate into the Chinese language the sacred books of Buddh. After an absence of fifteen years (some say twenty-six), he returned with copies of the original and a complete translation into Chinese. He brought over also a model of a Buddhist *sthupa* or tower. In commemoration of this work of merit, and also for the purpose of lodging these volumes in a suitable building, the happy idea hit the reigning emperor that he should erect a pagoda after an Indian model. So, in the third year of his reign (A.D. 639), a pagoda was built of brick, on the south side of the capital of Shen-ge, and in that building the sacred books of Buddha and other precious relics were lodged." This was not far from the spot where the Syrian or Nestorian monument was found, in which it is recorded, "A.D. 636 (or during the reign of the same monarch), a Christian teacher came from India to China; the emperor, after encouraging the doctrines, published a decree authorizing the preaching of Christianity among the Chinese."

But one remarkable line of evidence, that this style of building has throughout been particularly appropriated by the Buddhists, is its connection with the Buddhist relic called *Shay-le*. In two Chinese works I have consulted, it is asserted that "what is properly called a *t'ah* (pagoda) has a *shay-le*." Further, "a *shay-le* is a Buddhist word to denote a sacred relic of Buddha's body."* This word both Julien and Klaproth consider a transfer into Chinese of the Sanskrit (or, as Colonel Sykes proves, the Pali) name "sarira," which in the original means the relics of Buddh. Chinese writers give some most amusing descriptions of this curiosity. "Of the relic," says one, "there are three kinds; *e. g.* the *hair shay-le*, which is of a black colour; the *bone shay-le*, which is white; and the *flesh shay-le*, which is of a carnation hue. The relics of Buddh and of his disciples that have been apotheosized are of these three sets." These relics are reputed as scarce and rare. No new ones have recently been discovered. But whenever they have been found, they have been stored up in

* See p. 209, in Part Second.

crystal bottles and lodged in a temple or pagoda. Of course this offers a famous occasion for the priesthood to exercise their craft and imposition on the ignorant people. Most of them have the chameleon property of changing into the five colours, green, red, white, black, and yellow; indicative, however (as it is said), of the good or depraved qualities of the spectator! The miraculous effects of this charm fill many pages in some of the Buddhist writings.

The very devoted priests and disciples of the sect are likewise reputed as having encased in their craniums a scintillation of Buddha's *shay-le*.* On the decease of the devotee, the relic is believed to be proof against both rot and flame, though there be the ordinary distinction that "the *shay-le* of Buddh himself, if struck heavily with a mallet, is not frangible, while that of the most eminent among his canonized followers is easily broken." In the finest pictures, and sometimes the images of the Buddhist priests, there is a sort of luminous halo over the crown of the head, which they suppose to proceed from the *shay-le*. And it is believed of the padres of that sect, that the more they have of the *shay-le* in their golgothas, the larger and brighter will be their encircling halo of light. When any eminent disciple of the sect dies, his remains are consumed by fire. The ashes are then carefully examined in search of the remarkable curiosity that is believed to have been lodged in his skull, and to be indestructible even when it passes through the fire. A native author (who lived 300 years ago) says of the mysterious thing,—"In my neighbourhood there is a nunnery, one of whose inmates recently died. On burying her body, something of this description was said to be found. It was reported to resemble a louse in size; and further, that by the attraction of a single hair of a child's head

* See p. 242, in Part Third.

it could be raised up; but I cannot vouch for the truth of this!" "The *shay-le*, being the result of abstinence, self-command, and superior understanding, attained by pure and ardent devotion in the service of Buddha, can by no means easily be obtained."

The following account, drawn from native authorities, respecting the erection of the first pagoda in China is worthy of perusal:—"In the tenth year of the Emperor that sat on the throne about A.D. 250, a foreign priest of the Buddhist religion, named Kang-tsung-hwuy, appeared at Nanking, then the capital of the empire, and performed many strange and what seemed supernatural feats. The people represented the case to their sovereign. His Majesty immediately called the priest to an audience with him, and inquired if Buddha could communicate any divine emblems. He replied that Buddha had left some traces of himself on earth, though very mysterious. He had left numerous bone relics, the miraculous power of which was limitless. The Emperor then made special inquiry where these relics were to be found. To this the sacerdotal father replied that, if he himself were under the influence of Buddha's spirit to go in search, he was sure to find one. His Majesty, upon this, made a distinct promise, that if the priest succeeded in getting one such, he would erect an edifice called a pagoda. After twenty-one days of earnest research, the priest discovered one in a bottle, and immediately presented it to the Chinese sovereign. When taken into the palace, it lighted up all the building. In his eagerness to inspect the remarkable curiosity, the emperor poured it out of the bottle into a copper basin. The basin, however, was instantly smashed, both from the weight of the relic and the force with which it thumped on it. The king was greatly frightened at this supernatural specimen. The aged priest then advanced, to assure the monarch that, apart from these miraculous signs, there was something more astonishing about this bone of Buddh. It was that diamond or steel could not scratch it, fire could not scorch it, and the heaviest mallet could not smash it. The Emperor accordingly ordered a man of unusual strength to come forward and strike some heavy blows on the sacred *shay-le* with a huge sledge-hammer. The man did so, but to no purpose, except to destroy the hammer itself. The relic remained untouched, with an effulgence as bright as before, and dazzling every person's eye. Thereby the king's faith was confirmed, and, in fulfilment of his pledge, he erected a *t'ah* in which to keep the relic. This is the beginning of pagoda-building in China." This was the Nanking pagoda, that till recently had on its front the inscription, "The First Pagoda," which may have been intended to signify that it was first both in date and rank.

I see a contributor to the "Chinese Repository" has broached the opinion that the Chinese pagoda is not derived from India, but "that it is indigenous, and that even the unimaginative Chinese architect would have produced something better than the simple nine-storied pagoda, if he had tried to imitate the ornate pyramidal edifice of the Hindoo." In reply, I would remark that it must be allowed that the resemblance between the Chinese pagoda and the elegant pagodal building of modern Hindostan is very slight. Yet it may be presumed that the originals were similar; for the Hindoos may have improved in architecture, while in China, according to their almost universal preference for the "*status in quo ante*," the pagoda-tower all over the empire may be an exact imitation of the ancient specimens. Indeed, I think I may venture a little further, and say, that in all probability the fine and picturesque porches or towers over the gateways of the magnificent temples in India are innovations on the antique *sthoupas*; while the Chinese pagodas of the present day are imitations of models taken from the very earliest topes. Almost all the proofs already enumerated will second this opinion. Many, if not most, of the pagodas in the empire are of remarkable antiquity. The pattern is the same throughout the land, those of the latest date not different from those of the earliest origin. Some have been rebuilt but not remodelled, and others continue as they were from the first, unmoved, unchanged, except from the wear of time, weather, &c.

It is with some regret that I have to state that the Tai-ping insurgents not only, in their iconoclastic zeal, have disfigured, but by recent tidings, have completely destroyed the Nanking pagoda. In the first instance, their anti-idolatrous fury merely defaced the interior by fire, but, during 1856, their unbridled rage against one of their own leaders who had been suspected of conspiracy, and who, with his followers, had made the pagoda the rendezvous of the clique, led them to blow up the massive pile with gunpowder! "*Sic transit gloria mundi*" in China.

What a singular discovery will some day be made in the heaped ruins of such buildings, reputed as they are among the sacerdotal fraternity of Buddha, as the depositories of Pali inscriptions, çarîras of Buddha, Buddhist writings and other genuine Indian documents! These, we have undoubted authority for believing, were brought thither from Central India between the first and ninth centuries of the Christian era, and the preservation, or rather the procuring, of these will doubtless throw a flood of light especially on the religion and history of ancient India. Since foreigners of all countries and persuasions are now frequenting China, and permission for their free excursions throughout the interior can be withheld for but a few years longer, is it not suitable to invite their careful observation towards such extraordinary monuments of antiquity, the temples, monasteries, and pagodas of Buddhism? Some item in their respective histories may contribute to elucidate a dark, doubtful point in the early history of intercourse between Hindostan and China.

I am convinced that the Christianity of the inspired Bible is making due (in some places unexpected) progress in China, and I believe that in time it will "win and. conquer," and spread its happy influence all over the empire. Yet, may not the hope be expressed that, as every such Babel tower, or pagoda in China, shall lose its superstitious spell, Protestant missionaries, merchants, and travellers will do what they can to rescue the interesting memorials locked up in the towers of Buddhism "in the middle kingdom." These may add not a little to the information of our Western lands respecting the rise and progress, or the decline and downfall, of Buddhism in the two contiguous empires, India and China.

CHAPTER IV.

ROMISH MISSIONS AT SHANGHAI—OPENED MORE THAN 250 YEARS AGO—THEIR FIRST CONVERT A MANDARIN—VICISSITUDES IN THE HISTORY OF POPERY HERE—THE VILLAGE OF ZEE-KA-WEI—THEIR MODES OF OPERATION.

WANT of space and inclination prevents me entering at large into the history and the state of Romish missions in China. The theme would swell out into volumes; and to do it justice requires more ample and reliable materials than are at the command of Protestants. Under these circumstances, I purpose in the following pages to confine myself to the Shanghai branch of that mission; as any notice of this part of China would be defective without a glance at it.

So early as 1600, Popery singled out Shanghai for

the sphere of its zealous efforts in the empire of China, and as Count de Bessi, the Apostolic Vicar of Kiangnan, observed in his official despatch of September, 1844, it "became the theatre of the apostolic success of Father Matthew Ricci."

Among its first converts, first in date and first in eminence, Popery reckons a Shanghai family surnamed Seu. *Seu-kwangke*, the paterfamilias, was a mandarin of note, of great talent and extensive influence. At one time he bore the rank of *Koh-laou*, or one of the chief members of the Imperial Government; also the titles of "Duke, Guardian, and Tutor of the Sons of the Imperial House, and Chancellor of the National Institute." About the beginning of the seventeenth century, he came under the teaching of that laborious "missioner" Ricci, and was converted to the Romish faith. On profession of his new creed, *Seu* was baptized under the name of "Paul," as he desired to emulate the apostle of that name by abundant labours among his countrymen. This convert's energy and example greatly encouraged the Church of Rome. Ricci and his *confrères* were aided by his influence at court; for he wrote in defence of the faith,* and appealed to the Emperor himself in behalf of the missionaries. He devoted much of his property to the building of chapels. By his accurate knowledge of his native tongue, he clothed some Romish tracts in such a style as to secure the attention of the learned classes. He did not appropriate his talents merely to Christian writings. He was likewise an efficient coadjutor in promoting scientific publications, and he assisted Ricci in translating Euclid into Chinese.

Shortly after his adhesion, he saw the new religion encounter serious obstacles and actually checked by

* A copy of this apology is engraven on a marble slab, erected at the Jesuits' church outside the south gate of Shanghai.

court intrigue; but, after a persecution had raged for four years against the Popish missionaries and their churches, he obtained the reversal of the Imperial edict that had expelled the priests and disturbed the Christians. He lived to see the missionaries re-instated in Imperial favour mainly under his recommendation, and then expired in 1633,—his mantle falling on some members of his family, especially his youngest daughter, who adopted the Christian name Candida.

This lady appears to have been a remarkable woman. Though left a widow at an early age, with the charge of eight children, she gave herself up to the promotion of this form of Christianity. Duhalde says, she consecrated part of her fortune to the erection of thirty-nine churches in different provinces, and printing 130 varieties of Christian books for the instruction of the unconverted. The Emperor was so gratified with her reputed integrity and benevolence, as to confer on her the title "virtuous woman," accompanying his note of congratulation with a rich robe and head-dress, the ornaments in which, it is added, she disposed of to feed the poor. Like her father, she died lamented by all classes, especially by the missionaries, who in her lost their best Chinese friend.

Seu and his daughter have been apotheosized by Catholic families in China, especially those of Shanghai. Their remains were interred at or near a village on the west of Shanghai, five or six miles distant, called Seu-kia-hwuy,—colloquially Zee-ka-wei. The village derived its name from once having been the residence and possession of the Seu family. Part of his descendants now are Romanists, part have remerged into Chinese paganism. At the present day, a stone arch is pointed out in the heart of Shanghai, not far from the front of the city-provost's office, erected to the memory of Seu, with his name and titles carved thereon; where also in a temple there is a clay image of him as large as life, which, by Imperial appointment, receives divine honours.

It must be evident then, that, on the early arrival of the Romish mission in China, Shanghai figured prominently.

Since those days, Popery has undergone strange vicissitudes in the empire. Its church history here would make another *Yih-king*, or "Book of Changes." In consequence of her own political schemings, sanctimonious presumptions, and the divisions and dissent among her different orders, she has more than once lost her good footing and been driven into degradation, exile, or seclusion. For more than one hundred years now she has been striving to regain her position. To promote this object, no tool has been neglected, no weapon unused, no opportunity lost, no nook unsought, no subterfuge overlooked. As in every other place, although obliged to work underhand, she had for years been working at Shanghai, almost unobserved,—not only shunning observation, but adopting every semblance to prevent detection or even suspicion; till the making of peace, by the treaty of 1842, opened wider than before the intercourse between China and the West, when it was the commencement of a new epoch to the Romish church here. And no branch of her missions shared so much of the fresh impetus, on that day of revival, as the Shanghai Popish mission.

In 1844, in consequence of friendly correspondence on the subject with the French Commissioner Lagrène, the Chinese plenipotentiary Keying made a representation to Taoukwang, his Imperial master, on the toleration of Popery in China. That statesman's communication was thus worded:—"Your humble servant finds, on inquiry, that the religion of the Lord of Heaven* is

* "Lord of Heaven Religion" is distinctive now of "Popery."

that which is followed by every Western nation. Its great aim is to encourage virtue and suppress vice. Since its introduction into the middle empire during the former Ming dynasty, it has never been prohibited.* Subsequently to its introduction, however, in consequence of Chinese who professed this religion often practising wickedness under its guise, even seducing women and craftily extracting the pupils † of sick folks' eyes, government was under the necessity of making inquiry and inflicting prompt and summary punishment. During the reign of Kiaking, there were first laid down certain clauses for the punishment of these enormities. But this was to prevent Chinese under the covert of this religion practising vice. It was by no means an enactment condemnatory of the religion professed by the foreigners of the West. Now, as the French ambassador Lagrène has made the request that Chinese who profess this religion, and at the same time are upright in conduct, should be no longer considered criminals, it appears feasible. It is but fit, therefore, for me to request and earnestly implore the extension of Imperial favour and pardon hereafter in behalf of all people, natives or foreigners, without distinction, who may adopt and profess the religion of the Lord of Heaven, without irregular and improper conduct. Only, should any be chargeable with the seduction of women, or deceitfully puncturing the eyeballs of the sick, or walking in the old paths, or practising any other form of vice, let them be dealt with as by the former laws.

* This is opposed to the real facts of the case.

† This has been explained as a custom with some priests, who, when one was about to die, took a handful of cotton with a needle concealed in it. While rubbing the patient's eyes with the cotton, the eye was pricked with the needle to extract the humours therefrom, as it was supposed the cotton soaked in a dying man's eye-humour was a remedial medicine. But is not this a Chinese fable, founded probably on the practice of extreme unction administered in the Catholic system at the bed of death?

As to the French people, or any other foreign nation professing this religion, let them only be permitted to build chapels and conduct service at the five ports opened for general trade. They must not dare to go into the interior to propagate their religion. Should any act contrary to these treaty engagements, by overstepping the boundaries and bidding defiance, let the local officers at once seize them and hand them over to their respective consuls for restraint and correction. Let not the punishment of death be rashly inflicted, so that there may be a due display of gentleness and suavity. In this manner probably the good and the evil doers will not be confounded, and benevolent laws will be executed. The preceding request that all upright professors of this religion may be exempt from the charge of being criminals is most respectfully and dutifully laid before the throne, with the earnest prayer that the august Emperor would graciously grant the favour."

A prompt reply was received under the vermilion pencil, to the effect, "Let it be according to the counsel of Keying." This act of toleration was passed at the close of 1844. Only one month had expired when the proclamation fell into the hands of Count de Bessi, then bishop of the two provinces Shantung and Kiangnan, the seat of whose diocese was Shanghai. He was at the time on his diocesan journey northwards, but was so ecstatic on receipt of the above tidings, that he instantly despatched an encyclical letter in the Chinese language to "all his spiritual children," part of which I give :—"A special order from Lohing-sze (Count de Bessi), bishop of Shantung and Kiangnan, commanding all his spiritual children, and communicating for their information, that whilst he, the bishop, was at Soochow, preparing for his journey northwards, he suddenly fell in with the memorial of the governor-general of Canton, for which he returns thanks to Divine goodness, and feels penetrated with delight. The holy religion is most correct and true, and its professors certainly ought respectfully to maintain and diligently to learn it. Let them also pray that the holy religion may be greatly promoted, remembering that the kind consideration of the Emperor towards our holy religion springs entirely from the favour of the Lord of Heaven. After the reception of this order, let thanks be offered up to God for his mercies in the churches, for three Lord's-days in succession. While the faithful rejoice in this extraordinary favour,—let Ave Marias also be recited to display grateful feelings."

It is clear, from the above papers, that full toleration was obtained for the Romish creed, not only at the five ports, but also throughout the Chinese dominions.* The following year brought with it a strong proof of the genuine sincerity with which the grant was made. Many of the buildings in the country, formerly owned and occupied by Catholics for religious purposes, and seized or confiscated by Government, were restored; at least, the following act was promulgated with that view:—"With the exception of such as have been converted into temples or people's residences, let all the old churches of the religion of the Lord of Heaven that were built during the reign of the Emperor Kanghe (A.D. 1662—1723) and have been preserved to the present time, be restored to the professors of this religion in every place, if, on proper inquiry by official authorities, it be proven that they are their real possessions."

* Here I must observe that, in 1845, a proclamation appeared from the bureau of the same Chinese official, to certify that the rights that had been conceded to Romanists were alike secured for Protestants. A public instrument, specifically conceding to Protestants the privileges that had been obtained for Romanists by the French minister, was secured at that time, principally through the timely interference of Sir John Davis, the Governor at Hong-kong, and her Majesty's Plenipotentiary in China.

The effect of such acts was to stir up the native Romanists to great effort, aided by the counsel of foreign priests. When I first reached Shanghai, in the end of 1846, there was directly off the south-east corner of the city a very large native dockyard; but before I left Shanghai, at the end of 1853, it had been converted into the site of a cathedral, collegiate buildings, and a residence for the propagandist agents. The cathedral had already been erected and opened, and is now a spot where the Romish services are conducted in Chinese, partly by foreign, partly by native priests, as regularly and formally as at Lyons or Rome. This structure itself is very clumsy, heavy, and oppressive-looking; but, certainly, the single-eyed zeal, indomitable perseverance, and strict economy with which the progress of this erection was marked are beyond praise.

In consequence of the edict above quoted, certain possessions which at one time belonged to Roman Catholics at or near Shanghai have been restored, or they have obtained new sites, probably in compensation for property confiscated many years ago. In neighbouring towns and villages there is a considerable amount of land which, if not the property of the missions, is the property of "the spiritual children" connected with them, and completely under the control of their *shin-foos*, "spiritual fathers." Of these the most remarkable is the village Seu-kia-hwuy, already given as pronounced in the local *patois*, Zee-ka-wei.

In calling attention to this religious village, I must refer to a provision required in all the treaties,—English, American, and French,—that no foreigner is on any pretence to trespass beyond certain territorial limits. This prohibition was not ignored in either of the proclamations subsequently issued and above quoted. In the last-mentioned, the closing paragraph reads:—"But, that due distinctions may be made, foreigners, no matter of what nation, are, in accordance with existing regulations, prohibited from going into the interior to propagate their religion." In spite of these warnings, however, the following proclamation appeared in Shanghai, July 20, 1848, from which it will be evident that, five miles beyond the foreign boundaries, a sale of land was made and secured under the seal of Chinese authorities to a foreign bishop, distinctly designated a "Fuh-lan-see man." The said proclamation reads:—"Whereas it is authenticated that the constable of the sixth ward of the twenty-eighth tything has again reported the sale of land belonging to the people at Seu-kia-hwuy *to the French bishop Lo* (Count de Bessi) for the erection of a church and residence; and now that the said bishop or his agent is buying materials, and collecting artisans, and beginning the work, fearing lest ignorant villagers may oppose the carrying of brick, lime, wood, and other materials, or may take trouble and create disorder, or may steal the materials, or may there crowd together to get lodgings, and thus hinder the work; therefore, he (the said constable) has requested that a proclamation may be given for the purpose of prohibiting, &c. &c. Upon receiving the above report, it is proper to issue a proclamation, and I do hereby give this to the said constable and villagers for their information. People of the neighbouring villages, attend each one of you to your agricultural pursuits. If any worthless villains or vagabond beggars come from other places unto the said village and take up their lodgings there, hinder the work, or steal the materials, the said constable is hereby authorized to arrest them and deliver them over to my office, to be tried and punished according to law. The said constable also must not make this an occasion to create troubles. If he oppose, I will punish him. Let each and all respectfully obey. Oppose not.—A special proclamation." This is a point of some importance for the Protestant public to remember. Foreign priests of the

Popish persuasion have reclaimed landed property, have purchased new lands in their own name, and built chapels, &c. *beyond the boundaries defined for foreigners.* Besides which, it is universally known that Jesuit priests are in every part of the country prosecuting their missionary labours.

The Catholic village of Zee-ka-wei lies within a convenient walk of Shanghai, and is often visited by foreigners, which circumstance obliges the resident *padres* to be very cautious and chary, especially when they find Protestant missionaries are disposed to look in and announce themselves without disguise. On a certain occasion when I visited the colony, I found foreign priests, and other foreigners of a secular calling, on the premises. These offered every mark of courtesy, refreshments, &c., and apparently showed no reluctance to communicate information except on certain points.

The *school-house* was to me an object of some curiosity; but it was singular to watch the scrupulous jealousy with which permission to inspect it was granted. Before I could be admitted, there was to be some delay,—there were so many messages to and fro, and all in under-whispers. It was evident the desire was to smuggle the boys away from observation. Still, with all their manœuvre, when our party was admitted, it was found we were a little too soon. We met the lads just making their exodus, of various ages, good-looking, though evidently cowed. There were fifty in all, some of them *foreign boys* in native costume. They had foreign ushers and native teachers. The school-room, dining-hall, and sleeping-berths were nasty-looking apartments. In the school-house there were lying about Chinese books, Catholic catechisms, &c. Plates and pictures of Jesus, Mary, and some saints were hung on the walls,—one of Joseph, the husband of Mary, with the inscription on it, "Holy Joseph, pray for us." Two frames were stuck up containing the names of the scholars, and recording their good or bad marks, under these heads,—"recitation," "reading," "attending to instruction," "writing," "dining-hall," "school-house," "sleeping-room," "inattention," "correctness of behaviour," "respectful conduct." I examined the "school-library," which was rather meagrely supplied with books, English, French, and Italian. The only English work there was "Cobbett's Register!" Of other parts in the building, perhaps "the sculpture-room" was the most interesting. It was full of models, the principal one that of Xavier. There were three or four youths under instruction. The head artist was a Spaniard, who had been five years in China. The chapel was capable of holding 500 people, and fitted up mostly like a poor Catholic building anywhere else. There was a little gallery with a small seraphine in it. The priests in attendance were particular in uncovering the altar of its shields and curtains, to exhibit to us the Babe in the manger (this was on January 4, 1853), represented by a Chinese doll laid out upon a couch, rigged out with flowers and evergreens. On leaving the chapel, the senior Father L—— seized me by both hands, and begged that he might assure me he "did not worship any of *the images* in the chapel." On another occasion when I visited the chapel, I found a coffin stationed in the centre empty, but covered with a black cloth. Candles were arranged on either side, and all around there were fifty or sixty women and girls kneeling or squatting on cushions saying prayers, some using their beads, some their missals. A member of the Catholic Church had died, and prayers were said on behalf of the deceased. But the great point of interest about this village (to quote one of themselves*) "is connected

* Letter from "Father Fournier, Visitor of the Missions of the Society of Jesus in China, to Messrs. the Directors of the Work of the Propagation of the Faith," dated Zee-ka-wei, near Shanghai, Sep-

with the pupils of the college of Zee-ka-wei, who, together with the seminarists, are the hope of this mission. They afford us the greatest satisfaction by their love of labour, and their progress in the study of Chinese literature. So great is the docility and tractability of their dispositions, that the direction of the college is attended with no difficulty. A word suffices to maintain order and discipline. Their attachment to the fathers and the happiness they enjoy are so visibly expressed in their looks, that it is remarked by all strangers who visit our establishments. . . . . . This college will, I trust, furnish us with professors competent to teach the higher branches of education, well-instructed and zealous catechists, and even priests no less recommendable for their knowledge of the Chinese literature than for that of theology, in which they will be initiated at a later period."

The foregoing will illustrate some of the modes of operation superintended by the Romish Church in China, vigorously pursued at least in the diocesan city of Shanghai. "In his infidelium partibus," besides a bishop, they have numerous foreign teachers disguised as natives, and a large staff of Chinese agents. These live and labour chiefly in villages, that principally comprise "spiritual children," of whom they number in the Kiangnan vicarage above 70,000 souls! Under the supervision of the *confrères,* there are catechists and travelling agents. They maintain schools for girls and boys. They have chapels. They support monasteries. And recently, with some hope, and, as they believe, success, they have introduced "the institution of religious women."

There is a telling paragraph on that last-named scheme which I extract from the same letter already quoted:—"Together with the congregations and the

tember 20, 1855, and published in the May number of the "Annales" for 1856.

schools, the missionaries have to sustain and augment the piety of their neophytes, who constitute the society of Christian young women, that have always been regarded as the most precious portion of the church of Kiangnan. They are the first to frequent the sacraments, adorn the altars, instruct the catechumens, sing the prayers, and give an example of every virtue. From them are selected the schoolmistresses, the most zealous in the performance of every good work. A state of languor and indifference is observable wherever they are not; whilst life, fervour, and zeal indicate their presence wherever they are established. When asked the motives of their vocation, the peremptory and almost exclusive answer is, that they are desirous of following and walking in the footsteps of the Holy Mother; so sweet is the perfume of the virtues of Mary, even in this land of infidelity! How astonishing! in localities where there are at most only a few hundreds of the faithful, there are forty or fifty virgins whom neither promises nor threats can dissuade from that resolution they have taken from their infancy, to devote themselves to the service of God under the protection of Mary! It has always been believed that God made use of them to work out his secret designs, to deposit in the bosom of the church of China the precious germs of Christian perfection, and a predisposition for a religious life. This year has afforded us a convincing proof that this was the object of their vocation. We felt the want of governesses, who, being well informed, might assist us in the conversion of the infidels. A few virgins from the district of Poo-ni, amongst others, had afforded us an example of what the zeal of women may accomplish in China. Last autumn, when M. Maresca was making his pastoral visit in the district of Wongdam, we visited together the former establishment of the small seminary, deserted since the transference of the young Levites to Tsankouloo, near Shanghai. It occurred to us that this place might be turned to advantage, and on the 25th of March of the present year his lordship opened there, under the patronage of Mary, a school, the twofold aim of which is the education of orphans and the formation of school-mistresses selected from the female pupils who afford the most promising hopes of success. I cannot conjecture what may be the advantages of this establishment, which is only as yet an attempt. But it is somewhat remarkable that it has met with a good reception both from the idolaters and Christians. Not a single word of censure; on the contrary, numerous applications for admission have been sent from all the surrounding districts, made by young women jealous of their spiritual perfection. This new house is known by the appellation of '*the Convent of our Blessed Mother.*' The institution of religious women in China appeared hitherto, to many persons, a problem difficult to solve; and it may be that God is preparing the way to their establishment in an unforeseen manner."

This is a scheme to promote which the Romanists, during the year 1850, introduced eight foreign "Sisters of Mercy" into Shanghai. That introduction can readily be effected, especially where there already reside so many Popish families among the Chinese themselves, and in a country where Buddhist nunneries have been long extant, the female occupants who, in every respect (as to dress, appearance, manner, diet, penance, forbidding to marry, chanting prayers, &c.), so strikingly resemble the nuns and Sisters of Charity of the Romish profession.

As to their *publications*, they have numerous tracts, &c., for circulation, written in a good, easy style. Many of them, perhaps most, contain views which a Protestant could not deem exceptionable, saving that they are linked side by side with tales, fables, and fictions, absurd, monstrous, and blasphemous. Exactly like that new religious sect that lately has been figuring on the plains of China, the Taipingites, the Papists in China jumble up with truth more that is falsehood,—with what is solemn everything ludicrous,—with saving doctrines what is damning.

Among their books I have seen extracts from Scripture, but no book under the distinct designation of "The Holy Bible, containing the Old and New Testaments." One day that I visited the chapel at Zee-ka-wei, I saw represented in relief, on the wall over the altar-table, the two divisions of that Book,—the Old Testament open, but in the Hebrew text, and, what I thought too significant of the policy of this Church, the New Testament *shut!* The priests of Rome have for the last 250 years and more been labouring in this country, and had every facility for translating God's Holy Book, but I have not yet seen a copy of the entire version, nor more than portions only. Nor have I been able to ascertain from themselves that they have either completed it or attempted it. If they have, they certainly have *shut* it up, kept the translation under lock and key, to save it from the vulgar gaze, and withhold it from circulation. Their aversion to the circulation of Protestant Scriptures and tracts in Chinese can be pretty well understood from the annexed translation I give of a pastoral issued about the time I reached Shanghai, 1846, from the prolific pen of the then resident Bishop Bessi. I am aware that, because I published the same translation in the "Chinese Repository" of 1847, along with the Chinese original, "the lord bishop was displeased with the appearance of the translation, and pronounced some parts of it to be incorrect." But, as for the Chinese original itself, it was found in a Catholic chapel near Shanghai, I think at Zee-ka-wei, and was copied off by Dr. Medhurst, in the presence of witnesses. His lordship was requested to point out where there was any incorrectness in the original text or the translation, but has not favoured us with his strictures up to this date.

"LUDOVIC, *the Lord Bishop of this Diocese, takes occasion to issue this all-important Proclamation for the information of all the friends of the religion (of the Lord of Heaven).*

"Recently, in and about Shanghai, there have been persons who have been widely circulating books (written in imitation of those) belonging to our holy religion, at which our mind has been exceedingly pained; for, although in those books there are passages that accord with the doctrines of our holy religion, yet within their pages there are lurking heretical principles which poison and destroy men's souls—consequences by no means light and trifling.

"In the beginning, our Lord Jesus himself established the Church, a most righteous and a most perfect Church, one only, and not two churches. He then gave power to the chief of his disciples, Holy Peter, to receive and pass on the succession, and declared to Peter, saying, 'I have prayed for thee that (God would) for ever preserve thy faith.' Therefore, his successors have handed down no other faith, and the faithful everywhere all follow the commands of the supreme Pontiff. On which account all who heartily unite with the Pope are one; but such as do not give heed to the injunctions of the supreme Pope are heretics. Now, to desert and forsake the teaching of the high Pontiff, is not this to falsify and pervert his instructions?

"Ye are our sheep, and we the good shepherd. And fearing that, by accepting and pursuing those productions, ye may be a little disturbed with doubts and suspicions, to the great damage of your souls, we, therefore, issue this special proclamation, and moreover annex a few instructions in order, as follows:—

"Any adherent of our religion may not take and read these heretical writings, which have issued from Shanghai.

"Or, if any such have already accepted them, they must forthwith either burn them or deliver them up to their spiritual fathers.

"Any of the faithful who may be aware that other people have these heretical works in their possession, must advise them neither to detain them for pesusal, nor to present them to their neighbours, but to burn them up, or give them over to the spiritual fathers in their vicinity.

"Every one of our adherents is bound to spread abroad the orthodox religion of the Lord of Heaven, and always to love others as himself; and should he fall in with the members of any other sect who take in these heterodox publications, he ought to tell them most carefully and most plainly that their writings are decidedly erroneous, and do not, in all or anything, agree with the teaching of the religion of the Lord of Heaven; but, if men will follow such doctrines, they will fall into extreme error.

"Now, wherever there are corrupt and obscene books, there is every danger of injuring men's souls; but the heretical works, of which we have just spoken, are of one and the same class with corrupt and obscene writings; and a friend to (the true) religion must in no wise either receive them for perusal, or hold them in possession, because all corrupt or obscene works are of the devil; and both the recipients and the distributors of these works are undoubtedly the children of the devil; and all such will inevitably go down to hell!"

For a sample of their tampering with Scripture, take their translation of the Decalogue, *as found in their commonest manuals* and school-books at Zee-ka-wei:— 1. Reverently worship one God over all. 2. Do not call upon the holy name of God in uttering a vain oath. 3. Keep the worship day. 4. Honour father and mother. 5. Do not kill men. 6. Do not commit lewdness. 7. Do not steal or rob. 8. Do not bear false witness. 9. Do not desire another man's wife. 10. Do not covet another man's wealth or goods. In which it will at once be perceived how *the ten* commandments are made up, even after the second is smuggled away;—the tenth being divided into two commandments.

Then, their system of Mariolatry is as gross in China as in Italy or Ireland; in proof whereof read, if you can, this form of prayerful address to the Mother of Jesus, in their book of morning and evening prayers, which I translate from Chinese as it lies before me:—

"*Pray for us,*—

O holy Mary!
O holy Mother of God!
O holy Virgin of virgins!
O Mother of Christ!
O most beloved Mother of God!
O most pure Mother!
O most chaste Mother!
O Mother without wrinkle!
O Mother without stain!
O beloved Mother!
O admirable Mother!
O Mother of the creation!
O Mother of salvation!

("*Pray for us,*)—

O most wise chaste Woman!
O reverend chaste Woman!
O to be praised chaste Woman!
O omnipotent chaste Woman!
O all-benevolent chaste Woman!
O all-faithful chaste Woman!
O mirror of integrity!
O seat of perfect wisdom!
O source of our joys!
O thou concentration of the pure and subtile!
O most reverent vessel!
O vessel that contains all holy feelings!
O red gem of sublime rectitude!
O pagoda of crystal and ivory!
O temple of fine gold!
O ark of the covenant!
O gate of high heaven!
O most lustrous star!
O remedy for the sick!
O atonement for the guilty!
O comfort for the distressed!
O thou guide to those that enter our religion!
O Queen of all heavenly spirits!
O Queen of all holy ancestors!
O Queen of all the prophets!
O Queen of all the apostles!
O Queen of all who sacrifice themselves for righteousness' sake!
O Queen of all pure in heart!
O Queen of all virgins!
O Queen of all saints!"

Next, we have prayers without end to apostles, saints, and martyrs, among whom sits, as not the least, "Joseph the patron saint of China," to whom is addressed the following daily prayer "on account of the empire of China:"—"Most reverently I implore thee on my behalf to intercede with thy beloved son Jesus, that He forgive my sins; and I pray thee as the patron saint of China to intercede with God, that he look on the infidel inhabitants of China, and open their hearts to turn from evil and repent and obtain the virtues of knowledge, faith, hope, and love, until the whole empire devoutly worship God. O may our holy religion do great wonders! Let them not be deceived by devils. And after death let the people all together ascend to heaven and enjoy true bliss. Amen."

Last of all, I give a translation of one page of a pocket manual, popular among the faithful in Shanghai, that is entitled "The Righteous Acts of the Holy Road." The book is intended to be a guide to the devout, who would try to realize the sufferings of the Saviour. In their chapels they have (at least at certain seasons) fourteen pictures on the walls, descriptive of the several stages of our Lord's trials and sufferings, unto the death of the cross. By drawing attention to these, it is designed (as the book intimates) to "move the heart that is like iron or stone." Here is a translation of the thoughts to be cherished at the fourteenth spot or stage, which is illustrated in the picture-frame before which the devotee is supposed to be kneeling:—

"At this point we have presented to us a view of our Holy Mother, and sainted men and women, attending the body of our Lord to the tomb, and covering it over with a stone. Consider, O my soul, and think. The Holy Mother Mary and all the saints are using a great stone and shutting up the tomb, so that they no more can see the body of Jesus. What grief and anguish must have filled their hearts! Now ponder and think, if you have a heart still unmoved, as you come to this part of the scenery. Alas! it is only a proof that your conscience is seared, and you are an impenitent sinner. But oh, if your heart be like iron or stone, and your feelings have not yet been moved, do reflect on the sufferings which our Lord endured from Gethsemane to the tomb,—look at them minutely one by one. [After the relation of each successive suffering, the penitent has to say, 'O Jesus Christ, we revere and praise thee.'] On his way from the garden to the hall of Ananias the high priest, Jesus fell down seven times, wicked men trampled him under-foot 144 times, struck him with their hands 120 times, smote the palms of his hands 102 times, scourged him with 5,000 lashes, he fell three times while he bore his cross, he was overwhelmed with grief 72 times, the crown of thorns inflicted 1,000 wounds on his head, they spat on him 72 times, his hands and feet were pierced and bruised in 72 places, he sighed 109 sighs during his agonies, the wounds over his entire body amounted to 6,475, he spilt 230,000 drops of blood, and he shed for our sins 60,200 drops of tears."

In the notes faithfully and impartially given under this chapter, I have only spoken of Romanism as it is at Shanghai. But enough has been said here and also in a former part* to show that its policy under the garb of "the Propagation of the Faith," is throughout essentially one and the same in China, as it is in other countries of the world, and has been at all times.

CHAPTER V.

PROTESTANT MISSIONS AT SHANGHAI—COMMENCEMENT—OPERATIONS—STUDYING THE LANGUAGE—PREACHING—TRACT DISTRIBUTION—SCRIPTURE TRANSLATION—SCHOOLS—ROMANIZING THE CHINESE LANGUAGE—MEDICAL MISSIONS—A REVIEW OF FIFTY YEARS' PROTESTANT MISSIONS IN CHINA—ENCOURAGEMENTS IN THE WORK—THE CIVIL COMMOTIONS IN THE EMPIRE—PROBABLE RESULT OF THE PRESENT CONFLICT WITH FOREIGNERS.

No sooner had the treaty of Nanking been signed and sealed, than the eyes of Protestant missionaries, who were already stationed on the outposts of the empire, turned in the direction of Shanghai, as being "a great door and effectual opened unto them."

* Chapter ii., Part iv., page 355, where the alarming correspondence between Buddhism and Romanism is shown, in the section on Buddhism and its influences in China.

The city itself is but of an inferior class, and the natives of the district are not on a footing with their countrymen in the south of the empire for intelligence, energy, or independence of character; yet, there can be no doubt that the port of Shanghai is one of the principal entrances into the heart of the country. It communicates directly with Soochow (which may be reached by water within twenty-four or thirty hours), and, only 150 miles distant, with Hangchow, the capital of Chihkiang province,—two cities that for opulence, literature, fashion, and luxury, &c. have no other to compete with, in the words of their stale proverb,

"Above is heaven,
And below are Hangchow and Soochow."

Besides this ready intercourse with two large populous capitals, which claim headship over provinces embracing sixty millions of inhabitants, there is free and constant communication by sea with all the maritime ports along an entire coast above 1,000 miles in extent, from Canton in the south to Peking in the north, and up the Yang-tszekiang, as well as by an infinite number of secondary water-channels, with the middle provinces Hookwang, Nganhwuy, &c., where rich districts and fine cities (Nanking, Nganking, Woochang, Hankow, &c.) may be visited in a week or ten days. Possessed of these facile lines of communication with the coast and the interior, Shanghai could always add to its list of population an enormous accession of native travellers, merchants, and visitors, whose numbers have been vastly augmented (as the result has proved) by throwing open the port to foreign commerce. These and other considerations contributed to make this place a point of peculiar attraction to Protestant missionaries in China.

First and foremost to occupy Shanghai for a mission station was the London Missionary Society, two of whose labourers, the Rev. Dr. Medhurst and Mr. Lockhart, moved up thither in December, 1843, contemporaneously with her Majesty's consul, who planted the British flag at the same port. To own a conviction that has grown upon me ever since I landed there in 1846, the first occupation of this new field of missionary work could not have devolved on gentlemen more suitable and better qualified than those I have just named;—the one a veteran in the service, who, by his extensive knowledge of Chinese dialects and literature, could immediately communicate with natives from various parts of the empire, and by his advanced age (which in China always carries weight) could command respect and attention;—the other, skilful in medical practice, and versatile as well as prompt in schemes of benevolence, following up "the glad tidings" announced by his senior with visible assurances of the friendly intentions of "strangers from afar," and thus assuaging any feelings of animosity and prejudice that might have been entertained against the foreigner. Doubtless the incipient labours of these two esteemed individuals at that early period of foreign intercourse contributed essentially to secure a good footing at Shanghai for the London Society's as also every other mission.*

Since then several other missionary societies have selected the spot as the scene of their evangelical efforts; and their statistics show that, during the past thirteen years, ten distinct missionary societies have

* After penning the above lines the writer was called, along with a large body of admiring friends of various denominations, to mourn over the decease of that distinguished and laborious missionary, the Rev. Dr. Medhurst. After forty years of literary and active toil in the East, he returned to his native country in an extremely enfeebled state, and three days after landing he peacefully breathed his last, January 24, 1857. His removal has left a serious blank in the missionary circle in China; but, beneath the pressure of a truly woful sorrow, his brethren in the field can be sustained by that divine assurance—"Blessed are the dead that die in the Lord from henceforth; yea, saith the Spirit, that they may rest from their labours, and their works do follow them."

sent fifty-seven missionaries (with few exceptions married men); of whom there are at present at work there at least thirty-seven, the rest having been removed by death or illness, or other circumstances.

Speaking from personal acquaintance and experience of the general proceedings of the Shanghai missionaries, I may premise that, being unacquainted with the Chinese language, they have to postpone entering on the more arduous and direct labours of their vocation, until they are qualified for the task by duly acquiring the local *patois*. I make this almost needless remark for the purpose of alluding to what, I believe, is a misapprehension in Great Britain regarding the acquisition of the Chinese language. Judging from numerous inquiries that have been put to me on my return, I presume there is prevalent in all classes an impression that the Chinese tongue is not only odd and strange, but so hard of acquisition as to be almost unattainable except by men signally gifted. But I fear there is a good deal of exaggeration as to the difficulty of learning this language. I would not speak too lightly of the "book-language," to study which accurately and thoroughly will tax every power a man has of body and mind,—all his lifetime too. I refer specially to "the spoken language," or any of the common dialects of the people, to learn which with general accuracy one of ordinary abilities will only have to give a moderate share of study and labour. In former days, intercourse with the common people (which is the best medium of learning any colloquial) was fettered and prohibited; now it is the very reverse—open, easy, constant. A man cannot pick up the *patois* of the natives by sitting over his books, or chatting with his learned *siensang*. His best teachers of the local dialect are the common people in the suburbs, villages, market-places, and shops. To improve facilities of this nature will give any one all that readiness and fluency of speech which he covets. Therefore, I am not underrating the difficulty of learning any of the Chinese dialects, when I state that the acquisition of a local *patois* is not more arduous in China than in any Oriental state, provided one studies the Chinese colloquial as he would the French, Italian, or Bengalee.

In making specific mention of the labours of the Shanghai Protestant missionaries, there are five departments in which their exertions have been attended with encouragement and success, as well as trial and disappointment.

First: Preaching.—By this is meant oral instruction for the purpose of delivering the message of the Gospel; instruction given in public or in private, statedly or occasionally, in streets or in temples, in halls or other buildings hired or erected for the object. In this department of labour, various dialects are used at Shanghai, according to the nature of the audience,—perhaps the Mandarin tongue, perhaps the Fuhkien, but generally the Shanghai colloquial; so that every man may hear "in his own tongue wherein he was born" the great theme of evangelical truth. At none of the other ports of China, where missionaries are labouring, has this form of agency been developed in so extensive a manner; and the opportunities for it have been year by year immensely increased. Frequent and large audiences can now be readily collected in and about that city, partly, no doubt, from the natives' curiosity to see and hear "men from the West," and partly on account of the general respect in which foreigners are held there, and the remarkable confidence placed in the "teacher of the religion of Jesus." This teacher of a strange religion is respected and trusted, not merely because of his ability to converse in the language, but for his benevolent vocation,—as it is ascertained he leaves father, mother, and home to visit China, not as his other countrymen who pursue a mercantile trade and make their fortunes, but solely with the object of teaching the Chinese the way of salvation by Jesus Christ. Recently the audiences in the chapels and churches have increased considerably, since the piratical hordes have been expelled from the city; and the result has shown that those apprehensions were utterly groundless which were at one time entertained by a few, that, should the imperialist authorities resume their seals of office, there would be opposition to Protestant exertions amongst the people. The work of preaching is carried on with much facility and encouragement also in the country, where missionaries of various denominations, sometimes hand in hand, proclaim the Gospel 100 or 150 miles up in the interior.

Secondly.—The distribution of the Scriptures and Christian tracts is a handmaid to the former. In the preparation and gratis-circulation of fly-sheets, circulars, tracts, manuals, and pamphlets explanatory of the tenets of religion, Romanism and Buddhism too have been more than our compeers. But in the wide distribution of *God's holy oracles*, the Protestant missionary in China is at issue with Papacy, the *soi-disant* "religion of the Lord of Heaven." In 1853, intense excitement was produced in this mission, and vast encouragement given, by the liberal vote from the British churches of a million Testaments to the Chinese nation. It was a timely step, manifestly ruled by Providence; for, in all probability, had it not been taken in 1853, the next two years would have been so engrossed with the Russian war, as completely to shut "the middle kingdom" out of the mind's eye, or shut up the purse of British liberality.

The printing-presses, especially of the Bible Society, have been at full work in Shanghai during the last three years, casting forth, with all the rapidity consistent with accuracy and neatness, a portion of the million copies voted by Great Britain. These presses are set with moveable metal types from the fount invented and executed by the late Samuel Dyer, which, if for no other advantage but economy of time, labour, and money obtained thereby, deserves special commendation.

A more definite system of native *colportage*[*] has recently been set on foot, by which our Bibles and tracts may be more extensively spread; and I may also add that at present there is a more judicious caution observed in not giving our religious publications without due discrimination, or except to those who probably would make a proper use of them.

Tract and Scripture distribution is a scheme the importance of which cannot be overrated,—especially in a country like China,—where reading is extensively encouraged, and where even *paper*, with any form of written or printed character on it, secures for itself a notice that approaches superstitious reverence. Besides, there is the striking fact, that the book-language is one and the same throughout the eighteen provinces of China,—no matter how various and different the colloquials in these separate provinces. This arises from the pictorial complexion of the written language, each character representing an idea, and not essentially connected with sound; so that natives of different provinces, when unintelligible in conversation on account of their diversity of dialect, have merely to express themselves in writing; or, if in reading a native work, they are hard to be understood because of the same diversity of pronunciation, the difficulty is obviated by offering a copy of the book to the eye of their countrymen,—presuming of course that they are book-readers. In a field of such extent and population as we have in China, this peculiarity offers the singular facility, that in case our missionaries may not reach the utmost range of that empire, our tracts and publications may; or in case our missionaries were to reach its furthest limits, where they might in all probability be unable to pronounce or speak, to preach or converse in the *patois* of those localities, our Christian writings, clothed in the book-language, can be "seen and read of all men." Thank God for this channel of sending the "silent messengers" of peace throughout China!

Thirdly.—One special object to which the attention of missionaries at Shanghai has been directed since 1843, is *translation* into Chinese of works of general instruction on geography, medicine, astronomy, &c.,—especially religious writings, and supremely the Old and New Testaments. Under the former head I have spoken of their distribution; under this I call special attention to the translation of the Scriptures, as the latest version, and the most approved, that of "the Delegates," was completed at this station.

From the earliest date of our Protestant missions in China, the uppermost object has been to furnish the Chinese with a translation of the Bible in their own language. The difficulty of this task has been excessive. That the version made by Morrison and Milne, the first missionaries, should be imperfect, was a matter of course. In this work they had no opportunity of meeting together in session for any length of time: their separation from each other, at a distance of 2,000 or 3,000 miles, prevented those translators from united conference and revisions; the narrow and exclusive tone of the Chinese government forbade that intercourse with the people which is of essential aid in acquiring their language; and the multiplicity of other labours pressed too hard on their time and divided their strength. These and other unavoidable circumstances militated against the great object of these pioneers,—to give an accurate translation of the Scriptures. Although the work was completed before their decease, they did not believe that it was at all perfect.

To the last they lamented over its defects, and expired at their posts, breathing out the earnest wish that a revision might soon be effected. This duty devolved on their survivors and successors, though not until many years after. Meantime one or two new versions were attempted, but proved exceedingly defective, and very unsatisfactory.

When, upon the treaty of Nanking, the several missionary societies moved up to China, their agents felt more than ever the imperative necessity of revising, if not retranslating the Scriptures. A long experiment had clearly shown the insufficiency of the early translation; and now, more highly favoured with increased facilities for improving it, the missionaries could not fail to feel their own responsibility in this matter. A conference of the various missionaries, which met at Hong-Kong in the summer of 1843, brought the question to an issue, and they determined on a revision. After a good deal of delay, arising from correspondence and other circumstances needless to recount, a body of five delegates was appointed by missionaries at the various stations.

Seeing this delegation began, continued, and ended its labours at Shanghai, that station has secured no mean reputation in the history of evangelical missions to China. Its first session was in midsummer 1847; and, as the writer held an humble seat on this committee of five, he may be permitted to enter into a few interesting points.

Of the *quinqueviri*, the president was the late Dr. Medhurst, a man honoured by all who knew him, as *facile princeps* in the Chinese language. Under the able and skilful leadership of this linguist, who was elected as chairman, the translatorial engagements of the delegation were commenced upon the New Testament,—following the "*textus receptus*," in deference to the Bible Society's suggestion. Our sessions occurred daily, opened with reading a portion of the sacred Scriptures and prayer, and extended from ten o'clock A.M. to half-past two o'clock P.M. The method of proceeding in committee was to consider verse by verse, word by word, allowing each individual opportunity to propose any alteration that he might deem desirable. The several members of the delegation had their native tutors with them, three of whom* continued with us for six years in our daily sittings, rendering most valuable assistance. Each day, before adjournment, the portion of Scripture to be considered at the next meeting was specified, and a rough draft of its translation offered by the chairman so that each member might duly examine and compare the same.

The New Testament was completed in three years, or by the end of July, 1850, when the committee resolved, "That the version as it now stands be offered to the Bible Societies of Europe and America, and to all and every one of the Protestant missionaries at present engaged, or who hereafter may be engaged, in the work of evangelizing China; with the understanding that all parties who shall make use of this version shall refrain from altering the text as now given out by this committee, who reserve to a majority of their own body the right to make any alterations therein." As there was a difference of opinion amongst the missionaries throughout China as to the suitable terms by which to express βαπτιζω, Θεος, and Πνευμα, the delegates' version had blanks left for these words, leaving the responsibility of their renderings with the several parties, who might select their own terms;—"believing that said diversity of rendering will cause less injury if all parties use the same version, instead of having different versions as well as various renderings of these important words."

* Two of them have since been converted to the truth, and are now honouring the Christian faith by a consistent profession.

Upon entering on the translation of the Old Testament, three translators, the Rev. Dr. Medhurst, Rev. John Stronach, and myself, were formed into "the committee for translating the Old Testament under the auspices of the London Missionary Society," while the aim was, as before in the New Testament revision, "that the result of their labour should not be confined to the missionaries of the London Missionary Society, but should be offered to the Bible Societies of Europe and America, and to all the Protestant missionaries in China." Strong prudential reasons forced the translators to adopt that nominal structure; but the work of translation itself was uninterrupted, and was pursued precisely on the same rules and principles which guided us in the New Testament. We continued our labours until the spring of 1853, when the revised Old Testament was offered to the evangelical missionaries in China, on exactly the same broad and liberal conditions as the New Testament translation was given out. Within six years this improved version in Chinese of the entire Holy Scriptures was prepared and completed, and is now in the course of circulation.

Time would fail to dilate on one or two translations of a minor type, or smaller pretensions,—one perhaps preferred by one party for one feature, another for another. I can only add that there is much cause for regret that these sections, while they do offer the palm of superiority to the delegates' version, still will perpetuate differences and divisions by holding private crotchets rather than adopt a common version,—an object in missionary work pre-eminently desirable.

Fourthly.—As at all the other stations, the education of the youth of both sexes has occupied much of the attention of the missionaries at Shanghai. The chief of these schools is (as pointed out in the accompanying map) at Hung-k'ow, which by this time has well-nigh become a missionary colony. It sprang up ten years ago, under the able and experienced management of the Rev. Dr. Boone, bishop of the American Episcopal missions in China. A passing visitor at Shanghai should visit this establishment; it will well repay an hour or two's examination. Although some members of this mission are engaged in preaching, &c., the sum of their labours is directed specially to moulding the youthful mind, in which department of missionary work great success has attended the efforts of the Christian Church all over the world. A year ago there were about 200 boys educated here, and about 80 girls under the matronly care of some judicious female teachers. They are instructed in the various branches of elementary knowledge, but mainly in religious instruction.

At this establishment English is taught as well as their native tongue. But in our mission schools in China, probably experience has taught that it is more judicious not to make the study of the English language so much an essential and uniform branch of education for all the youth, as a means of stimulating those that give promise, or of rewarding them.

Of the system of "Romanizing the Chinese language," the introduction of which has been attempted in some of our schools, I must explain that it is a scheme for expressing Chinese sounds in Roman letters, and writing books, but not in Chinese characters. But is it not a pity to waste time, expense, and labour on such an experiment? Is this the most expeditious method of doing the most extensive good in the shortest time? Native children taught after this fashion cannot have time to learn the native mode of acquiring their book-language. Then, the Romanized Chinese writing will be confined to an infinitesimal part of 360,000,000, and only to the unit educated and trained in that system. But scholars under such a training cannot be of service among their countrymen at large: the innovation cannot possibly upset the antique language of the books; it cannot reform the stereotyped idiographs of China; it unfits the Chinese youths educated in it for usefulness among their countrymen as merchants, or even clerks; it un-Chineses them, and will not really secure respect for them as Christian teachers. Why adopt, encourage, and pursue it? Besides, is it not waste of a missionary's time and talents? The new-fangled scheme may seem fine, and be easy to one disposed to be indolent, perhaps idle; but it will not answer if one wants to work earnestly and to some purpose among the people. He must grapple with the language of the Chinese in its native type—in all its forms and shapes, and in their own writing, if he will write, write for them what they can read and understand as a body.

Fifthly.—Another object which has attained some conspicuousness at Shanghai is the Medical Mission, in which the practice of medicine is carried on among the natives free and without distinction. Without any slight to others who have opened similar institutions, I must be permitted to specify that this plan has been carried out from the first opening of the London Mission, with marked promptness, unflagging regularity, and great success, under the direction of Wm. Lockhart, Esq. The Medical Hospital connected with the London Mission Society's premises is supported chiefly by the foreign residents. By such means crowds are daily collected together; and, while attention is paid to their bodily wants, a preacher is at hand to drop a hint and speak a word in season that may, under the Divine blessing, lead the sufferer to seek the balm of Gilead for the diseased spirit.

The report of last year, Jan. 1st to Dec. 31st, 1856, gives the following review of its history:—"During a period of thirteen years, considerably more than 150,000 persons have been attended to for various diseases; patients have come to the hospital, not only from the immediate neighbourhood, but also from many different towns and cities in distant parts of this and the surrounding provinces, and great numbers of sailors from the Shantung and Fuhkien junks constantly resort to the hospital for relief."

Seeing it is now quite half a century since the Protestant mission in China was opened, it is but natural to take a rapid survey of the progress of Christian missions in that empire up to the present date.

Since the commencement of the work, at a time when every conceivable difficulty existed arising from natural prejudice and hostility to foreigners, the country has been opened, ingress has been obtained, native bigotry in many places has been superseded by respect and confidence, a footing for the foreigner has been secured in some of the largest cities, the interest of the Western world has been awakened in behalf of China, numerous missionary societies have entered the field, and every appliance is now at work to promote the chief end of evangelization, with many signs of success and triumph. Then, as to missionary labour in China, hitherto this department of enterprise has been that of *pioneering*, for which service above 190 men have enlisted and left their native shores. Their employ has been (if we may say so) the work of "navvies,"—to clear the ground, raise the sod, cut down jungles, dig trenches, throw up earthworks, sink mines, blast rocks, bore tunnels, level the roads, lay the sleepers, set the rails, &c.; and, but for these predecessors in the field (many of whom have already been called to their rest and reward), all this preliminary and necessary rough work would have been undone—and unbegun. Therefore, the fifty years' history of our Chinese missions, though not exhibiting that kind of fruit we had expected, is full of encouragement of another sort we did not look for; and we call on all, "Jubilate Deo, jubilate."

Still, this cheerful review of the past and survey of

the present state of our missions in China cannot entirely dispel the anxious cloud that naturally comes over us, as we look at the vastness of that territory, and, pointing to its enormous population, think — There, not only is there " one other man there yet,"—there are nearly 400 millions there yet,—men, women, children, —men and brethren of the same family with ourselves, and of like capacities,—born for similar ends, destined to live in eternity as we are, for whom the same means of salvation are provided, who must perish unless made partakers of like grace! There, there are yet 400 millions undelivered—unemancipated by the liberty with which Christ can make them free!

Was there ever a louder call from any family of man for the sympathy and pity of Evangelical Christendom than from China? The sole aim of Christian missions here is to save, sanctify, and elevate the Chinese mind; and the only effective means at command are Gospel truth and Gospel institutions.

In carrying out this heaven-born project, the Church of Christ finds in China that God's providence has already anticipated her wants, by providing some efficient aids and appliances, or at least by removing some obstacles in this which meet her in other fields. A voice has already been crying in that wilderness, " Prepare the way of the Lord, make straight in the desert a highway for our God." Some valleys have been exalted, some hills made low, some crooked paths made straight, some rough places plain. For instance, the people are not scattered over the face of the land, and to be reached with difficulty; but they are collected in throngs, live in crowds, and are influenced in masses. Civilization of a high type has thriven for centuries here, and there is nothing like savage and wild barbarism; we have not to tame the cannibal, clothe the naked, teach them the blessings of social life, or the advantages of clothing, housing, commerce, trade, and the arts.

Education is appreciated and popular, and instruction has been encouraged for ages by the people, officials, sages, and emperors; so that the missionary has not to coin a book language for them, or discover to them the secrets of writing, or open up to them the mysteries of the press, &c. In preparing Christian books for the hundreds of millions of Chinese, we have not to grapple with and master fourteen or twenty separate and different languages, as in British India; her books only speak one tongue; and nothing like religious caste obtains, for idolatry itself has but a slender hold.

In such a condition of society, however, the missionaries of the Christian Church come in direct contact with the human mind in every form of its depravity,—godless, atheistic, worldly, sensual, proud, and conceited; hard, unimpressible, indifferent, attached to ancient forms, detesting change, deficient in principle, wanting in manliness, obsequious, plausible, and formal. These are characteristic features daily encountered by every preacher of righteousness on Chinese soil; who finds, too, that nothing of human authority, learning, or eloquence, can affect these dark outlines of character, and that only the omnipotence of God's Spirit through the simple Gospel can change them for the better.

The task of evangelizing the Chinese is by no means easy; but, at the present time, encouragement dawns on this missionary field of a decided form, in large audiences, several inquirers, an eager desire for the Scriptures, hopeful conversions, zealous adherents to the truth, and churches increasing in their most holy faith.* There is no doubt but the force of truth will

* In a late communication from Amoy, summing up the favourable results of the various missions there, it is stated that, "connected with this mission station, including the city of Amoy and towns embraced within a circuit of thirty miles around it, there are at present 363 Chinese Christians. So mightily has the Word of God grown and prevailed."—*London Missionary Society's Report for* 1857.

triumph in China as elsewhere, so "that at the name of Jesus every knee should bow and every tongue confess that Jesus is Lord of all, to the glory of God the Father."

PART FIFTH.

STATE AND PROSPECTS OF CHINA

CHAPTER I.

NATIVE INSURRECTIONS IN CHINA—LOCAL RISINGS AT CANTON, AMOY, AND SHANGHAI, AND THEIR SUPPRESSION—THE TAIPING REBELLION—RISE, PROGRESS, CHECK, RELIGIOUS CHARACTER, AND PROBABLE RESULTS.

FOR several years past, troubles of a menacing form have been thickening within the very borders of China.

These various political agitations have had some points in common, though they have been totally distinct and unconnected in their leaders, in their claims, and in their creeds. If we might, for convenience sake, divide them into the greater and the lesser agitations, we would begin with the lesser, although they are in point of date the most recent.

Along the line of coast from the port of Canton to the mouth of the Yangtsze-Kiang, extending over eight hundred miles, there have been, since 1852, three seditious risings among the natives; one at each of the three seaports of China most famous for native traffic, and for foreign trade and commerce. The ports we mean are Amoy in the province of Fuhkien, Canton in that of Kwangtung, and Shanghai in Kiangsoo.

Although this spirit of insubordination burst out in the month of May 1853, it had long been fermenting upon the eastern coast of the empire. In no other quarter, indeed, has the reigning government had to deal with more perpetual annoyances. Nor have foreigners anywhere met with insults of so aggravated a character as they continually have encountered along this coast. Perhaps this is not to be wondered at. The spirit of daring independence, adventure, and knavery had long been growing among this maritime population, born upon the sea coast or on its rugged islands, bred up among fishermen, sailors, smugglers, and pirates, trafficking with foreigners or engaged in the opium trade; and of late, especially since 1840, when the power of England exposed the weakness of the native government, this tone of defiance has risen to a pitch beyond precedent.

However, after long delay and much bloodshed on either side, these maritime tumults were suppressed, the unruly were disbanded, the peaceful natives returned to their former residences, public security was restored, trade revived, and the Imperialists appeared to re-establish their authority.

But the political movement of the more extensive and formidable cast, is that which has often been emphatically designated by foreigners, either "the revolution in China," or "the Nanking rebellion." To give it the former designation, however, imposes on it a universality to which it has no pretensions; and to name it by the latter, conveys an erroneous impression as to the original site of the outbreak. More properly, it should be spoken of as "the Kwangse insurrection," that province having been the nursery of the rising, and the hot-bed where the combustible elements that had been smouldering in the south and south-western parts of China, since 1842, were collected. Upon the termination of the war with England in that year, when amicable relations with foreign Powers were restored, it is unquestionable that the national executive fell back into more than its usual self-satisfaction and security. Military authority and municipal surveillance became exceedingly relaxed. It is equally certain that the hardy, independent, and turbulent among the people, eager for opportunities to realize their political projects, had perceived the late exposure of the impotence of the Imperial Government, and watched with pleasure the progress of that languor, which ever since had been creeping over the various boards of the administration.

While the Emperor Taoukwang still lived (he died in 1850), various riots and extensive robberies, "occasioned by certain banditti belonging to the Kwangse province," were reported to his Majesty, as noted in the *Peking Gazette*. These were looked upon by "the Great Eye," as trivial affrays, to be put down by a puff of the Imperial breath, or extinguished by one stroke of the vermilion pencil. But down to the middle of 1851, those bands continued to occasion no little annoyance in Kwangse, spreading disorder beyond the boundaries of that into the adjoining provinces, Kwangtung (*i. e.* Canton) and Hoonan.

The agitation then began to assume the more decided form of an irruption. From the mountain lines of Kwangse, it crept northwards through the heart of the empire. As this invading force advanced, its leaders endeavoured to adopt something like an organized plan of campaign,—proclaiming the foundation of a new dynasty as their prime object. High-sounding claims were announced. Violent complaints against the existing monarchy were raised. Thrilling appeals were made to all classes, in one form most inviting, in another most appalling. These demands gained currency through the press—a medium not idle among the Chinese, and in some respects the most popular and effective instrument in that country. Passing from city to city, from province to province, the quiet and peaceable natives were startled and cowed. The Imperialist soldiery, whether composed of "tigers" or "village braves," was, before these rebels, in most instances little better than the wooden regiments that amuse the children in our nurseries. The crowds of idle and indolent vagabonds which infested the rural and suburban population found proper aliment in this commotion, and joined the movement in gangs. Still, this threatening insurrection took eighteen months to pass out of Kwangse, through the Hoonan province, up to the banks of the river Yangtsze,—a distance not exceeding 700 miles. Its approach created great alarm everywhere. Although the local authorities must have heard the wild rumours that floated on long before the actual appearance of the invaders, yet it does not appear that even the more cautious and courageous of the Imperial servants made any timely and vigorous preparation for resistance. The consequence was that, at the approach of the formidable host, whose numbers, large as they were, were enormously exaggerated by a timid and flying mob, numerous villages and walled towns were at once deserted by their inhabitants, and almost as speedily by their grotesque militia, after a show of military manœuvres which they took care to exhibit at a convenient distance from the enemy.

As it is not our purpose to weary our readers by a minute itinerary of the line of march pursued by the insurgents, we shall take them at once to Nanking, which fell on the 19th March, 1853. Early in the morning of that day the insurgents sprung a mine, which caused a breach of thirty yards' width under the wall of the city, near its northern angle. The assault was then made, and, after a slight resistance, the rebels entered, took possession of the capital, and have ever since made it their head-quarters. Near the close of the same month, they made for the citadel of Chinkiangfoo, at a distance of fifty miles from Nanking. In the beginning of April, the conquerors proceeded to the two walled cities, Kwachow and Yangchow, nearly opposite to Chinkiang upon the northern bank of the

Yangtsze. These likewise fell without defence. Having taken possession of these important cities on the two banks of the river, they got complete command of the great channel of communication between the north and south of China by way of the grand canal, called by the natives "the transport grain canal," from its chief use. Before advancing farther up the country, they took the precaution to establish a sort of regular government at "the heavenly capital," as they name Nanking, and to strengthen the various fortifications there, as well as in the other cities upon the north and south banks, with the evident intention of permanently occupying these important heads of the canal. But, while the insurgents were engaged in these precautionary measures, the Imperialist hosts came down upon their head-quarters, —pitching their tents, however, at a respectful distance from the Nanking walls, on the west, south, and eastern faces, and anchoring flotillas eight or ten miles both above and below the capital, so as to command the main channel of communication from west to east by way of the Yangtszekiang, whose waters flow along the northern face of Nanking. It would appear that the greater part of this besieging army has been lying here for nearly the space of six years,—as if with no other object than to keep the insurgents within the stone walls of the "heavenly capital," and prevent them from marching forth in masses to ravage the surrounding country. But, in spite of this parade of the Imperial forces, the insurgents, after some delay, managed to elude the besiegers, and sent detachments, according to all accounts, large and strong, to the south, the west, and the north. The division intended for the north moved leisurely, and for some time unimpeded, through the province of Shantung. It crossed the Yellow River, and penetrated the Chihli province till within 100 miles of Peking, the metropolis of the empire. At last the rebels found they had "gone too far north," for nothing but a succession of reverses awaited them there. Their hitherto victorious bands now met with a continued series of defeats. Their battalions were repulsed, broken up, and dispersed. Whole companies were cut to pieces, and the survivors fled whither they could. The same fate befell the southern and western detachments.

Thus the prestige of the usurper *Taiping* began to decline at the close of the year 1854, though then still in occupation of Nanking and the neighbouring fortress at Chinkiang; nor has his cause since revived, notwithstanding the very crippled state of the Imperial forces.

The history of the two following years of this strange movement was remarkable only for a serious division in the camp of its leaders, which (whatever may have been the direct cause) resulted in disasters the most terrific to the insurgents themselves. Two of the grand confederates, the Eastern and Northern kings, who had been most in the confidence of the Chief Hungsewtseuen, were seized as conspirators, and put to death as traitors, along with a large body of their immediate partisans, who had taken refuge in the far-famed Porcelain Tower of Nanking, but who were blown up at one and the same time with the pagoda.*

The convulsions of that juncture did not lead to the immediate downfall of the *soi-disant Taiping* dynasty, but they by no means promoted its interests or strengthened its repute. And we now find these insurgents nearly in the same position which they held in 1853, or occupying a small section of the valley of the Yangtszo river, running, perhaps, 350 miles along its southern bank from Chinkiang in Kiangsoo province, up to Kewkiang, on the northern margin of the Poyang lake in Kiangse.

Other parts of the inland country have been visited by the spasmodic efforts of upstart agitators; but we

* *Vide* account of destruction of this pagoda at p. 391.

must hesitate to identify these with the *Taiping* men, although they are alike led on by the lowest motives and impulses, and are bent on plunder and power.

It is impossible to predict the future course of politics in China; but it is not improbable that the result of the *Taiping* insurrection, and of the disturbances we have alluded to, may ultimately contribute to the entire disorganization of the empire, and the breaking up of China into a number of states never to be reunited under one sovereign. This, however, will be a work of years; and, meantime, foreign elements will be introduced, which doubtless, must increase the complications already threatening.

Notwithstanding that the Chinese nation has a name for lethargy, approaching to stolidity, yet, for two or three centuries, civil commotions of some sort have been continually breaking out in different provinces of the country, and although these have been one after the other put down, their frequent occurrence in various parts indicates that, in that overgrown empire, there are elements of life and social energy not easily to be crushed. What has rendered the recent disturbances among the Chinese themselves unusually formidable to their government, is, that they are distinct, separate, and unconnected with each other; showing that the spirit of national independence, or the desire for it, is not confined to one spot, but has been spreading among the people.

The reigning government, entitled "the Ta-tsing dynasty," may not be overthrown by any of these stirring movements; nor, if so, is it at all probable that a mere change of ruler would directly induce an improved state and administration of affairs. Hope of improvement in China is not in any organized form of agitation, but in the fact that *thought* is beginning to circulate among the people. New ideas have been infused into the popular mind. Since free intercourse with foreigners was opened in 1842, the "schoolmaster has been abroad" in China, and self-dependence, so manifest in their various insurrections, has begun to assume a higher tone among the people. Such agitations, like storms and hurricanes, will clear the atmosphere. Upheavings of such a type must arouse thought and feeling, teach the people to act for themselves, and complete the destruction of the fossil remains of prejudice, bigotry, and superstition. Any shaking in the nation is a symptom of the secret workings in a vast laboratory, preparatory to some new and marvellous result; and we cannot but believe that all the tossings up and down of China (most of them concealed from foreign observation), will end in the creation of what will be "very good;"—just as our entire globe, after the countless and terrible convulsions of nature had swept over it, at length presented a form of which even the Great Creator was pleased to say, "Behold, it is very good!"

Of the most conspicuous of the movements named above, viz., "the *Taiping* rebellion," it was its religious element that, four years ago, excited the curiosity and interest of Christendom more than anything else.

From original documents upon our table we find, that among their articles of faith they recognize the primary truth that there is but one God, and beside him none else; they declare that idolatry in any shape is derogatory to the honour of the Supreme Being, and a violation of his commands; that the ten commandments, as delivered in the Mosaic dispensation, are obligatory upon all people; that Jesus came into the world to save sinners; that the future lot of the wicked is eternal damnation, but the righteous have the bliss of heaven in reserve for them; that the Holy Spirit influences men's hearts; and that to the Trinity, God the Father, the Son, the Spirit, solemn worship is due.

Besides these, the following Scripture facts are mentioned in their writings: the creation in six days, the deluge, the giving of the decalogue, the miraculous and divine interpositions in behalf of the Israelites; the descent of Jesus into our world, his benevolent mission, his death on the cross, the sun being darkened at his crucifixion, his resurrection, and his presence in heaven. They have the decalogue also, not in full, but abridged. They profess faith in the existence and the validity of the Scriptures of the Old and New Testaments, portions of which (*e. g.* the Pentateuch, Judges, Joshua, and the Gospel of Matthew), as printed and distributed by themselves, have fallen into the hands of foreigners.

At first sight, the system seemed to offer some hope that it might prove effective in diffusing the principles of the Christian faith. A further examination of their writings and papers, however, has not only disclosed that their notions of Christianity are of a very loose and confused description, but has revealed the most revolting and blasphemous fables, interwoven with Scripture facts and Bible truths, all which have been evidently assumed for the purpose of ambition and intolerance.

It is too painful, not to say disgusting, for us to retail their silly vile tales;* moreover, it is impossible to read these assumptions of superhuman power and of divine authority, without feeling that Hungsowtseuen deserves to be classed among the grossest fanatics or impostors who have appeared in the world, and that all attempts to palliate his frauds are futile and mistaken. Is his assumption of being in a peculiar sense "*the second* Son of God," of having many visions

* Should any one be disposed to peruse a more lengthened opinion upon the insurgents in China, I must apologize for referring to an article written by me, headed "Political Disturbances in China," and inserted in the *Edinburgh Review*, October, 1855, No. 208; from which I have to acknowledge the introduction of a few paragraphs in the above notes.

and divine revelations, or of holding repeated intercourse with the Divine Being, in colloquies and special interviews, but a venial offence? Is his claim to universal homage, on the plea that he has been anointed to his sacred kingship by the hands of God, and has received direct orders to that effect from the lips of the Eternal, to be regarded merely as one of his "tolerabiles ineptiæ?" Can the good though imperfect passages in his writings be brought forward as outshining those that are thick with darkness and full of blustering blasphemy? It is true, he has the reputation of being a fierce iconoclast, he publishes some Christian truths, and is said to distribute portions of our Scriptures; but his imperfect acquaintance with the religion of Jesus is not sufficient to counterbalance the frightful pretensions which are unblushingly made throughout his own books and proclamations: so that the only consistent and straightforward explanation of the case is to put the chief of this movement down as in every respect a pretender.

There is little doubt that the movement was from the first, as it is now in an enfeebled form, a grasping at power and property.

But this extraordinary revolution has not yet been consummated, nor is there much prospect, according to the information we at present possess, of the Kwangse rebels winning the prize. *Vincit qui patitur.* For a revolution to be effective in China,—effective in reforming every branch of the government and in improving all classes of the people—we believe it will have to call in the aid and the influence of the foreigner. The limited freedom, which has been secured to foreign visitors on the soil of China during the past fifteen years, is itself a change which has probably had no small influence on the country, and there is reason to hope that its results are not unwelcome to the people.

CHAPTER II.

BRIEF DESCRIPTIONS OF HONG-KONG, MACAO, AND CANTON.

ANY vessel bound to the port of Canton has to enter the delta of the "Pearl River," the area of which is largely occupied with isles and sandbanks. This extensive estuary forms a rough triangle, measuring about 100 miles in length on each side. Few rivers can be more protected than this, for during the late visit of Admiral Seymour, the forts along its banks amounted to thirty. It is fed by large and numerous branches, some of which run two and three hundred miles into the interior of the country.* When your ship has passed through the mouth of this wide embouchure, you may (if you please) turn to the right to the English island of *Hongkong*, which lies S.E. by E., at a distance of nearly ninety-five miles from Canton, or, to the left, to the Portuguese settlement of *Macao*.

The name *Hongkong* is the foreign corruption of *Heongkong*, and that again is the vulgar pronunciation in local patois of *Hiangkiang*, which is by interpretation "Scented stream," or further (as might be suggested by a fruitful imagination), "a series of spicy cascades, eau-de-cologne, or lavender water,"—in which case fancy would certainly be more romantic than fact. Properly, this designation belongs to a small stream on the southern side of the island, which had been long frequented by ships' boats for the purpose of taking in its fine pure water; but now the name is given by foreigners to the whole island.

The island itself is nine miles in length, nearly the same in breadth, and about twenty-six in circumference.

* See description at pp. 305, 306.

THE ISLAND OF HONG-KONG.

It presents a very uneven and exceedingly barren surface, consisting chiefly of rugged and rocky ranges of hills, with narrow ravines, through which streams of excellent and never-failing water flow. To give a notion of the ridges and peaks upon so small an island, I annex the names and heights of some:—Victoria Peak, 1,825 feet; High West, 1,174; Mount Gough, 1,575; Mount Kellett, 1,131; Mount Parker, 1,711; Pottinger Peak, 1,016. There are only a few spots that are arable, and these are cultivated with rice, peas, and potatoes. The botany of the island is scanty, and the curious fact is mentioned by Fortune, that the most ornamental flowering plants on its face are to be found high up the mountains, from 1,000 to 2,000 feet above the sea-level.

There are some patches of level beach land, as at *Chek-choo* on the south-western point, *Shek-pai-wan* on the west, *Tai-tam* on the eastern end of the island, which several sites were at first considered as the more likely to be eligible for foreign residences; but hitherto few of the colonists have erected dwelling-houses out of that district called *Victoria.* This lies on the north face of the island, at the base of that lofty peak represented in the opposite engraving, and called by the same name.

Victoria, the capital of the colony and the seat of the government, extends nearly three miles from east to west,—part of the central grounds being occupied by government, for military barracks and hospitals, commissariat buildings, the colonial church, officers' quarters, post-office, and harbour-master's depôt, all which are overlooked by the government-house itself, higher up the hill.

West and east of this central portion, almost close to the sea-beach, stretch the private residences of foreigners, commercial houses, club-house, exchange, two or three chapels, with public market-places. The Chinese colonists occupy ground principally to the west of the central division,—modelling their houses after the native fashion. In the year 1849, the town of Victoria in the colony of Hongkong was ordained a city, and the island and its dependencies were erected into a bishop's see and diocese, to be called the bishopric of Victoria.

It was the shelter, security, and convenience offered by the harbour immediately before Victoria, that induced the English government to select this for a British settlement; for it has one of the noblest roadsteads in the world, with a safe and wide passage at both ends, east and west, as well as an anchorage for the largest fleet afloat. This island and harbour were both ceded to the crown of England in January, 1841, and again confirmed by the treaty of Nanking in August, 1842. Before the cession, the native population on the island amounted to no more than two thousand,—and these chiefly a set of low, poor, and degraded quarrymen, smugglers, fishermen, or pirates. But since "the colony of Hongkong" was opened, there has been an immense accession of Chinese immigrants, whose numbers, by the last census, exceed 60,000.

The government of the colony is vested in a Governor, a Lieutenant-Governor, and a Legislative Council of three official and two non-official members.

Hongkong lies exactly opposite to the main-land of China; at the eastern point of which there is seen the town of "Nine Dragons," or Kow-loong, where the Canton authorities, when they had the will for it, had one way of annoying English residents by stopping the supplies of provisions in regular demand by the islanders; but of this method of irritating their neighbours they have recently been taught to be a little more cautious.

Macao (pronounced *Macow*) is forty miles to the westward of Hongkong, a Portuguese settlement at precisely the same distance from Canton as Hongkong.

The position of Macao is agreeable to the English sojourner, as it has a pleasant variety of hill and dale in its little territory, and is nearly surrounded with water and open to sea-breezes on every side. But, apart from its having no good harbour whatever, it has the great drawback of a mongrel Portuguese society, and a low-caste pig-headed class of Chinese. Besides, to some of the present generation of English residents in China, there can be anything but associations of a comfortable kind connected with Macao, recollecting as they must the unfriendly policy which the Portuguese on the spot pursued some sixteen or seventeen years since, and the bitterly hostile bearing which the Chinese of the settlement were encouraged to assume towards the "red-haired English."

Macao is a peninsula, not more than eight miles in circuit. It is attached to the south-east point of a large island, called in the Chinese tongue "Hiangshan," or, as if again to delude the fancy, "the fragrant hill." The connecting band is a narrow isthmus, which, in the native topography, is designated "the stalk of a water-lily!" In 1840, a low wall stretched across this isthmus, the foundation-stones of which had been laid about three hundred years ago, with the undisguised object of limiting the movements of foreigners, pedestrian or equestrian. This was the notorious "barrier" which, during the Chinese war of 1840 and 1841, was a source of great uneasiness to the Portuguese settlers of Macao, and the occasion of repeated fits of jealousy between Chinese and English. As large numbers of the peasantry had to pass the "barrier-gates," with provisions for the mixed population at Macao, it was a frequent manœuvre with the Chinese authorities, out of revenge on the English, to stop the market supplies by closing this gate, and setting over it a guard of half-starved and ravenous militia.

But to leave Macao and make for Canton, your ship

starts and glides by the notorious "Bogue Forts," threads her course through an involved network of islets and mudbanks, and at last drops anchor twelve miles from Canton, off the small island of "Whampoo."

At Whampoo our near approach to the city of Canton is indicated by the numerous and grotesque "egg-boats," "sampans," "bumboats," and other small fry of that class, which are constantly ferrying between the two places, not to mention the mastheads of junks lying abreast of Canton, and the flagstaffs of Chinese, British, and other ensigns, which on a clear day are visible at some distance. (The reader is reminded that we speak of Canton "as it was" under the native *régime.*)

The name "Canton" is given by foreigners both to that city and to the province of which it is the capital; but it is a European corruption of "*Kwang-tung,*" the native term to denote "Broad East."

The proper names applied by the inhabitants themselves to their capital are various: thus, in speaking to their fellow-citizens they merely call it "Sang-ching," an equivalent to "our capital:" in conversation with natives of neighbouring provinces, they designate it "Kwang-tung-sang-ching," "the capital of Canton;" while poetically it is described as "the city of rams," "the city of the genii," "the city of grain."

The origin of such romantic epithets is traced by the people to the following legendary incident.

They say that, after the foundation of the city (which dates so far back as 2,000 years ago), five genii, clothed in garments of five different colours, and riding on rams of five different colours, met at this place. Each of them bore in its mouth a stalk of grain having six ears, and presented them to the tenants of the soil, to whom they spake in these words:—

"May famine and dearth never visit you!"

Upon this, the said rams were immediately petrified and converted into perpetual monuments of stone. And should any foreign archæologist now at Canton be disposed to push his inquiries immediately on the spot, and place himself under a native guide, he may find these five stone rams in "the Temple of the Five Genii," which stands hard by the city-gate of the same name.

The city of Canton lies on the northern bank of "the Pearl River," in a plain which extends to the foot of "the White Cloud Mountains," the highest point of which is said by the natives to rise 1,200 feet above the level of the river.

Immediately abreast of Canton, there stand, in the bed of the stream, two tiny forts, which were long held by the mandarins but are now occupied by the allied forces of Great Britain and France. The one still goes by the name "Dutch Folly,"* the other (on a peninsula) by that of "French Folly." Exactly behind these, as you face the city, there stretches the island of Honan, separated from the opposite bank by the river, which here does not much exceed the width of the Thames at London Bridge. "Honam" (as it is called in the Canton patois), ever has and ever will afford, from its isolated position, some pleasant walks for recreation, particularly to foreigners, after their day's toil in the counting-house or the factory. The island has a considerable town on it; but, besides a few walks, there is the large "Joss-house," a Buddhist temple, whose shady grounds cover about seven acres, and which, surrounded by a wall, has its gardens, courts, monastery, idols, and images—all within the enclosure. To saunter in the cool grounds of this temple is a favourite pastime for the natives who have means and leisure for it.

* A slight allusion is made to it at page 306.

But, as you return to the city, the river-scene cannot but attract the eye as most diverting and instructive; for you have presented to you, in more than a miniature scale, "Life in China on a river." You have, indeed, lying before you a *floating town*, consisting of wood-huts and houses, built on rafts or on piles driven into the banks, with boats of every conceivable shape and use, linked and lashed together, rising and falling with ebb and flow; in fact, it is an *aquarium* of human occupants,—male, female, veteran and infant,—skimming and skipping about,—in search of indulgences, lawful and criminal, or in pursuit of their daily bread, —all exhibiting a marvellous ingenuity, an untiring industry in the same avocations that engross their neighbours on "*terra-firma*."

The suburbs of Canton extend all round the city, and stretch full four miles along the river-bank, particularly towards the west of the city. The native streets and buildings of this portion differ very little, if at all, from those within the walls.

Hitherto, the foreign residences have been chiefly confined to the western suburbs,—nearly opposite to "Dutch Folly." The range of buildings usually known as "the foreign factories," had a river frontage of 800 feet, within which lot there was an area of about 100 feet in depth, laid out as a garden. These buildings were at first called "*factories*," by the foreign merchants themselves, from appearing in China as "factors," or agents for others in a distant country; but to the present day they are spoken of as "hongs" by natives and foreigners,—"hong" being the Chinese name for "a row," "a series," or "a succession," of large, lofty apartments. The latter term is by no means inappropriate, as the factories were built in rows, one behind another. On this account, the front "hong" looked out on the river, while the "hong" in the rear had not an agreeable prospect. Some, indeed, were dark, prison-like blocks, that had to be reached by a dismal tunnel through the centre ground story; the rooms on either side of this passage being occupied by compradores and servants. However, they were strongly built, of stuccoed brick, upon granite foundations, rising some two, some three stories high, though they have, during the last eighteen months suffered from war and pillage.

"The White-cloud Hills," in the rear, command the city. From these heights (which used to have their forts and camps of Man-tchoo soldiers) there is a view of the country round, but particularly of the doomed city beneath, and its expanse of red-tiled roofs and low houses,—relieved occasionally by military towers, solitary pagodas, Buddhist temples, and official flag-staffs, &c.

The entire circuit of city and suburbs cannot be far from ten miles, embracing a land and water population amounting probably to a million; but the circumference of the walled city may not be above six or seven miles.

That part of Canton which is surrounded by a wall, is again divided into the "Old City" and the "New City" by a wall running straight from east to west. The northern, or the "Old City," which "rests on the brow of the hill" already named, is the larger division, having famous pleasure-grounds, tea-gardens, and some wide streets, with not a few official houses.

South of the partition is the "New City," whose outer wall is about 100 yards distant from the river side, —the intervening space being entirely occupied with suburban houses and hongs.

The city walls have a foundation of sandstone, and are built both of brick and stone; the thickness varying from 25 to 30 feet, and the height from 28 to 40 feet. In many places the houses of the poor are built so close to the walls, inside and outside the city, that they can scarcely be distinguished. On the wall, circling the city, there are twelve large gates, and four in the partition wall; sixteen in all, some of them bearing high-sounding titles, of "Mighty Peace," "Eternal Rest," "Everlasting Purity," &c. The interior of Canton is intersected by ditches, canals, and streets,—the latter also dignified by the equally inappropriate names of "Warlike Dragon," "Golden Lily," "Flower Street," &c. These streets are about 8 feet wide, flagged chiefly with granite, and generally thronged with a motley group. At any busy hour of the day, vociferating porters of merchandize and nimble sedan-carriers, in noise and bustle, make up for the deficiency of carts and conveyances; but the crushing and jostling of numerous passengers and various venders, pedlars, and beggars, which occurs every day in every one of these thoroughfares, we shall not attempt to describe, but leave the reader to imagine from the accompanying sketch of "a street in Canton."

Such is a brief description of Canton "as it was" up to the close of 1858; but the Canton "*that is to be*," we leave the future to unveil.

CHAPTER III

CANTON RUPTURE WITH FOREIGNERS—DELAY IN SETTLING IT FORTUNATE ON TWO GROUNDS—THE POPULAR FEELING AT NORTHERN PORTS FAVOURABLE TO FOREIGNERS—ACCOUNT OF BRITISH ACTION AGAINST CANTON DOWN TO THE BEGINNING OF 1858—CAPTURE OF YEH.

THE late *embroglio* at Canton (of which every one knows) has awakened more discussion in England than it has in China, and excited more alarm in our Parliament than in the Imperial cabinet at Peking. But, believing that our British authorities on the spot (with

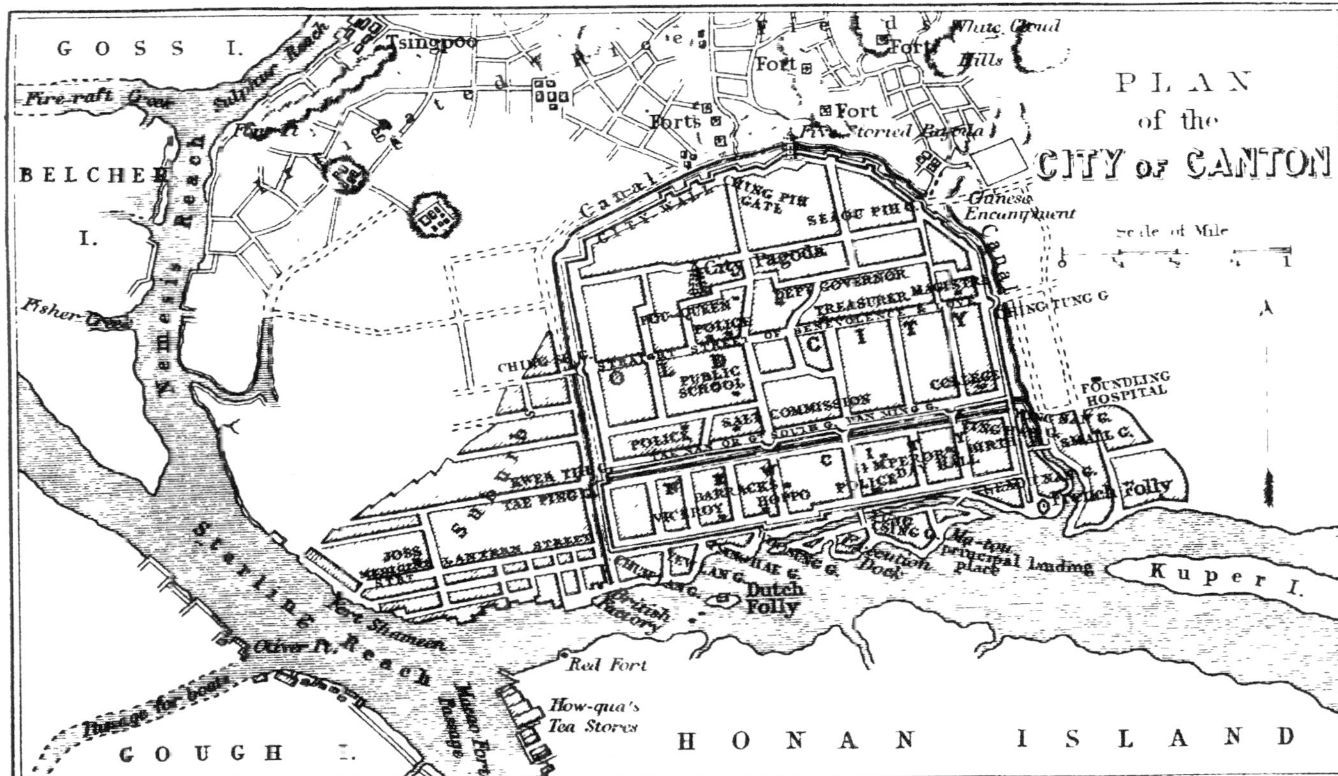

L. M. Becker Sc.

London G Routledge & Co Farringdon St

all their faults) were fully justified in the vigorous course which they adopted in October 1856, and which, but for a mistaken spirit of leniency, their predecessors ought to have taken long since and so saved us this rupture, I cannot but express a hope that the amazing interest awakened in British hearts by the recent occurrence will not subside or vanish into vapour.

During the greater part of 1857, the terrible affairs in India have driven those of China very much into the background; but every one must be aware of the urgent causes that compelled the British Government to relinquish for a time its original plans, and divert a portion of the resources put at its disposal for the purpose of rectifying the anomalous state of foreign relations upon the coast of China.

Perhaps this interruption to the rigorous proceedings of Britain in China may be regarded as fortunate on two accounts.—First—Lord Elgin has been saved from repeating the mistake of former plenipotentiaries,—that of attempting to visit Peking in person, and of appealing to his Imperial Majesty before decided operations had been taken against Canton, and an impression made upon the insolent officials and insulting rabble of that province and city.

Among the foreign residents in China there was reason to fear that his lordship, on the threshold of his career, was somewhat disposed, first of all, to visit the *Peiho*, and seek an interview with the occupant of the "dragon throne;" the failure of which policy any one acquainted with the tone of the Peking cabinet might easily have predicted. However, the grave complications in India drew off his lordship's attention from the north of China, and withdrew the land forces from the south of the empire, on which military strength he was in a measure dependent in pursuing the scheme of visiting the Gulf of *Pihchelee*.

Meantime, it appears, that gulf has been visited by His Excellency Count Poutiatine, the Russian envoy, who had been deputed by his government to wait upon his Majesty of Peking. He was detained twenty days at the mouth of the *Peiho*, and was not invited up to the capital, only one hundred miles distant. He found the entrance to that river strongly and newly fortified. By last accounts, the Russian ambassador had returned to the South of China, having completely failed in the diplomatic mission of the Czar,—affording a further confirmation to our objections to the shores of *Teentsin* as a place for negotiations, until at least the offending natives and authorities of Canton city shall have received their merited chastisement; when in all probability the British ambassador will be received in the city of Peking with all the honours due to his position as the representative of the British empire.

Secondly.—But this strange and unexpected interruption to warlike operations intended against Canton has developed the fact—or, rather, has most fully confirmed the opinion, which from the earliest period of the rupture has been entertained by foreign residents on the spot,—that the present dispute is essentially local and confined to the "Pearl River," on whose banks the notorious Cantonese have so long flourished.

It is true that the Imperial will coincides with the sullen and stubborn bearing of Commissioner Yeh;—for, to the scanty papers that have appeared in the *Peking Gazette* anent the Canton troubles, the short verdict has been appended from the vermilion pencil, "*We entirely agree.*" Nevertheless, there is the following singular anomaly, at this moment unfolded to view:—For the past fourteen months, hostilities of the most irritating kind have continued in the southern part of the Chinese empire, by which Canton, the capital of one of the most important provinces, has been cut off from all seaward communication, and its external commerce, hitherto very lucrative, has been totally annihilated; and during that same term, the enmity shown by the natives of that region against the English has been inveterate, and no means of expressing it have been spared, open or secret, foul or fair. Yet, at the other ports where British residents have established themselves, as merchants or missionaries, not a ripple of ill-feeling has disturbed the face of society. There continues as before, the smooth flow of peaceful intercourse between British officials and Chinese mandarins, which latter indeed have become, if anything, more civil and courteous. Mercantile transactions at *Shanghai, Ningpo, Amoy,* and *Fuh-chow* have been conducted with as much amity and security as if the port of Canton belonged to another sphere, and as if its inhabitants had as little to do with the other parts of China, as the natives of "Central Africa," or the citizens of the "Salt Lake Union."

Not only so; but the majority of natives at those four ports, have been chuckling at the prospect of their Canton neighbours getting a "thrashing,"—detested as they are everywhere for their pride, insolence, and tyranny,—and they have been disappointed by the delay of the castigating process. Moreover, there is this significant fact that, at the very time when Mr. Yeh, of Canton, was vomiting forth fury and hatred at the English, and encouraging their poisoning, kidnapping, and beheading,—the Chinese authorities at Shanghai, 800 miles nearer Peking, were acknowledging, in a manner noble and generous, the services of one of H.M.'s naval officers in rendering the navigation of the *Yang-tze-kiang* more safe and easy. We quote the account of this act of kindness, as given in the *North China Herald,* of September last:—

"We are glad to learn that the services of Mr. Carr, Master of H.M.S. *Pique,* in laying down the buoys at the entrance of the Yang-tsze-keang, have not been overlooked by the Chinese authorities. Mr. Carr was occupied for some time, at the beginning of this year, in directing the placing of these marks; and the benefit which has resulted to the shipping at this port has been unequivocal. Instead of the numerous mishaps to both outward and inward bound vessels we were formerly called upon to report, comparatively few have come to our notice since these useful guides have been established. That the Chinese authorities should be the first to acknowledge Mr. Carr's services, in the way of a testimonial, is all the more creditable to them, as they derive no direct benefit from them. The acknowledgment is in the form of a handsome Gold Chronometer Watch, by Frodsham, valued at 70 guineas, and has on its inner lid the following inscription:—

"FROM HIS EXCELLENCY LAN, TAOUTAE
of Shanghae,
To GEORGE L CARR,
Master, Royal Navy,
As a mark of his appreciation of the services rendered
by him on laying down the Buoys in the
River Yang-tsze-keang,
1857."

Further, we have pleasure in quoting from the December number of the *Missionary Magazine* of the London Missionary Society, the following corroborative remarks of the point now adduced:—

"If proof were wanting that the political disturbances prevailing at Canton excite no interest or sympathy among the people of China beyond the city and provinces where those disturbances have arisen, we might adduce the fact that Mr. Wylie, of the Shanghae mission, has not long since returned from a three weeks' journey to the interior, in the course of which, though everywhere recognized as a foreigner, he experienced no incivility either from the authorities or the people. Mr. Wylie himself, at the close of his journal remarks:—'I have mentioned six walled cities, all of which I entered on my return, and walked about them with great freedom; and although frequently betrayed by my foreign features, I did not once hear the *offensive epithet* applied to me north of the Yang-tsze, nor any symptom of disapprobation at my presence. The small stock of books I endeavoured to make the most of, distributing them as favours to particular parties, and in many instances they were doubtless appreciated. Although the similarity of our books to the rebel publications was readily observed, yet that did not prove any bar to their reception, nor did it at all excite suspicion; indeed, none were more eager to obtain them than officers and soldiers in the Imperial service.

" 'There are three different kinds of offices from which every boat must receive permits to pass: 1. The regular custom-houses, where there is a search for goods of any kind that may be concealed (and should Bibles be taken on a large scale, they will probably have to pay customs). 2. The subscription-offices, where a special tax is levied for carrying on the war, according to the value of the boat and its contents. 3. The examination-houses, where every boat is searched to see that no improper persons pass. We had to pass in all thirteen of these offices, nor was there the least difficulty. In some cases the officers took no notice; in others, when spoken to, I always announced myself as an Englishman, and stated clearly the object of my trip, and never did I hear any token of disapprobation. On the other hand, several of them seemed much interested on the occasion, and had evidently the desire that such visits should be repeated. I received marked civility from them on every occasion, and all things conspired to show that the mandarins are evidently desirous of cultivating a friendly feeling with us at present; and, should we obtain their countenance, there is little fear of our maintaining amicable terms with the people.' "

There is no question that the present conflict is one with the officials of Canton, and that the brush of contest has ere this commenced in that same locality. It is to be hoped it will end there satisfactorily to the interests of justice and humanity. Our moral prestige protects us in the north; but any weakness or shortcoming of ours at Canton will be utterly ruinous to the influence which we have peaceably won at the northern ports.

Ever since the matter of the *Arrow*, which gave proper occasion for pressing upon the native authorities the treaty rights of Great Britain,—there has been with the English a broken series of land-skirmishes, boat-fights, naval cruizes, junk-burnings, battery-explodings, and river-blockades,—in which have been exhibited the extraordinary feats of daring heroes and the bold adventures of valorous tars; whilst, on the part of the Cantonese, there have been rewards for English heads, kidnappings of English persons, wholesale poisonings, and a few midnight assassinations.

At length, in the middle of December 1857, the first act in the move was evident in the following general order issued to the British fleet.

"GENERAL ORDER.

"The period being now at hand for commencing active operations against the city of Canton, the Commander-in-Chief has to call the serious attention of the captains, officers, seamen, and marines of the squadron to the necessity of carefully protecting the lives and property of the peaceable and unarmed inhabitants, not only on the ground of humanity, but likewise on that of policy, which renders it so important to retain the goodwill of those classes of the Chinese population, whose material interest and predilections separate them from the high mandarins and the military powers of Canton, against whom alone hostile actions will be directed.

"The Rear-Admiral has also to impress upon the officers and men who may so soon be actively employed, his determination to discountenance and prevent all looting or plundering, both as demoralizing and as subversive of the discipline that is so essentially necessary to success. He trusts that the officers, by precept, and especially by their example, will carry out his views and instructions.

"The Commander-in-Chief takes this opportunity of expressing his warmest thanks to the commodore, captains, commanding officers, seamen, and royal marines of the squadron for the patient endurance they have evinced during the last twelve months, in the monotonous and frequently harassing duty of keeping open the navigation of the river; and he further assures them that, whatever may be the nature of expected operations, he shall enter upon them with the strongest confidence in their ready and gallant co-operation for the maintenance of the honour of the British flag and the success of our arms.

"M. Seymour,
"Rear-Admiral, Commander-in-Chief."

The attacking force before Canton in that month, consisted of eight men-of-war, aggregating 250 guns; nine steam-vessels with 149 guns, and nineteen gunboats. Exclusive of these there were:—

Troops from the garrison at Hong-Kong, with artillery and engineers	800
Royal Marines	2,500
Naval Brigade	1,500
Chinese and Malay coolies, attached to the artillery, medical, and commissariat staffs	987
Total	5,787

The French have throughout cordially acted with the British, and in this concerted attack on the city of Canton, the French navy in those waters has not only aided in the strict blockade, but has furnished nearly 1,000 men, from its naval and marine brigades, to assist the British in their movement upon "the city of Rams."

After due arrangements had been made before the walls of Canton, an officially-appointed messenger was sent ashore under a flag of truce, on the 12th of December, to deliver the demands of the English and French plenipotentiaries—Lord Elgin and M. Bourbillon. The summary of these claims was, probably, that the terms of the Nanking treaty should be carried out at Canton as at the other ports—its gates opened to foreign ingress, and that compensation should be done for damage to British property for the last fifteen months. Ten days were given the stubborn Chinese *Yeh* to accede to their terms; at the expiration of which *interim* (should no favourable reply be received), a positive attack would be made upon the city. In proof of their real earnestness in urging their demands, the Island of Honan, facing the city, was occupied by the allied forces on the 16th of the same month. This island, which is above a mile and a half wide, and about five miles long, lies exactly in front of Canton and in the middle of the enormous volume of water that flows past that city, seeking the ocean through various channels.*

In former days, the suburb of "Honan" offered to foreigners a few walks for recreation, and native citizens, too, used to frequent its fields in the afternoon, or saunter in the cool grounds of its great temple. But at the close of 1857, these limits were occupied by English and French garrisons—a prelude to something decisive on the part of the foreigners.

* *Vide* Map of Route from Canton to Hongkong.

During the "days of grace," which had been offered to *Yeh*, by the allied plenipotentiaries for compliance with their demands, strenuous efforts were made on the part of the English, by printed placards and proclamations, to inform the natives of the real *casus belli*, and to advise them to remove from the vicinity of danger; and, amongst other *colporteurs*, Consul Parkes and Captain Hall were engaged in this dangerous labour of "tract-distribution." According to the correspondent of a public paper, the following amusing incident occurred,—amidst the hazard and terror that prevailed around in the native community:—In one of their rapid descents, Captain Hall caught a mandarin in his chair, not far from the city gate. The captain pasted the mandarin up in his chair with the barbarian papers, pasted the chair all over with them, and started the bearers to carry this new advertising van into the city! The Chinese crowd, always alive to a practical joke, roared, —and well they might. However, the belligerent bill-stickers of *Yeh's* school brought in some Chinese counter-proclamations. Arrogant to the last, these papers said that the rebellious English, having seduced the French to join in this rebellion, it became necessary to stop the trade altogether, and utterly to annihilate these barbarians.

But the truce had expired; and, during the last few days of 1857, the bombardment commenced in earnest, though studiously repressed, so as not to injure the place more than was necessary to insure compliance. For this purpose, the English and French squadrons (specified above) took up their position directly opposite to Canton, exactly between that city and Honan, half a mile up and down the stream, moored stem and stern, *with their broadsides* toward the Canton shore. Thus, there yawned upon that city the mouths of more than 400 guns and mortars of tremendous calibre, which only waited the signal to pour forth their terrible contents upon the ill-fated capital. The bombardment was so arranged as to touch chiefly the city walls, the official residences, and the hill forts; and, in the words of the "General Order before Canton," "the bombardment was to be in very slow time, and not to exceed, for each gun employed, sixty rounds during the first twenty-four hours."

So, on Monday morning, the 28th of December (when the dawn had scarcely broken), the fire began slowly and regularly. For hours the squadrons continued their leisurely fire, but there was no sign of yielding. About mid-day the debarkation of the land-force began. The landing-place was at Kuper Creek, to the east of the city. The object was to seize, first, a fort called Lin's Fort, on the east, and then the hill defences to the north of the city. The force was divided into four divisions. Three were in advance. The right brigade was of English sailors; the centre was made up of the 59th regiment, artillery, sappers, and marines; and to the left were the French, about 900 strong. The fourth division, composed entirely of marines, was the reserve, commanded by Colonel Holloway. Darkness put an end to the operations of the 28th, and during the night the effects of the fire were seen in the blazing houses throughout the city. The destruction at certain points seems to have been very great, but it is thought that only inferior dwellings near the walls perished. On the 29th the assault on the hill defences was made; and with a few serious casualties, the landing-force secured its objects early that day. Consequently, by the last day of the old year, Canton was between two fires and at the mercy of the conquerors; for the force in the river was evidently powerful enough to destroy the city in a few days,—the "yamun" and most of the public buildings being near the river, and exposed to the full fire of the fleets; and the whole east and north of the city was commanded by our troops, of whom no less than 3,000 men had landed on the Monday (December 28), taken Lin's Fort, which commands the place from the east, and the next day had captured the whole of the hill forts to the north.

The operations seem to have been singularly well planned and entirely successful: the whole appears to have been conducted with a view to occasion the smallest possible sacrifice of life to friends or foes; so that we may hope the victory has been a cheap one.

As for the Cantonese, they seem to have taken the matter very composedly. *Yeh* remained throughout in his cantonment, stern and stubborn to the last. The native soldiers were occasionally seen walking sentry, or flaunting about with varicoloured signal-flags; though, in some cases, they stood manfully to their guns, but only ran away at the last moment "to fight another day." The people of the city had mostly removed quietly away to some safe retreat,—at least those that could do so; and of those that preferred to remain, there were Chinamen who seemed glad enough to be near the Englishmen, going from boat to boat with bananas for sale, and tunngans and lichees, as though these "red-haired devils" had been settled there for lifetime. There were coolies and bearers too, who, as long as they got their daily rations of food and cash, were content and jolly, grinning and chattering all day long to the great amusement of "John Bull;" and there were others on the river-banks watching the flight of shot and shell with the utmost composure; while some people in their native boats were moving up and down the river, like lightermen, in the usual routine of their daily calling.

For nearly a week after the bombardment of the city, the allied forces were occupied in securing the positions they had gained within and without the walls, and the estimate of killed and wounded in the assault did not exceed 140 British and 30 French.

But on Tuesday, January 5, an expedition into the city was planned and executed, chiefly to capture the native officials of high rank, who, it appeared, were still lurking about its interior. The buildings in which they had taken refuge were pointed out from the hill-top to Captain Key, of the *Sanspareil*, and, having obtained the admiral's sanction, he mustered his brigade of blue-jackets and marched into the city. Mr. Consul Parkes was attached to this party, and rendered most effective assistance in the seizure. After one or two vain searches, at last they reached an official residence, called a *yamun*. On bursting open the doors of this building, the retreating figure of the High Commissioner was the signal for a general rush after him, as he attempted to scramble over a low wall. An ambitious *aide-de-camp* of Yeh's staff protested very strongly that the captive was the wrong man, and tried to pass himself off as the commissioner, loudly stammering out—"*Me* Yeh; *me* Yeh." But it was of no avail. The prize was caught; and the stout viceroy found himself in the embrace of Captain Key and the commodore's coxswain, who had outrun the others, and ranged up one on each side of him. Instinctively, the blue-jackets threw up their caps and gave three regular British cheers. Yeh was soon identified by many Chinese, who instantly fell on their knees—as they used to do when he was their lord—saying he was the Governor-General, &c.

Meantime, the Lieutenant-Governor of Canton and the Tartar general were both captured in their own *yamuns*, and made prisoners without opposition; and thus the three principal officers of Canton province were taken without bloodshed,—a remarkable fact, and a proof of the weakness, or the faithlessness, of their attendants.

Yeh is described as a man of short stature, gross, fat, and portly in person, with a huge, sensual, flat face. He holds his head haughtily; his eyes are restless, roving, and ferocious; his dress is after the fashion of a first-style mandarin:—yet withal, this man is not the hero some have taken him to be. He has shown himself to be a fierce, insolent, determined, and violent despot; but he has not been a courageous man. In a most cowardly way he strenuously denied his identity, and he trembled fearfully when brought face to face with his foes. As with all Chinese mandarins, there is about him too much of affected dignity to inspire respect in his captors. After he felt safe in their hands, he assumed to be very merry, and appeared to enjoy the questions put to him; but this laugh must have been simulated, to hide the chagrin he naturally felt at being catechized by persons he had so long pretended to despise. He ridiculed the idea of giving up his seals of office to the foreigners, as also that of being carried off on board ship. He told the British plenipotentiary that he did not see the necesity of his going on board ship, and added that he could do everything that was required as well on shore. But, on finding that his triumphant captors were inexorable, it is said, he added —"Very well, I will accept their polite invitation; for, indeed, I shall be happy to go on board and see one of your men-of-war!"

He was finally removed, under a strong guard, to one of her Majesty's vessels appointed to receive the Imperial prisoner. He was allowed three servants to accompany him on board ship, whom he selected from a number who seemed inclined to follow him into captivity.

Immediately on the removal of Yeh to his prison-ship, a release was offered the other two high mandarins mentioned above, on condition that they would aid in restoring quiet in Canton and in re-establishing the government. At first they refused to have anything to do with the proposed *régime;* but soon their scruples were overcome, and the lieutenant-governor and Tartar general were reinstalled in office, under the supervision of a commission of two British and one French officers, —the wisdom of which policy admits of serious doubt, especially in connection with a people like the Cantonese, and a cabinet like that of Peking, both which are sure to turn round and convert this into a victory over the barbarians! However, time will tell.

Such, then, is a brief history of the assault and capture, by a force of some 6,000 foreigners, of the provincial city of Canton, which has hitherto been considered by the natives as impregnable. The Chinese nation will scarcely believe it. Even at Hong-Kong, which is within 100 miles of Canton, it is said, the first reports were listened to by the Chinese with incredulity, as a fable of the foreigners to cover a defeat. But they will soon know, see, and feel the truth for themselves.

What effect this reverse of fortune at Canton will have at Peking it is quite vain to attempt to surmise; but the foreign plenipotentiaries, British and French, will doubtless avail themselves of an opportunity so favourable for placing our relations with China on a firmer and a more friendly footing than that which led to the unfortunate affairs at Canton. Nor is this all. They are there to obtain for their countrymen free entrance into the empire.

The advantages sought for are not to be gained by diplomacy, or by negotiation, or by request. They can be secured from the Chinese cabinet only *by active, vigorous, resolute determination.*

INDEX.

COX AND WYMAN, PRINTERS, GREAT QUEEN-STREET, LONDON.

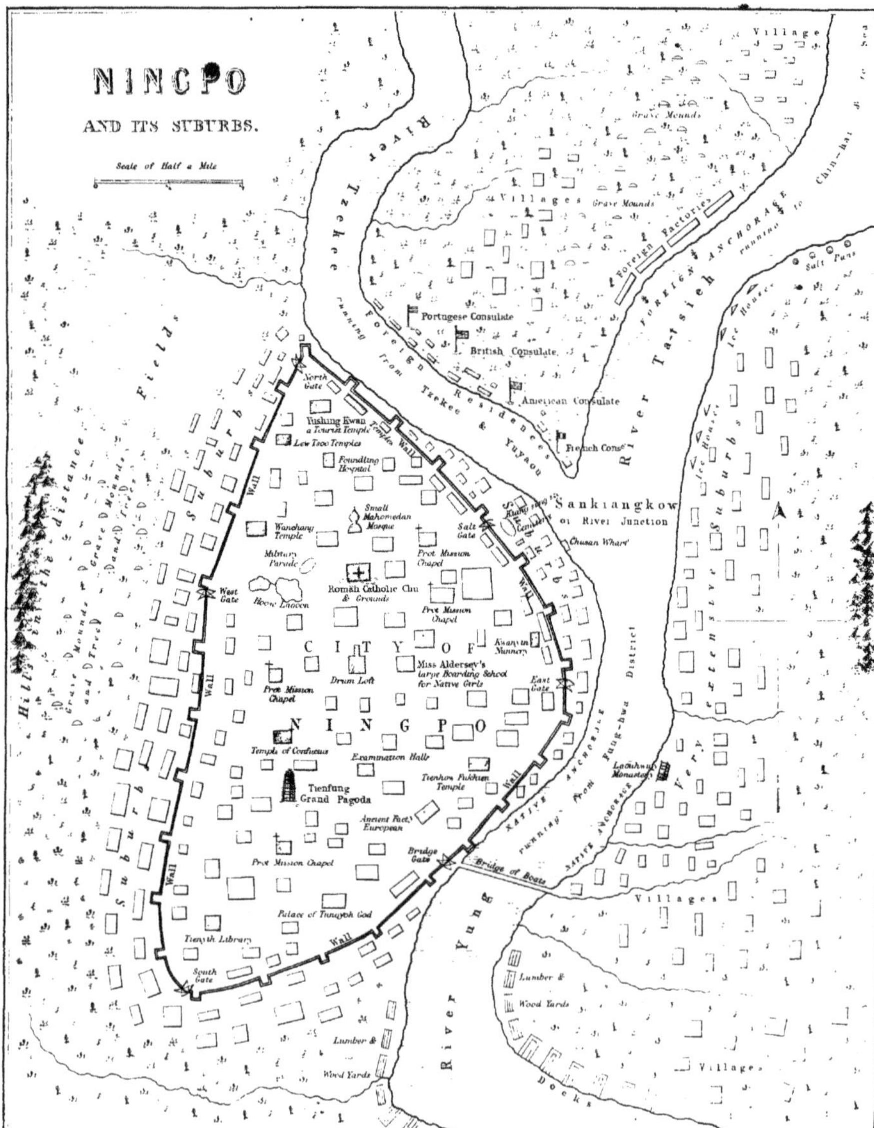

London, George Routledge & Co. Farringdon Street

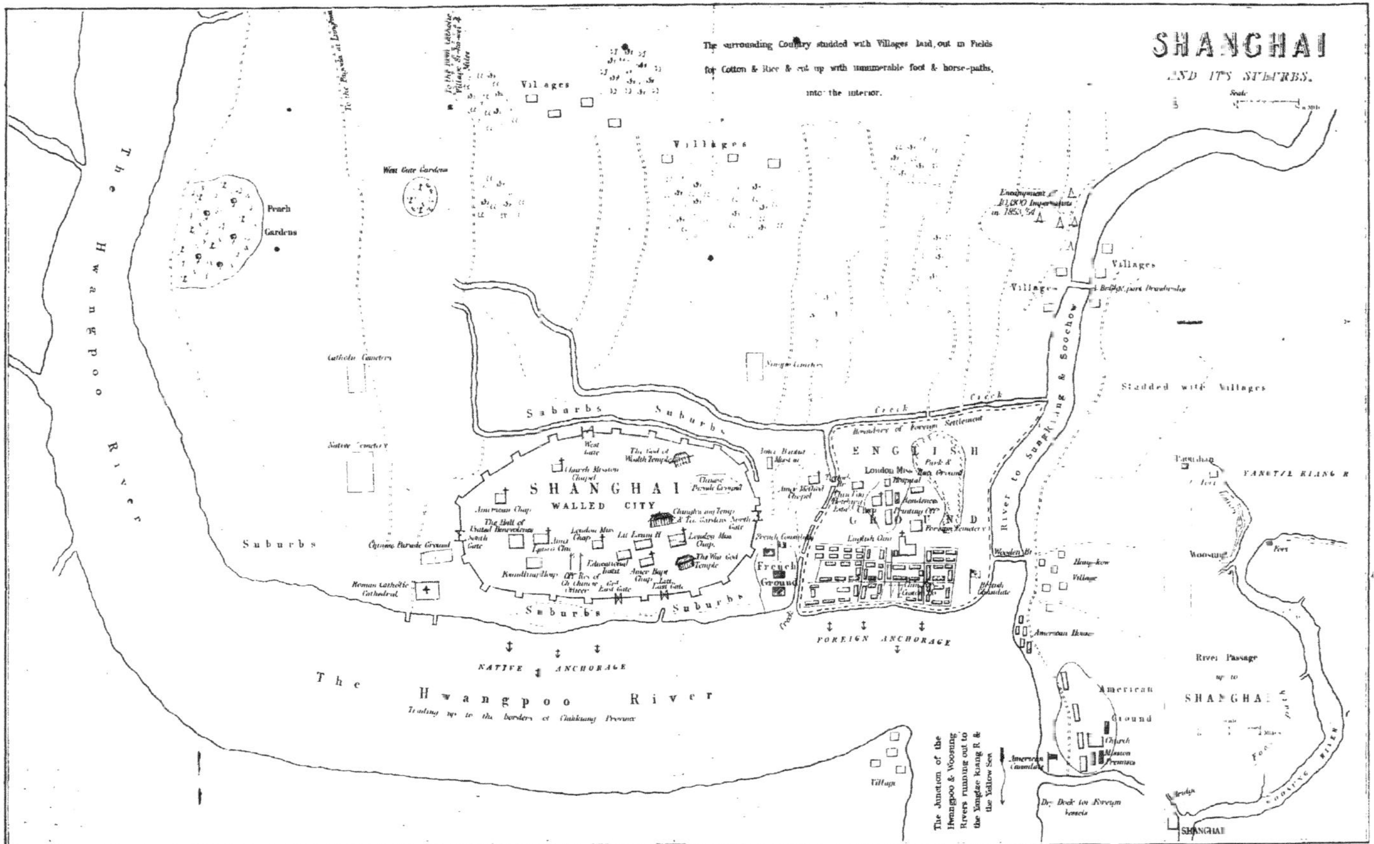
SHANGHAI
AND ITS SUBURBS.
Scale
The surrounding Country studded with Villages laid out in Fields for Cotton & Rice & cut up with innumerable foot & horse-paths, into the interior.
The Hwangpoo River
Peach Gardens
West Gate Gardens
Catholic Cemetery
Native Cemetery
Villages
Suburbs
SHANGHAI
WALLED CITY
American Chap.
South Gate
West Gate
The God of Wealth Temple
Chinese Parade Ground
Roman Catholic Cathedral
NATIVE ANCHORAGE
FOREIGN ANCHORAGE
The Hwangpoo River
Trading up to the borders of Chekiang Province
French Ground
ENGLISH GROUND
Boundary of Foreign Settlement
Creek
River to Sungkiang & Soochow
London Miss. Hospital
English Chur.
British Consulate
Wooden Br.
Hang-kew Village
American House
American Ground
Church
Mission Premises
American Consulate
Dry Dock for Foreign Vessels
Village
The Junction of the Hwangpoo & Woosung Rivers running out to the Yangtze kiang R & the Yellow Sea
Studded with Villages
YANGTZE KIANG R
Fort
Woosung
River Passage up to SHANGHAI
WOOSUNG RIVER
Bridge
SHANGHAI
London, George Routledge & Co., Farringdon Street

CPSIA information can be obtained
at www.ICGtesting.com
Printed in the USA
LVHW040110080123
736651LV00002B/53

9 783375 127091